THE NIGHTMARE BRIGADE

VOL. 2 INTO THE WOODS

Story
FRANCK THILLIEZ

Art
YOMGUI DUMONT

Color
DRAC

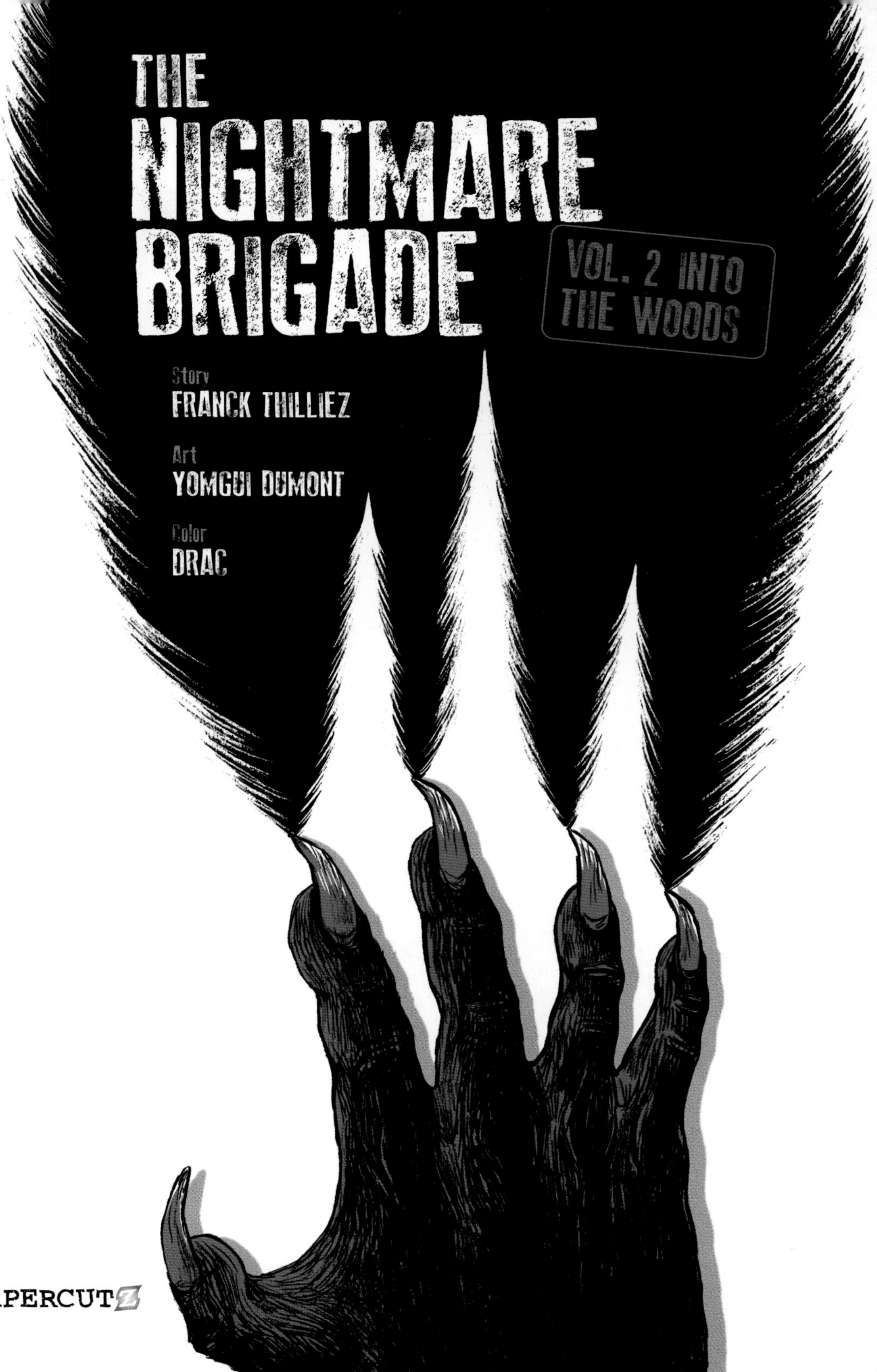

PAPERCUTZ

THE NIGHTMARE BRIGADE

Vol. 2
Into
The
Woods

To all those who made my dreams possible.
— **Franck Thilliez**

Thanks to the Jungle team for supporting this awesome series.
A big thumbs up to Marie, whom we'll all miss ;-)
Thanks to Anne-Charlotte for her zen-ness even in the midst of wrapping up.
Thanks to Franck for his twisted meninges.
Thanks to Drac & Co for their colorful delusions.
Thanks to Aude for everything else and to my Perrine for her impatience
("So, when's that coming out?").
I dedicate [the first half of] this volume to my daughter Léonie, who doesn't have
nightmares anymore, but whom I'll always watch over, just in case! I dedicate
[the second half of] this book to Michèle and Jean who, sometimes
without knowing it, opened doors to imagination for me.
— **Yomgui Dumont**

Thanks to Yomgui, Franck, Reiko, Julien, and Anne-Charlotte.
— **Drac**

English translation and all other editorial material © 2022 by Papercutz
All rights reserved.

La Brigade des Cauchemars [The Nightmare Brigade] #3 "Dossier no 3 Esteban"© 2019
Éditions Jungle
La Brigade des Cauchemars [The Nightmare Brigade] #4 "Dossier no 4 Melisandre"© 2020
Éditions Jungle

Story: Franck Thilliez
Art: Yomgui Dumont
Color: Drac
Color Assistance: Reiko Takaku, Julien Langlais

JayJay Jackson — Production
Joe Johnson — Translation
Wilson Ramos Jr. — Lettering
Stephanie Brooks — Assistant Managing Editor
Zachary Harris — Editorial Intern
Jim Salicrup
Editor-in-Chief

Special thanks to: Clélia Ghnassia, & Moïse Kissous

HC ISBN: 978-1-5458-0896-2
PB ISBN: 978-1-5458-0895-5

Printed in China
June 2022

Papercutz books may be purchased for business or promotional use. For information on
bulk purchases please contact Macmillan Corporate and Premium Sales Department at
(800) 221-7945 x5442.

Distributed by Macmillan
First Papercutz Printing

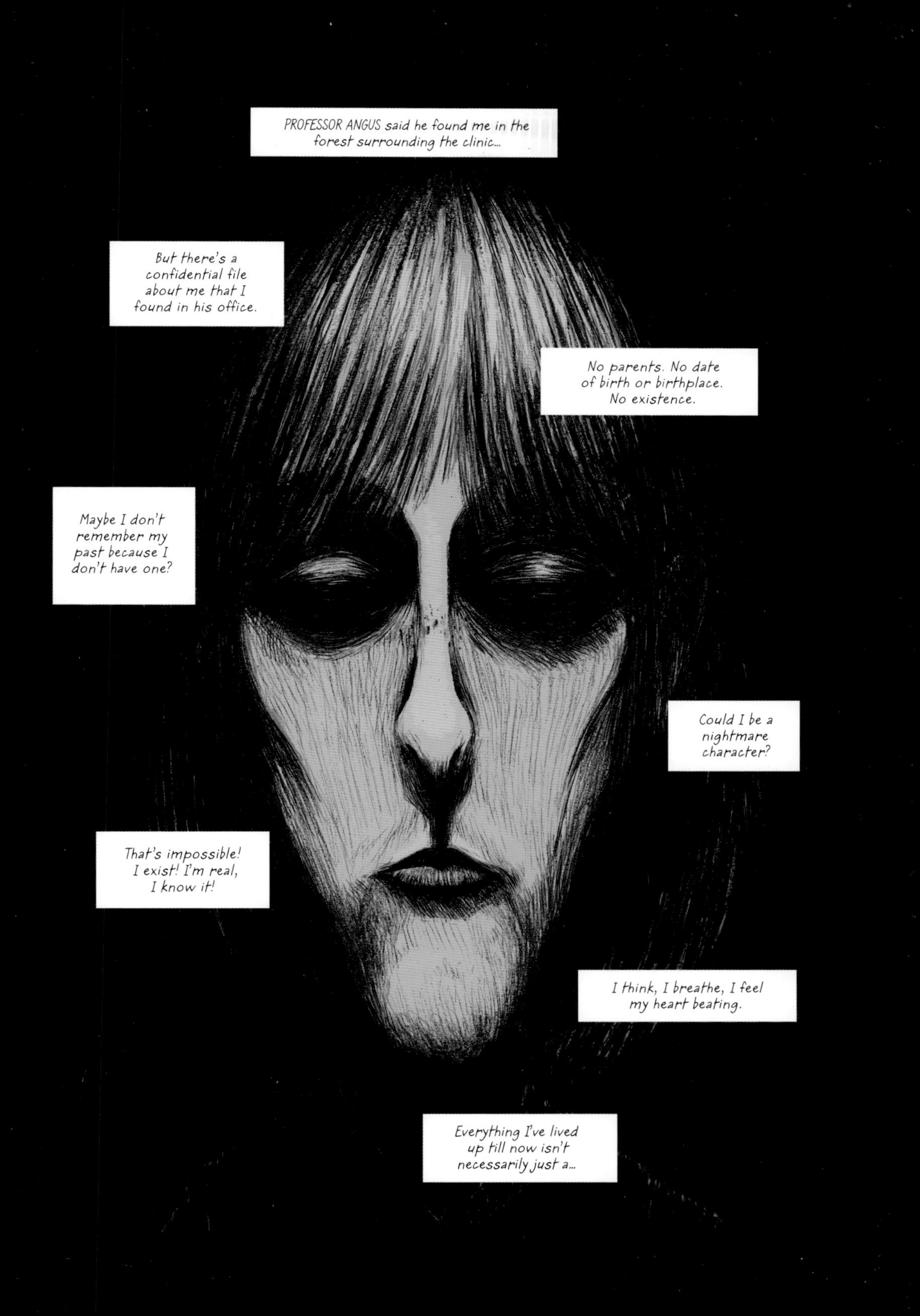
PROFESSOR ANGUS said he found me in the forest surrounding the clinic...
But there's a confidential file about me that I found in his office.
No parents. No date of birth or birthplace. No existence.
Maybe I don't remember my past because I don't have one?
Could I be a nightmare character?
That's impossible! I exist! I'm real, I know it!
I think, I breathe, I feel my heart beating.
Everything I've lived up till now isn't necessarily just a...

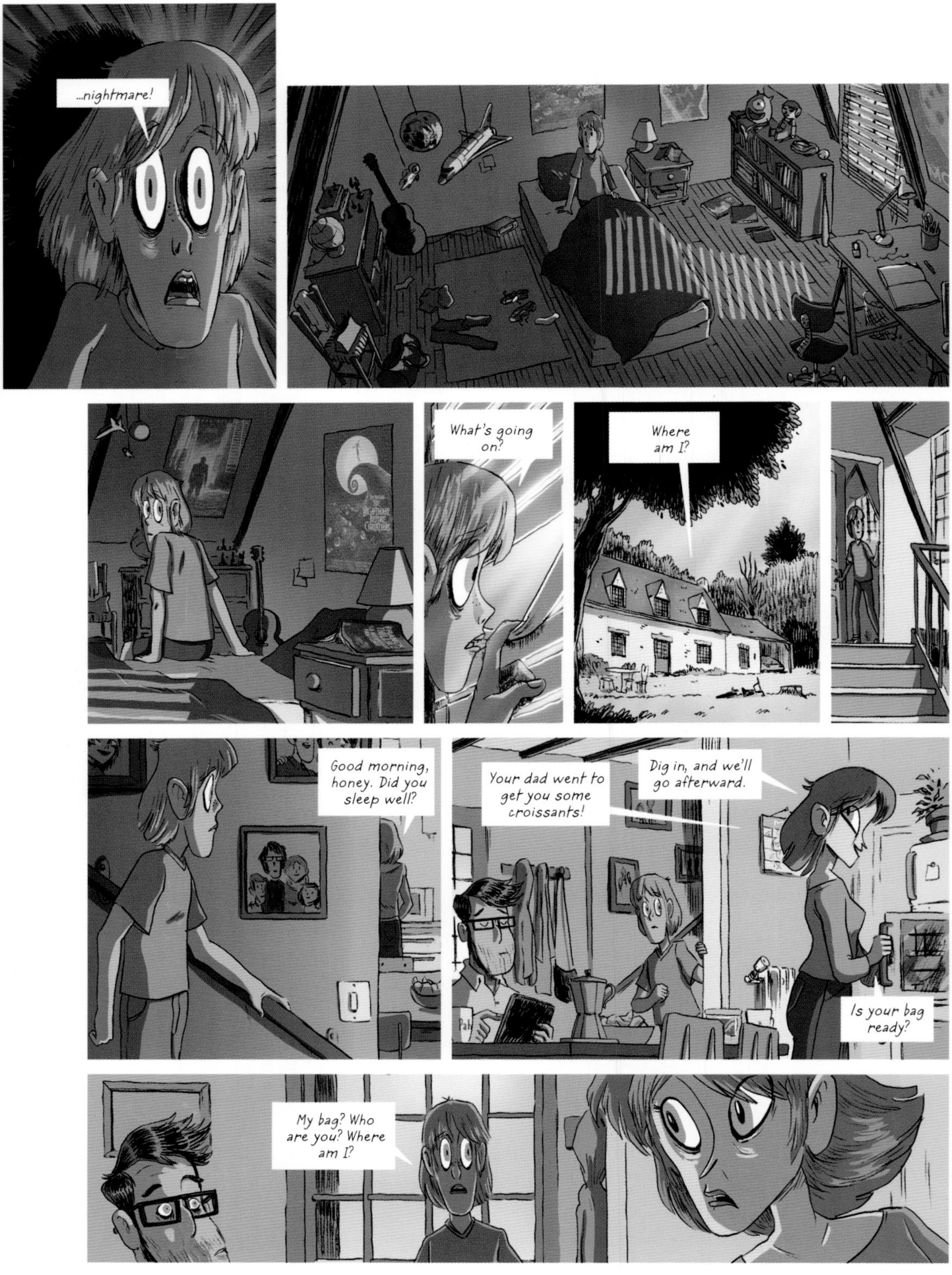
...nightmare!
What's going on?
Where am I?
Good morning, honey. Did you sleep well?
Your dad went to get you some croissants!
Dig in, and we'll go afterward.
Is your bag ready?
My bag? Who are you? Where am I?

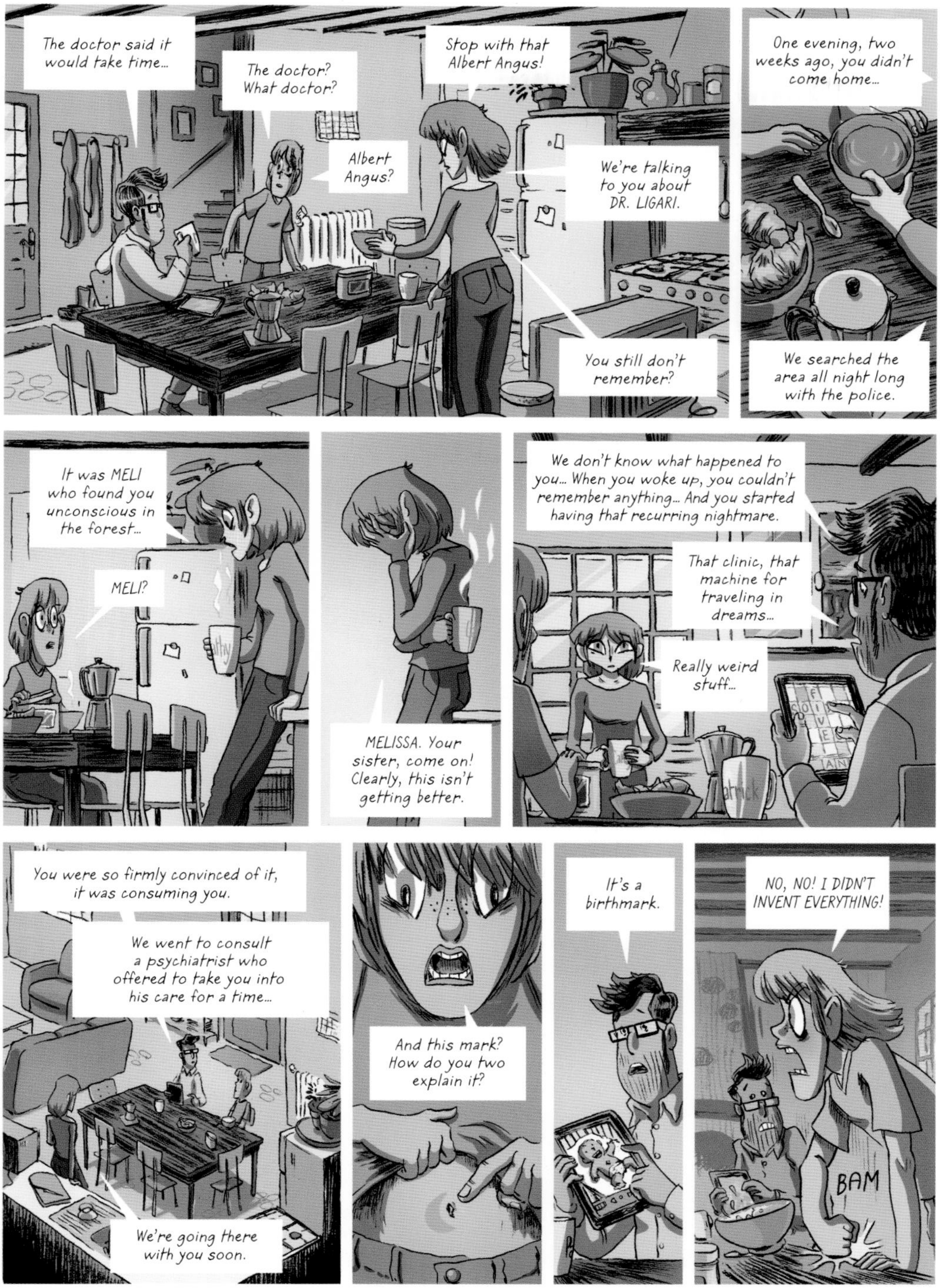
The doctor said it would take time...
The doctor? What doctor?
Albert Angus?
Stop with that Albert Angus!
We're talking to you about DR. LIGARI.
You still don't remember?
One evening, two weeks ago, you didn't come home...
We searched the area all night long with the police.
It was MELI who found you unconscious in the forest...
MELI?
MELISSA. Your sister, come on! Clearly, this isn't getting better.
We don't know what happened to you... When you woke up, you couldn't remember anything... And you started having that recurring nightmare.
That clinic, that machine for traveling in dreams...
Really weird stuff...
You were so firmly convinced of it, it was consuming you.
We went to consult a psychiatrist who offered to take you into his care for a time...
We're going there with you soon.
And this mark? How do you two explain it?
It's a birthmark.
NO, NO! I DIDN'T INVENT EVERYTHING!
BAM

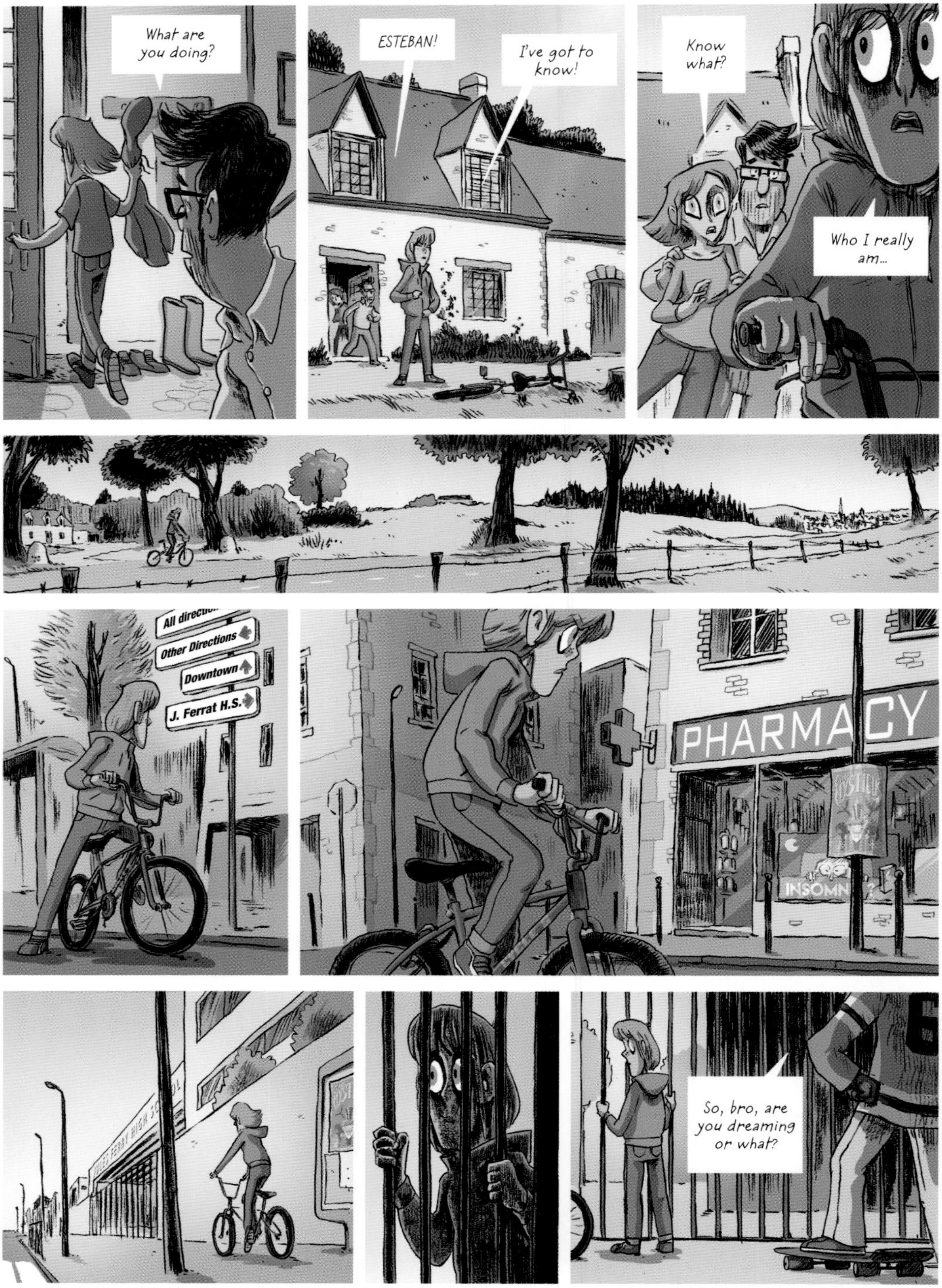
What are you doing?
ESTEBAN!
I've got to know!
Know what?
Who I really am...
All direction
Other Directions
Downtown
J. Ferrat H.S.
PHARMACY
INSOMN ?
So, bro, are you dreaming or what?

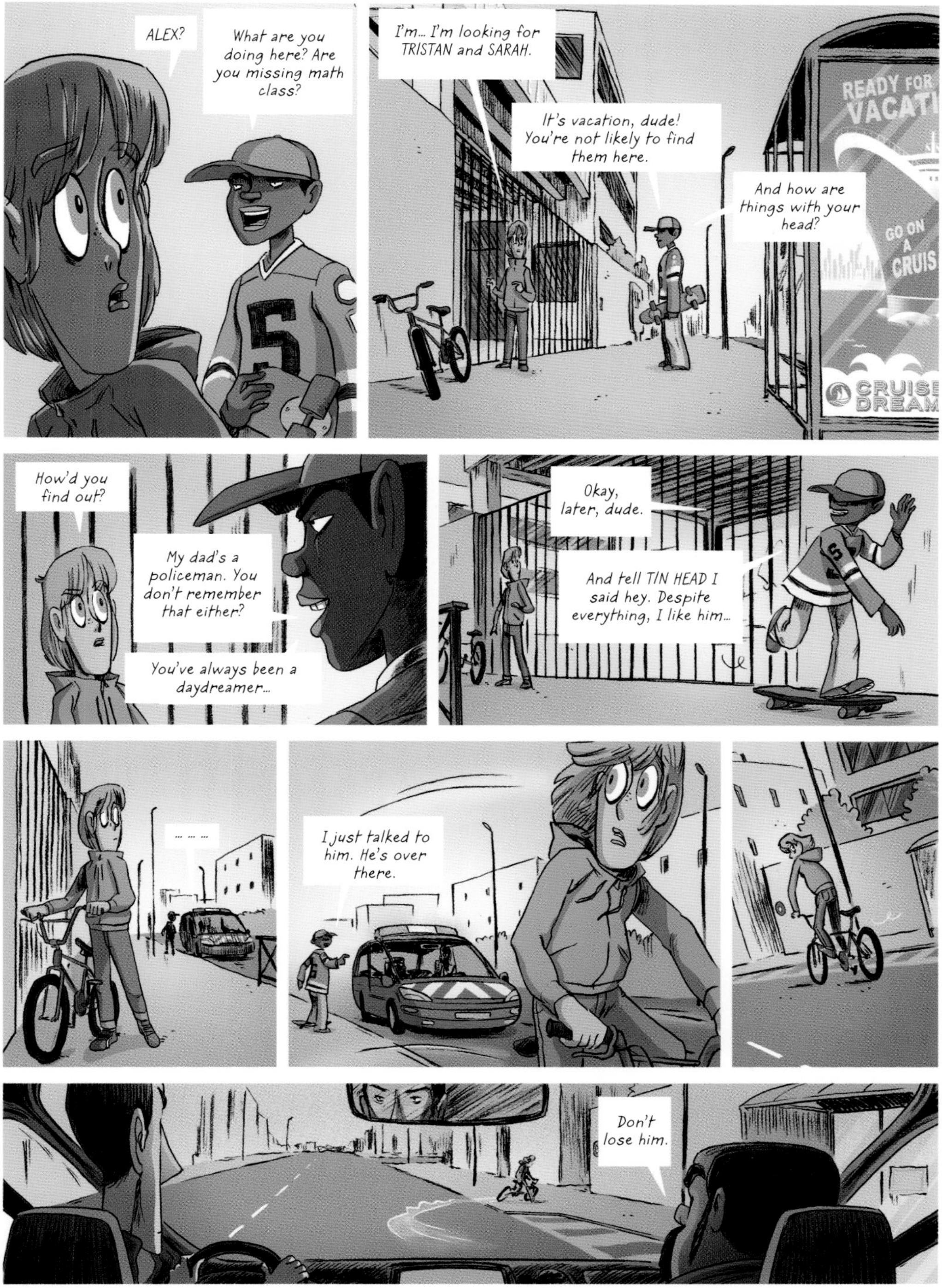
ALEX?
What are you doing here? Are you missing math class?
I'm... I'm looking for TRISTAN and SARAH.
It's vacation, dude! You're not likely to find them here.
And how are things with your head?
READY FOR VACATI
GO ON A CRUIS
CRUISE DREAM
How'd you find out?
My dad's a policeman. You don't remember that either?
You've always been a daydreamer...
Okay, later, dude.
And tell TIN HEAD I said hey. Despite everything, I like him...
... ...
I just talked to him. He's over there.
Don't lose him.

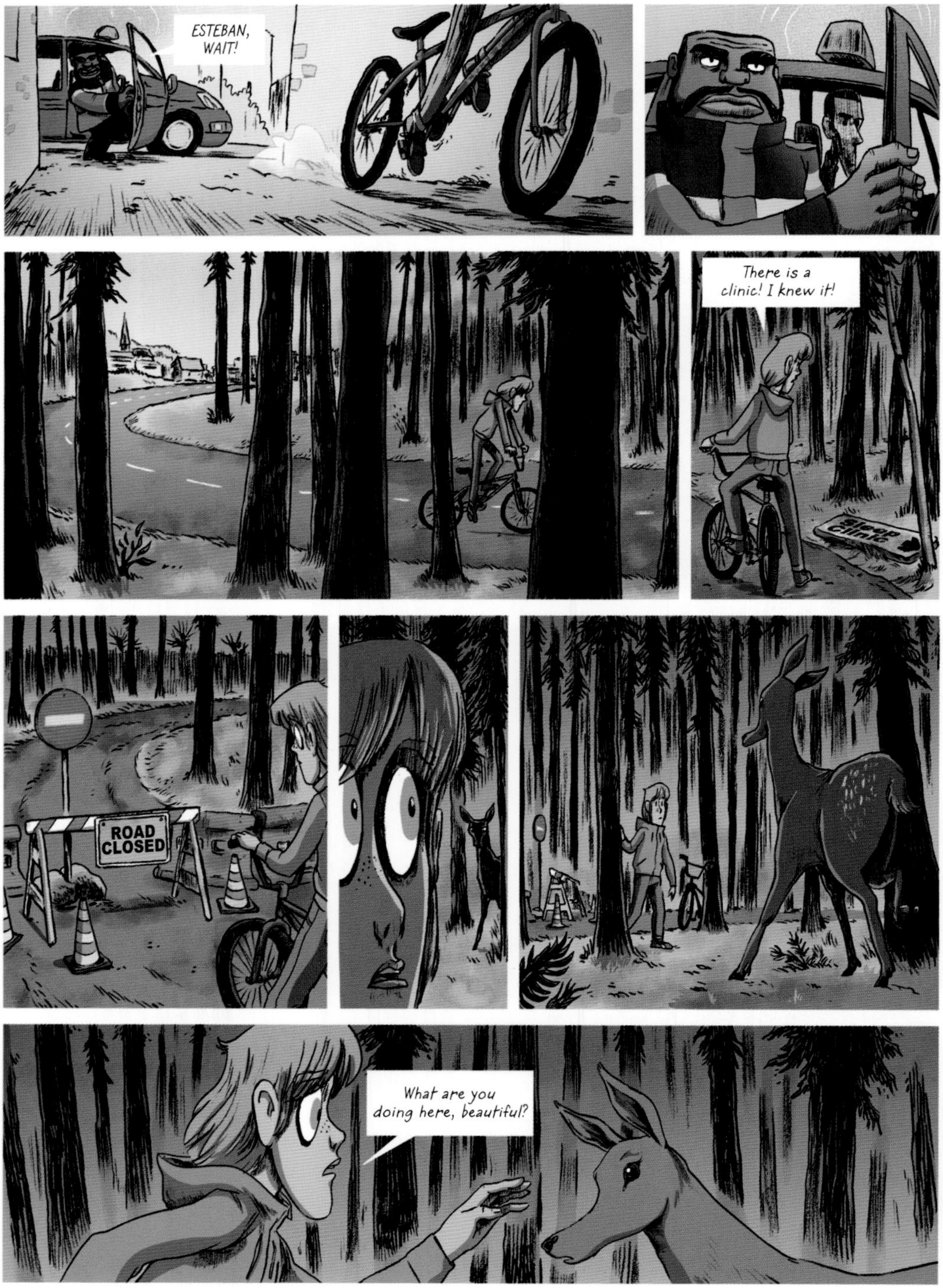
ESTEBAN, WAIT!
There is a clinic! I knew it!
Sleep Clinic
ROAD CLOSED
What are you doing here, beautiful?

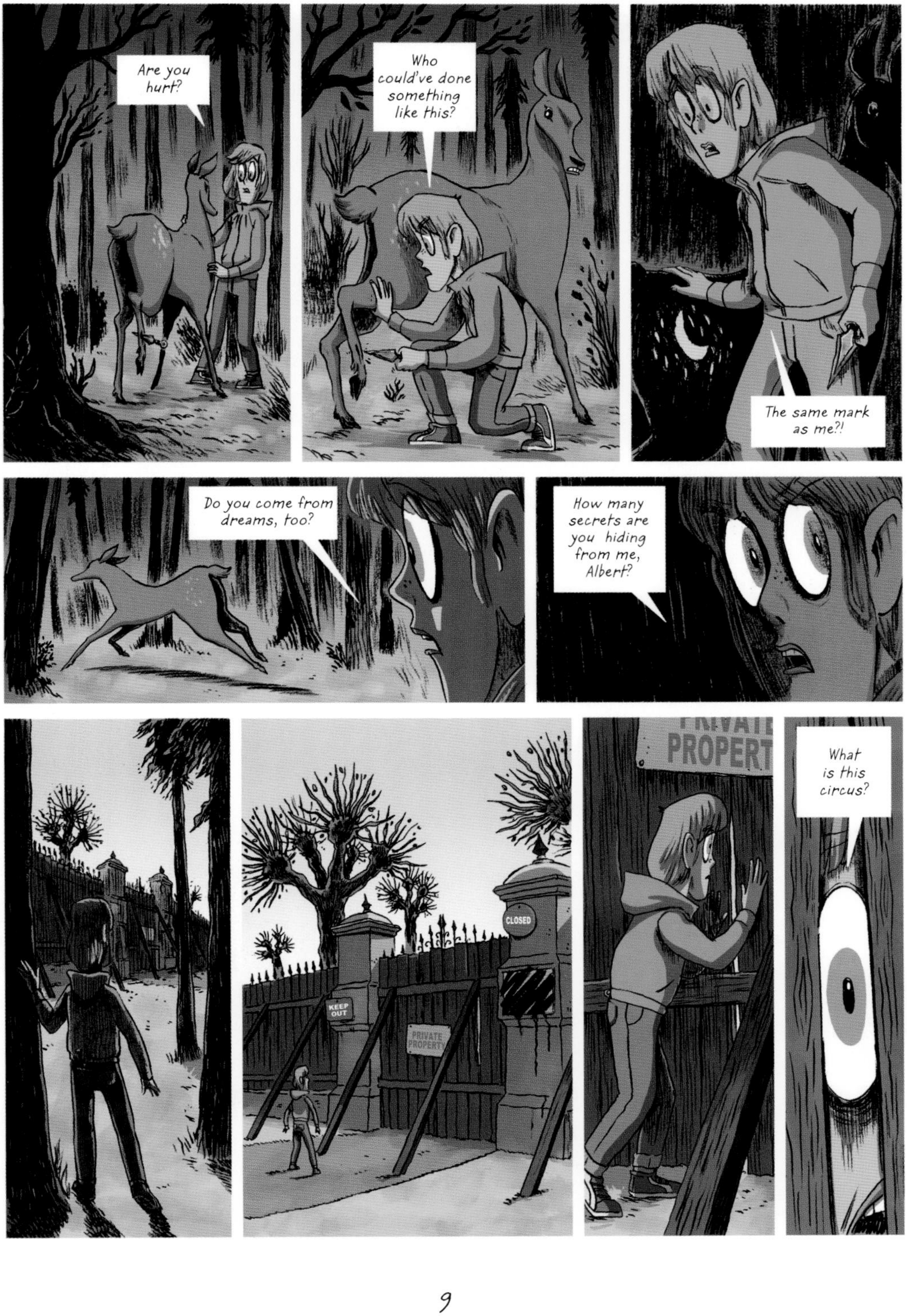
Are you hurt?
Who could've done something like this?
The same mark as me?!
Do you come from dreams, too?
How many secrets are you hiding from me, Albert?
KEEP OUT
PRIVATE PROPERTY
CLOSED
PRIVATE PROPERT
What is this circus?

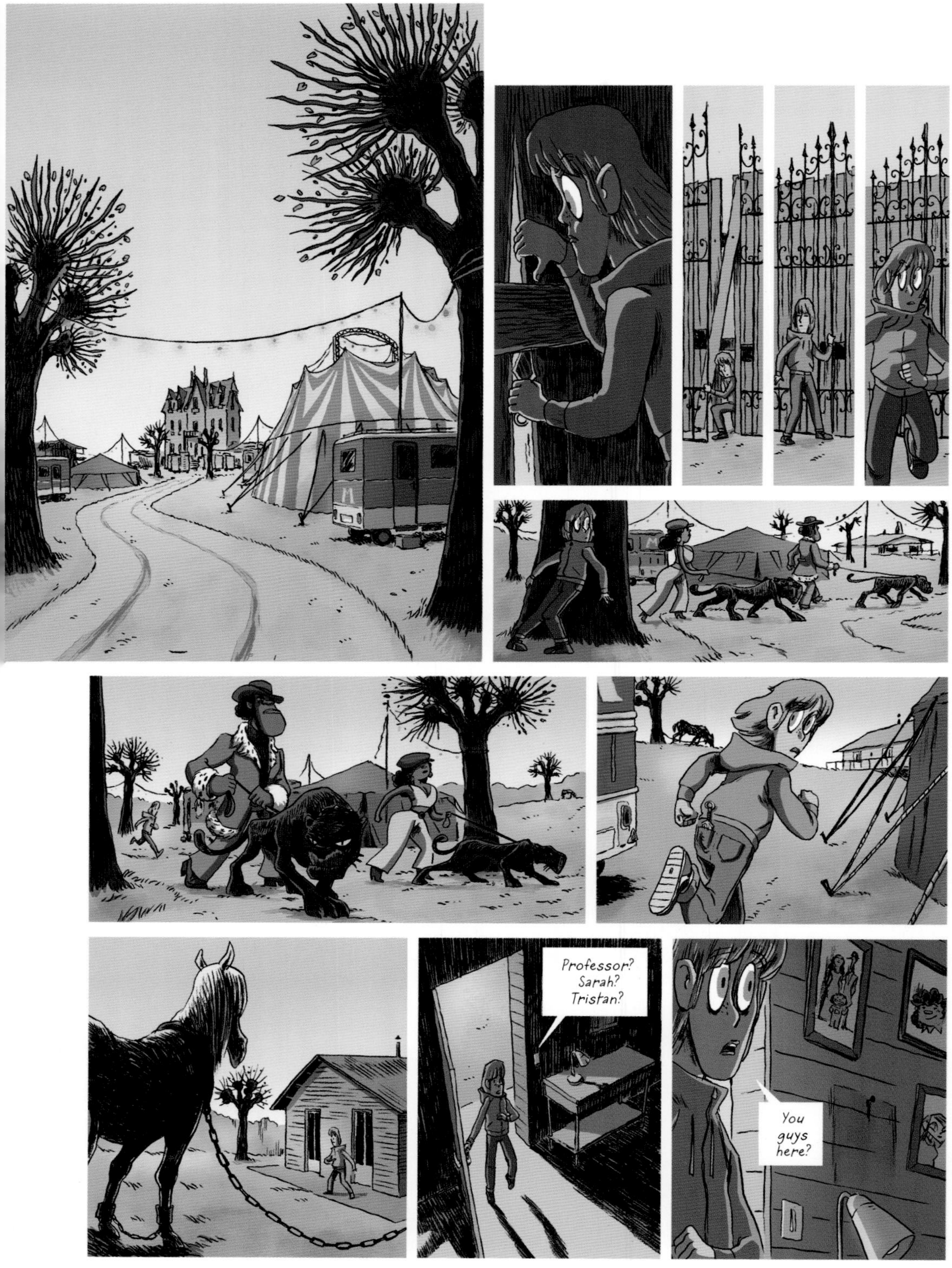
Professor? Sarah? Tristan?
You guys here?

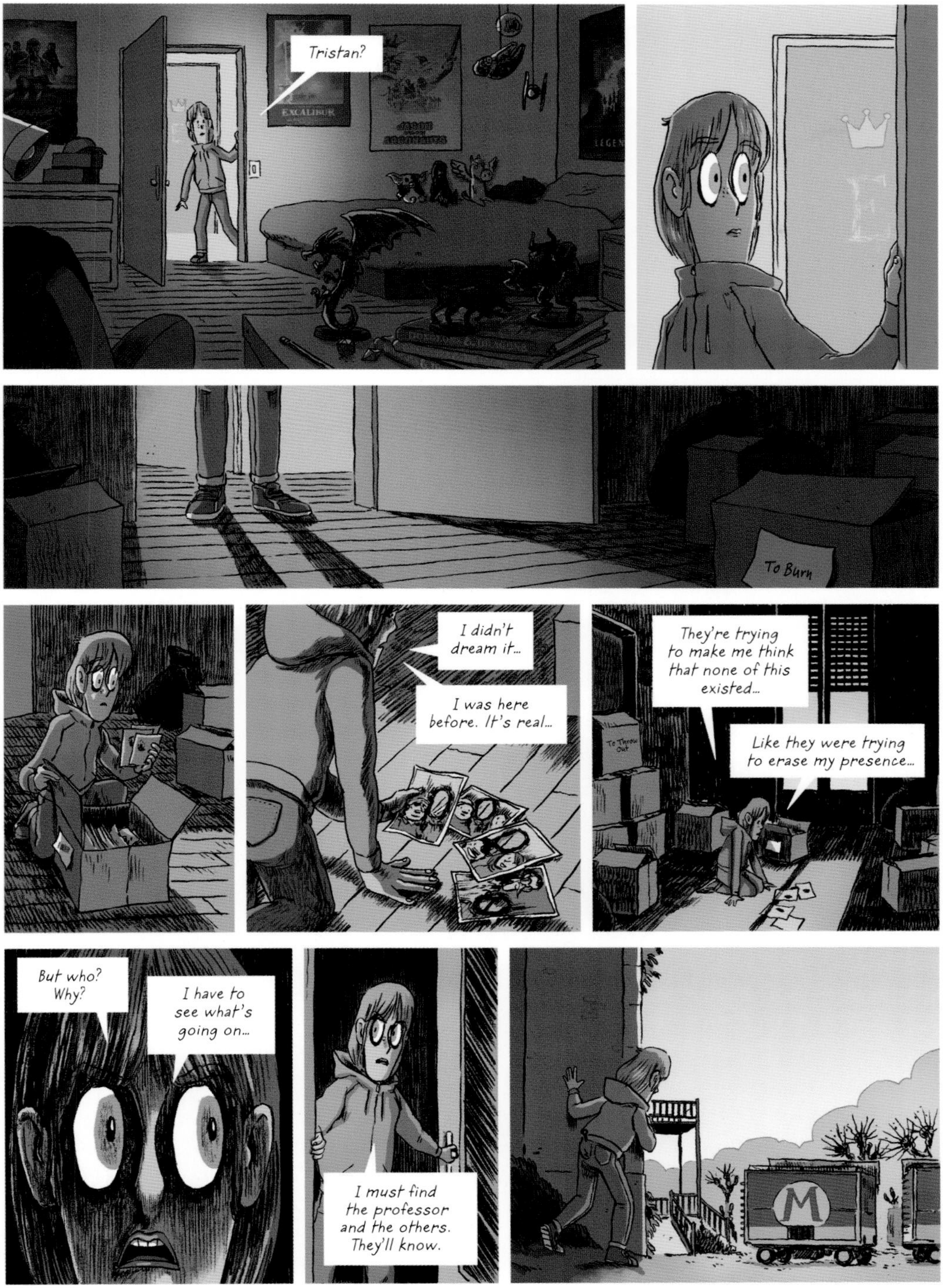
Tristan?
EXCALIBUR
LEGEN
To Burn
I didn't dream it...
I was here before. It's real...
They're trying to make me think that none of this existed...
To Throw Out
Like they were trying to erase my presence...
But who? Why?
I have to see what's going on...
I must find the professor and the others. They'll know.
M

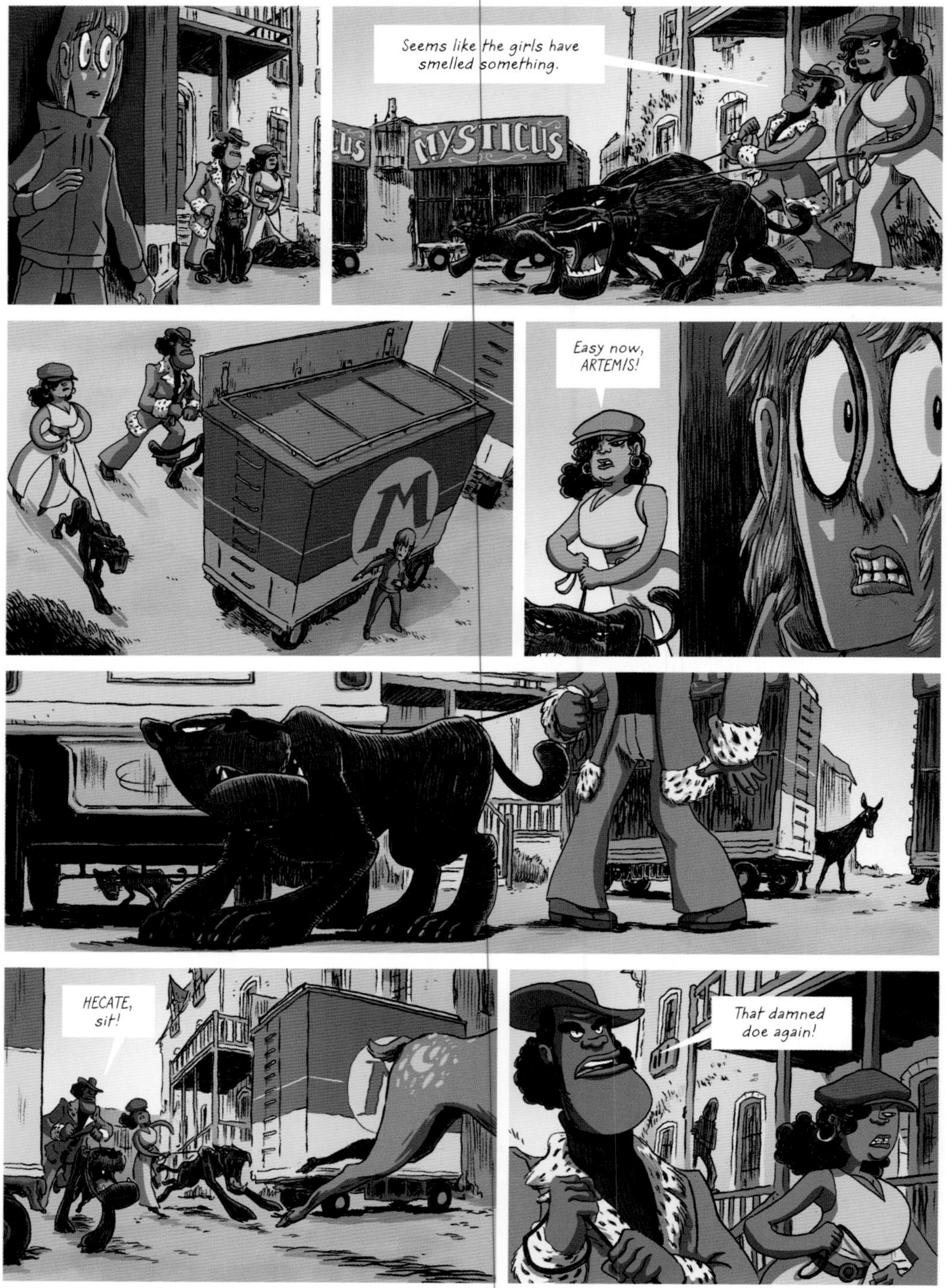
Seems like the girls have smelled something.
MYSTICUS
Easy now, ARTEMIS!
HECATE, sit!
That damned doe again!

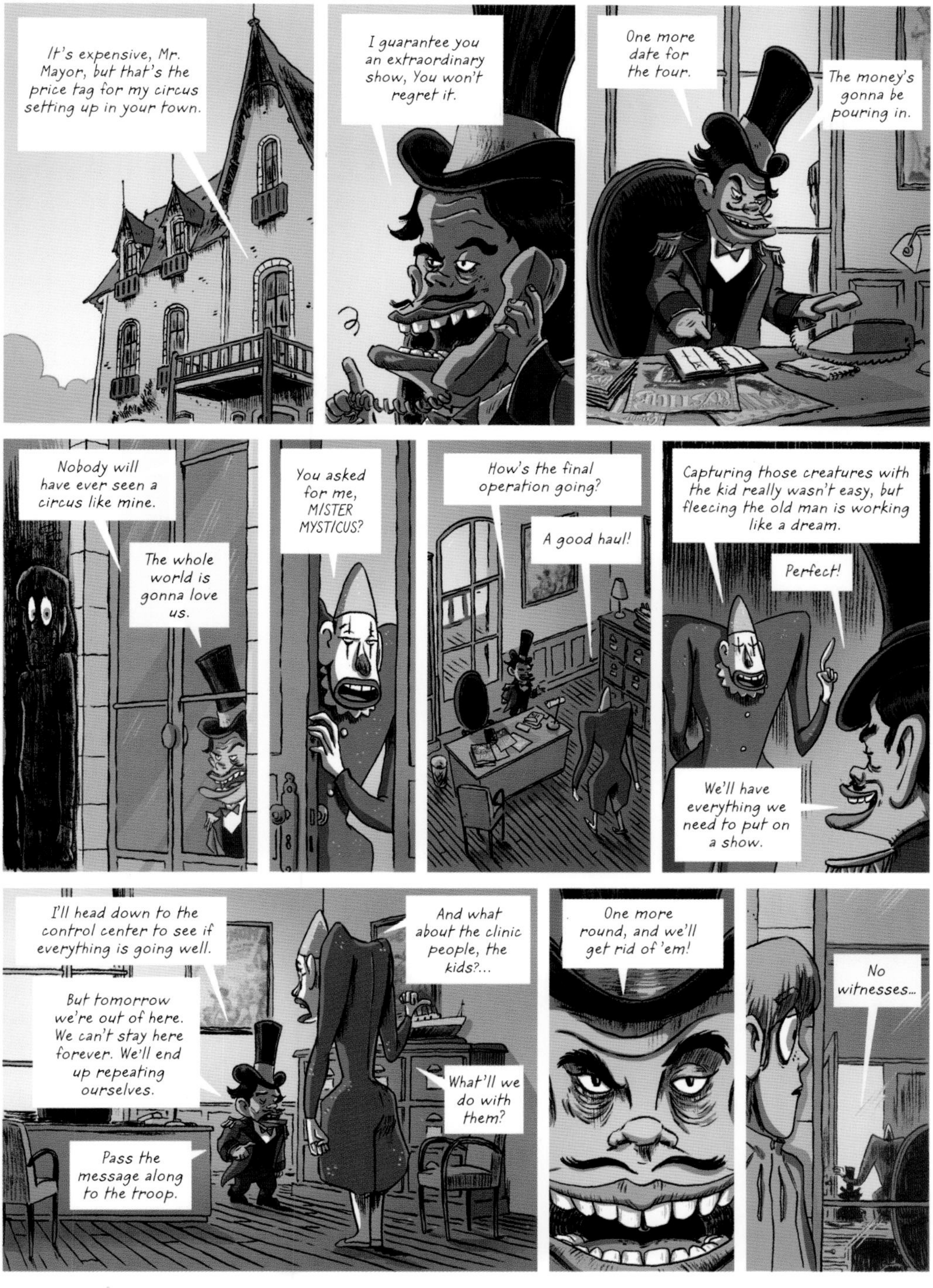
It's expensive, Mr. Mayor, but that's the price tag for my circus setting up in your town.
I guarantee you an extraordinary show, You won't regret it.
One more date for the tour.
The money's gonna be pouring in.
Nobody will have ever seen a circus like mine.
The whole world is gonna love us.
You asked for me, MISTER MYSTICUS?
How's the final operation going?
A good haul!
Capturing those creatures with the kid really wasn't easy, but fleecing the old man is working like a dream.
Perfect!
We'll have everything we need to put on a show.
I'll head down to the control center to see if everything is going well.
But tomorrow we're out of here. We can't stay here forever. We'll end up repeating ourselves.
Pass the message along to the troop.
And what about the clinic people, the kids?...
What'll we do with them?
One more round, and we'll get rid of 'em!
No witnesses...

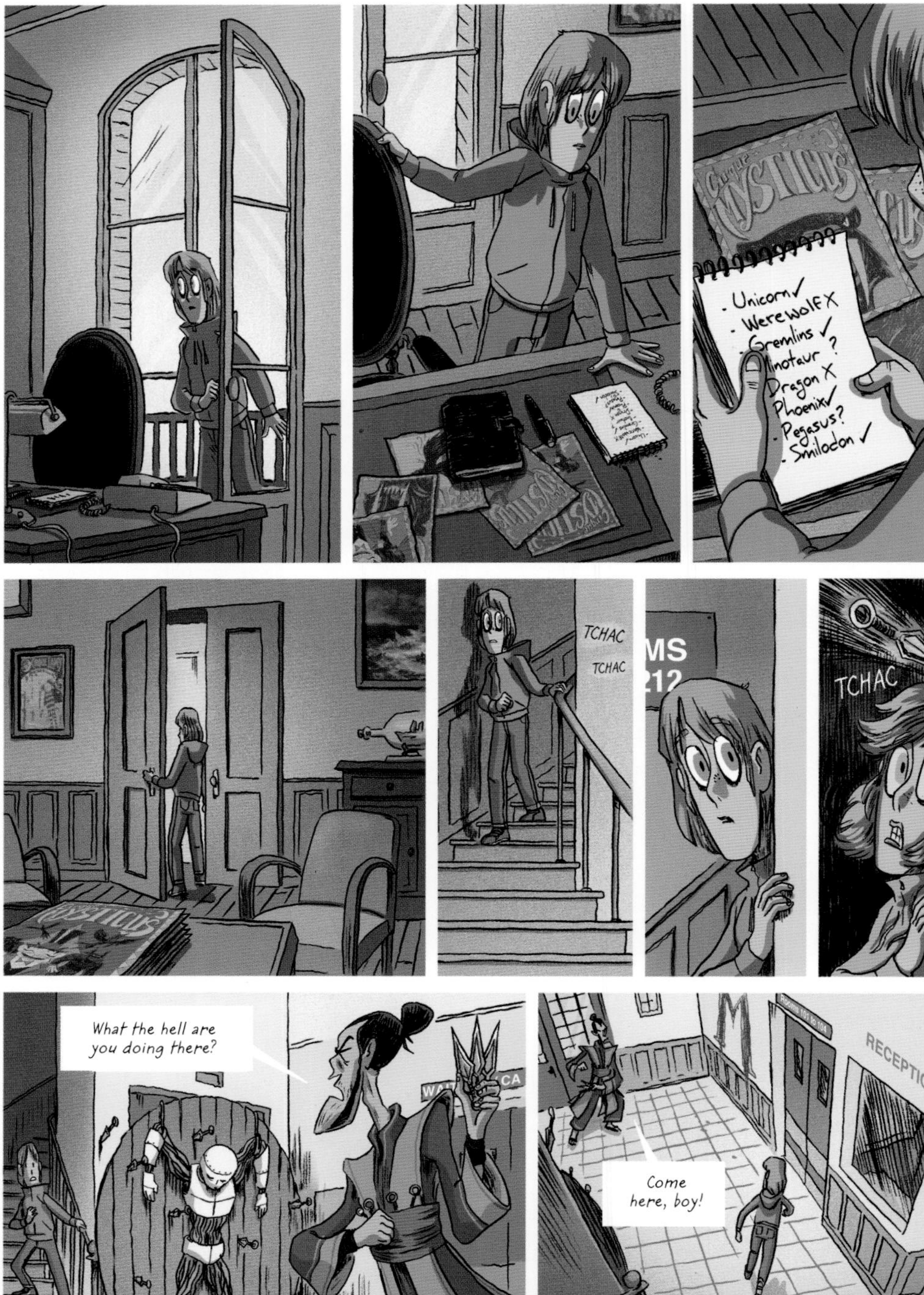

- Unicorn ✓
- Werewolf X
- Gremlins ✓
- Dragon X
- Phoenix ✓
- Pegasus?
- Smilodon ✓
TCHAC
TCHAC
TCHAC
What the hell are you doing there?
RECEPTION
Come here, boy!

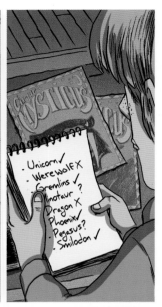

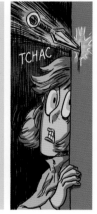

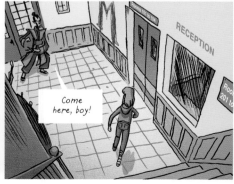

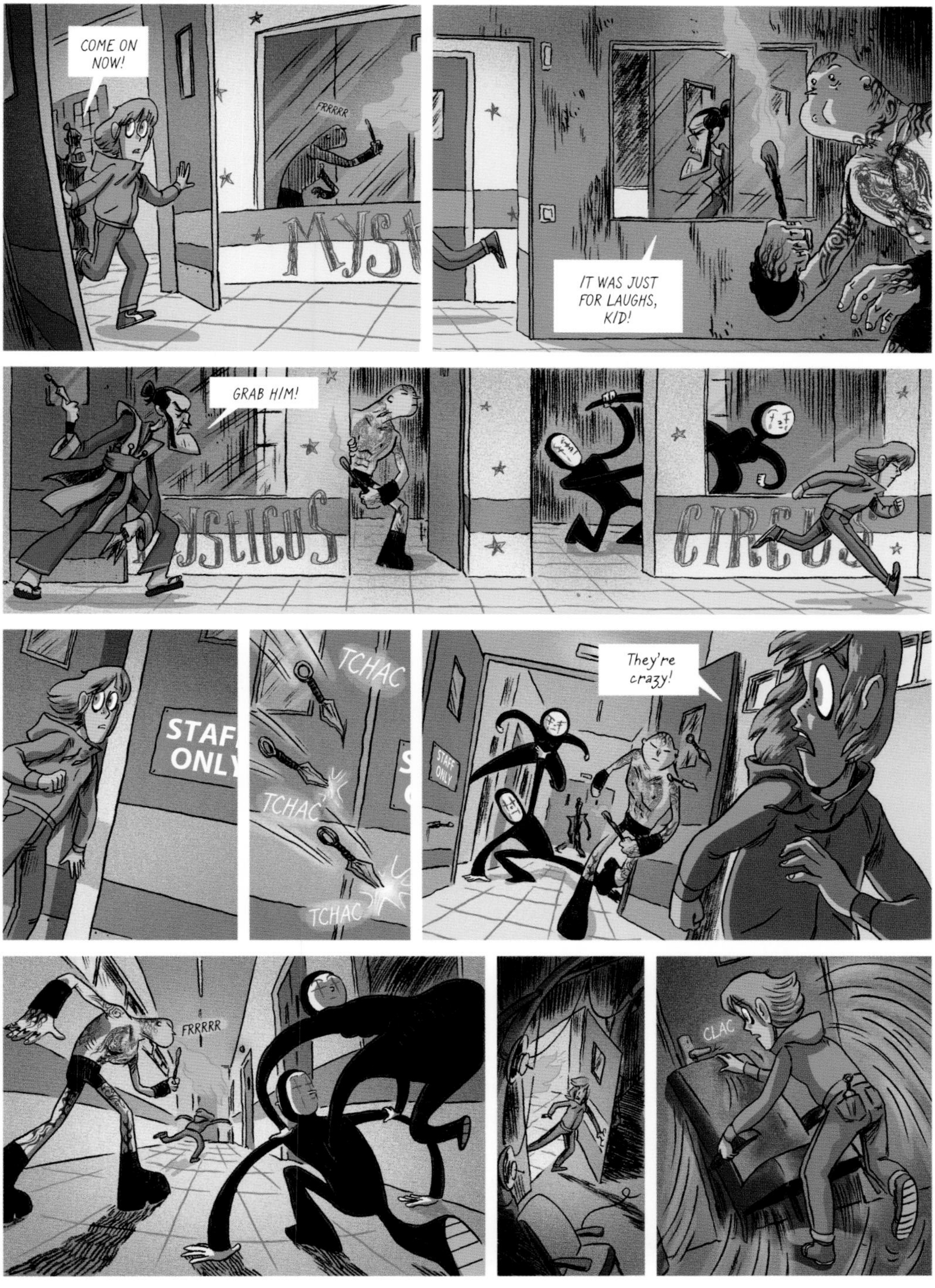
COME ON NOW!
FRRRRR
IT WAS JUST FOR LAUGHS, KID!
GRAB HIM!
STAFF ONLY
TCHAC
TCHAC
TCHAC
They're crazy!
STAFF ONLY
FRRRRR
CLAC

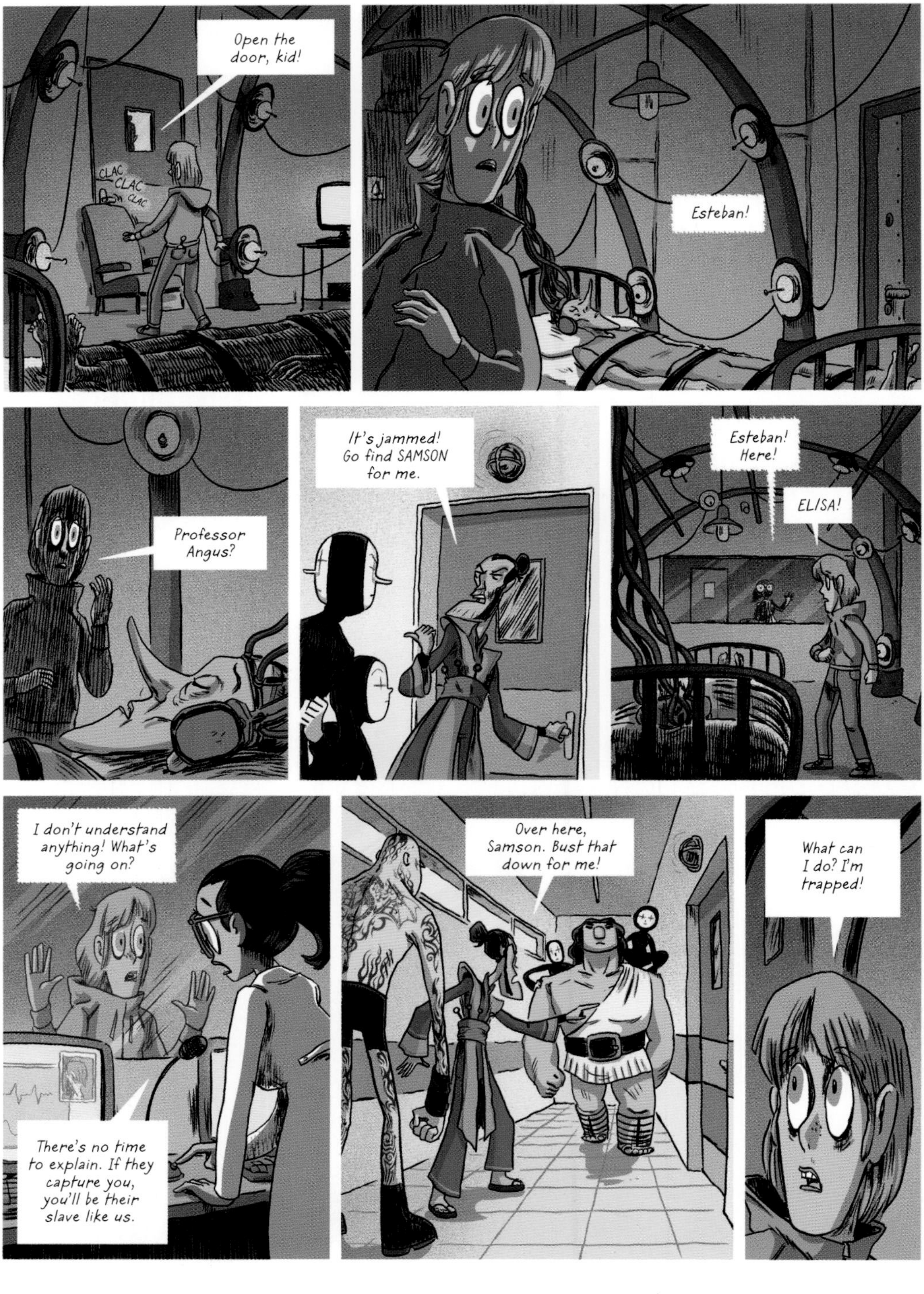
Open the door, kid!
CLAC CLAC CLAC
Esteban!
Professor Angus?
It's jammed! Go find SAMSON for me.
Esteban! Here!
ELISA!
I don't understand anything! What's going on?
There's no time to explain. If they capture you, you'll be their slave like us.
Over here, Samson. Bust that down for me!
What can I do? I'm trapped!

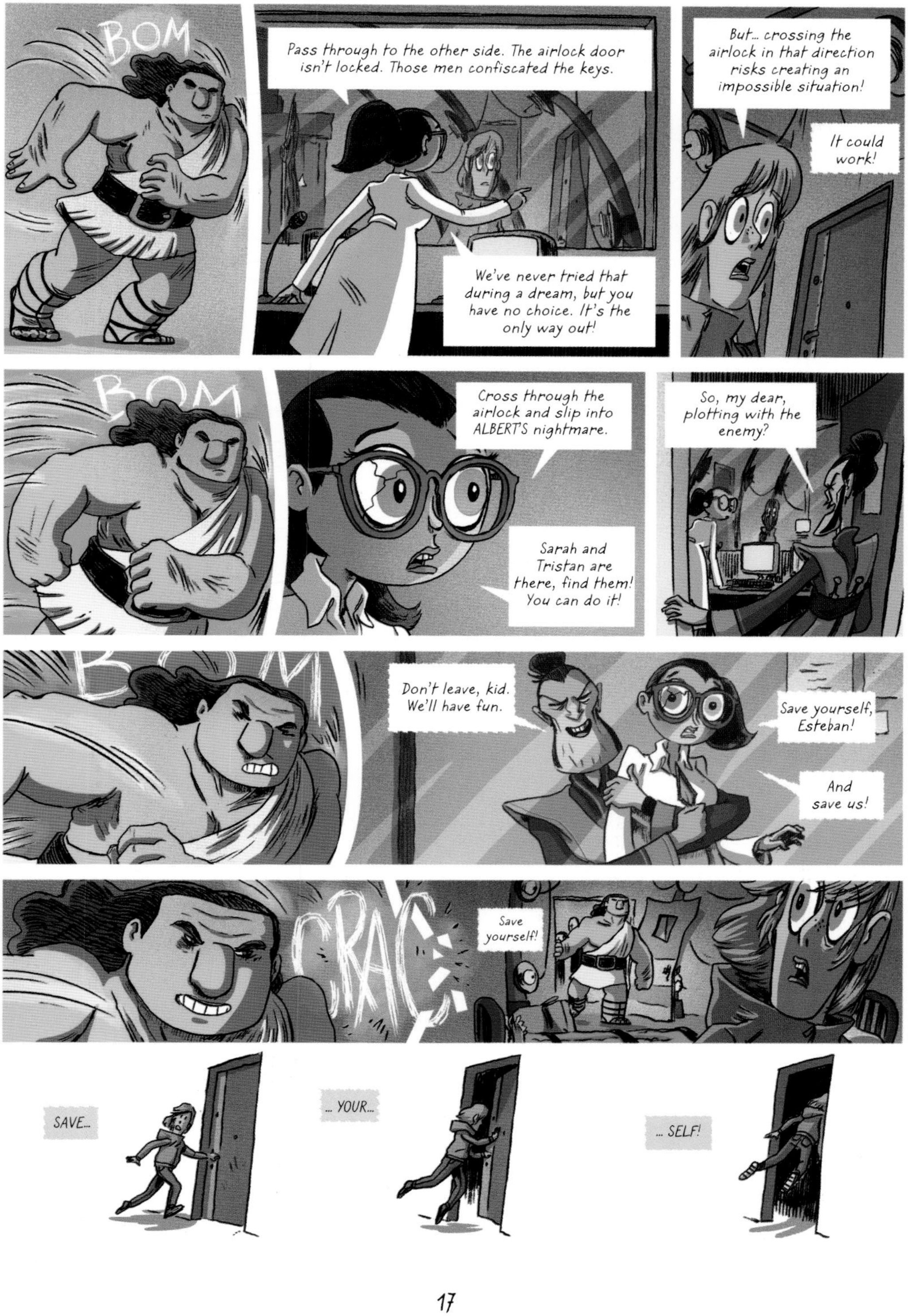
BOM
Pass through to the other side. The airlock door isn't locked. Those men confiscated the keys.
We've never tried that during a dream, but you have no choice. It's the only way out!
But... crossing the airlock in that direction risks creating an impossible situation!
It could work!
BOM
Cross through the airlock and slip into ALBERT'S nightmare.
Sarah and Tristan are there, find them! You can do it!
So, my dear, plotting with the enemy?
BOM
Don't leave, kid. We'll have fun.
Save yourself, Esteban!
And save us!
CRAC
Save yourself!
SAVE...
... YOUR...
... SELF!

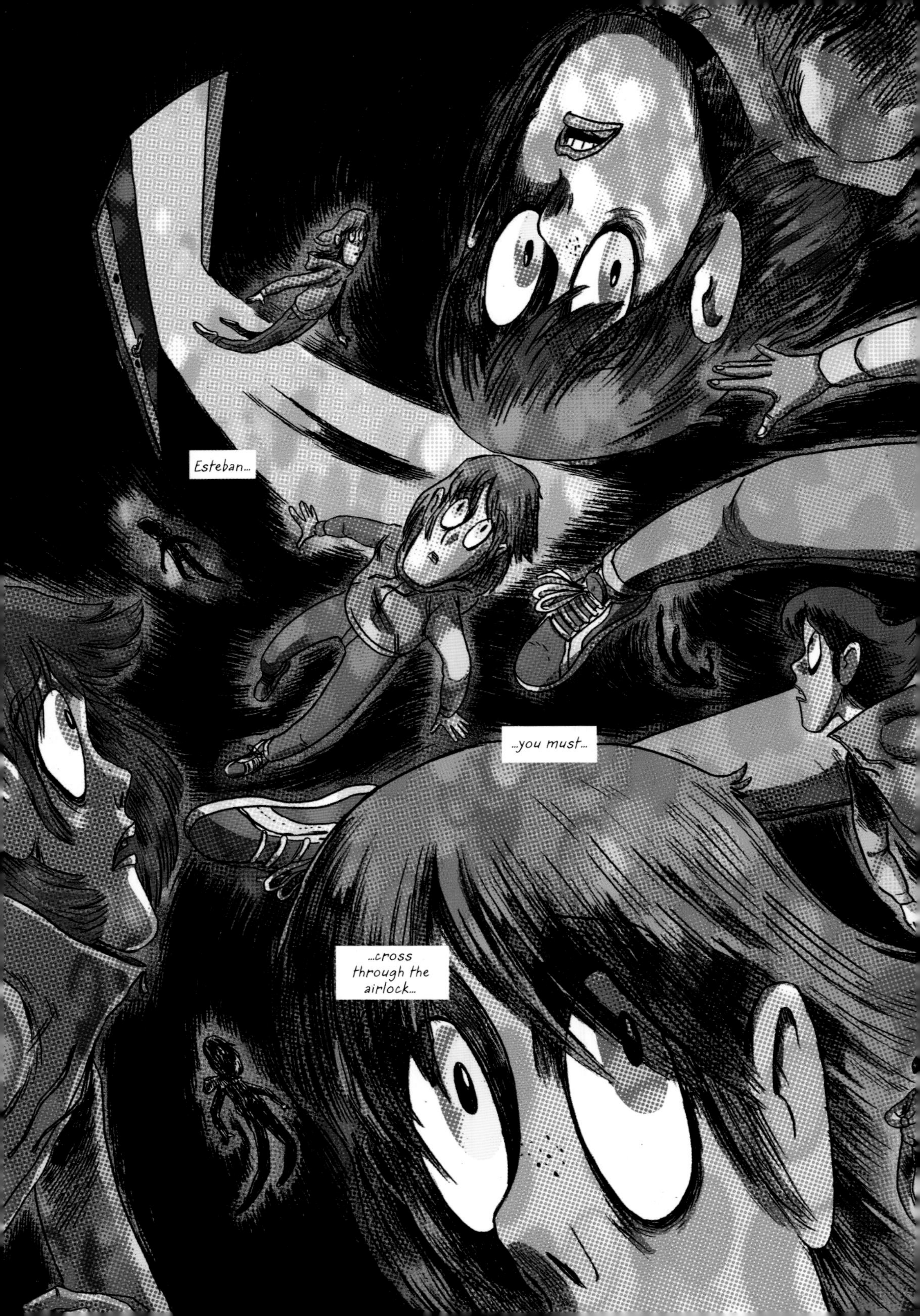
Esteban...
...you must...
...cross through the airlock...

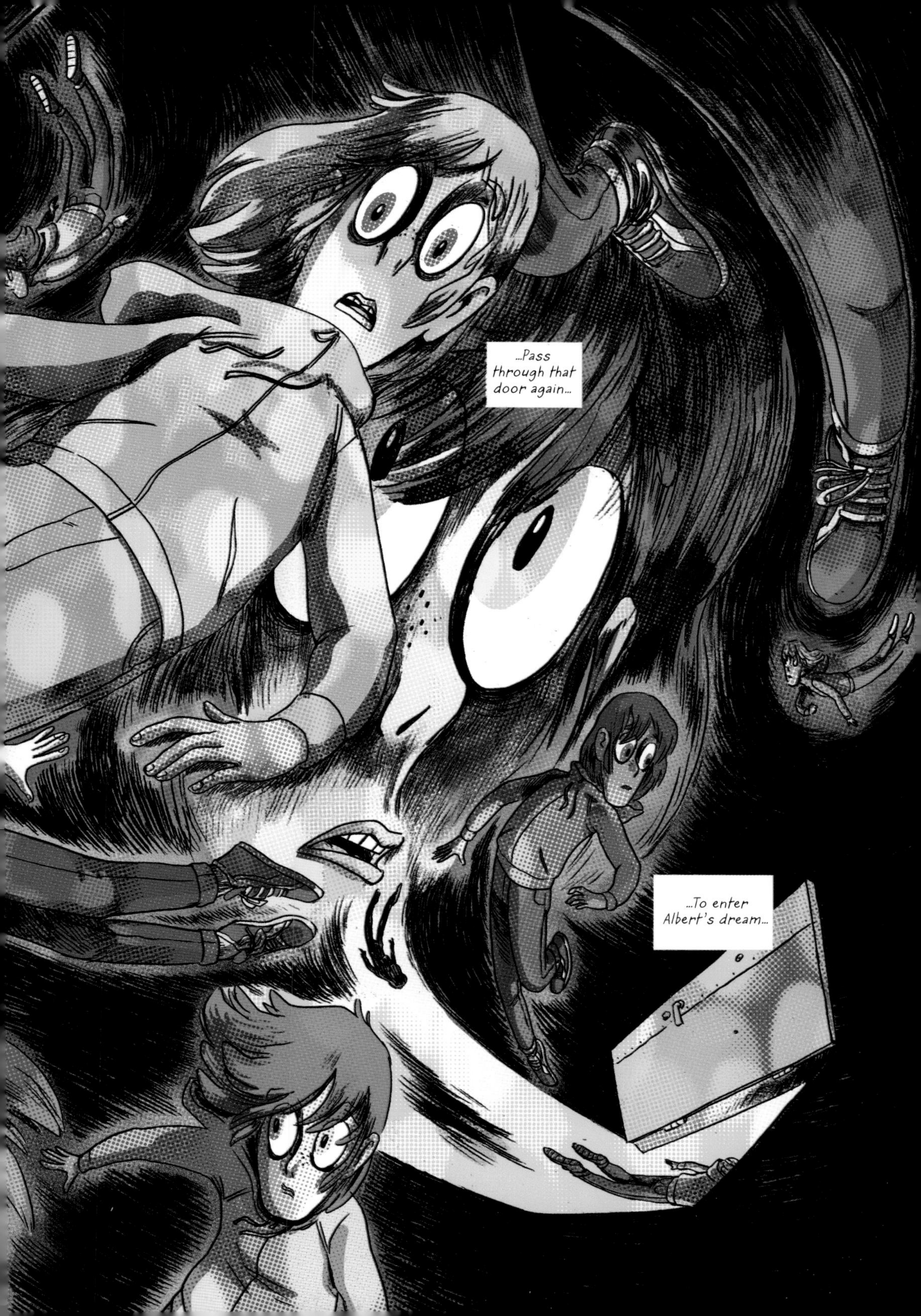
...Pass through that door again...
...To enter Albert's dream...

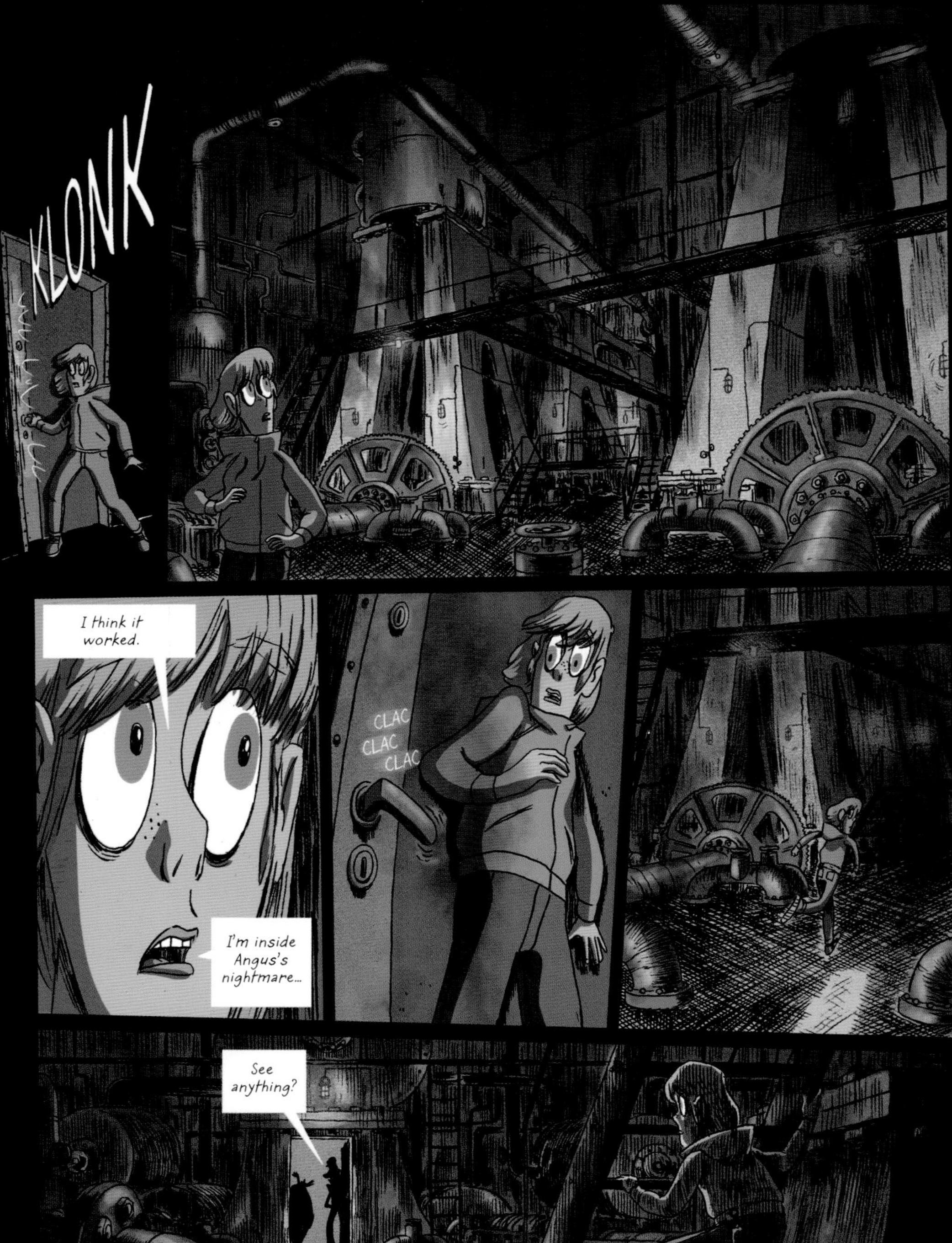
KLONK
I think it worked.
I'm inside Angus's nightmare...
CLAC
CLAC
CLAC
See anything?

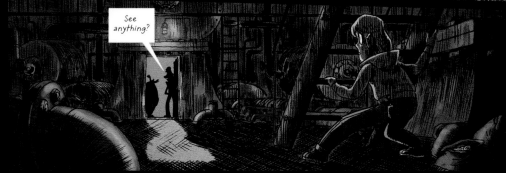

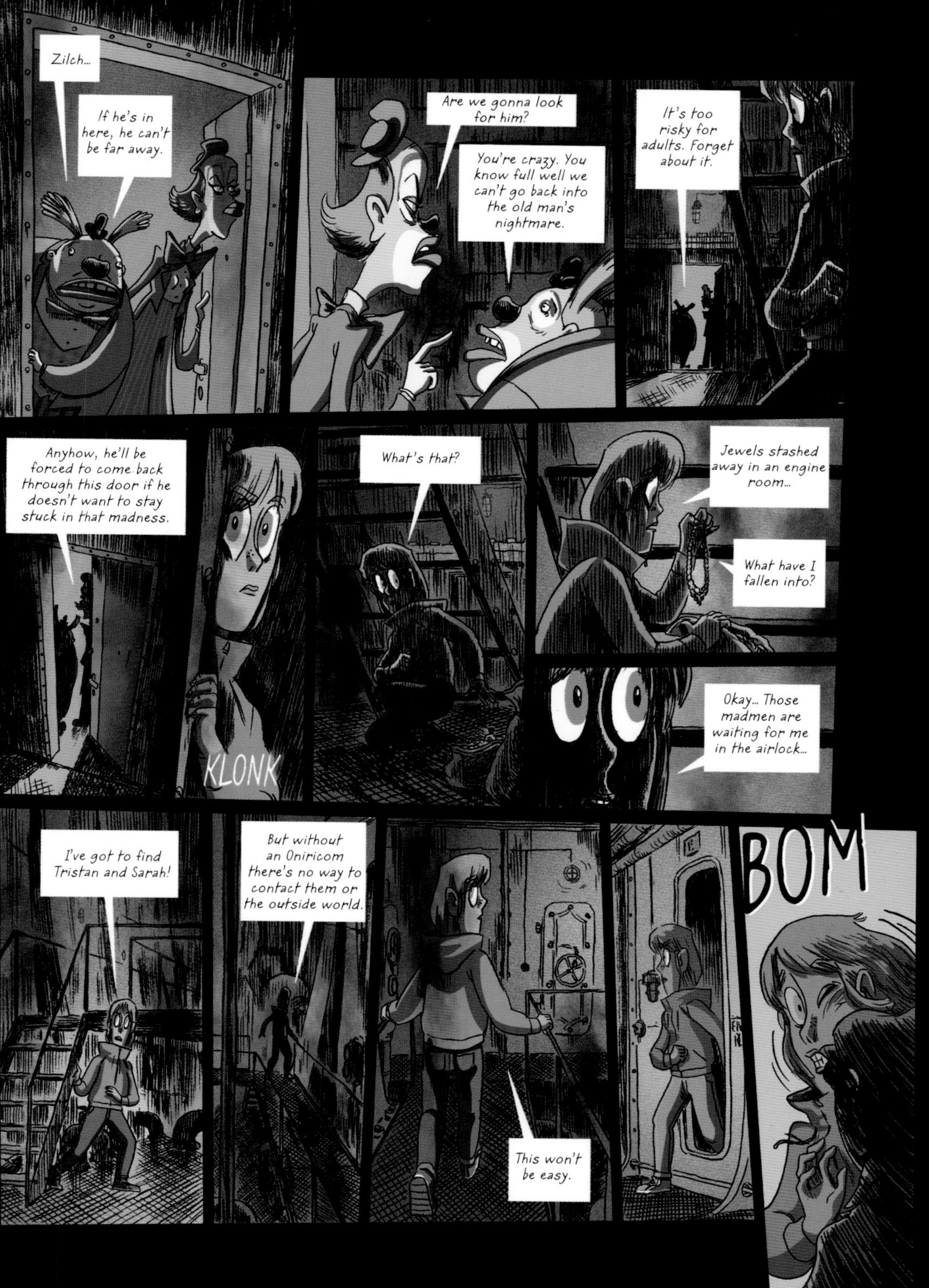
Zilch...
If he's in here, he can't be far away.
Are we gonna look for him?
You're crazy. You know full well we can't go back into the old man's nightmare.
It's too risky for adults. Forget about it.
Anyhow, he'll be forced to come back through this door if he doesn't want to stay stuck in that madness.
KLONK
What's that?
Jewels stashed away in an engine room...
What have I fallen into?
Okay... Those madmen are waiting for me in the airlock...
I've got to find Tristan and Sarah!
But without an Oniricom there's no way to contact them or the outside world.
This won't be easy.
BOM

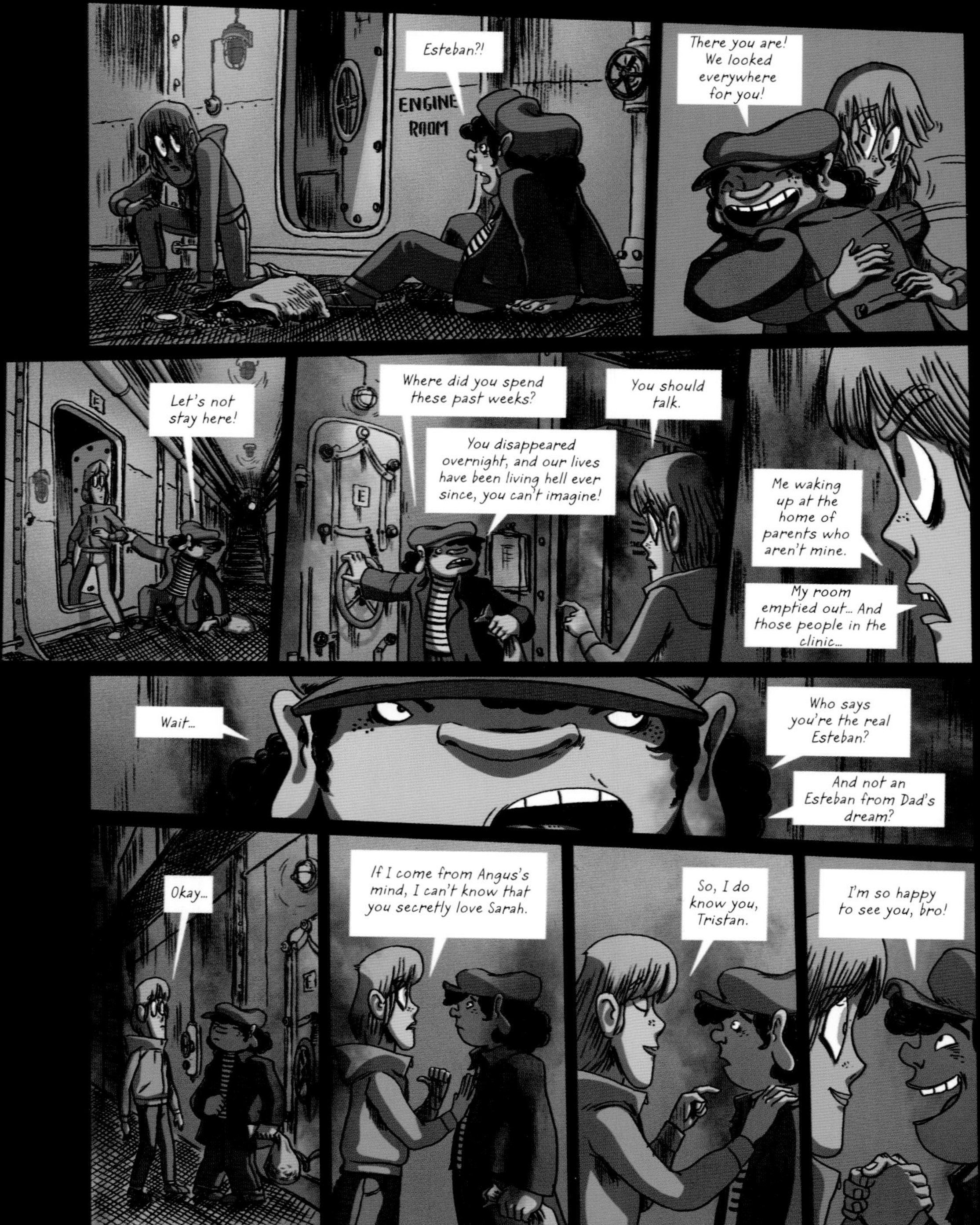
ENGINE ROOM
Esteban?!
There you are! We looked everywhere for you!
Let's not stay here!
Where did you spend these past weeks?
You disappeared overnight, and our lives have been living hell ever since, you can't imagine!
You should talk.
Me waking up at the home of parents who aren't mine.
My room emptied out... And those people in the clinic...
Wait...
Who says you're the real Esteban?
And not an Esteban from Dad's dream?
Okay...
If I come from Angus's mind, I can't know that you secretly love Sarah.
So, I do know you, Tristan.
I'm so happy to see you, bro!

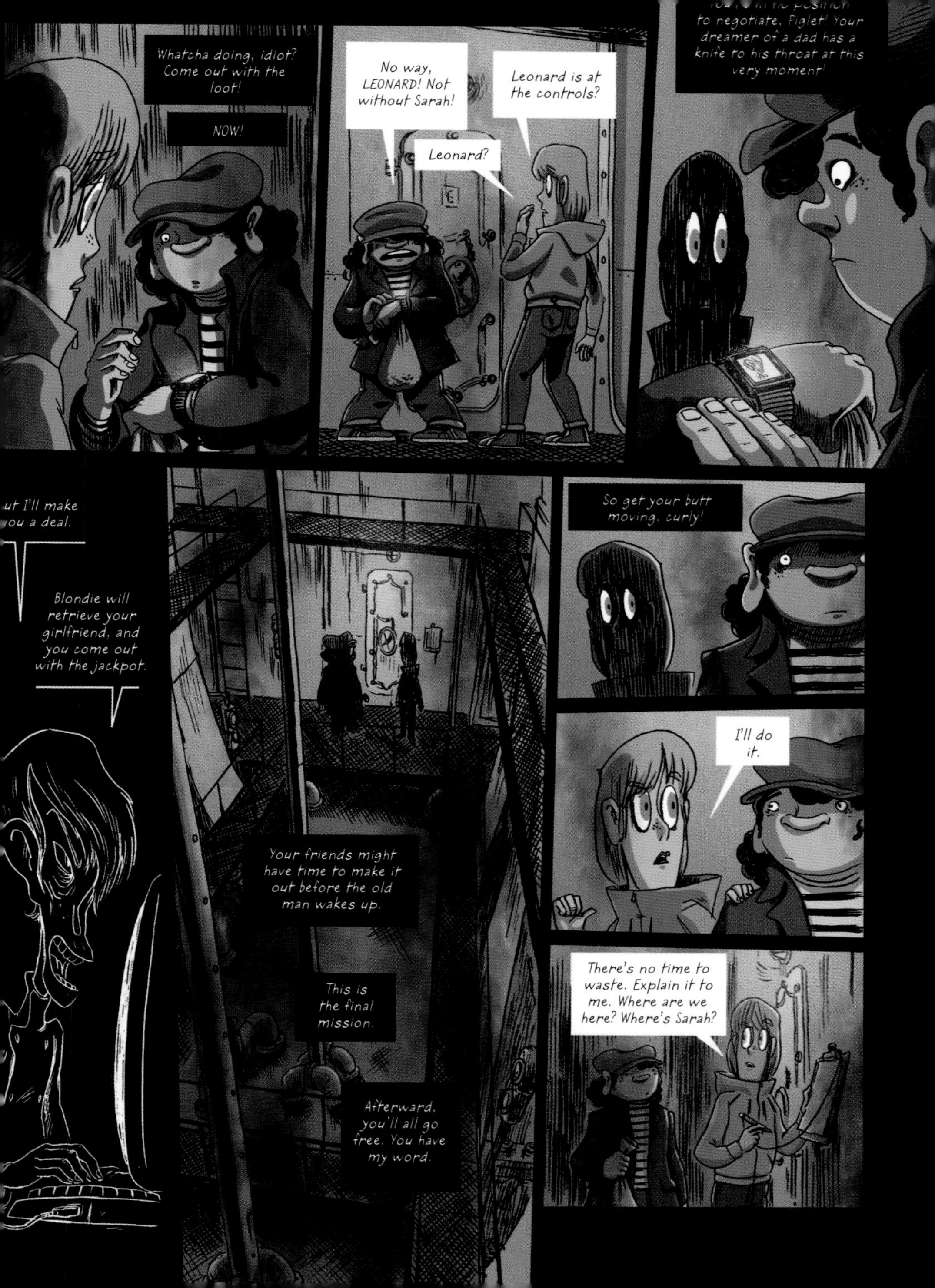

Whatcha doing, idiot? Come out with the loot!
NOW!
No way, LEONARD! Not without Sarah!
Leonard?
Leonard is at the controls?
to negotiate, Piglet! Your dreamer of a dad has a knife to his throat at this very moment!
ut I'll make you a deal.
Blondie will retrieve your girlfriend, and you come out with the jackpot.
Your friends might have time to make it out before the old man wakes up.
This is the final mission.
Afterward, you'll all go free. You have my word.
So get your butt moving, curly!
I'll do it.
There's no time to waste. Explain it to me. Where are we here? Where's Sarah?

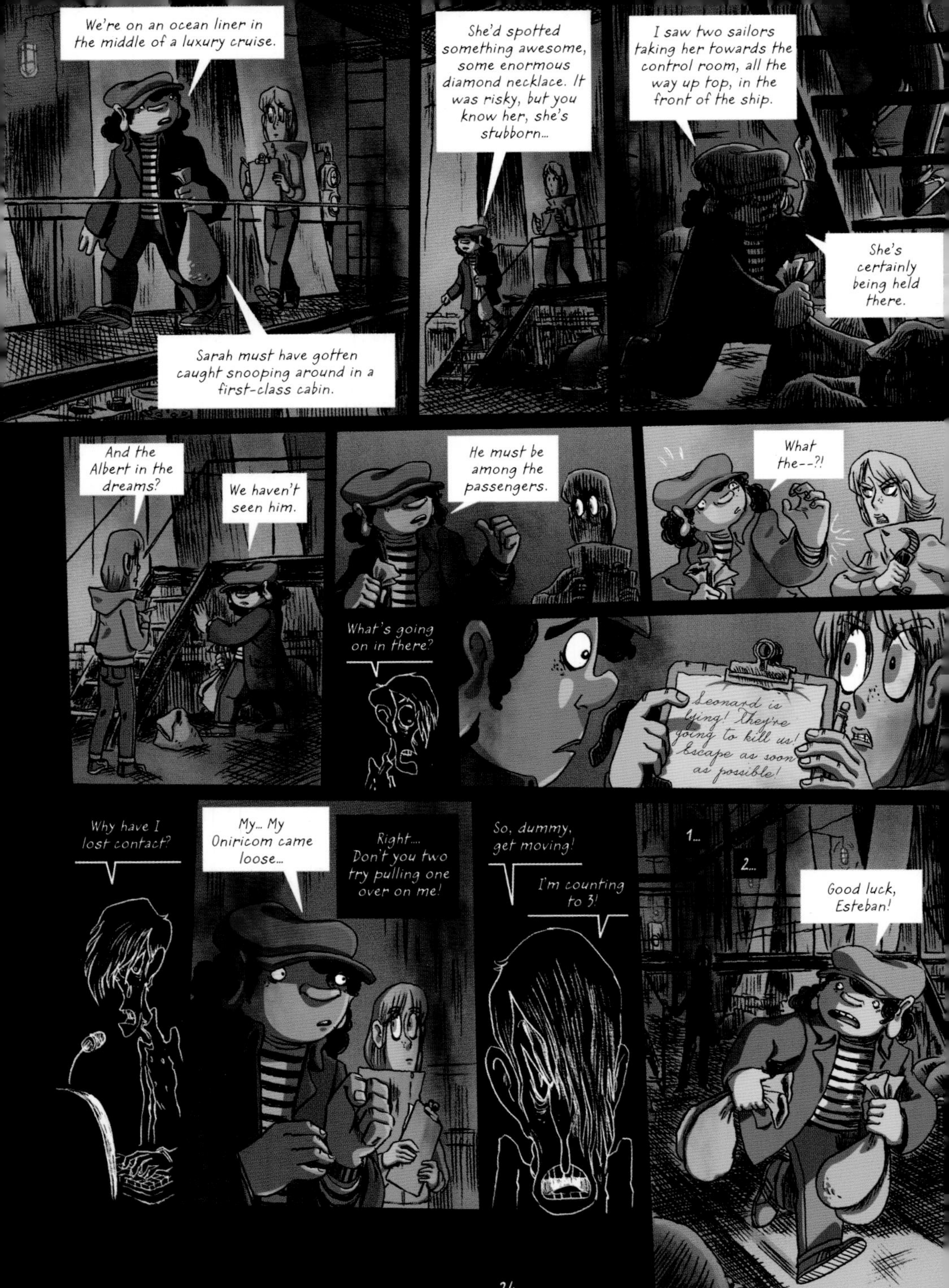

We're on an ocean liner in the middle of a luxury cruise.
Sarah must have gotten caught snooping around in a first-class cabin.
She'd spotted something awesome, some enormous diamond necklace. It was risky, but you know her, she's stubborn...
I saw two sailors taking her towards the control room, all the way up top, in the front of the ship.
She's certainly being held there.
And the Albert in the dreams?
We haven't seen him.
He must be among the passengers.
What the--?!
What's going on in there?
Leonard is lying! They're going to kill us! Escape as soon as possible!
Why have I lost contact?
My... My Oniricom came loose...
Right.... Don't you two try pulling one over on me!
So, dummy, get moving!
I'm counting to 3!
1...
2...
Good luck, Esteban!

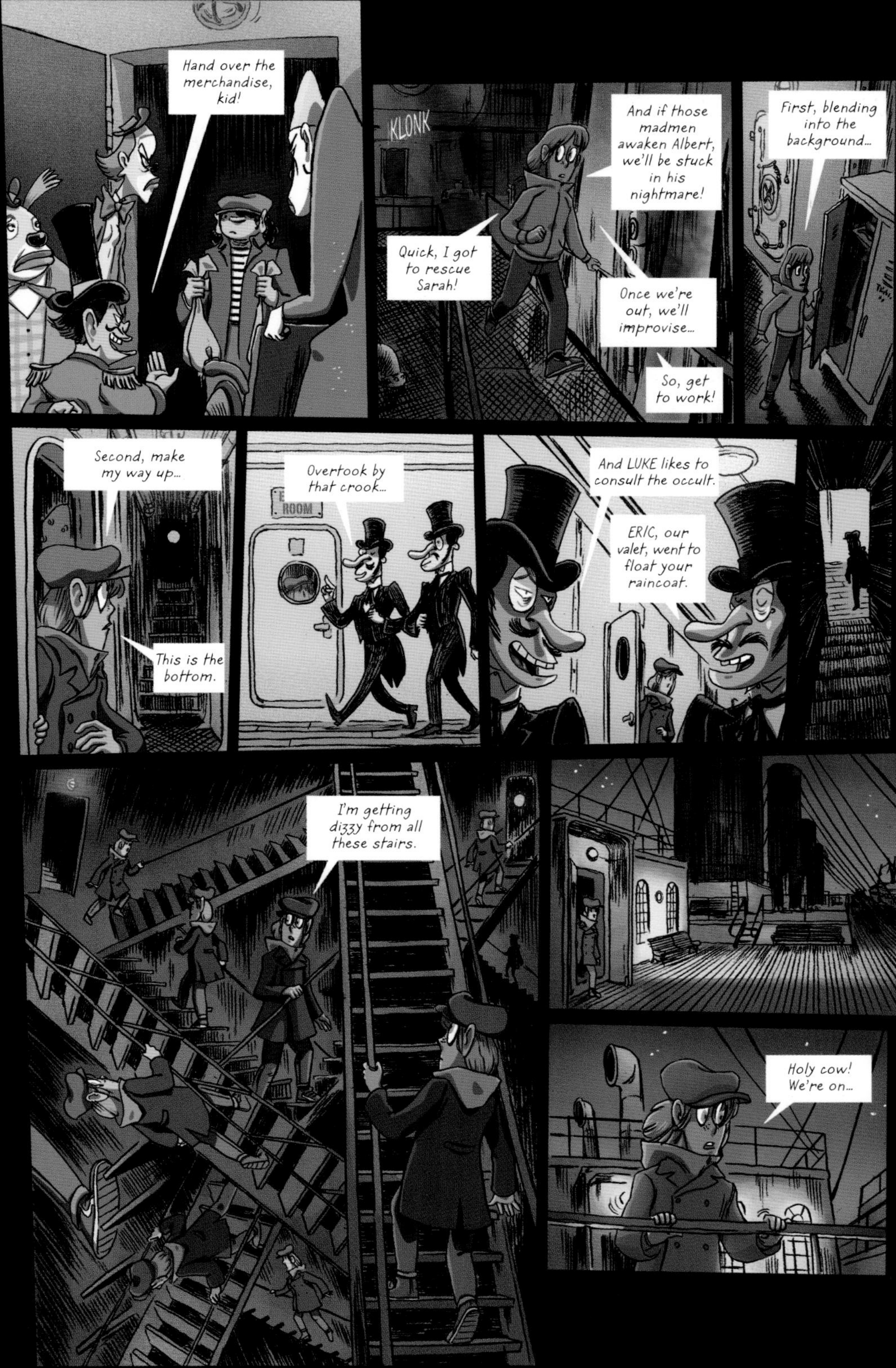
Hand over the merchandise, kid!
KLONK
Quick, I got to rescue Sarah!
And if those madmen awaken Albert, we'll be stuck in his nightmare!
Once we're out, we'll improvise...
So, get to work!
First, blending into the background...
Second, make my way up...
This is the bottom.
Overtook by that crook...
ROOM
And LUKE likes to consult the occult.
ERIC, our valet, went to float your raincoat.
I'm getting dizzy from all these stairs.
Holy cow! We're on...

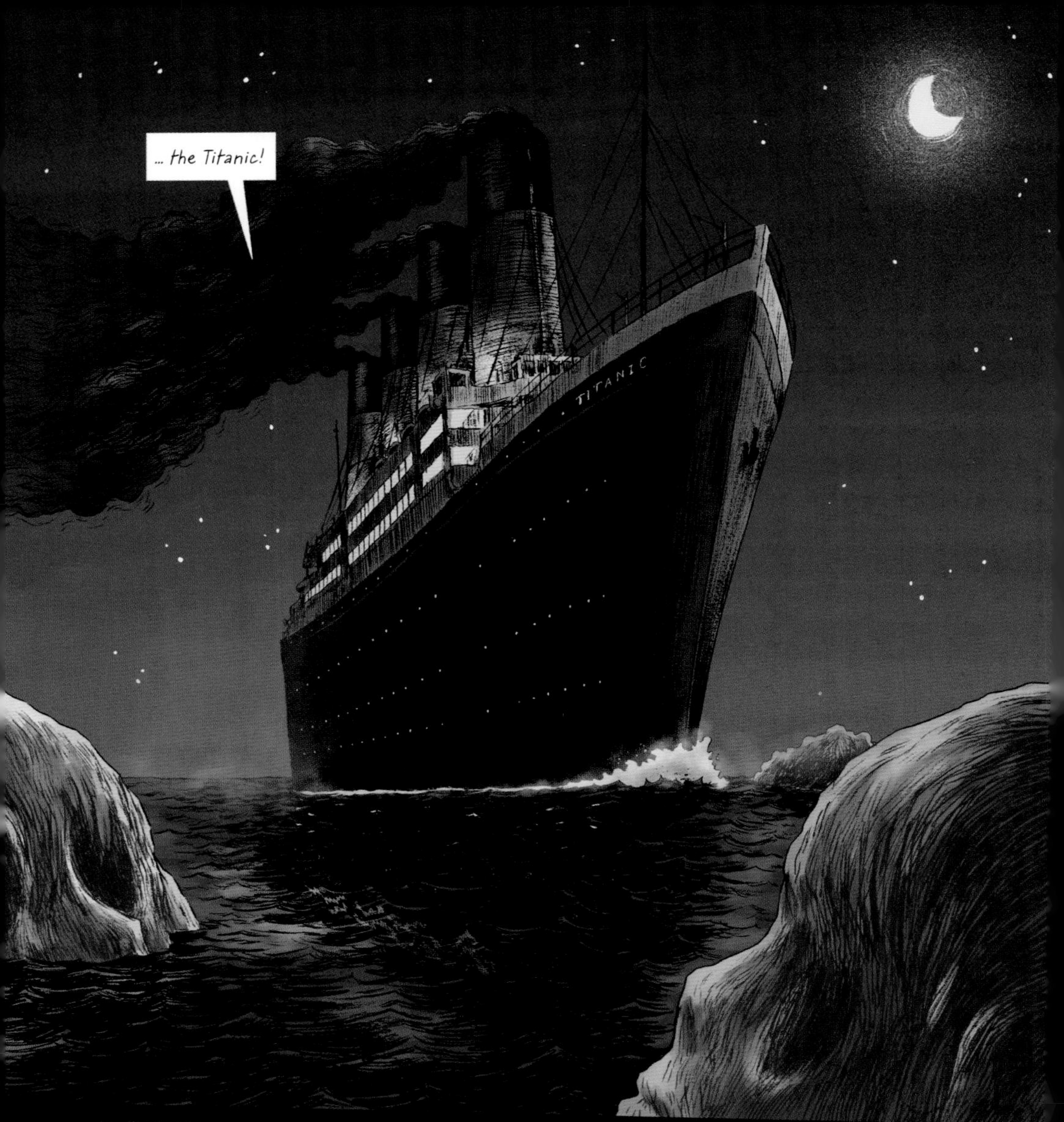
... the Titanic!
TITANIC

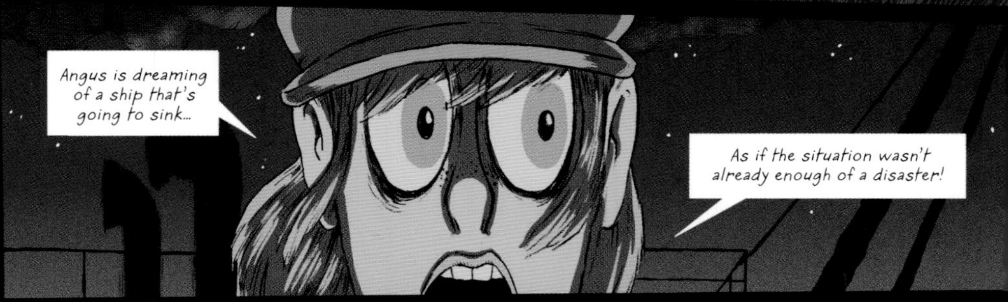
Angus is dreaming of a ship that's going to sink...
As if the situation wasn't already enough of a disaster!

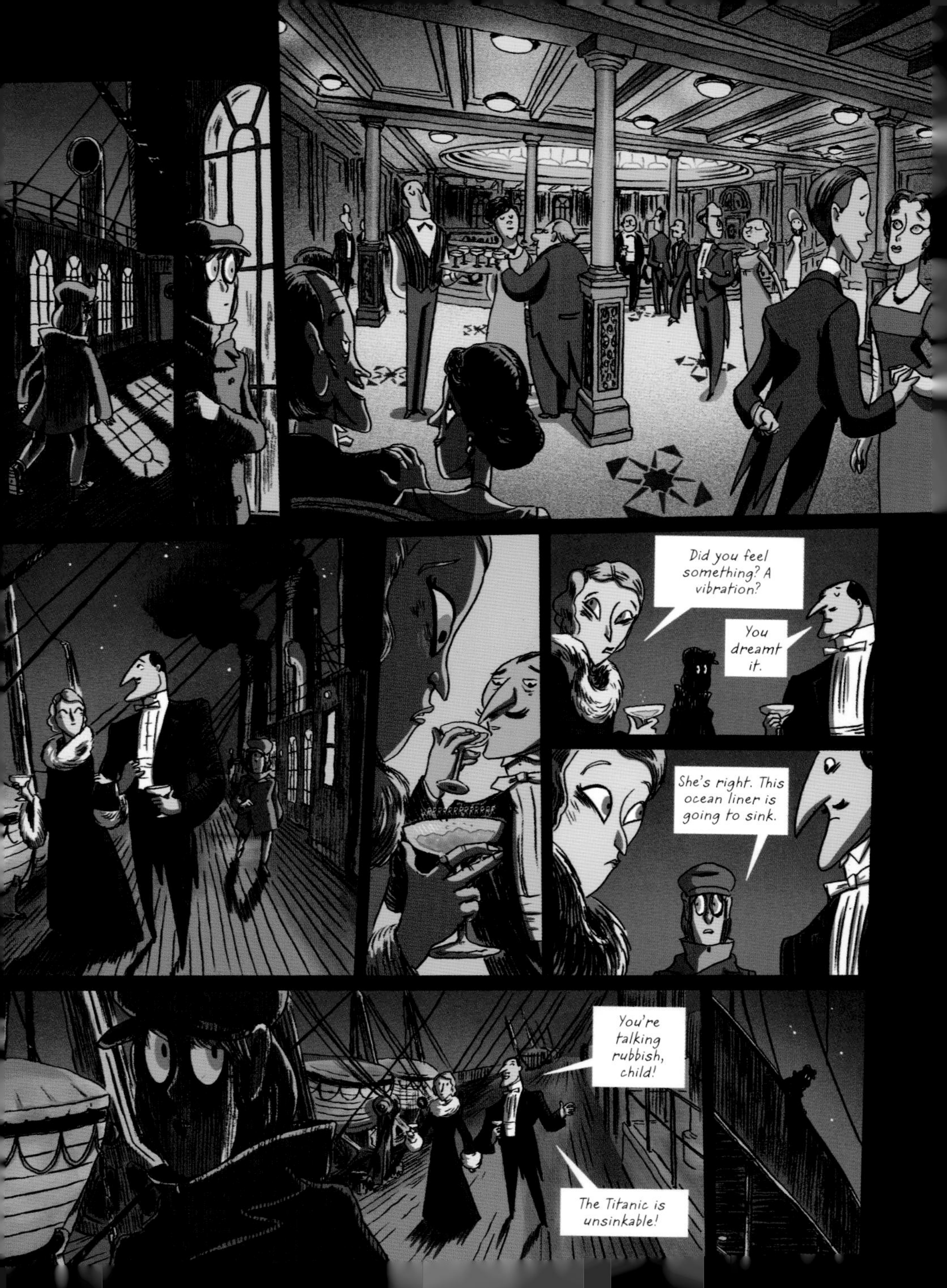
Did you feel something? A vibration?
You dreamt it.
She's right. This ocean liner is going to sink.
You're talking rubbish, child!
The Titanic is unsinkable!

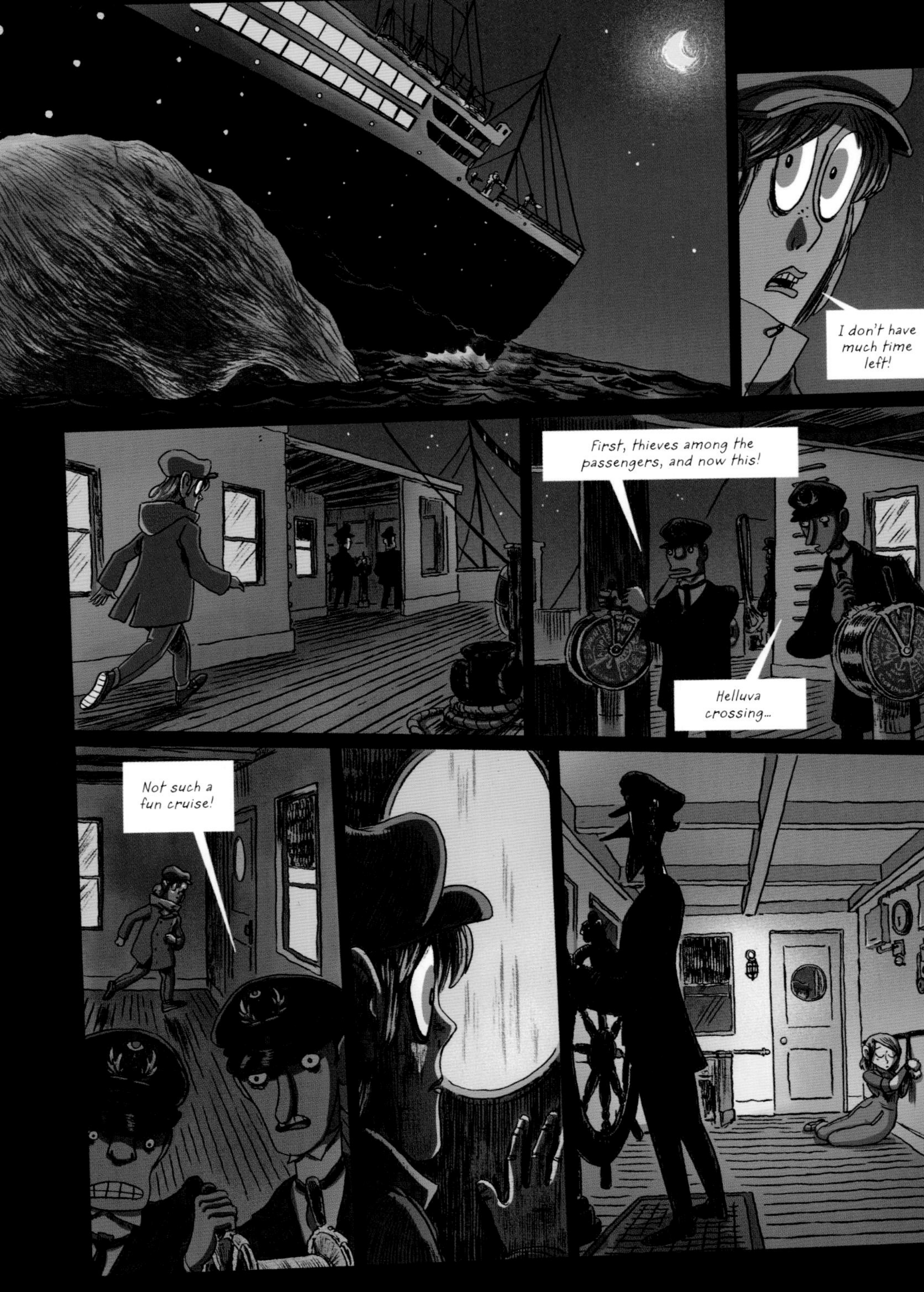
I don't have much time left!
First, thieves among the passengers, and now this!
Helluva crossing...
Not such a fun cruise!

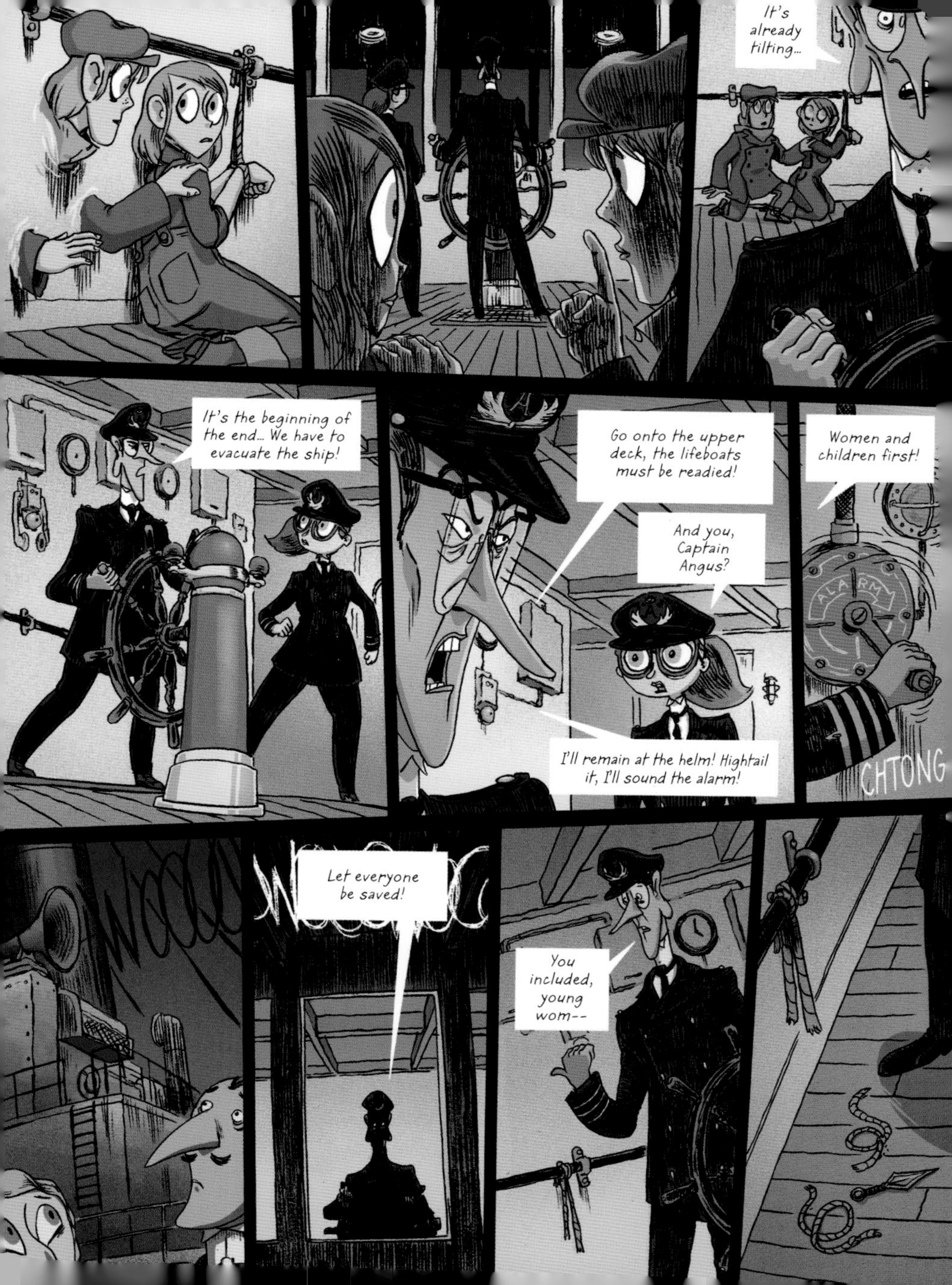
It's already tilting...
It's the beginning of the end... We have to evacuate the ship!
Go onto the upper deck, the lifeboats must be readied!
And you, Captain Angus?
I'll remain at the helm! Hightail it, I'll sound the alarm!
Women and children first!
ALARM
CHTONG
Let everyone be saved!
You included, young wom--

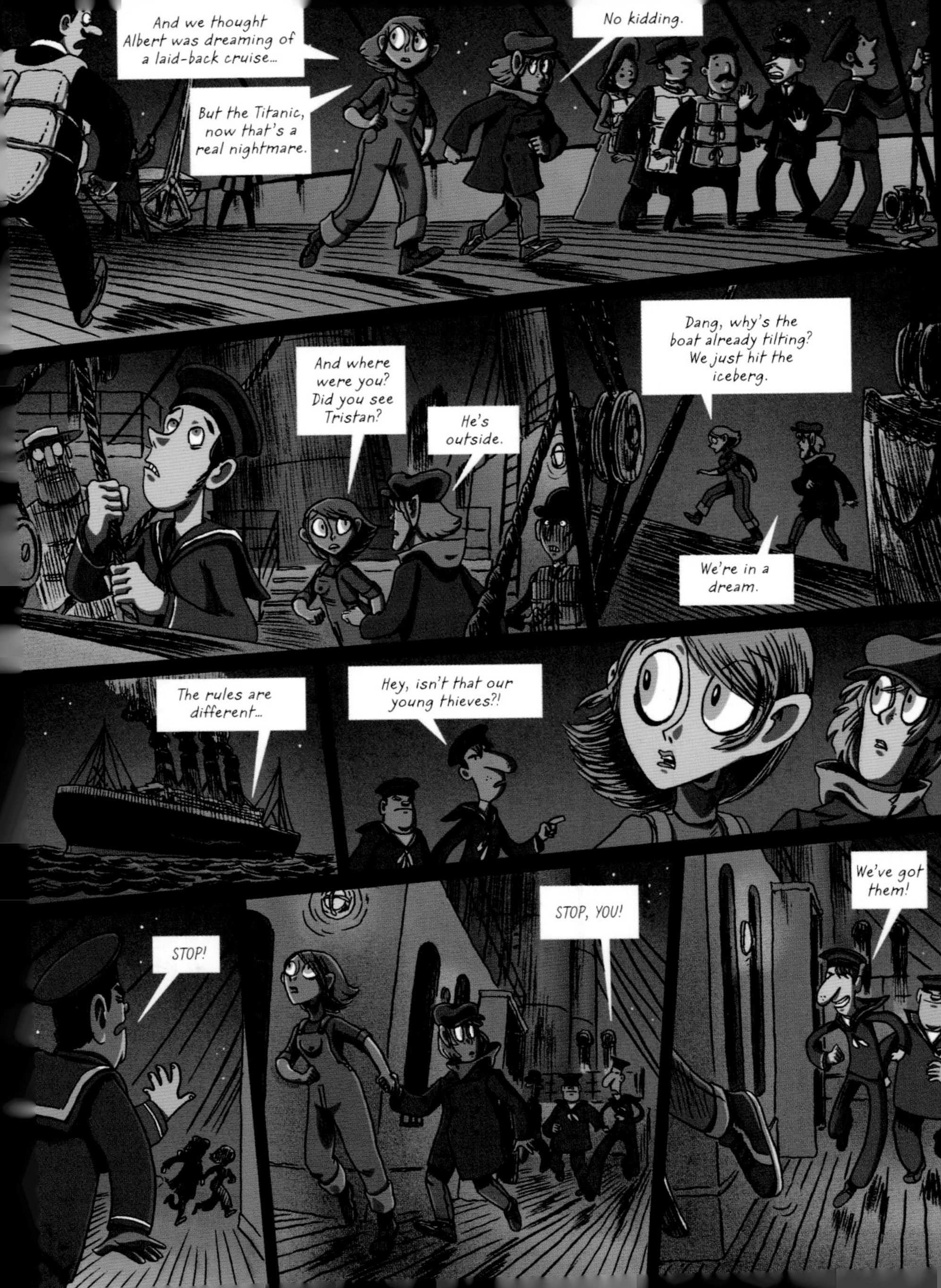

And we thought Albert was dreaming of a laid-back cruise...
But the Titanic, now that's a real nightmare.
No kidding.
And where were you? Did you see Tristan?
He's outside.
Dang, why's the boat already tilting? We just hit the iceberg.
We're in a dream.
The rules are different...
Hey, isn't that our young thieves?!
STOP!
STOP, YOU!
We've got them!

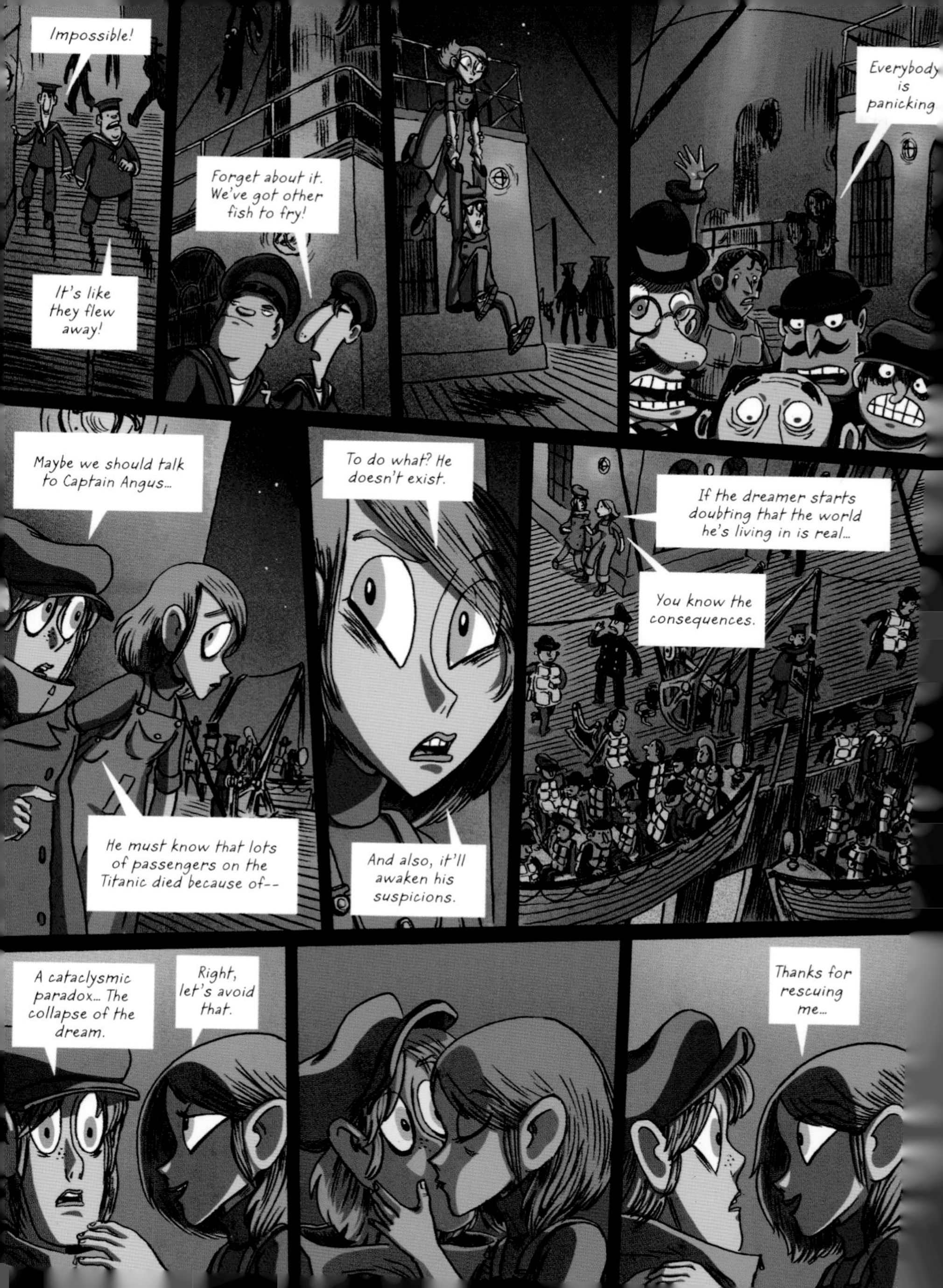

Impossible!
It's like they flew away!
Forget about it. We've got other fish to fry!
Everybody is panicking
Maybe we should talk to Captain Angus...
He must know that lots of passengers on the Titanic died because of--
To do what? He doesn't exist.
And also, it'll awaken his suspicions.
If the dreamer starts doubting that the world he's living in is real...
You know the consequences.
A cataclysmic paradox... The collapse of the dream.
Right, let's avoid that.
Thanks for rescuing me...

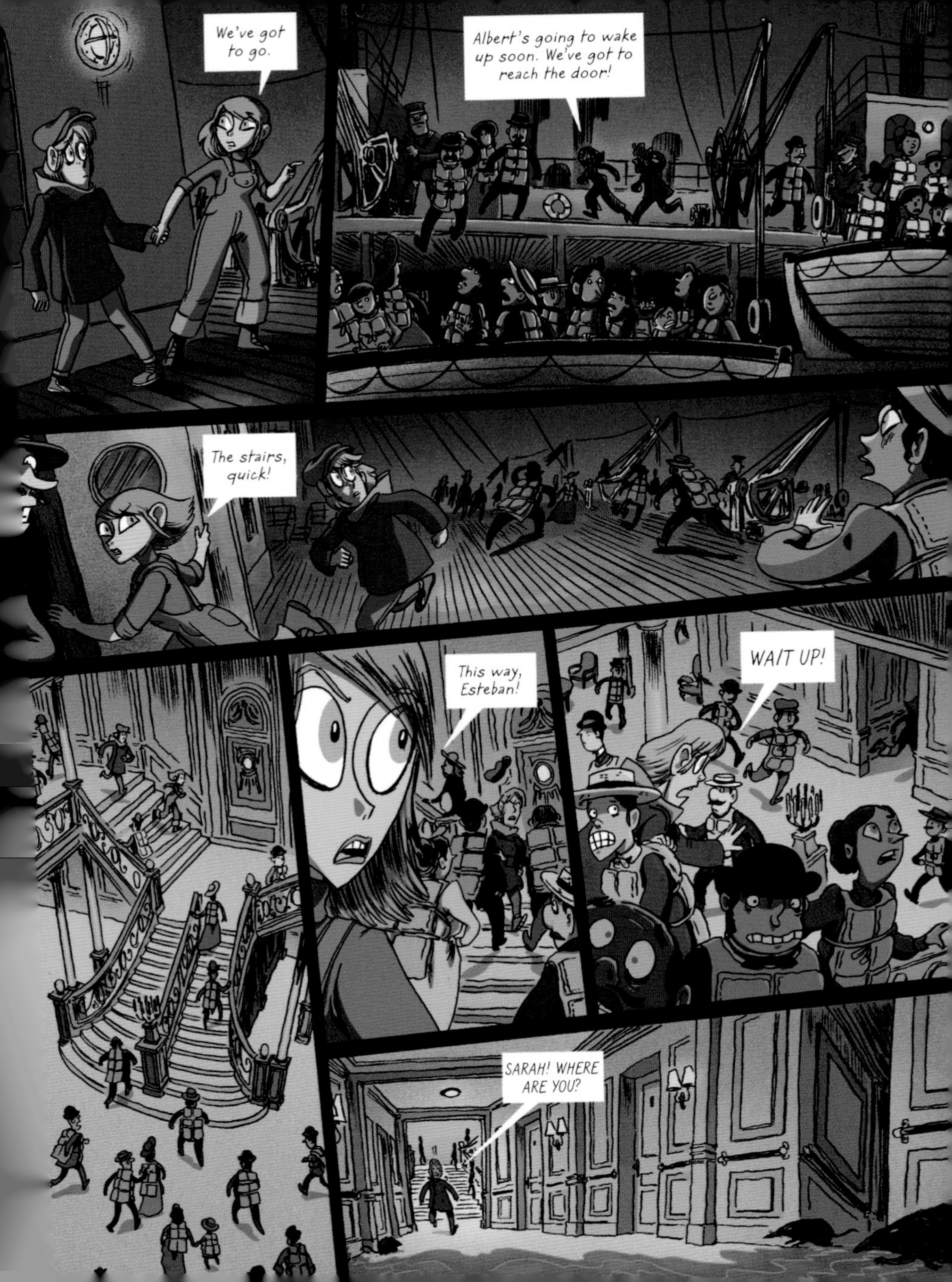
We've got to go.
Albert's going to wake up soon. We've got to reach the door!
The stairs, quick!
This way, Esteban!
WAIT UP!
SARAH! WHERE ARE YOU?

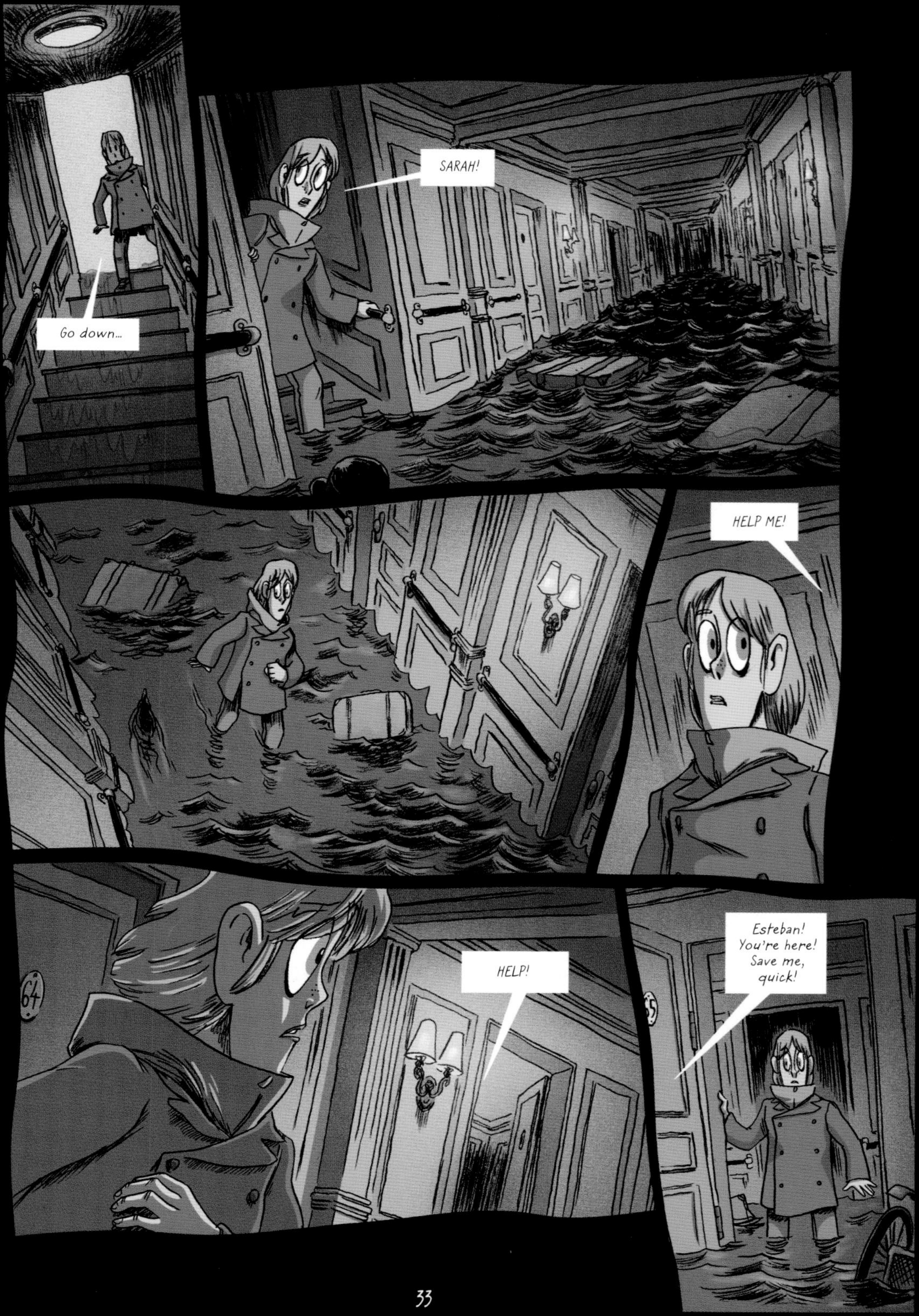
Go down...
SARAH!
HELP ME!
HELP!
Esteban! You're here! Save me, quick!

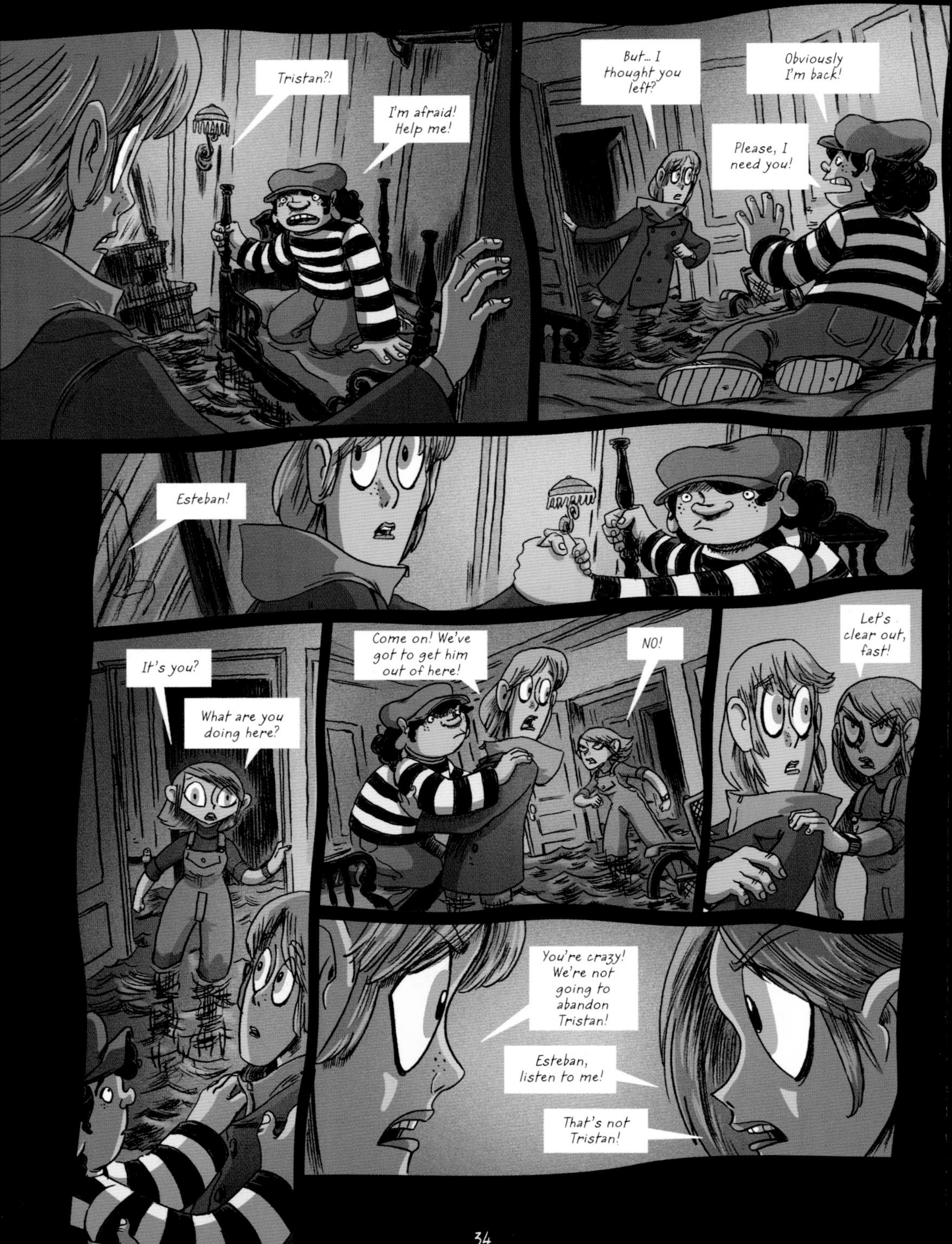
Tristan?!
I'm afraid! Help me!
But... I thought you left?
Obviously I'm back!
Please, I need you!
Esteban!
It's you?
What are you doing here?
Come on! We've got to get him out of here!
NO!
Let's clear out, fast!
You're crazy! We're not going to abandon Tristan!
Esteban, listen to me!
That's not Tristan!

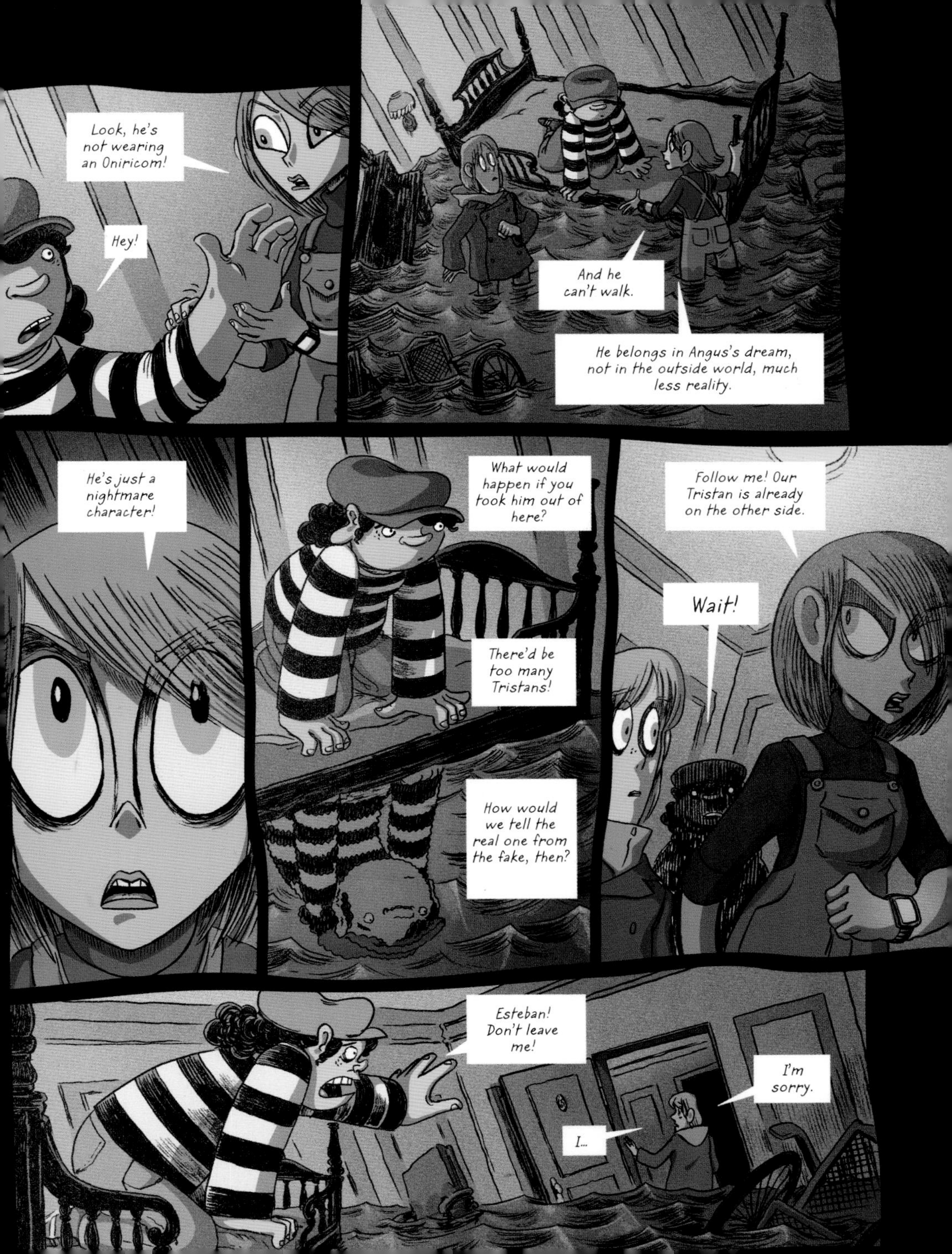
Look, he's not wearing an Oniricom!
Hey!
And he can't walk.
He belongs in Angus's dream, not in the outside world, much less reality.
He's just a nightmare character!
What would happen if you took him out of here?
There'd be too many Tristans!
How would we tell the real one from the fake, then?
Follow me! Our Tristan is already on the other side.
Wait!
Esteban! Don't leave me!
I...
I'm sorry.

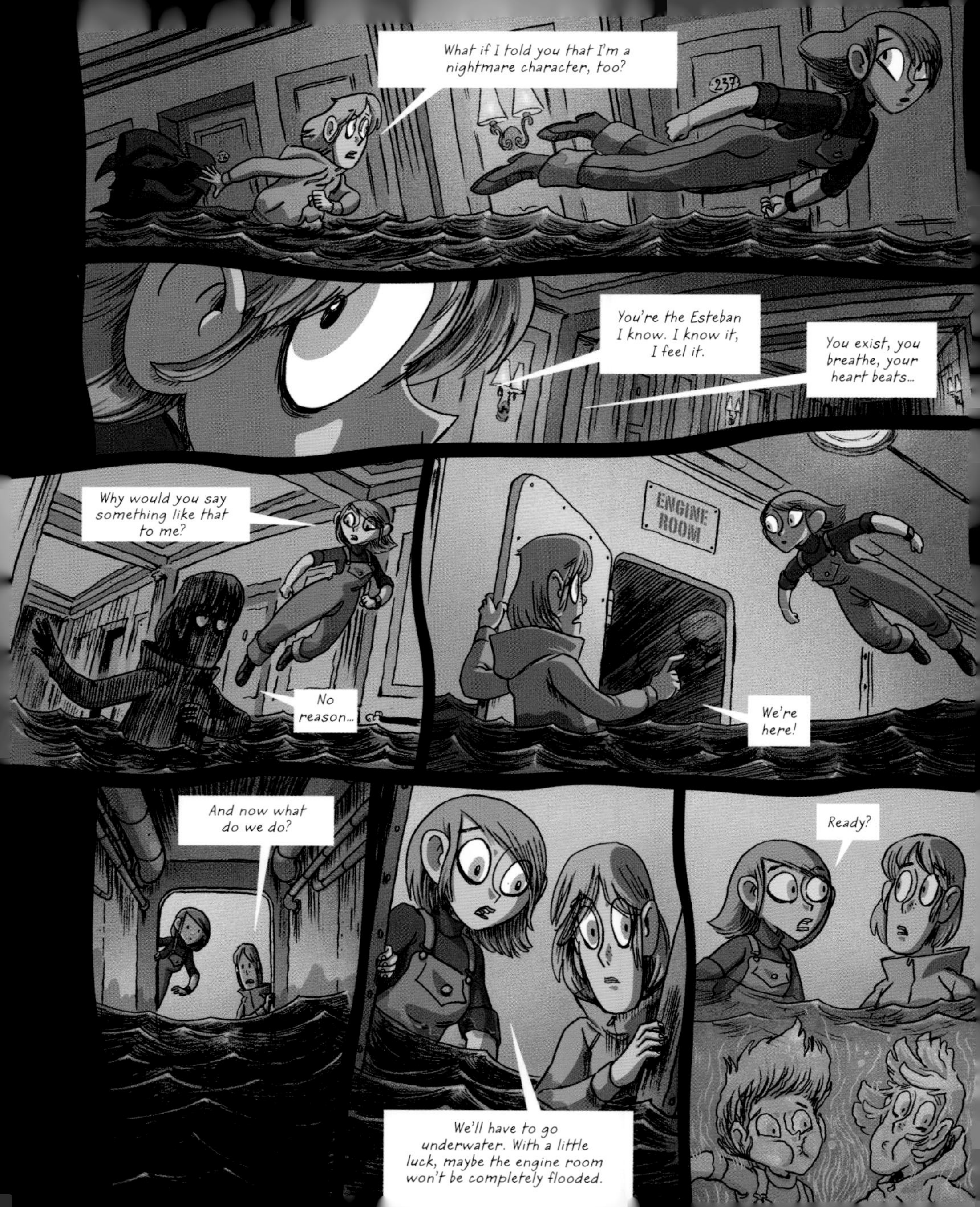
What if I told you that I'm a nightmare character, too?
237
You're the Esteban I know. I know it, I feel it.
You exist, you breathe, your heart beats...
Why would you say something like that to me?
No reason...
ENGINE ROOM
We're here!
And now what do we do?
We'll have to go underwater. With a little luck, maybe the engine room won't be completely flooded.
Ready?

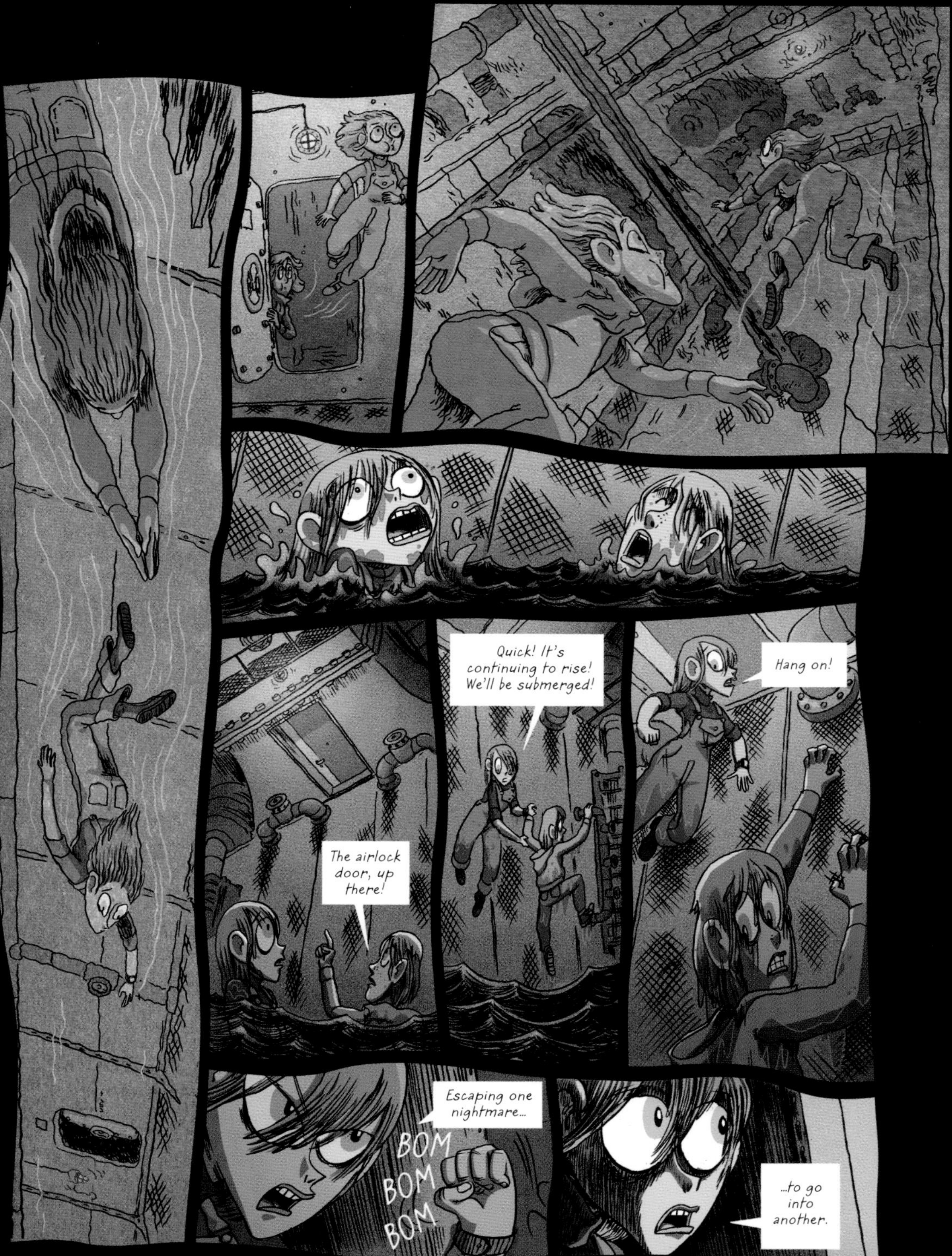

The airlock door, up there!
Quick! It's continuing to rise! We'll be submerged!
Hang on!
Escaping one nightmare...
BOM
BOM
BOM
BOM
...to go into another.

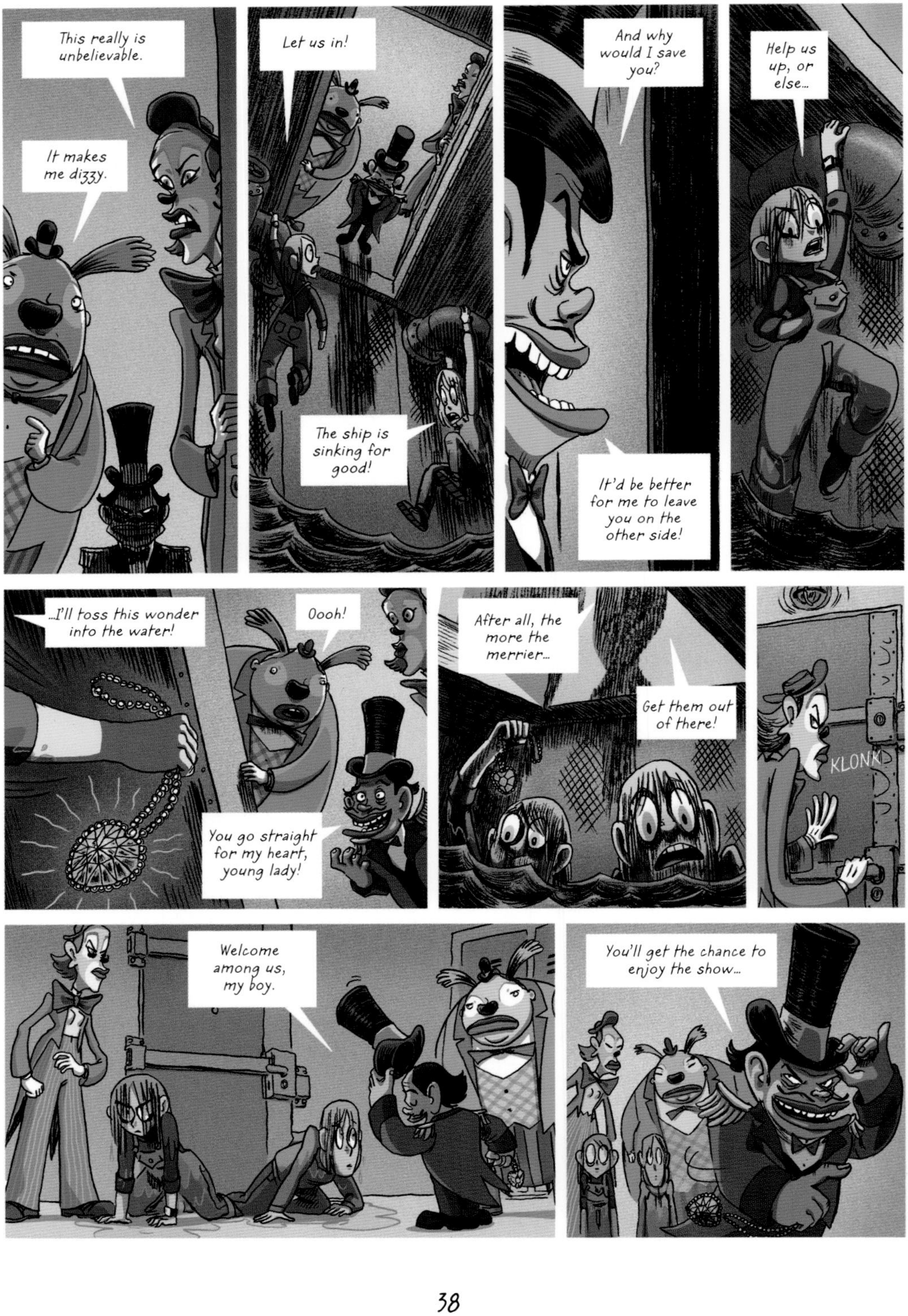
This really is unbelievable.
It makes me dizzy.
Let us in!
The ship is sinking for good!
And why would I save you?
It'd be better for me to leave you on the other side!
Help us up, or else...
...I'll toss this wonder into the water!
Oooh!
You go straight for my heart, young lady!
After all, the more the merrier...
Get them out of there!
KLONK
Welcome among us, my boy.
You'll get the chance to enjoy the show...

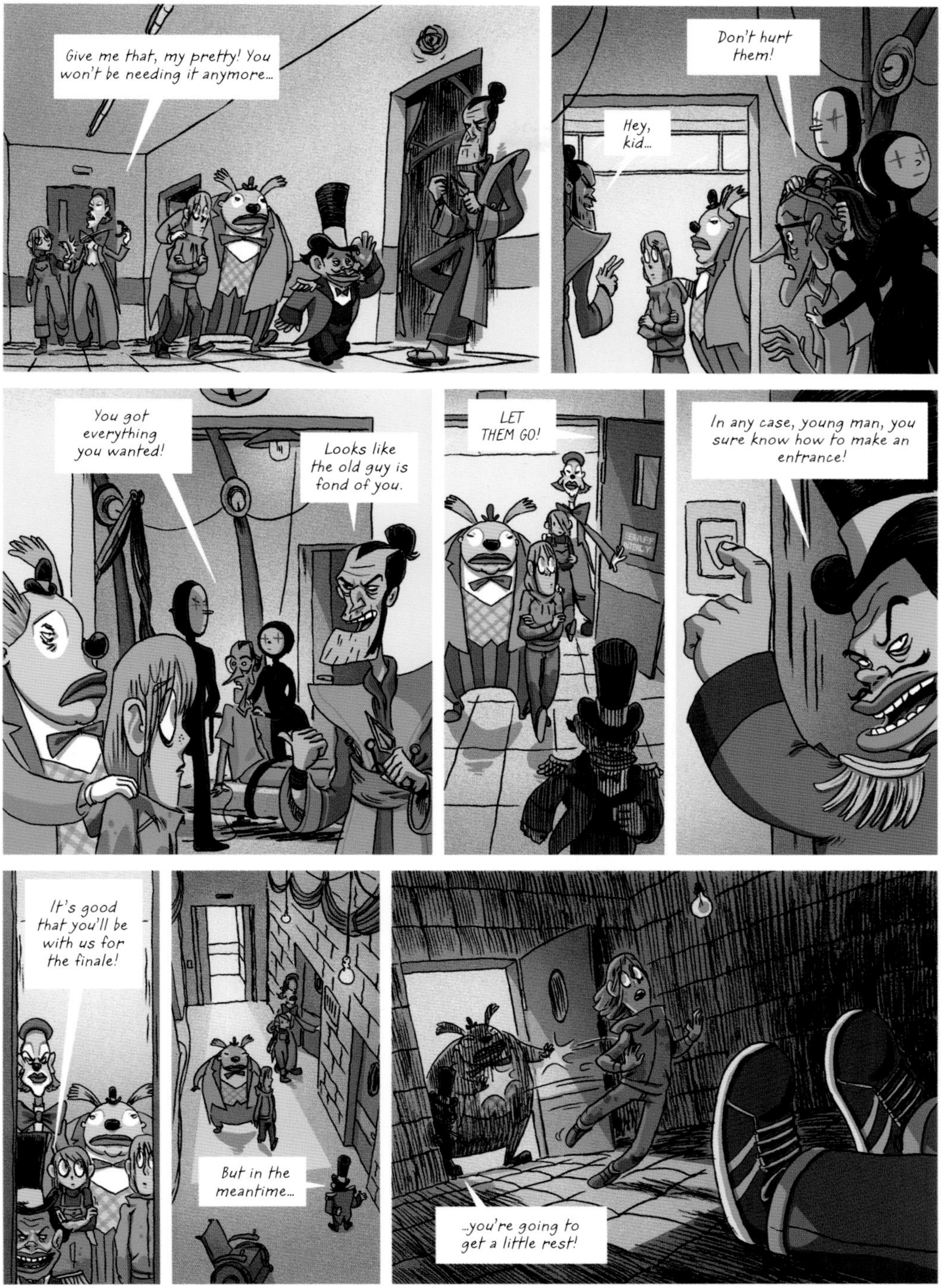
Give me that, my pretty! You won't be needing it anymore...
Don't hurt them!
Hey, kid...
You got everything you wanted!
Looks like the old guy is fond of you.
LET THEM GO!
In any case, young man, you sure know how to make an entrance!
It's good that you'll be with us for the finale!
But in the meantime...
...you're going to get a little rest!

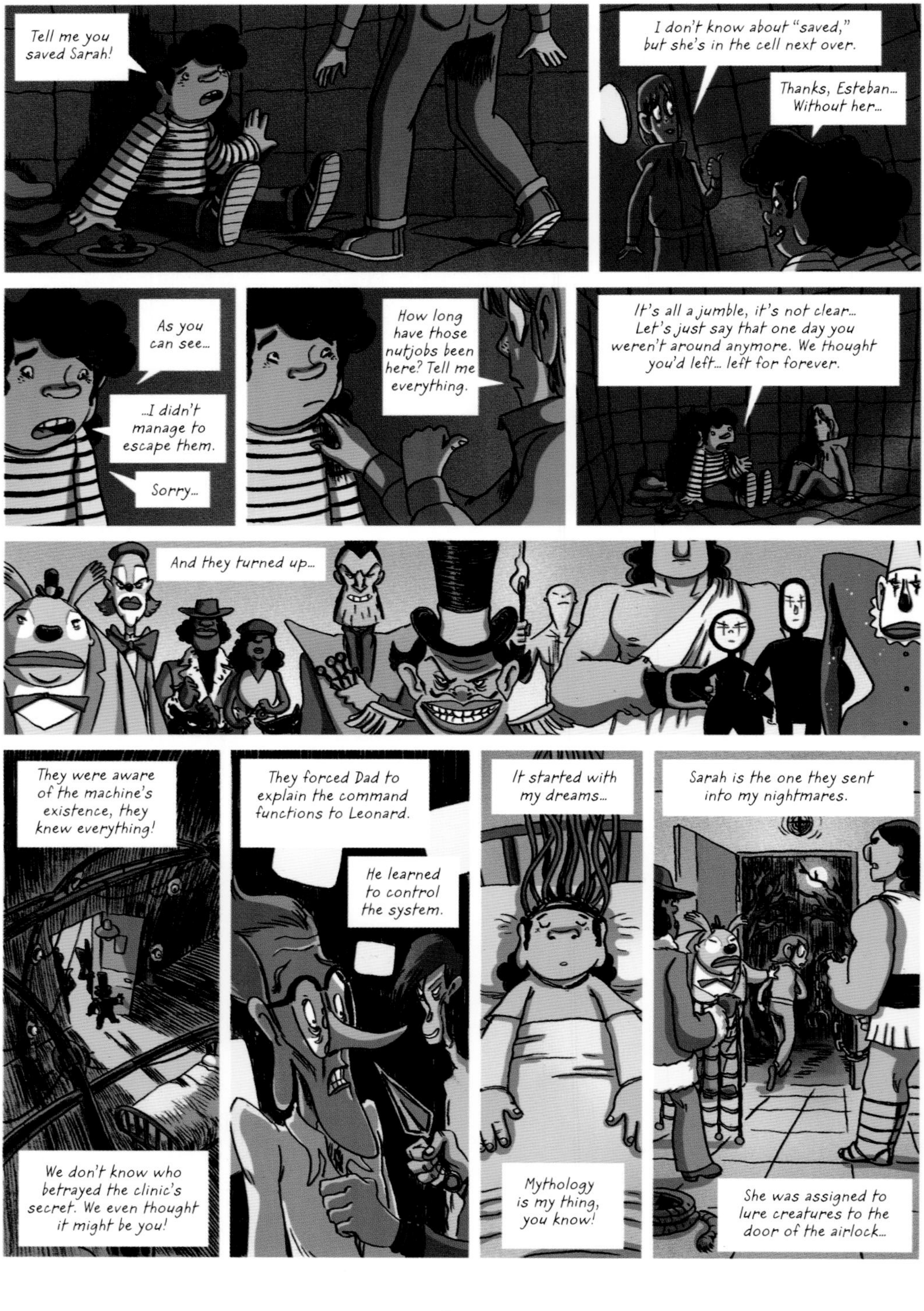
Tell me you saved Sarah!
I don't know about "saved," but she's in the cell next over.
Thanks, Esteban... Without her...
As you can see...
...I didn't manage to escape them.
Sorry...
How long have those nutjobs been here? Tell me everything.
It's all a jumble, it's not clear... Let's just say that one day you weren't around anymore. We thought you'd left... left for forever.
And they turned up...
They were aware of the machine's existence, they knew everything!
We don't know who betrayed the clinic's secret. We even thought it might be you!
They forced Dad to explain the command functions to Leonard.
He learned to control the system.
It started with my dreams...
Mythology is my thing, you know!
Sarah is the one they sent into my nightmares.
She was assigned to lure creatures to the door of the airlock...

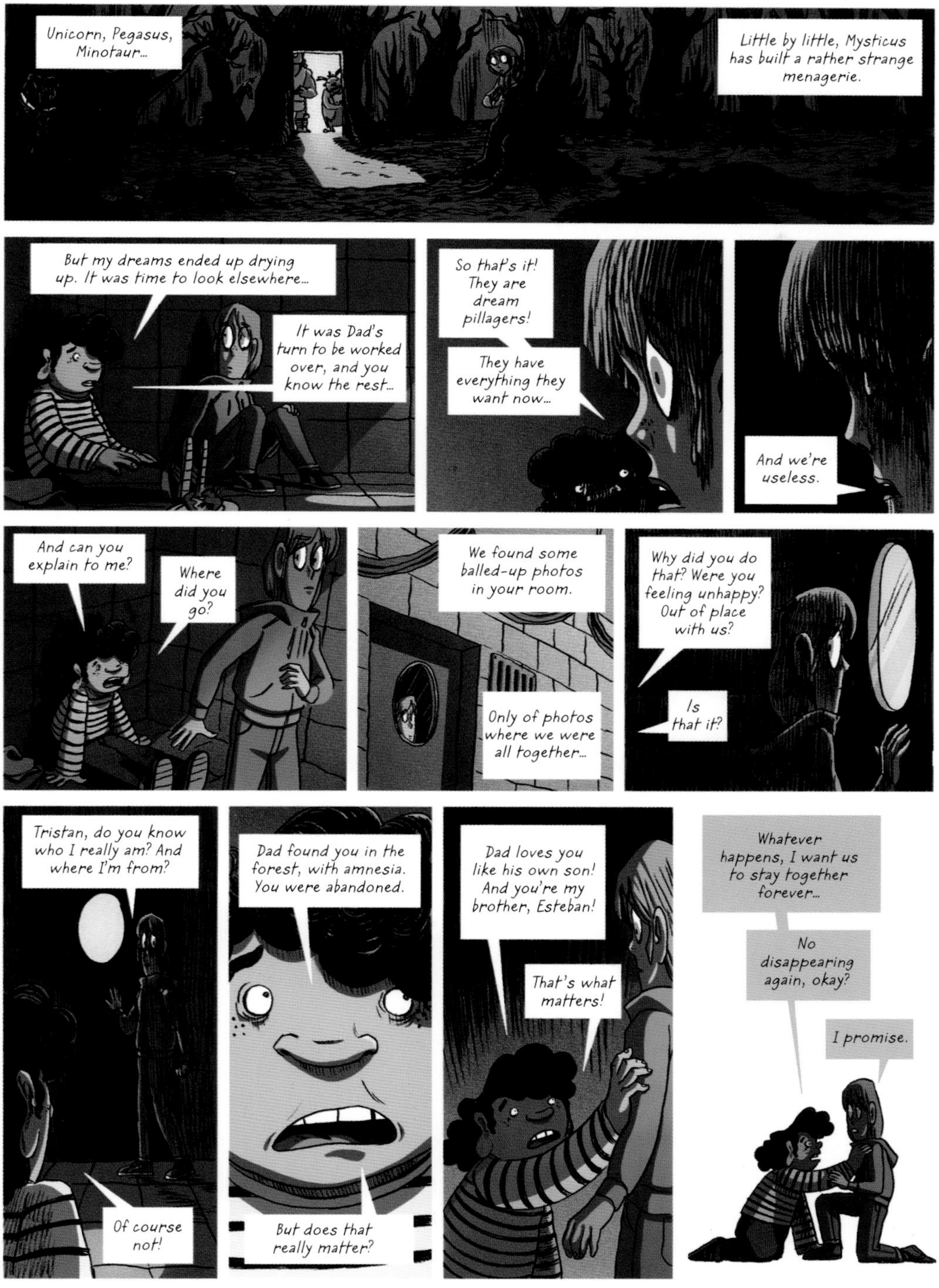

Unicorn, Pegasus, Minotaur...
Little by little, Mysticus has built a rather strange menagerie.
But my dreams ended up drying up. It was time to look elsewhere...
It was Dad's turn to be worked over, and you know the rest...
So that's it! They are dream pillagers!
They have everything they want now...
And we're useless.
And can you explain to me?
Where did you go?
We found some balled-up photos in your room.
Only of photos where we were all together...
Why did you do that? Were you feeling unhappy? Out of place with us?
Is that it?
Tristan, do you know who I really am? And where I'm from?
Of course not!
Dad found you in the forest, with amnesia. You were abandoned.
But does that really matter?
Dad loves you like his own son! And you're my brother, Esteban!
That's what matters!
Whatever happens, I want us to stay together forever...
No disappearing again, okay?
I promise.

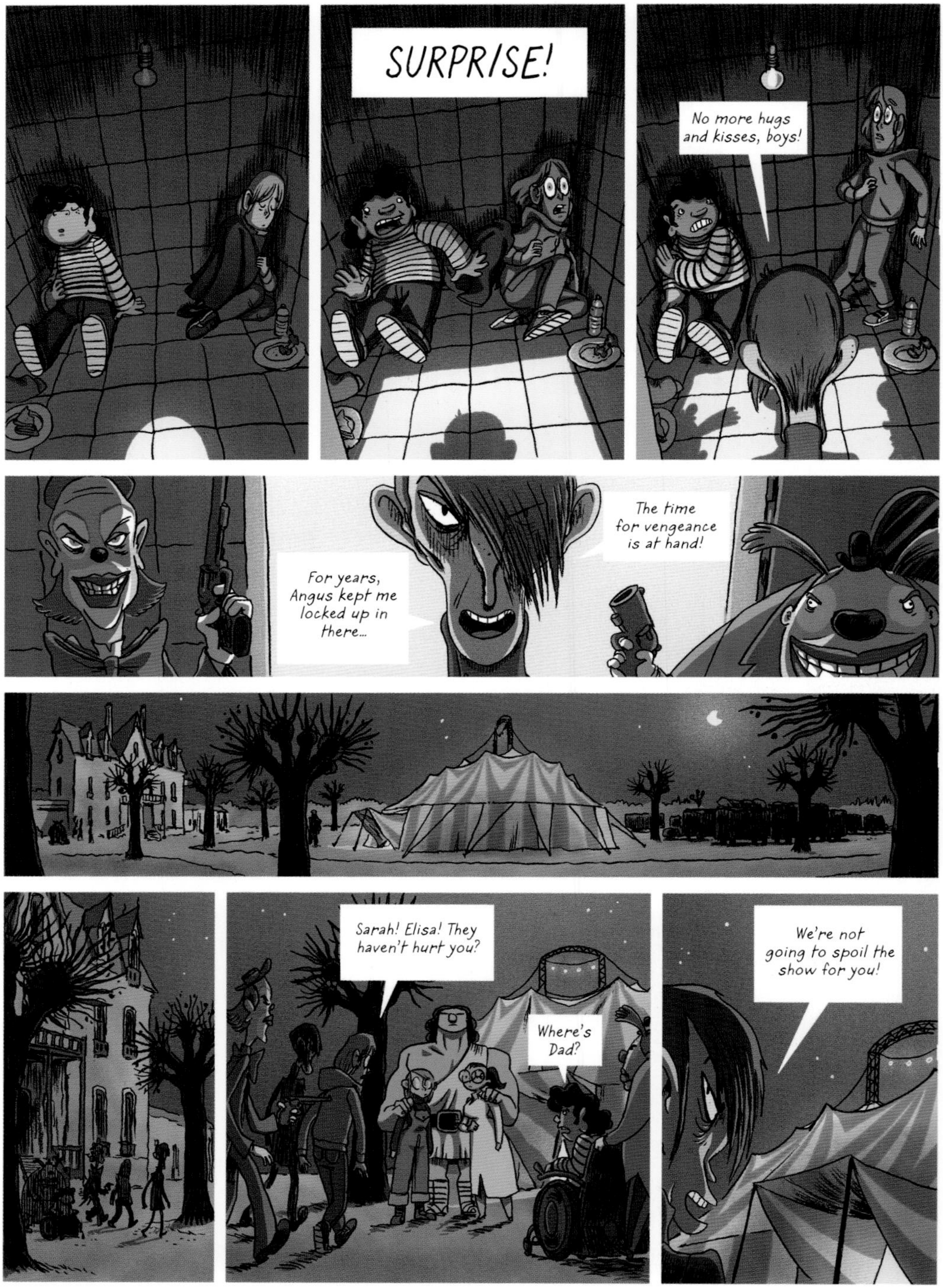
SURPRISE!
No more hugs and kisses, boys!
For years, Angus kept me locked up in there...
The time for vengeance is at hand!
Sarah! Elisa! They haven't hurt you?
Where's Dad?
We're not going to spoil the show for you!

Sit!

Very funny...

My friends!

Tomorrow, we'll start traveling the world.

Thanks to you, people will be paying out the nose for our circus tickets!

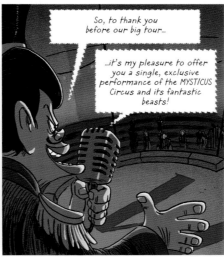

So, to thank you before our big tour...

...it's my pleasure to offer you a single, exclusive performance of the MYSTICUS Circus and its fantastic beasts!

Let YOUR show begin!

43

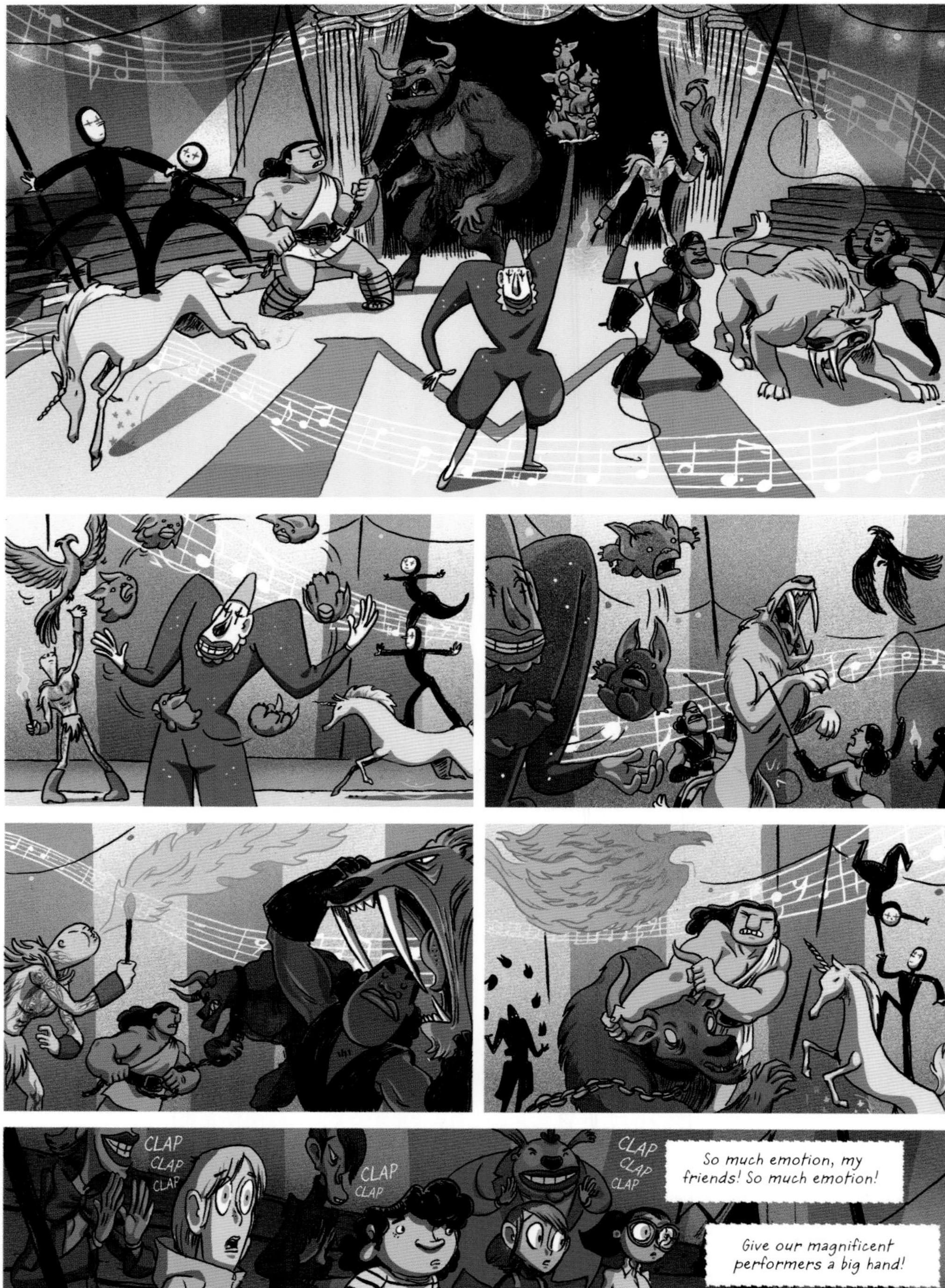
CLAP
CLAP
CLAP
CLAP
CLAP
CLAP
CLAP
CLAP
So much emotion, my friends! So much emotion!
Give our magnificent performers a big hand!

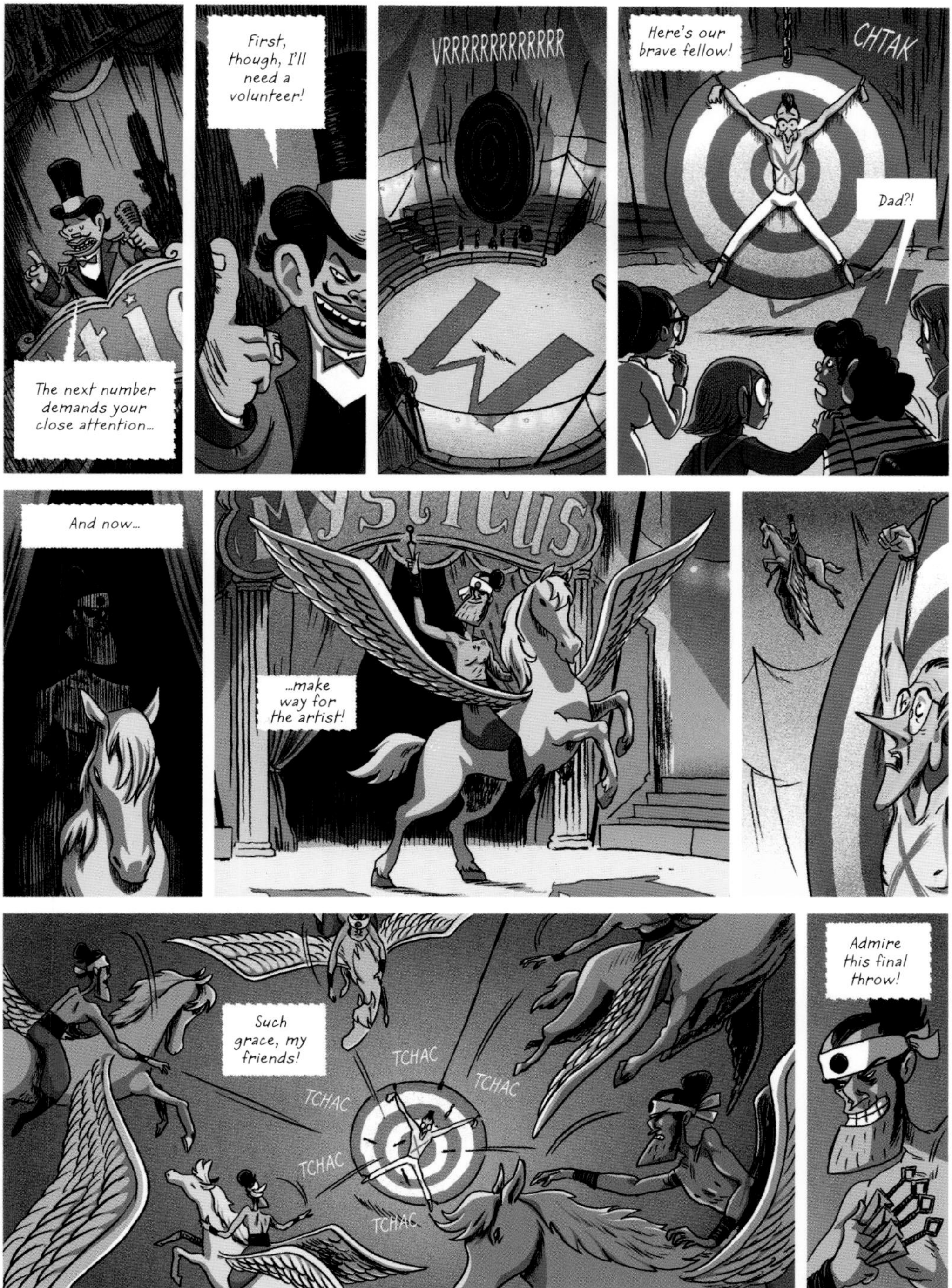
The next number demands your close attention...
First, though, I'll need a volunteer!
VRRRRRRRRRRRR
Here's our brave fellow!
CHTAK
Dad?!
And now...
...make way for the artist!
Such grace, my friends!
TCHAC
TCHAC
TCHAC
TCHAC
TCHAC
Admire this final throw!

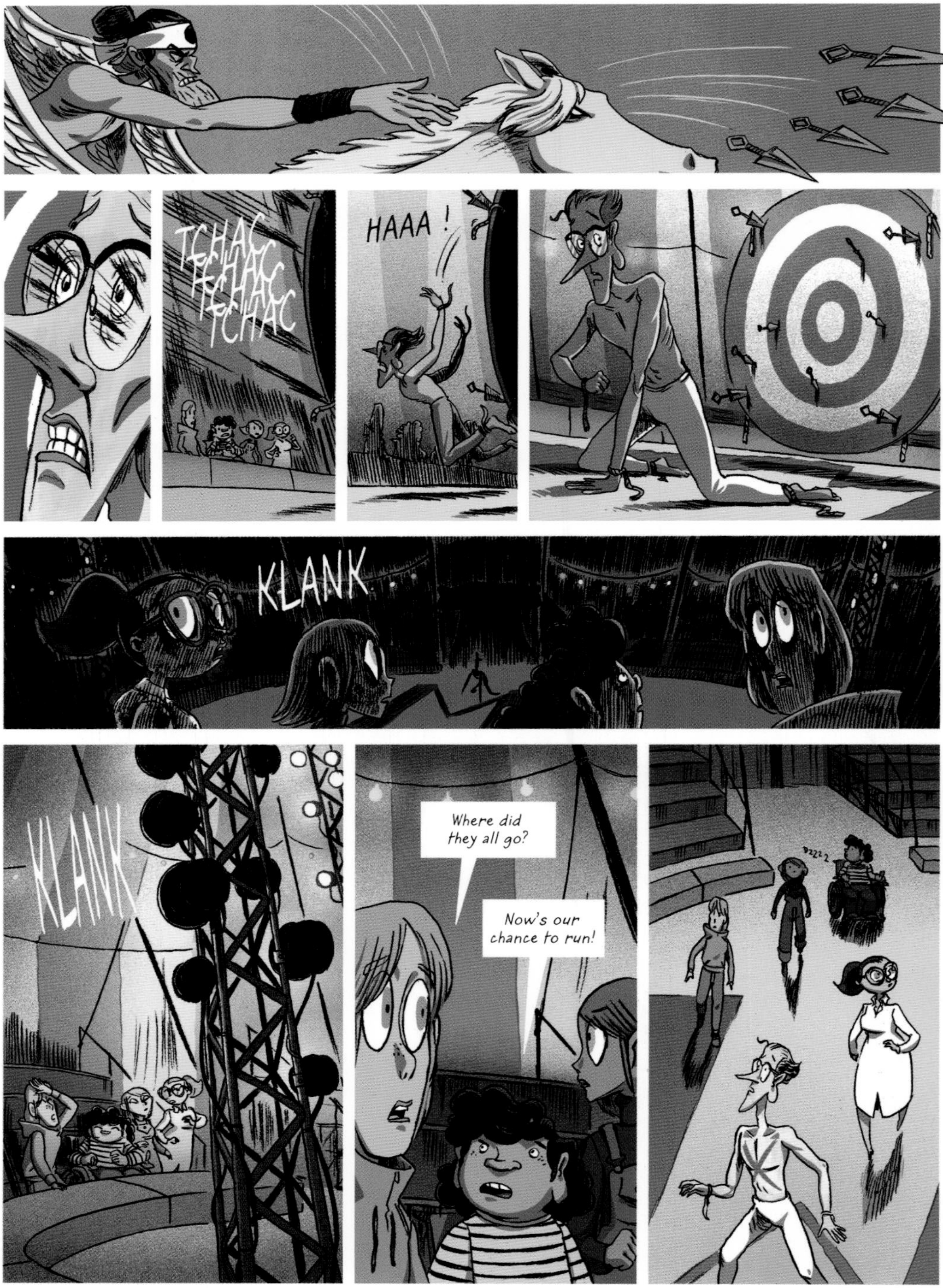
TCHAC TCHAC TCHAC TCHAC
HAAA !
KLANK
KLANK
Where did they all go?
Now's our chance to run!

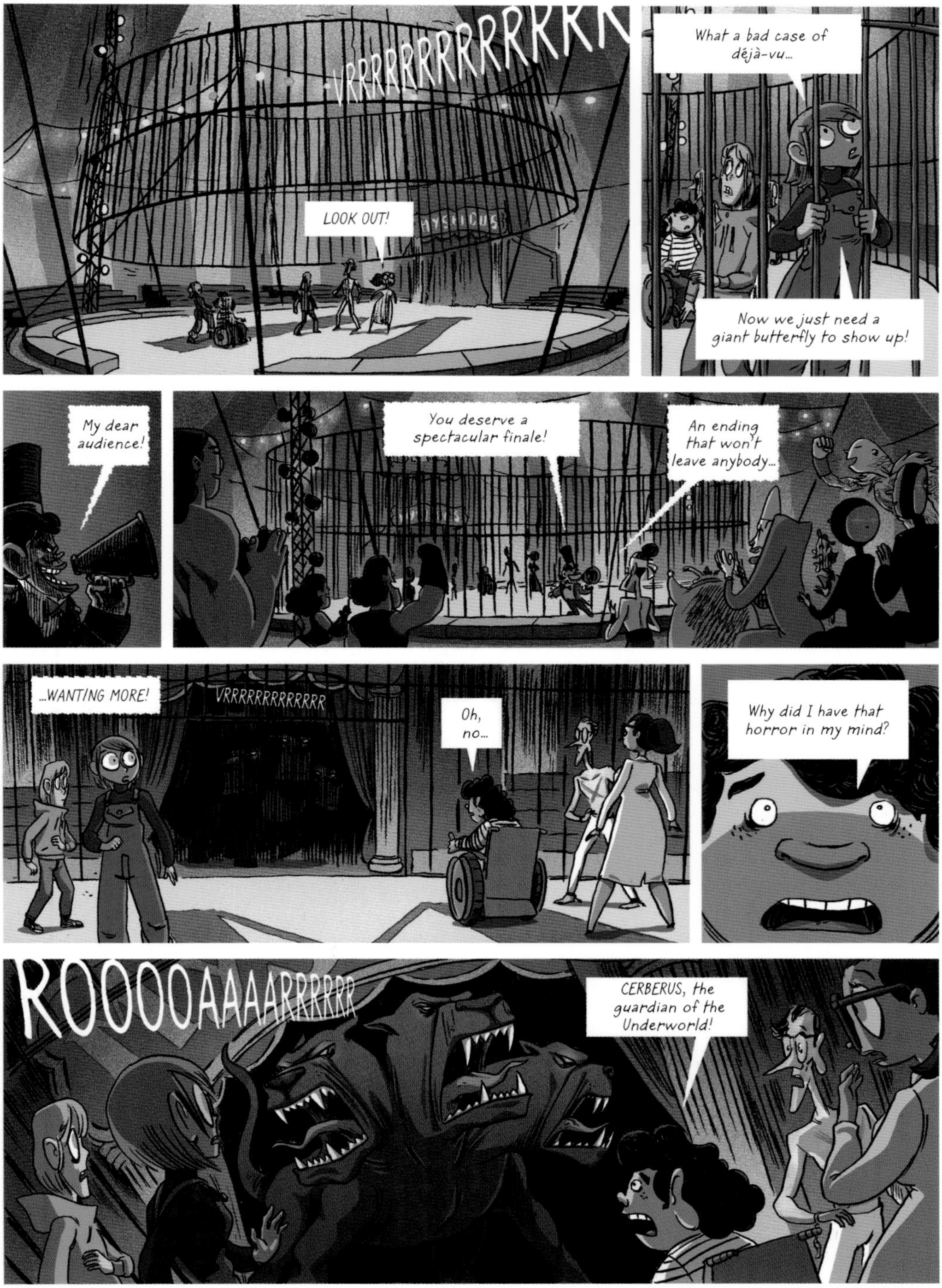
VRRRRRRRRRRRRK
LOOK OUT!
What a bad case of déjà-vu...
Now we just need a giant butterfly to show up!
My dear audience!
You deserve a spectacular finale!
An ending that won't leave anybody...
...WANTING MORE!
VRRRRRRRRRRRR
Oh, no...
Why did I have that horror in my mind?
ROOOOAAAARRRRR
CERBERUS, the guardian of the Underworld!

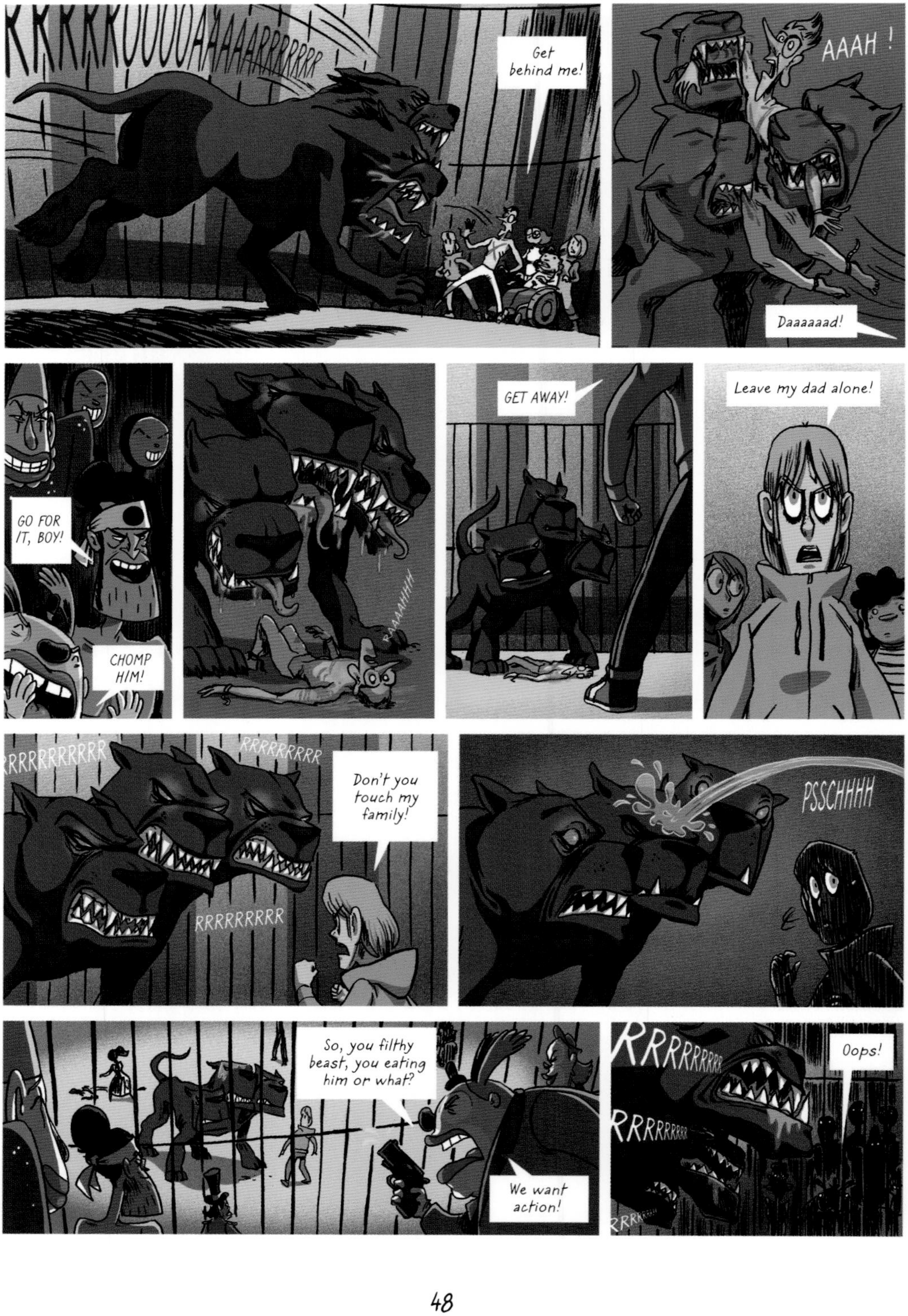
RRRRRROOOOAAAAARRRRRRR
Get behind me!
AAAH !
Daaaaaad!
GO FOR IT, BOY!
CHOMP HIM!
RAAAAAHHH
GET AWAY!
Leave my dad alone!
RRRRRRRRRR
RRRRRRRRR
Don't you touch my family!
RRRRRRRRR
PSSCHHHH
So, you filthy beast, you eating him or what?
We want action!
RRRRRRRRR
Oops!
RRRRRRRRR
RRRRRRR

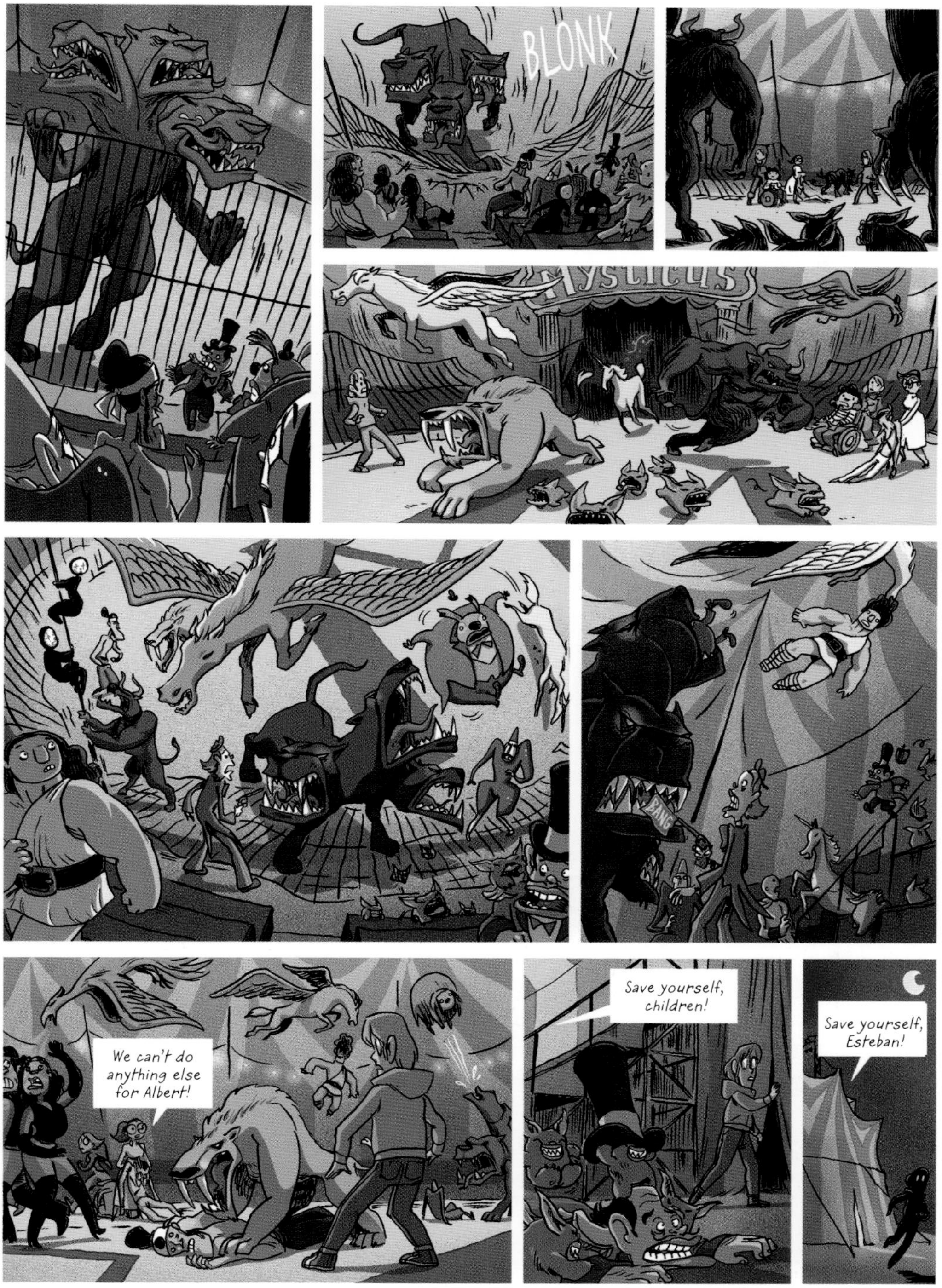
BLONK
Mysticus
BANG
We can't do anything else for Albert!
Save yourself, children!
Save yourself, Esteban!

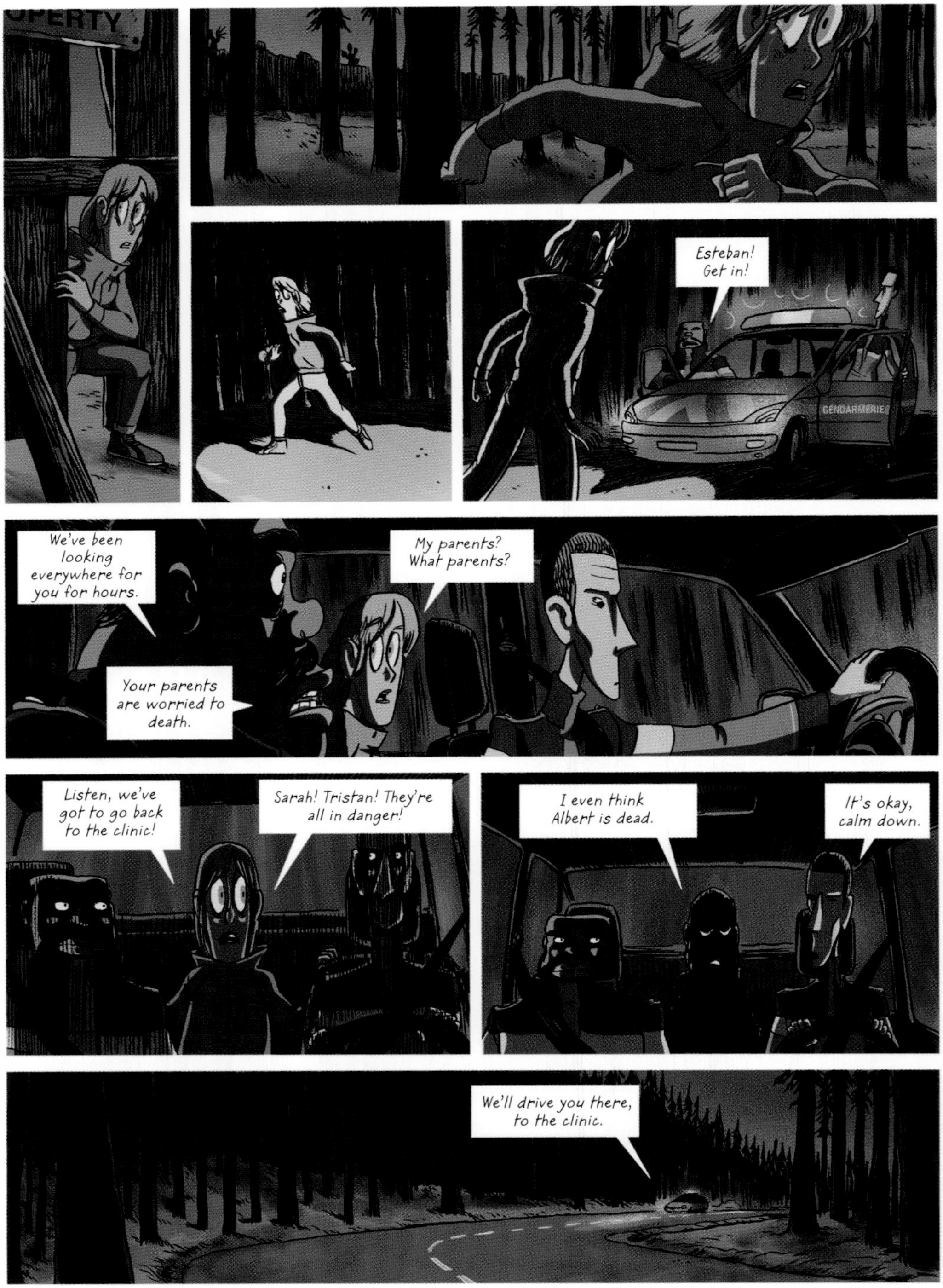
PERTY
Esteban! Get in!
GENDARMERIE
We've been looking everywhere for you for hours.
Your parents are worried to death.
My parents? What parents?
Listen, we've got to go back to the clinic!
Sarah! Tristan! They're all in danger!
I even think Albert is dead.
It's okay, calm down.
We'll drive you there, to the clinic.

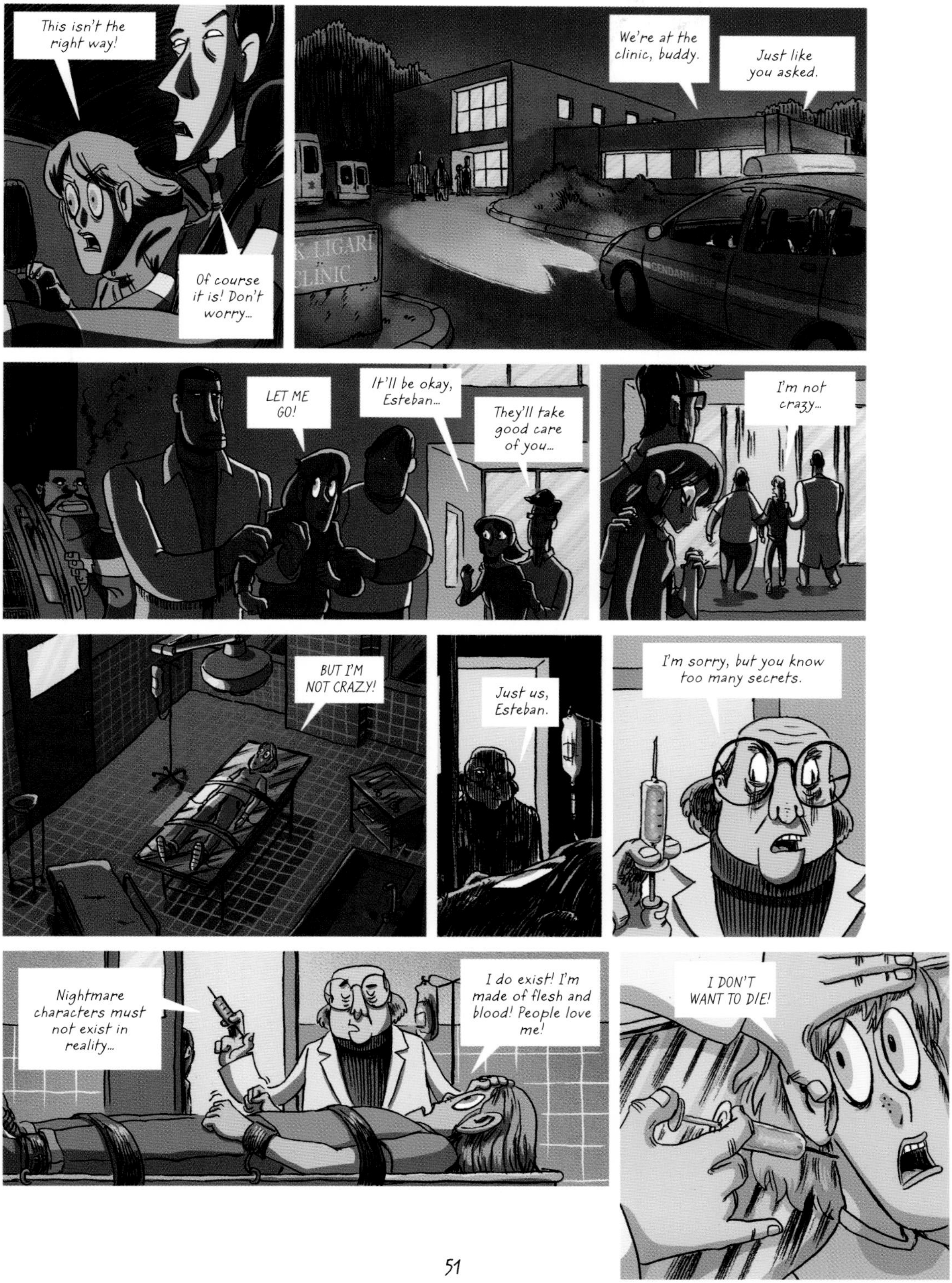
This isn't the right way!
Of course it is! Don't worry...
We're at the clinic, buddy.
Just like you asked.
K. LIGARI CLINIC
GENDARMERIE
LET ME GO!
It'll be okay, Esteban...
They'll take good care of you...
I'm not crazy...
BUT I'M NOT CRAZY!
Just us, Esteban.
I'm sorry, but you know too many secrets.
Nightmare characters must not exist in reality...
I do exist! I'm made of flesh and blood! People love me!
I DON'T WANT TO DIE!

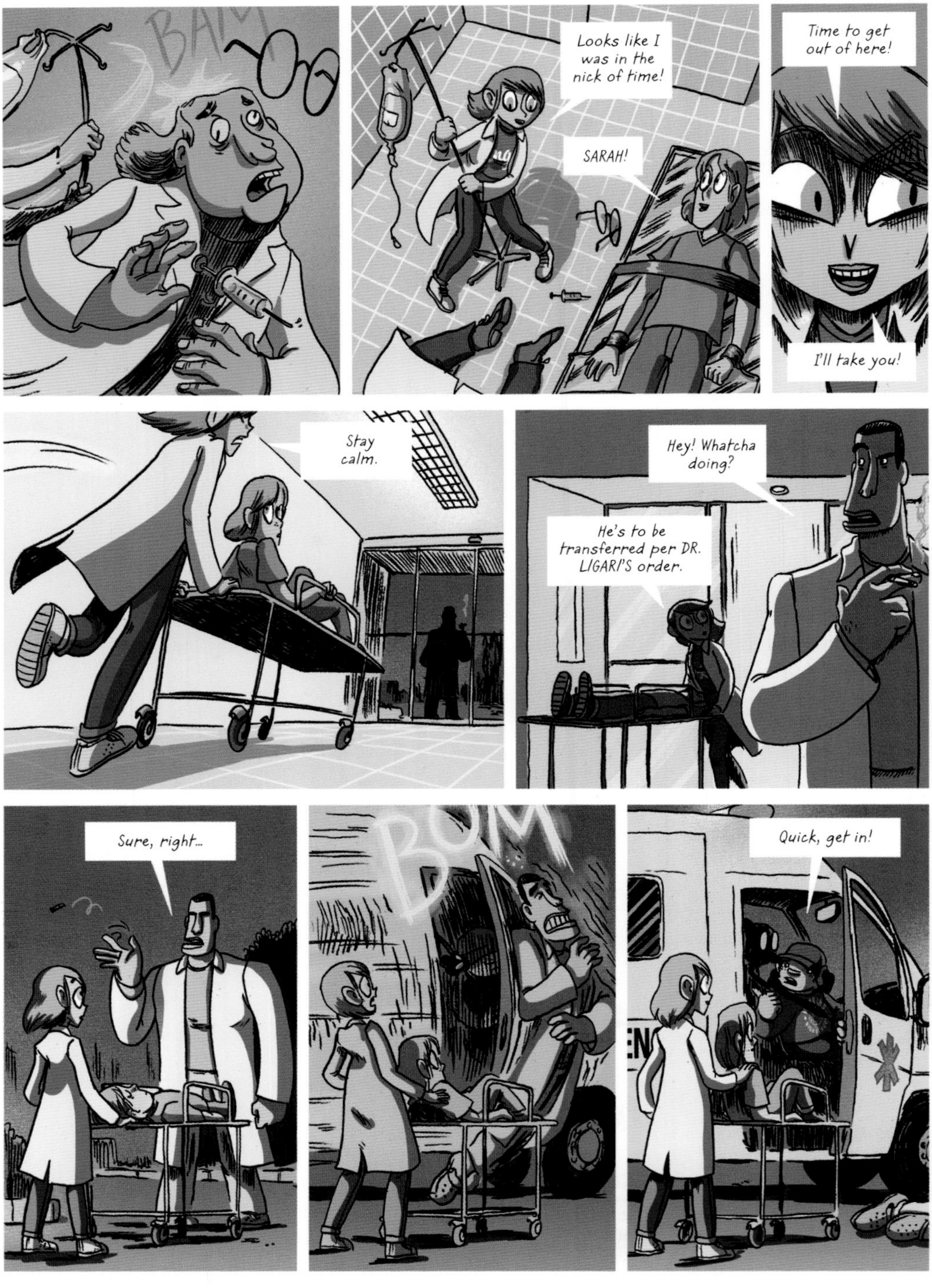
BAM
Looks like I was in the nick of time!
SARAH!
Time to get out of here!
I'll take you!
Stay calm.
Hey! Whatcha doing?
He's to be transferred per DR. LIGARI'S order.
Sure, right...
BOM
Quick, get in!

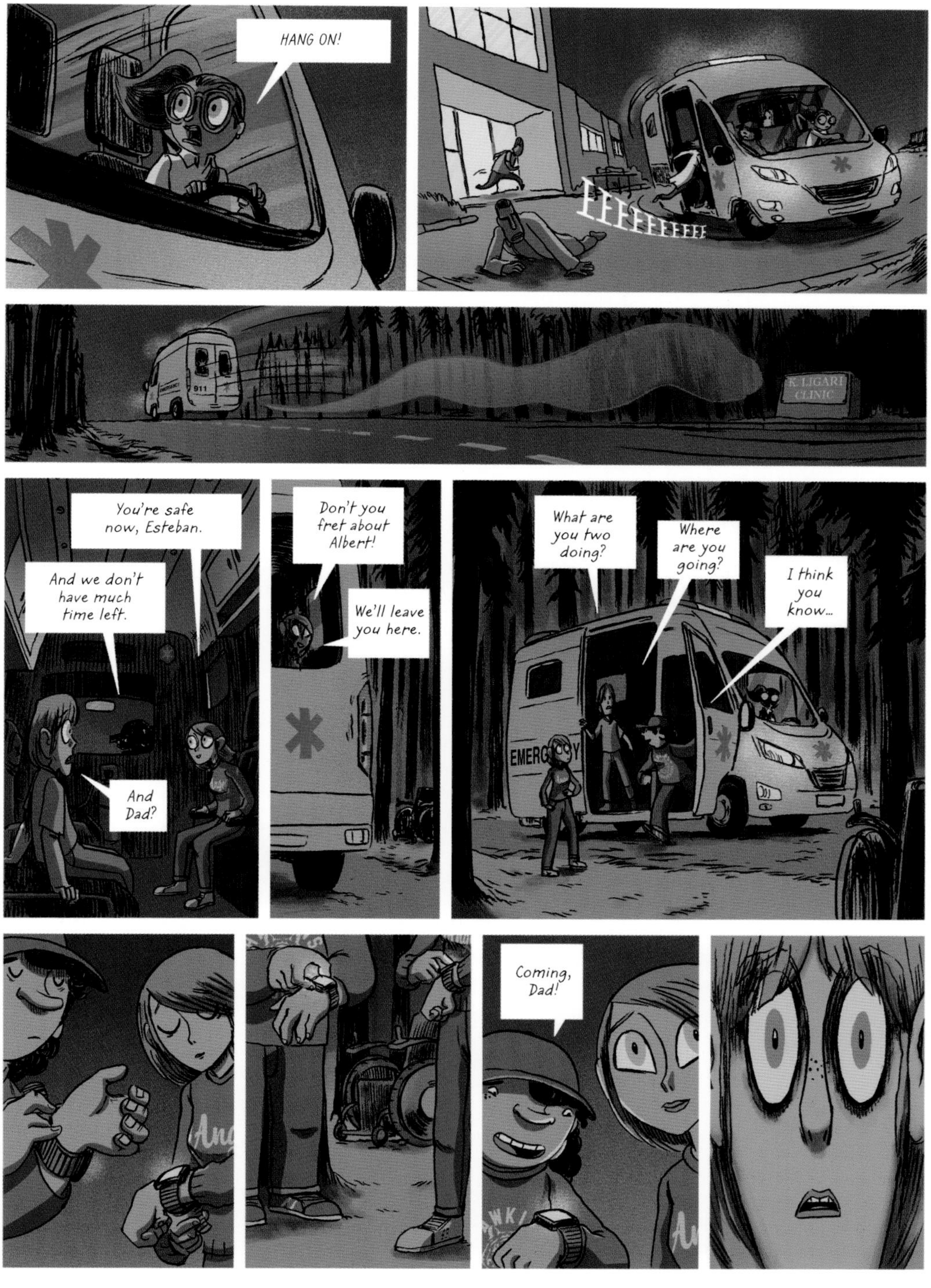
HANG ON!
K. LIGARI CLINIC
You're safe now, Esteban.
And we don't have much time left.
And Dad?
Don't you fret about Albert!
We'll leave you here.
What are you two doing?
Where are you going?
I think you know...
Coming, Dad!

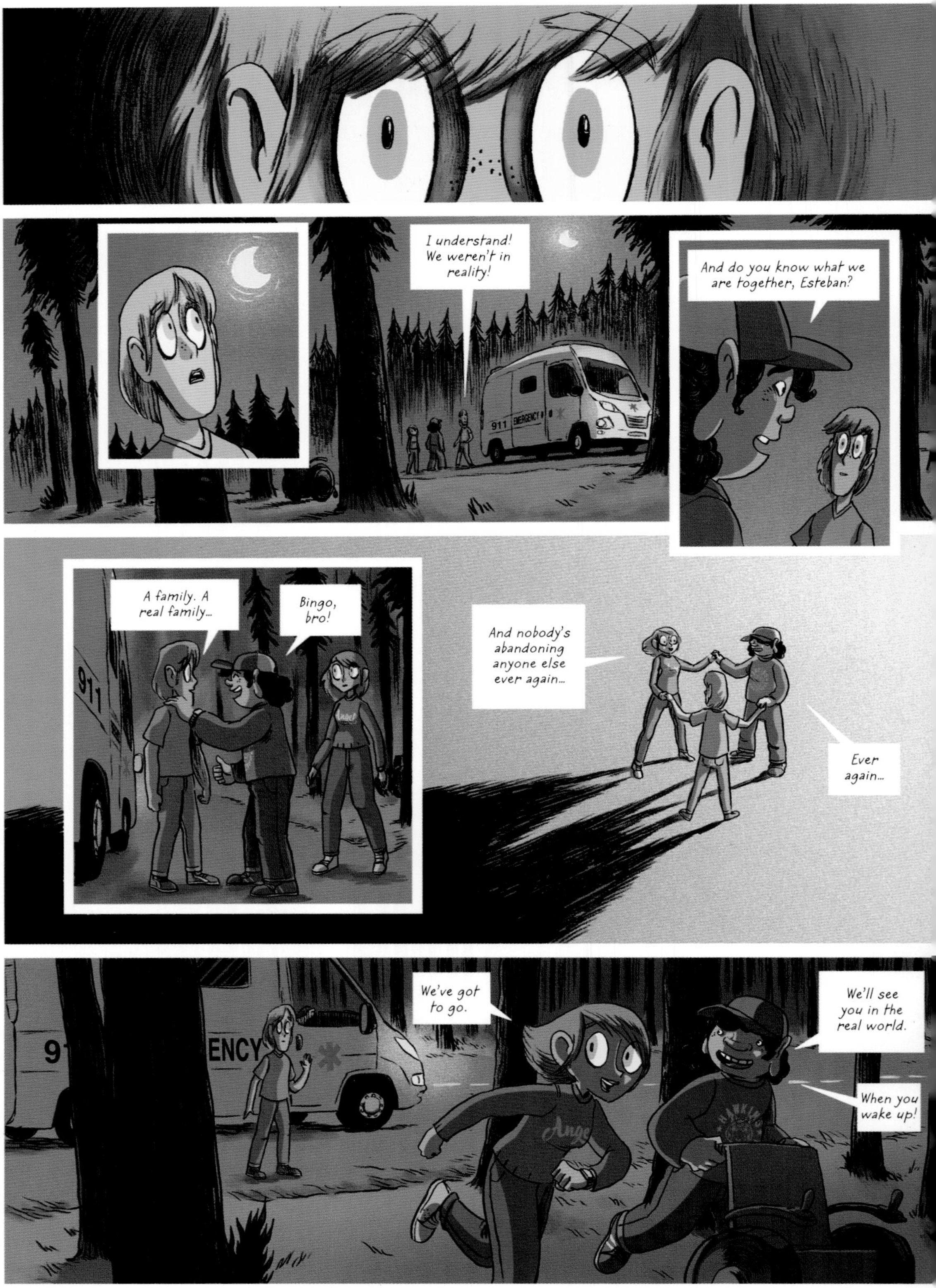
I understand! We weren't in reality!
And do you know what we are together, Esteban?
911
EMERGENCY
A family. A real family...
Bingo, bro!
And nobody's abandoning anyone else ever again...
Ever again...
We've got to go.
We'll see you in the real world.
When you wake up!
ENCY

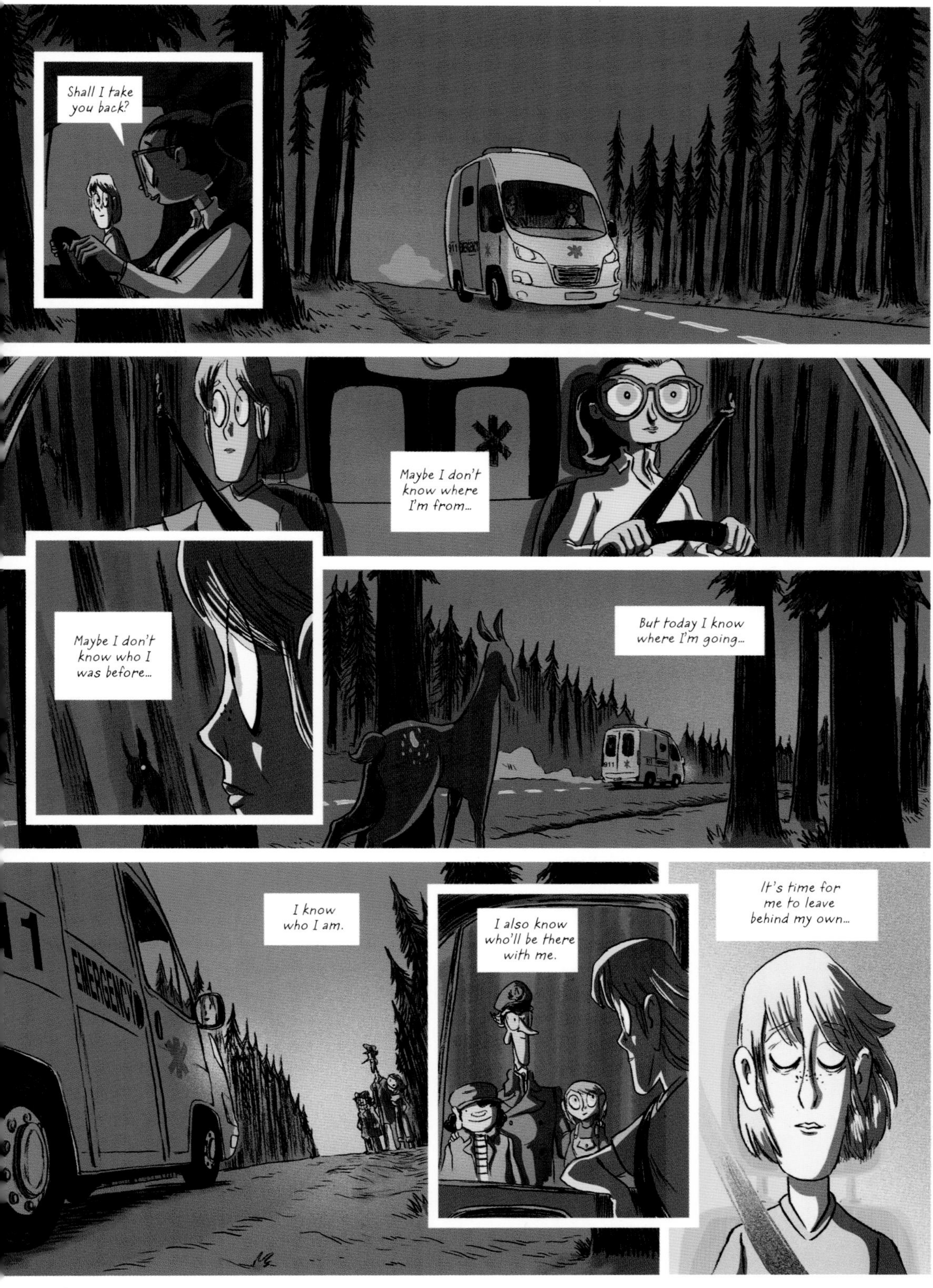
Shall I take you back?
911 EMERGENCY
Maybe I don't know where I'm from...
Maybe I don't know who I was before...
But today I know where I'm going...
I know who I am.
EMERGENCY
I also know who'll be there with me.
It's time for me to leave behind my own...

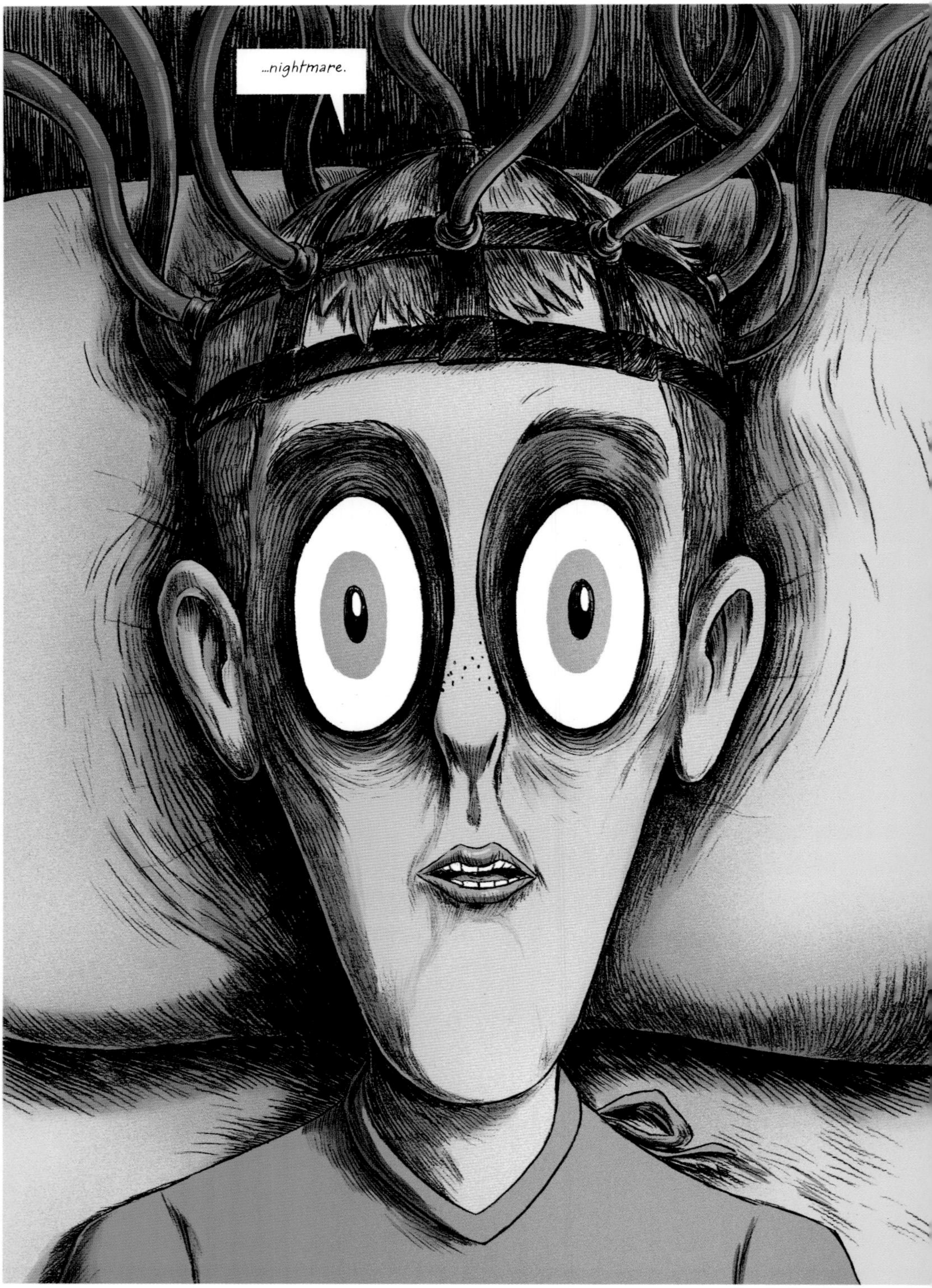
...nightmare.

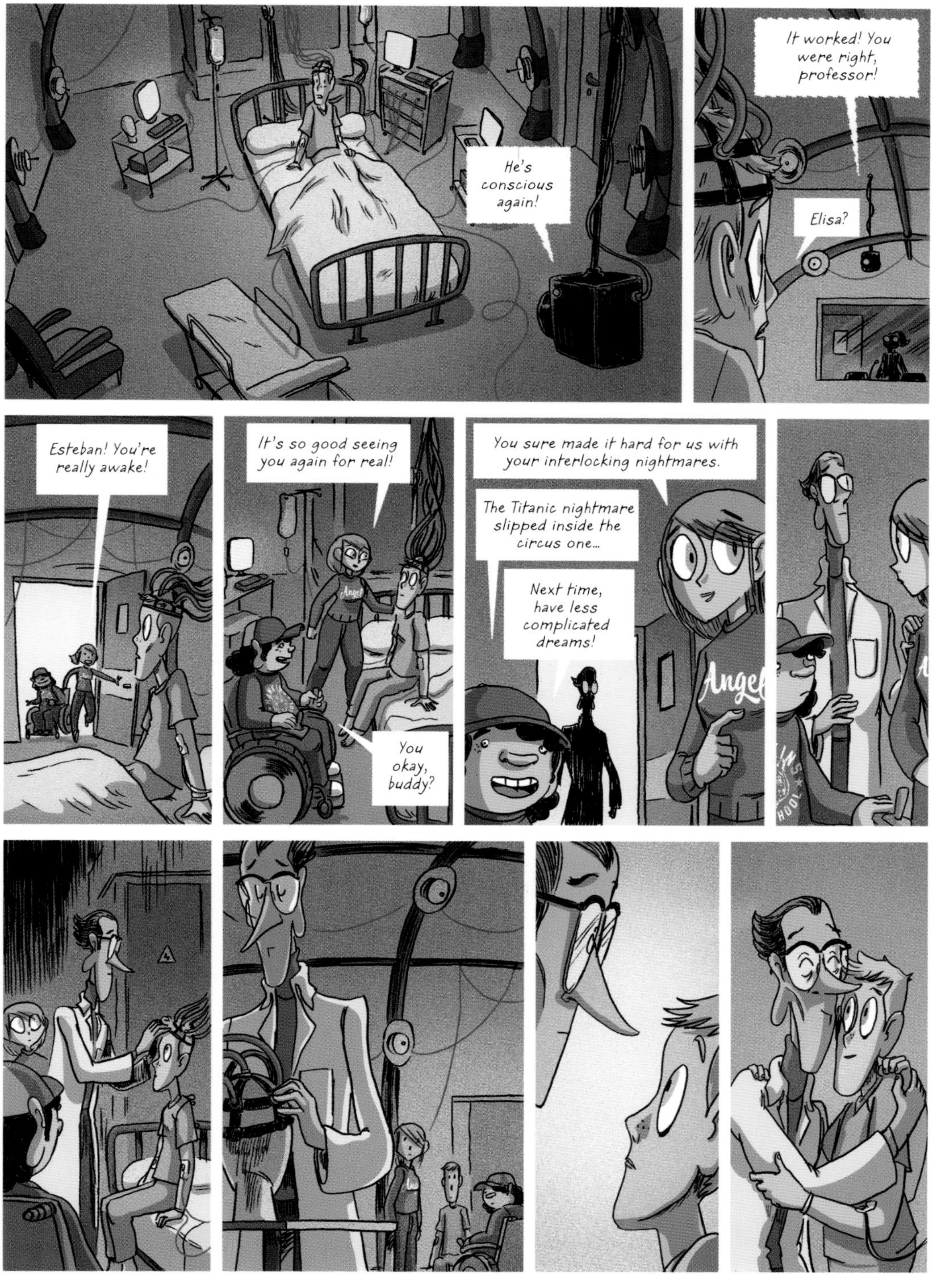
He's conscious again!
It worked! You were right, professor!
Elisa?
Esteban! You're really awake!
It's so good seeing you again for real!
You okay, buddy?
You sure made it hard for us with your interlocking nightmares.
The Titanic nightmare slipped inside the circus one...
Next time, have less complicated dreams!
Angel
Angel

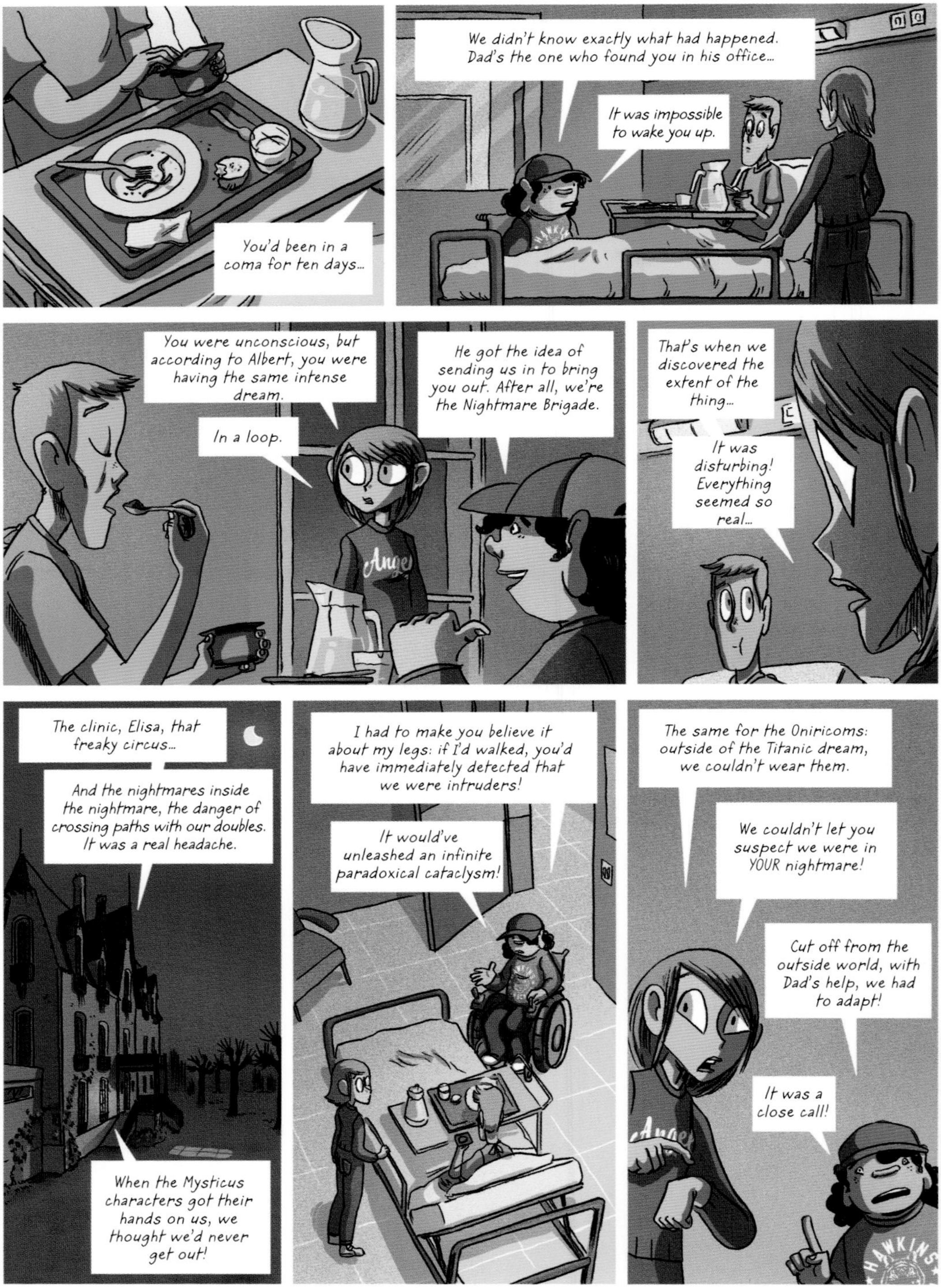
You'd been in a coma for ten days...
We didn't know exactly what had happened. Dad's the one who found you in his office...
It was impossible to wake you up.
You were unconscious, but according to Albert, you were having the same intense dream.
In a loop.
He got the idea of sending us in to bring you out. After all, we're the Nightmare Brigade.
That's when we discovered the extent of the thing...
It was disturbing! Everything seemed so real...
The clinic, Elisa, that freaky circus...
And the nightmares inside the nightmare, the danger of crossing paths with our doubles. It was a real headache.
When the Mysticus characters got their hands on us, we thought we'd never get out!
I had to make you believe it about my legs: if I'd walked, you'd have immediately detected that we were intruders!
It would've unleashed an infinite paradoxical cataclysm!
The same for the Oniricoms: outside of the Titanic dream, we couldn't wear them.
We couldn't let you suspect we were in YOUR nightmare!
Cut off from the outside world, with Dad's help, we had to adapt!
It was a close call!

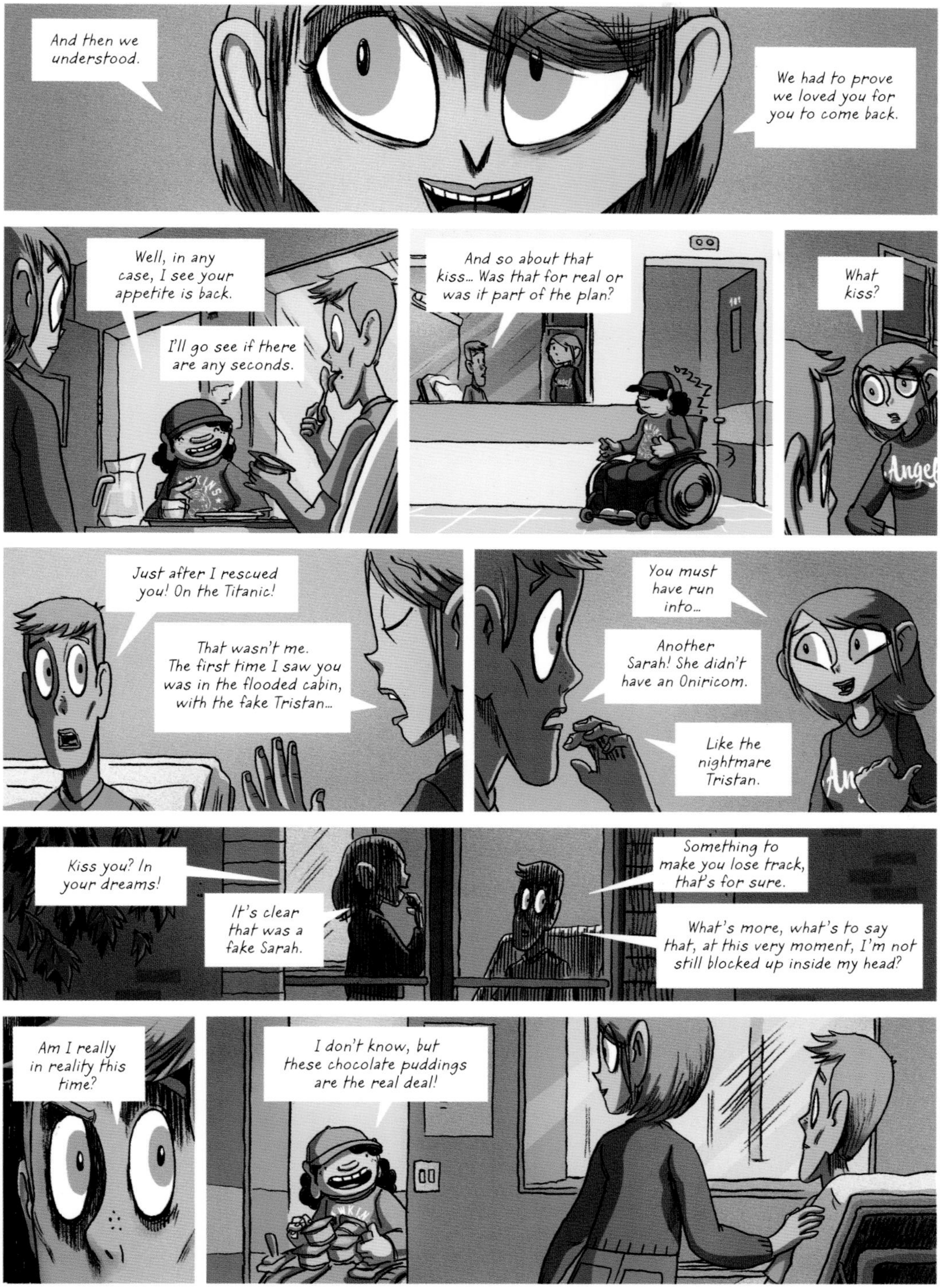
And then we understood.
We had to prove we loved you for you to come back.
Well, in any case, I see your appetite is back.
I'll go see if there are any seconds.
And so about that kiss... Was that for real or was it part of the plan?
What kiss?
Just after I rescued you! On the Titanic!
That wasn't me. The first time I saw you was in the flooded cabin, with the fake Tristan...
You must have run into...
Another Sarah! She didn't have an Oniricom.
Like the nightmare Tristan.
Kiss you? In your dreams!
It's clear that was a fake Sarah.
Something to make you lose track, that's for sure.
What's more, what's to say that, at this very moment, I'm not still blocked up inside my head?
Am I really in reality this time?
I don't know, but these chocolate puddings are the real deal!

A few days later...

TOC
TOC
TOC

Come in!

May I come in, Albert?

Of course, Esteban. Have a seat.

I was wondering when you'd decide to come by.

How are you feeling?

Better.

Listen, I know you have lots of quest--

Let me talk.

I just wanted to tell you thanks.

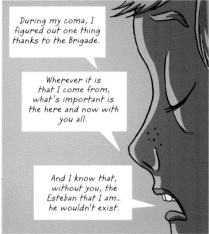

During my coma, I figured out one thing thanks to the Brigade.

Wherever it is that I come from, what's important is the here and now with you all.

And I know that, without you, the Esteban that I am... he wouldn't exist.

My goodness, have you grown up...

...my son.

I'm so happy you came back.

Me too, Albert.

Just one last thing...

Do know that I'm ready to find out where I'm from.

A truly real person must have dreamt of me.

And one day, you'll have to tell me who that person is.

60

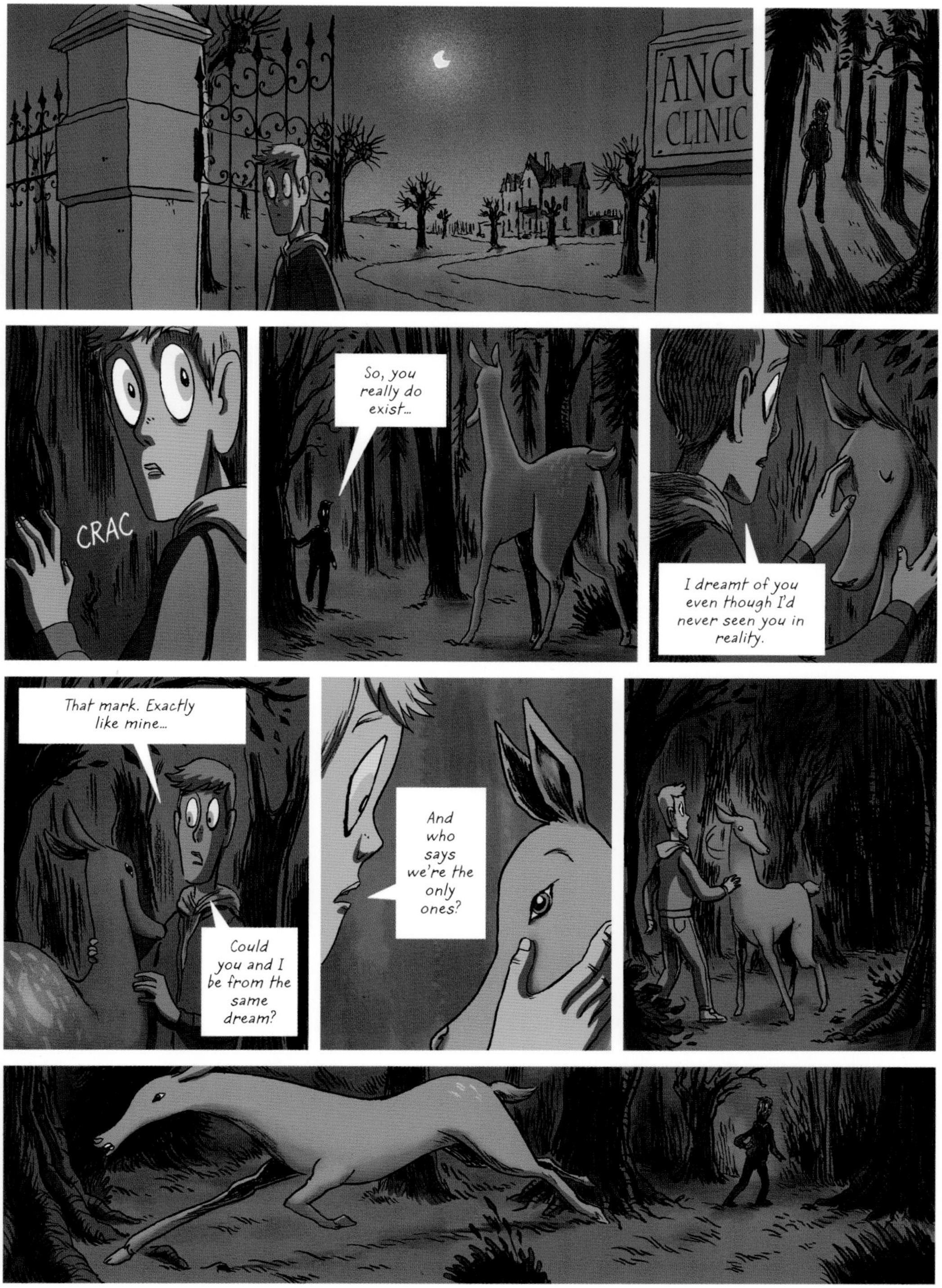
ANGU
CLINIC
CRAC
So, you really do exist...
I dreamt of you even though I'd never seen you in reality.
That mark. Exactly like mine...
Could you and I be from the same dream?
And who says we're the only ones?

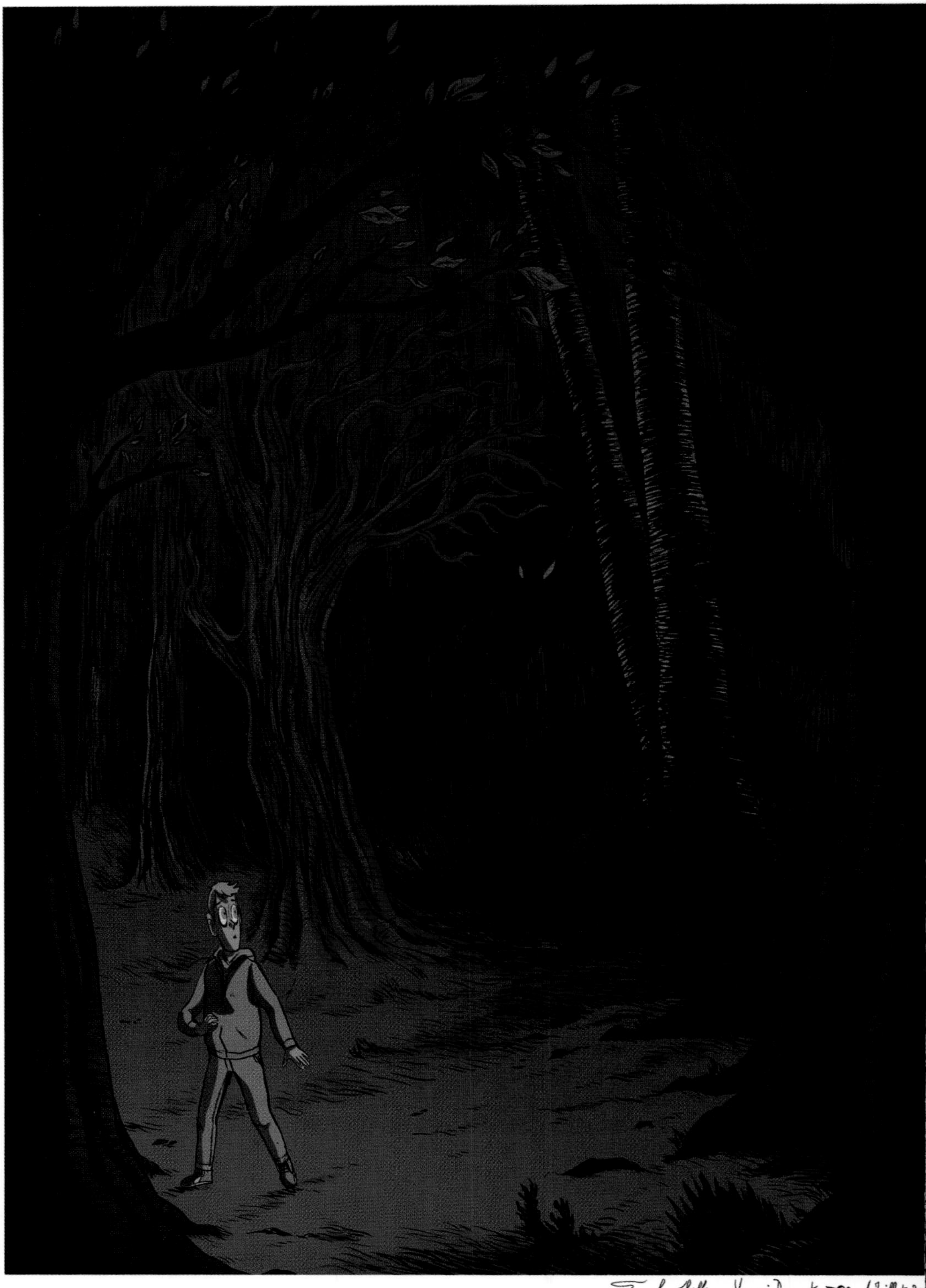

Franck Thilliez - Yomgui Dumont - DRAC / Juillet 20

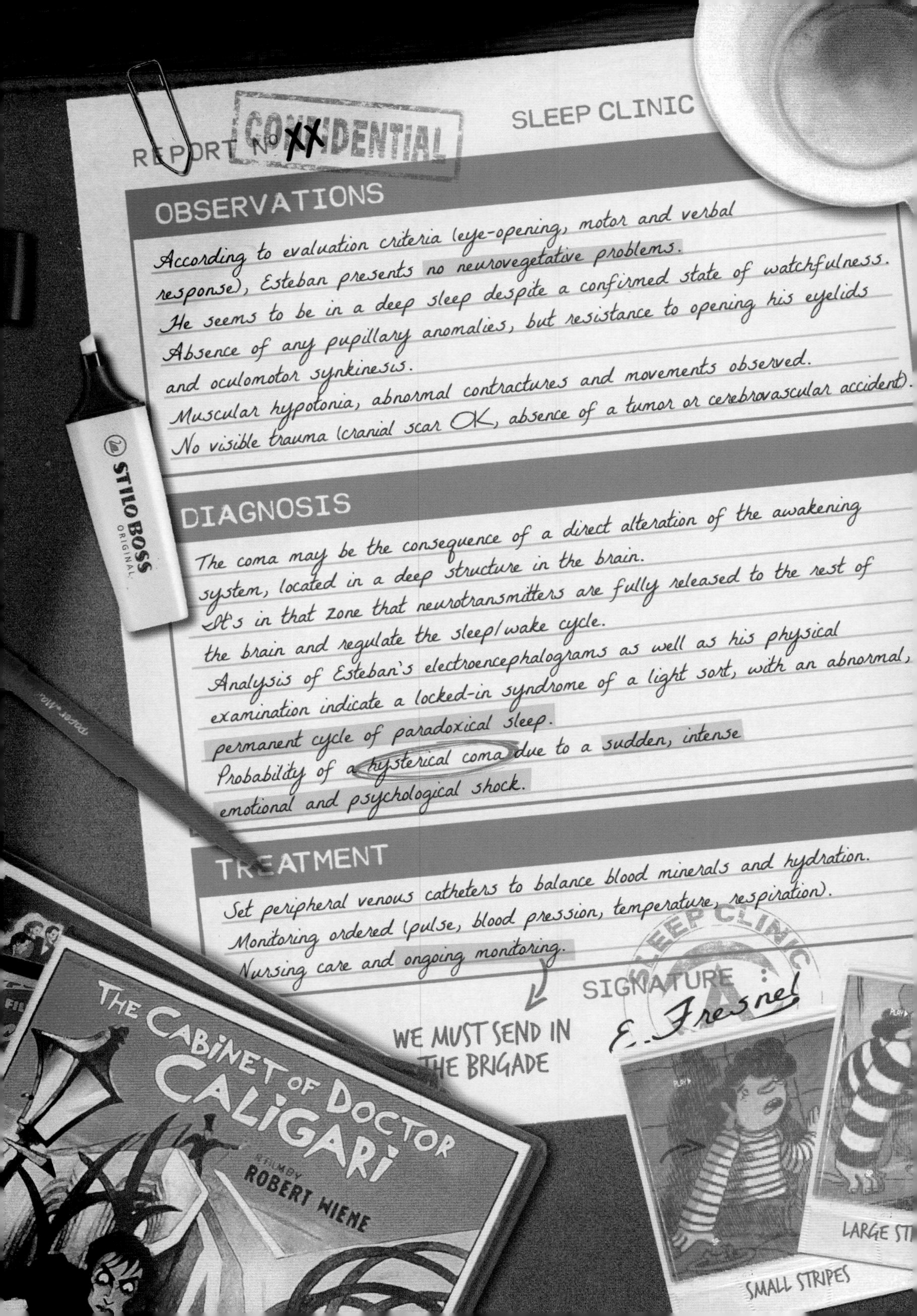
SLEEP CLINIC

REPORT N° XX

CONFIDENTIAL

OBSERVATIONS

According to evaluation criteria (eye-opening, motor and verbal response), Esteban presents no neurovegetative problems.
He seems to be in a deep sleep despite a confirmed state of watchfulness.
Absence of any pupillary anomalies, but resistance to opening his eyelids and oculomotor synkinesis.
Muscular hypotonia, abnormal contractures and movements observed.
No visible trauma (cranial scar OK, absence of a tumor or cerebrovascular accident).

DIAGNOSIS

The coma may be the consequence of a direct alteration of the awakening system, located in a deep structure in the brain.
It's in that zone that neurotransmitters are fully released to the rest of the brain and regulate the sleep/wake cycle.
Analysis of Esteban's electroencephalograms as well as his physical examination indicate a locked-in syndrome of a light sort, with an abnormal, permanent cycle of paradoxical sleep.
Probability of a hysterical coma due to a sudden, intense emotional and psychological shock.

TREATMENT

Set peripheral venous catheters to balance blood minerals and hydration.
Montoring ordered (pulse, blood pression, temperature, respiration).
Nursing care and ongoing montoring.

SIGNATURE: E. Fresnel

SLEEP CLINIC
WE MUST SEND IN THE BRIGADE
STILO BOSS ORIGINAL
THE CABINET OF DOCTOR CALIGARI
A FILM BY ROBERT WIENE
SMALL STRIPES
LARGE ST

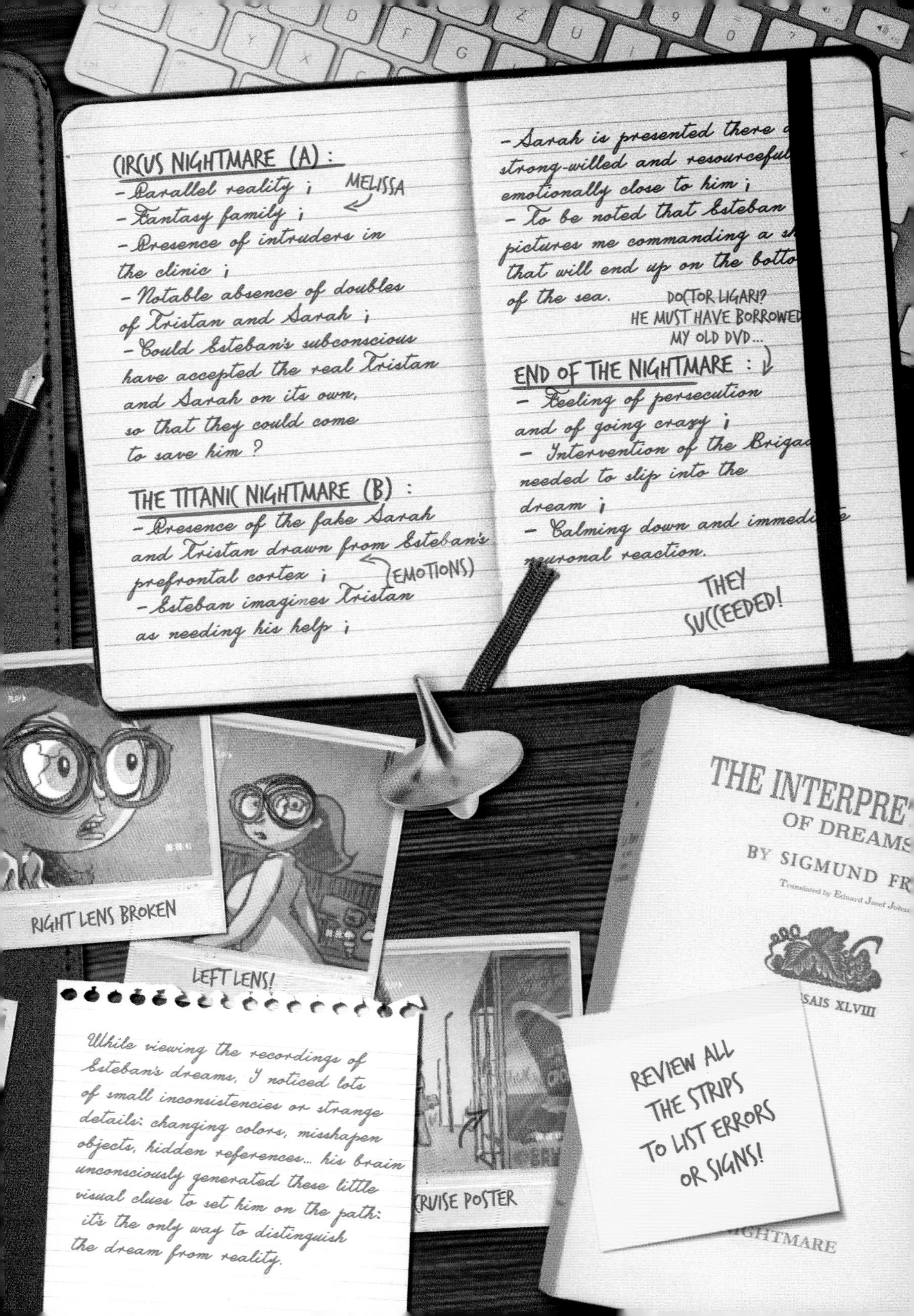
CIRCUS NIGHTMARE (A) :
- Parallel reality ;
MELISSA
- Fantasy family ;
- Presence of intruders in the clinic ;
- Notable absence of doubles of Tristan and Sarah ;
- Could Esteban's subconscious have accepted the real Tristan and Sarah on its own, so that they could come to save him ?
THE TITANIC NIGHTMARE (B) :
- Presence of the fake Sarah and Tristan drawn from Esteban's prefrontal cortex ;
(EMOTIONS)
- Esteban imagines Tristan as needing his help ;
- Sarah is presented there a
strong-willed and resourceful
emotionally close to him ;
- To be noted that Esteban
pictures me commanding a sh
that will end up on the botto
of the sea.
DOCTOR LIGARI? HE MUST HAVE BORROWED MY OLD DVD...
END OF THE NIGHTMARE :
- Feeling of persecution and of going crazy ;
- Intervention of the Brigad
needed to slip into the dream ;
- Calming down and immedi te neuronal reaction.
THEY SUCCEEDED!
RIGHT LENS BROKEN
LEFT LENS!
CRUISE POSTER
While viewing the recordings of Esteban's dreams, I noticed lots of small inconsistencies or strange details: changing colors, misshapen objects, hidden references... his brain unconsciously generated these little visual clues to set him on the path: it's the only way to distinguish the dream from reality.
THE INTERPRE
OF DREAMS
BY SIGMUND FR
Translated by Eduard Josef Joha
SAIS XLVIII
HTMARE
REVIEW ALL THE STRIPS TO LIST ERRORS OR SIGNS!

WATCH OUT FOR PAPERCUTZ

"Is this the real life?
Is this just fantasy?
Caught in a landslide
No escape from reality"
—Freddie Mercury, Queen

Welcome to the sleep-induced second volume of THE NIGHTMARE BRIGADE "Into the Woods," by Franck Thilliez, Yomgui Dumont, and Drac, brought to you by Papercutz, those daring dreamers dedicated to publishing great graphic novels for all ages. I'm Jim "Sleepy" Salicrup, the Editor-in-Chief and Former Out Patient of the Professor Albert Angus Sleep Clinic. I'm here to offer up another look into dreams, as written by one of my favorite poets, as well as to point you to another Papercutz publication that can offer more information, in a most entertaining way, on one of the locales found in this volume of THE NIGHTMARE BRIGADE. But first, the poem…

Dream-Land
By Edgar Allan Poe
By a route obscure and lonely,
Haunted by ill angels only,
Where an Eidolon, named NIGHT,
On a black throne reigns upright,
I have reached these lands but newly
From an ultimate dim Thule—
From a wild weird clime that lieth, sublime,
Out of SPACE—Out of TIME.

Bottomless vales and boundless floods,
And chasms, and caves, and Titan woods,
With forms that no man can discover
For the tears that drip all over;
Mountains toppling evermore
Into seas without a shore;
Seas that restlessly aspire,
Surging, unto skies of fire;
Lakes that endlessly outspread
Their lone waters, lone and dead,—
Their still waters—still and chilly
With the snows of the lolling lily.

By the lakes that thus outspread
Their lone waters, lone and dead,—
Their sad waters, sad and chilly
With the snows of the lolling lily,—
By the mountains—near the river
Murmuring lowly, murmuring ever,—
By the grey woods,—by the swamp
Where the toad and the newt encamp,—
By the dismal tarns and pools
Where dwell the Ghouls,—
By each spot the most unholy—
In each nook most melancholy,—
There the traveler meets, aghast,
Sheeted Memories of the Past—
Shrouded forms that start and sigh
As they pass the wanderer by—
White-robed forms of friends long given,
In agony, to the Earth—and Heaven.

For the heart whose woes are legion
'T is a peaceful, soothing region—
For the spirit that walks in shadow
'T is—oh, 't is an Eldorado!
But the traveler, travelling through it,
May not—dare not openly view it;
Never its mysteries are exposed
To the weak human eye unclosed;
So wills its King, who hath forbid
The uplifting of the fring'd lid;

And thus the sad Soul that here passes
Beholds it but through darkened glasses.

By a route obscure and lonely,
Haunted by ill angels only,
Where an Eidolon, named NIGHT,
On a black throne reigns upright,
I have wandered home but newly
From this ultimate dim Thule.

Thank you, Mr. Poe. If I shared your view of Dream-Land, I don't think I'd ever want to go to sleep. And speaking of sleep, when Esteban, on page 20, stumbled into the engine room of the most famous shipwreck of all time, chased by crazed clowns, no less, I wish I could've handed him a copy of MAGICAL HISTORY TOUR #9 "The Titanic." Because in that Papercutz graphic novel, written by Fabrice Erre and drawn by Sylvain Savoia, is everything Esteban would've needed to know about that historic ship. So, while I can't give it to Esteban, although maybe I can in a dream, I can suggest that you check out this wonderful graphic novel for the full factual story of that fabled sunken ship. And if you want to make one of my dreams come true, you'll want to pick up the very next volume of THE NIGHTMARE BRIGADE, available soon at booksellers and libraries everywhere.

Thanks,
Jim

FABRICE ERRE • SYLVAIN SAVOIA
Magical
History Tour
NICO
ANNIE
The Titanic
Shipwreck of a Giant
PAPERCUTZ

STAY IN TOUCH!

EMAIL:	salicrup@papercutz.com
WEB:	papercutz.com
TWITTER:	@papercutzgn
INSTAGRAM:	@papercutzgn
FACEBOOK:	PAPERCUTZGRAPHICNOVELS
FANMAIL:	Papercutz, 160 Broadway, Suite 700, East Wing, New York, NY 10038

Go to papercutz.com and sign up for the free Papercutz e-newsletter!

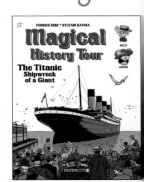

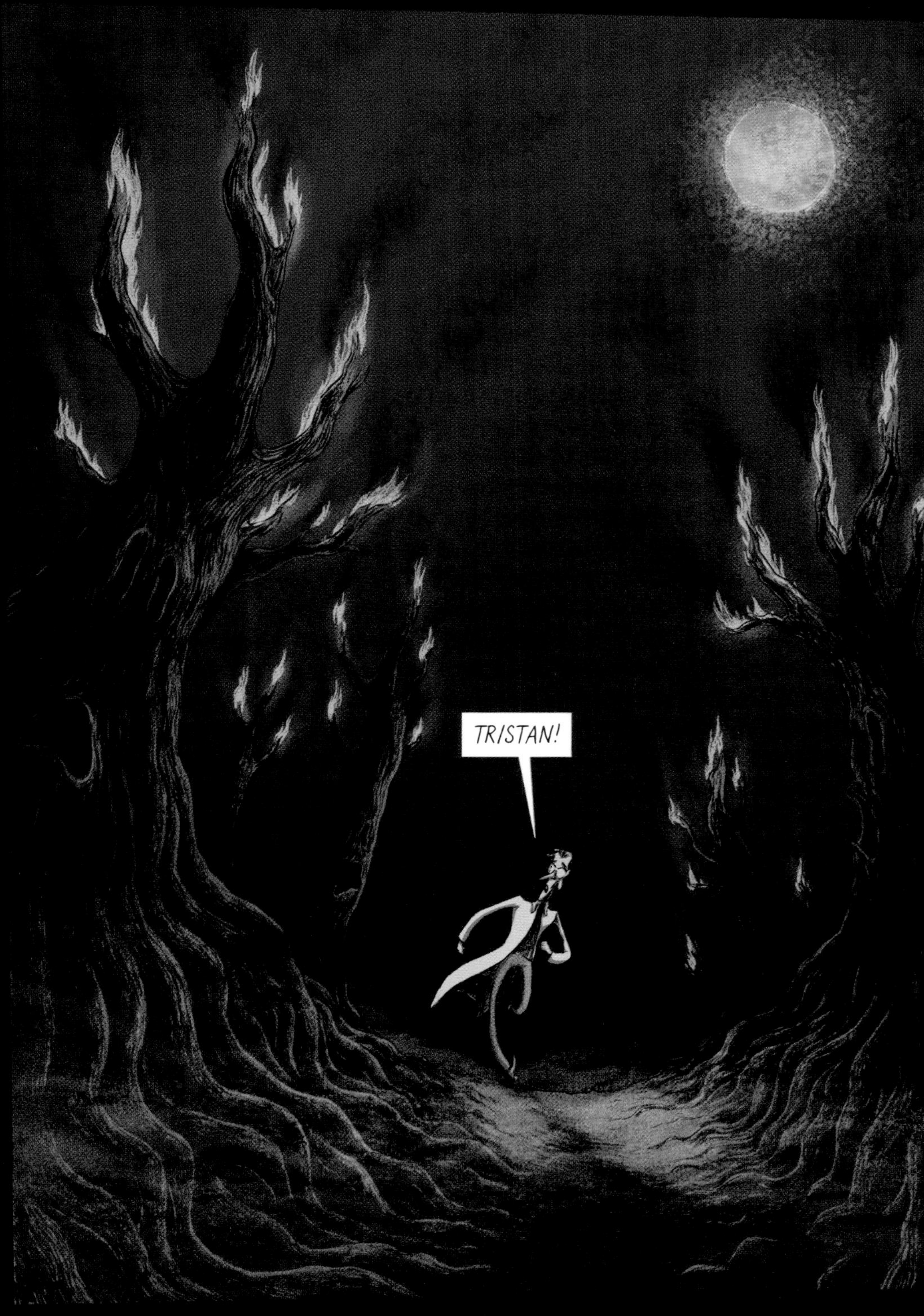
TRISTAN!

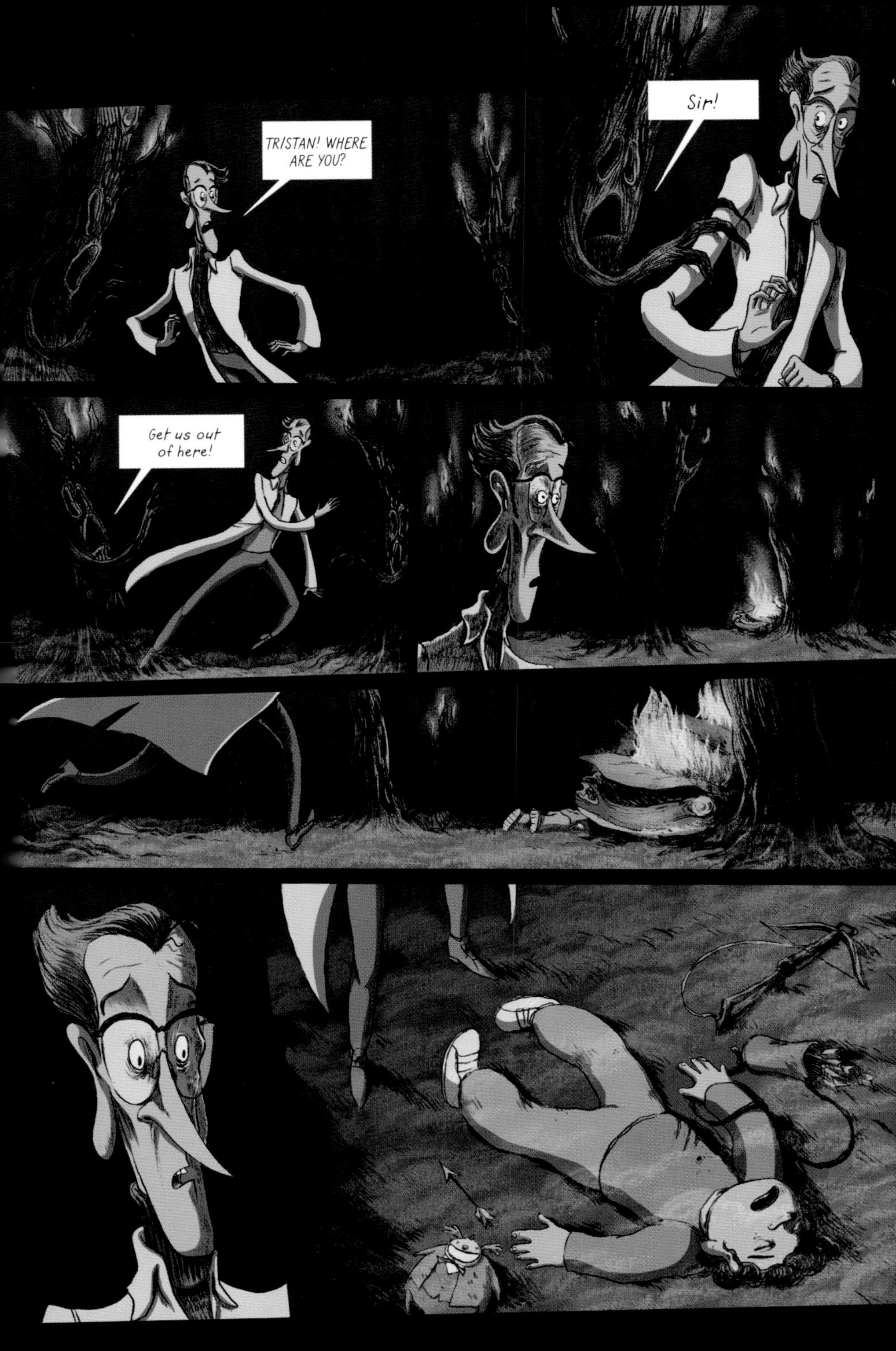
TRISTAN! WHERE ARE YOU?
Sir!
Get us out of here!

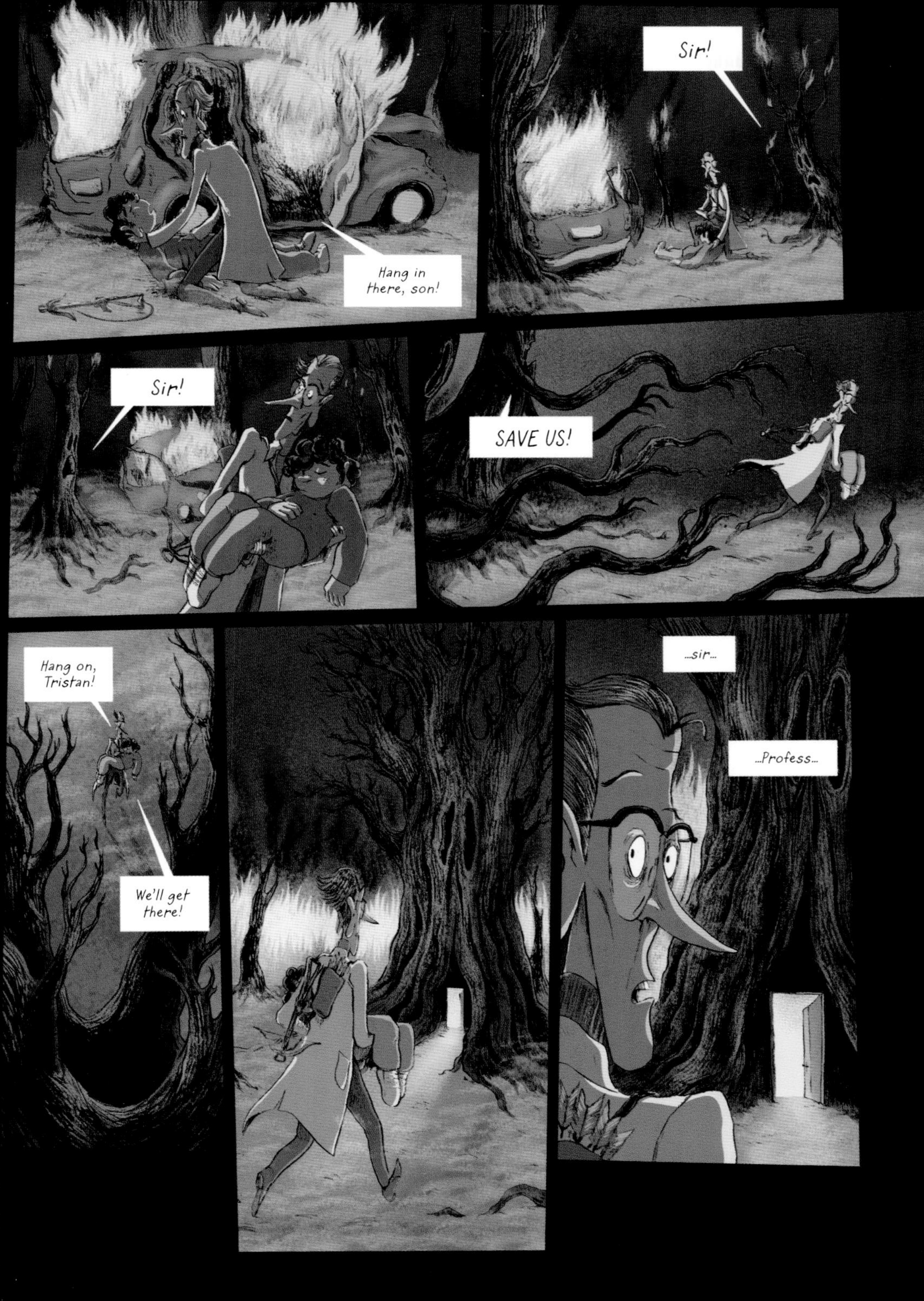
Hang in there, son!
Sir!
Sir!
SAVE US!
Hang on, Tristan!
We'll get there!
...sir...
...Profess...

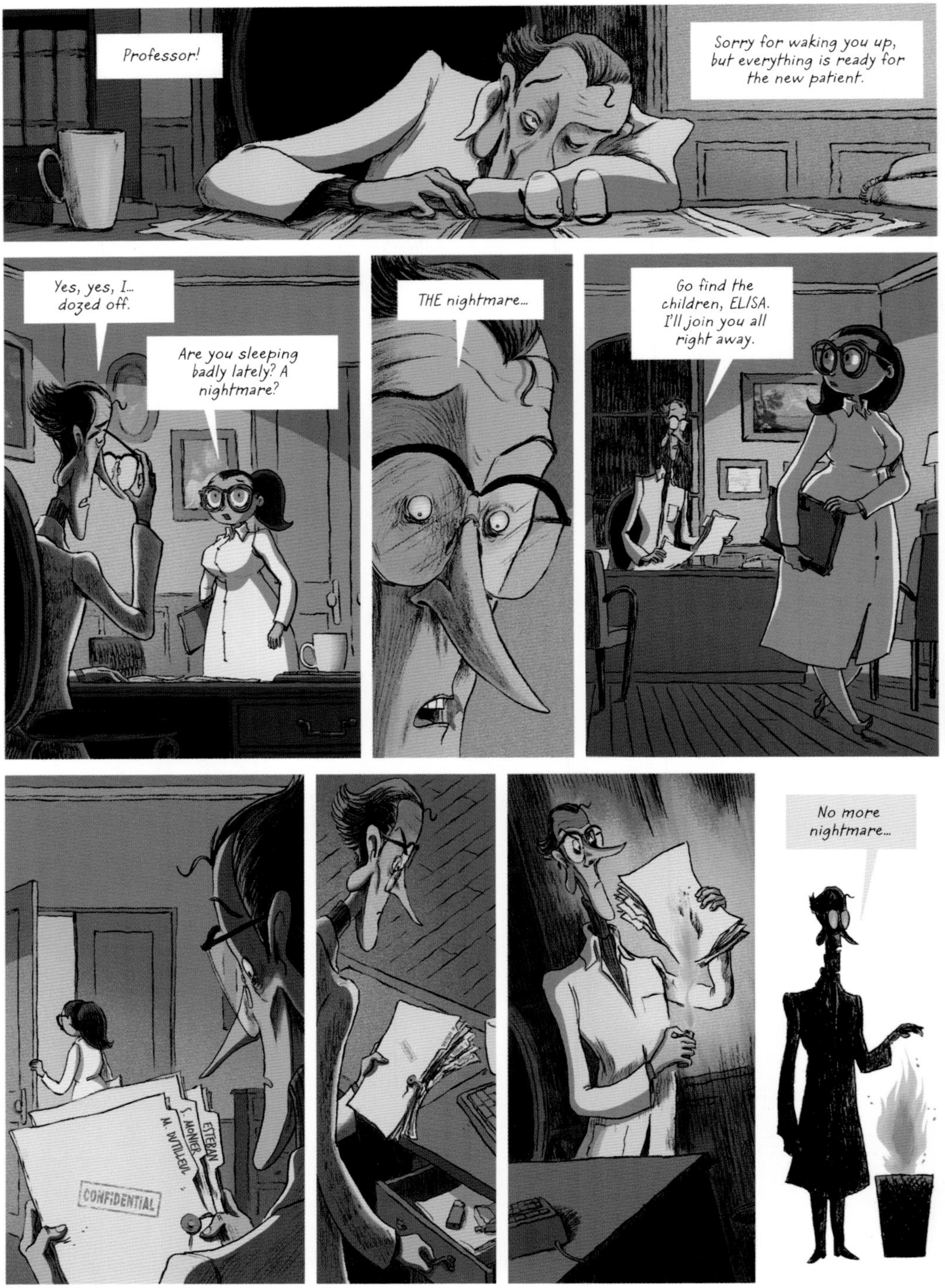
Professor!
Sorry for waking you up, but everything is ready for the new patient.
Yes, yes, I... dozed off.
Are you sleeping badly lately? A nightmare?
THE nightmare...
Go find the children, ELISA. I'll join you all right away.
ESTEBAN
S. MONIER
M. DUTILLEUL
CONFIDENTIAL
No more nightmare...

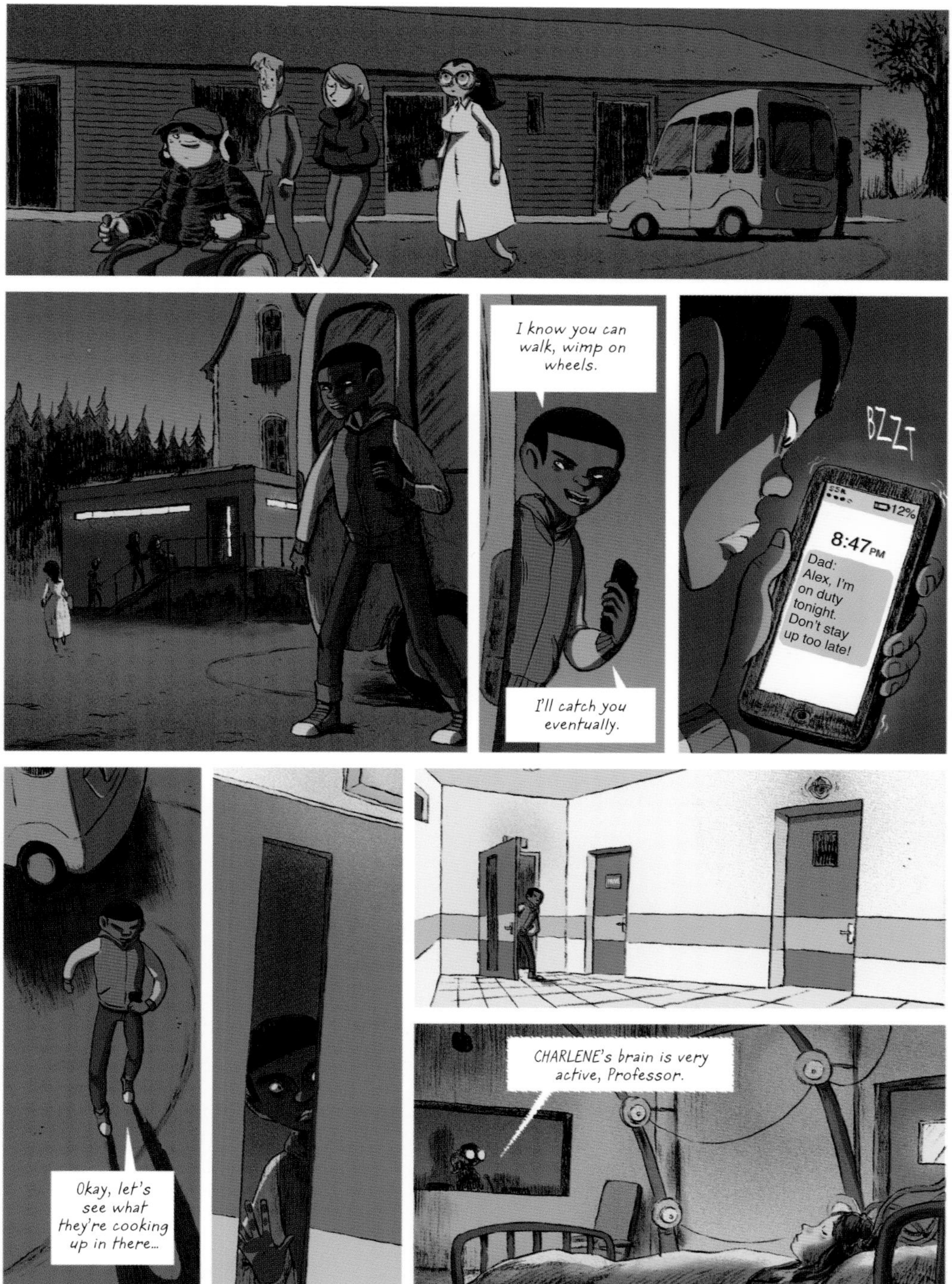
I know you can walk, wimp on wheels.
I'll catch you eventually.
BZZT
12%
8:47PM
Dad: Alex, I'm on duty tonight. Don't stay up too late!
Okay, let's see what they're cooking up in there...
CHARLENE's brain is very active, Professor.

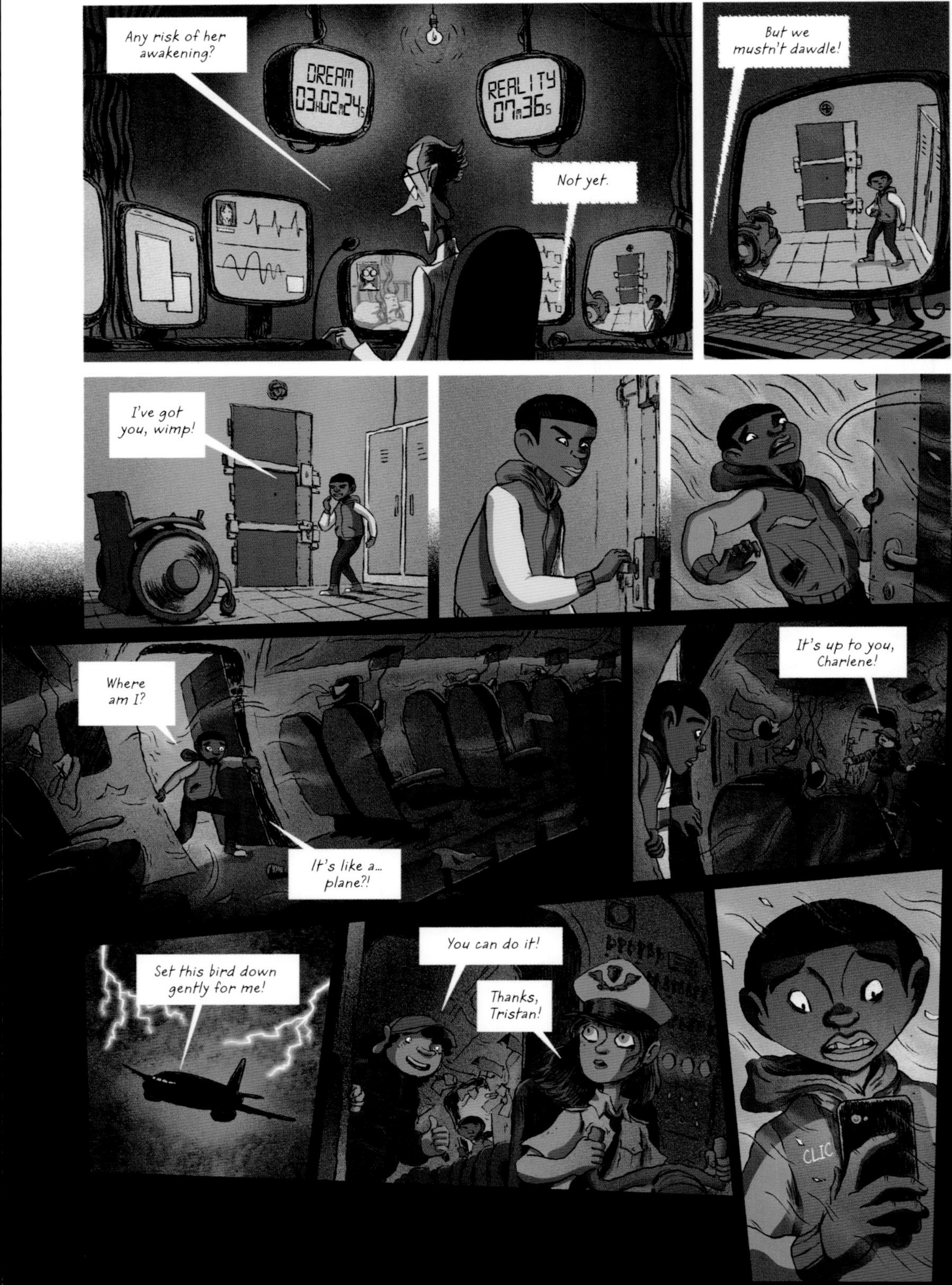
Any risk of her awakening?
DREAM 03H02M24S
REALITY 07M36S
Not yet.
But we mustn't dawdle!
I've got you, wimp!
Where am I?
It's like a... plane?!
It's up to you, Charlene!
Set this bird down gently for me!
You can do it!
Thanks, Tristan!
CLIC

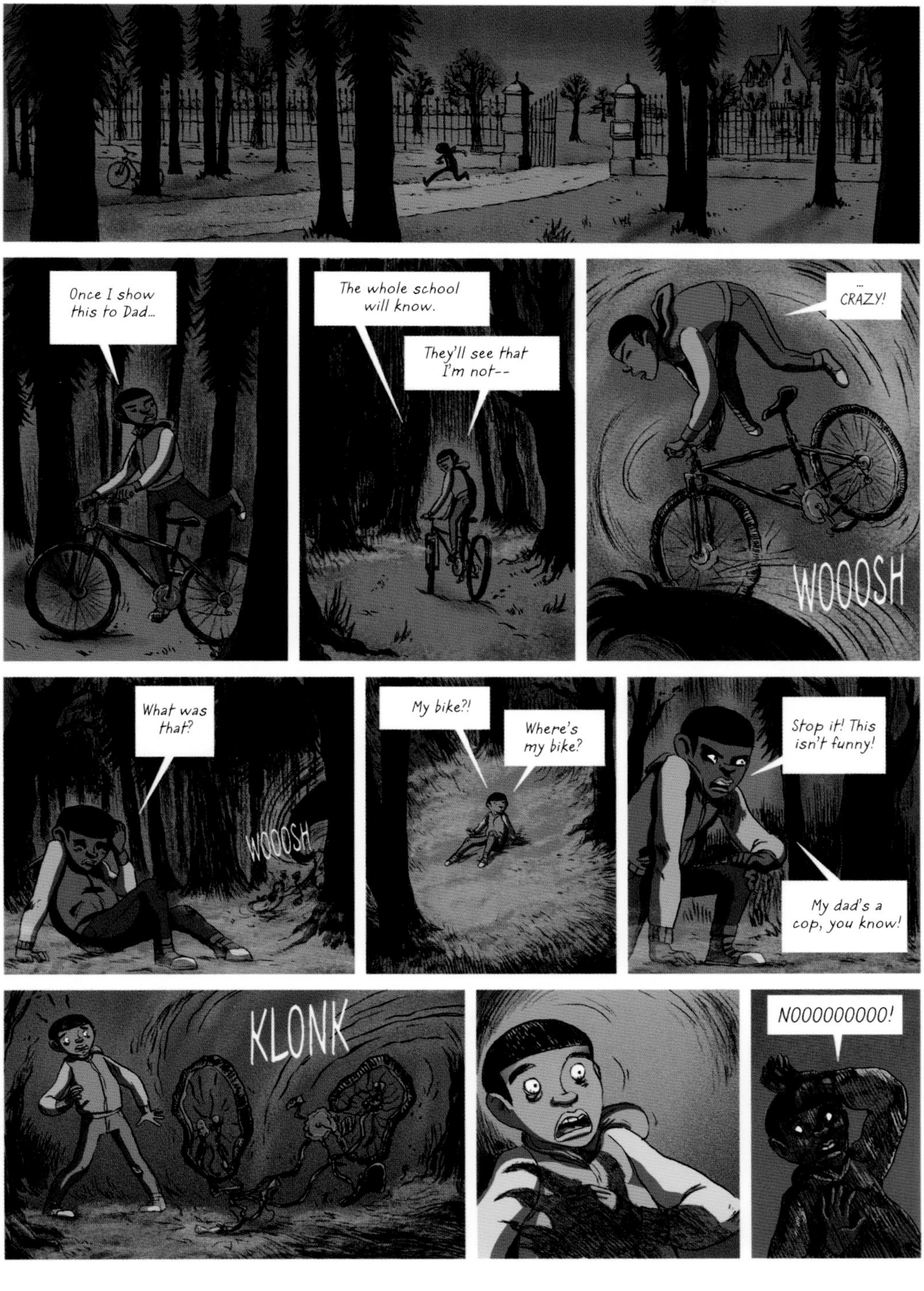
Once I show this to Dad...
The whole school will know.
They'll see that I'm not--
... CRAZY!
WOOOSH
What was that?
WOOOSH
My bike?!
Where's my bike?
Stop it! This isn't funny!
My dad's a cop, you know!
KLONK
NOOOOOOOOO!

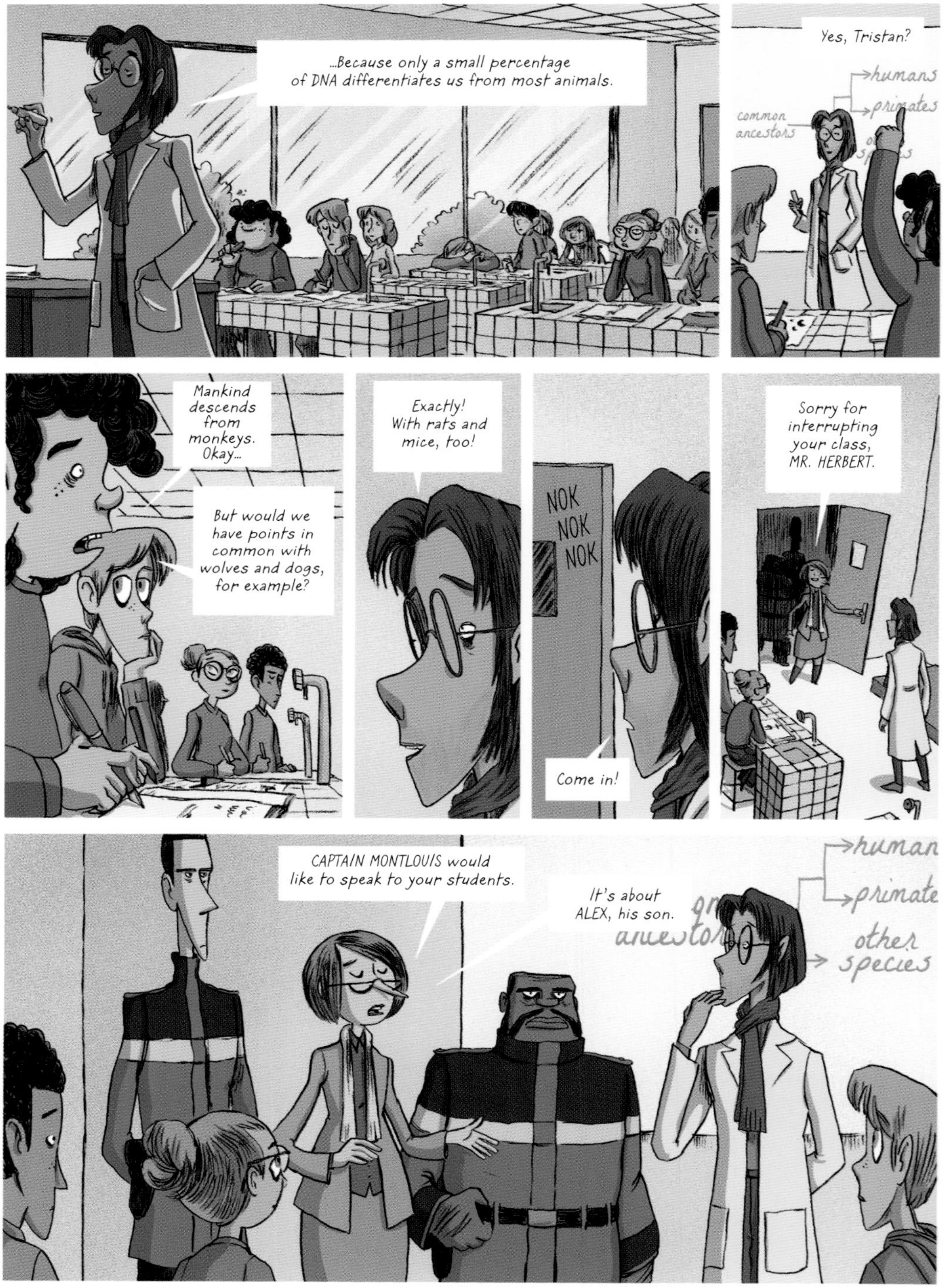
...Because only a small percentage of DNA differentiates us from most animals.
Yes, Tristan?
humans
primates
common ancestors
Mankind descends from monkeys. Okay...
But would we have points in common with wolves and dogs, for example?
Exactly! With rats and mice, too!
NOK NOK NOK
Come in!
Sorry for interrupting your class, MR. HERBERT.
CAPTAIN MONTLOUIS would like to speak to your students.
It's about ALEX, his son.
other species

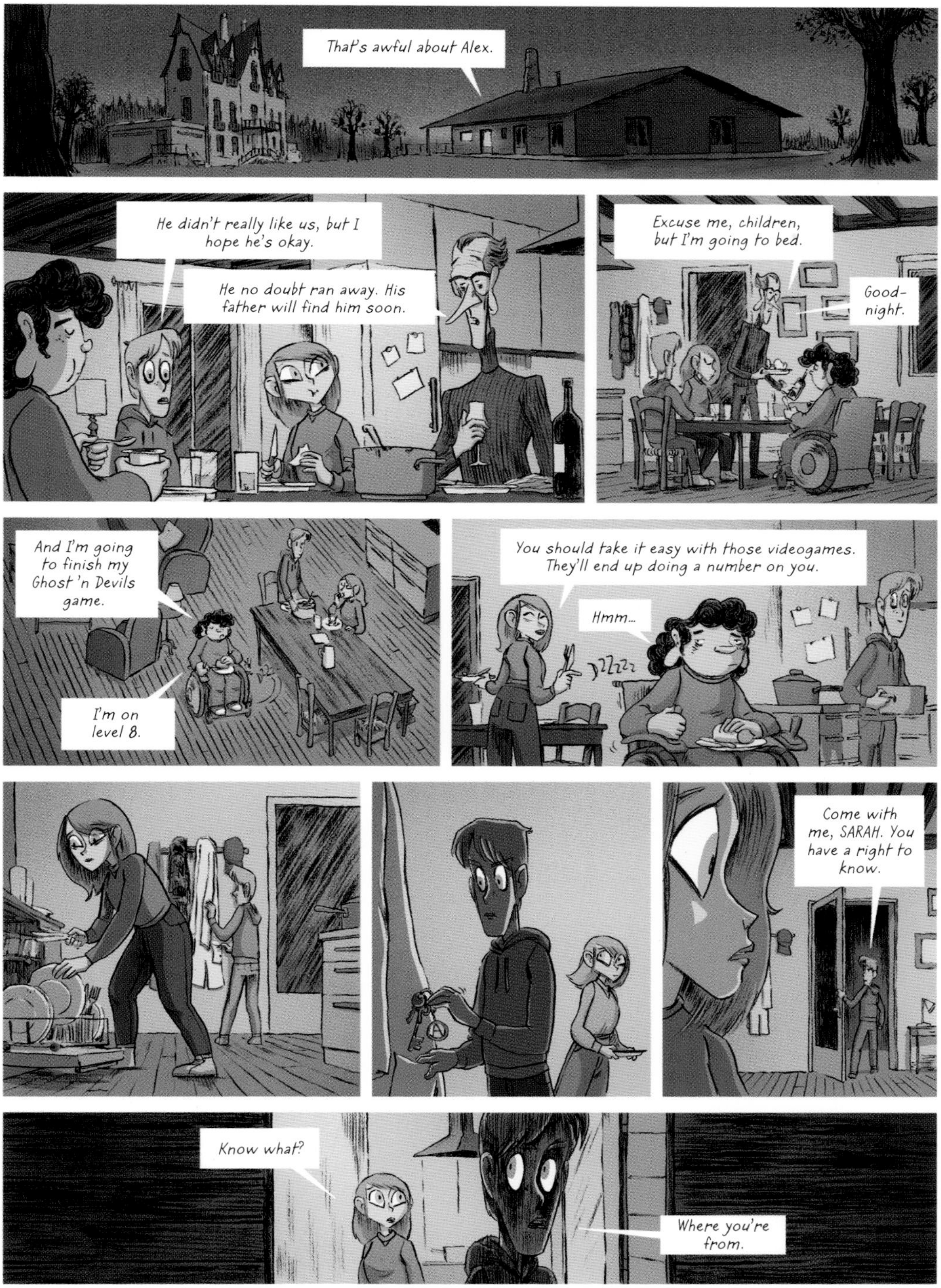
That's awful about Alex.
He didn't really like us, but I hope he's okay.
He no doubt ran away. His father will find him soon.
Excuse me, children, but I'm going to bed.
Good-night.
And I'm going to finish my Ghost 'n Devils game.
I'm on level 8.
You should take it easy with those videogames. They'll end up doing a number on you.
Hmm...
ZZZZZ
Come with me, SARAH. You have a right to know.
Know what?
Where you're from.

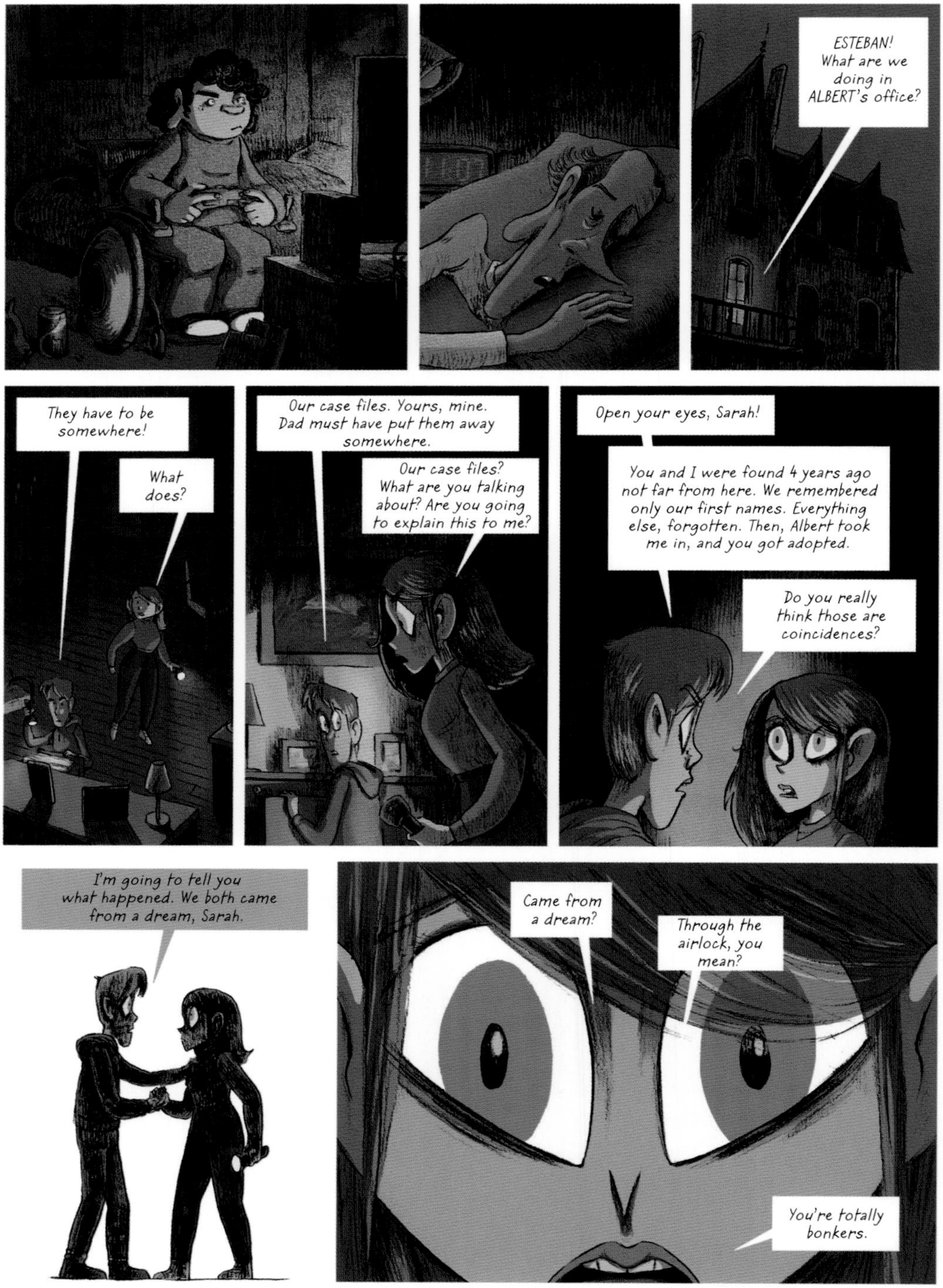
ESTEBAN! What are we doing in ALBERT's office?
They have to be somewhere!
What does?
Our case files. Yours, mine. Dad must have put them away somewhere.
Our case files? What are you talking about? Are you going to explain this to me?
Open your eyes, Sarah!
You and I were found 4 years ago not far from here. We remembered only our first names. Everything else, forgotten. Then, Albert took me in, and you got adopted.
Do you really think those are coincidences?
I'm going to tell you what happened. We both came from a dream, Sarah.
Came from a dream?
Through the airlock, you mean?
You're totally bonkers.

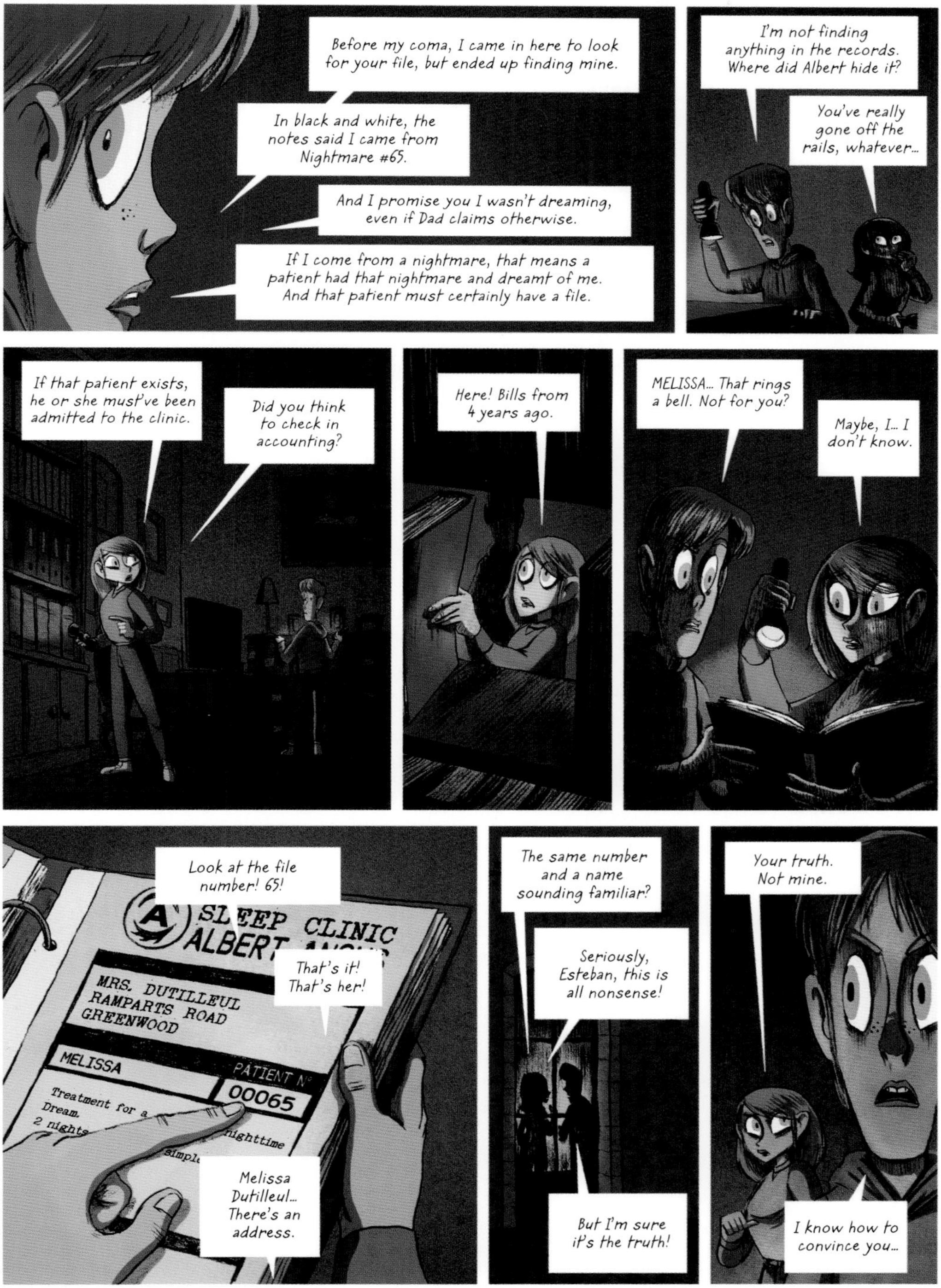

Before my coma, I came in here to look for your file, but ended up finding mine.
In black and white, the notes said I came from Nightmare #65.
And I promise you I wasn't dreaming, even if Dad claims otherwise.
If I come from a nightmare, that means a patient had that nightmare and dreamt of me. And that patient must certainly have a file.
I'm not finding anything in the records. Where did Albert hide it?
You've really gone off the rails, whatever...
If that patient exists, he or she must've been admitted to the clinic.
Did you think to check in accounting?
Here! Bills from 4 years ago.
MELISSA... That rings a bell. Not for you?
Maybe, I... I don't know.
Look at the file number! 65!
SLEEP CLINIC
ALBERT
That's it! That's her!
MRS. DUTILLEUL
RAMPARTS ROAD
GREENWOOD
MELISSA
PATIENT N°
00065
Treatment for a Dream.
2 nights
nighttime
Melissa Dutilleul... There's an address.
The same number and a name sounding familiar?
Seriously, Esteban, this is all nonsense!
But I'm sure it's the truth!
Your truth. Not mine.
I know how to convince you...

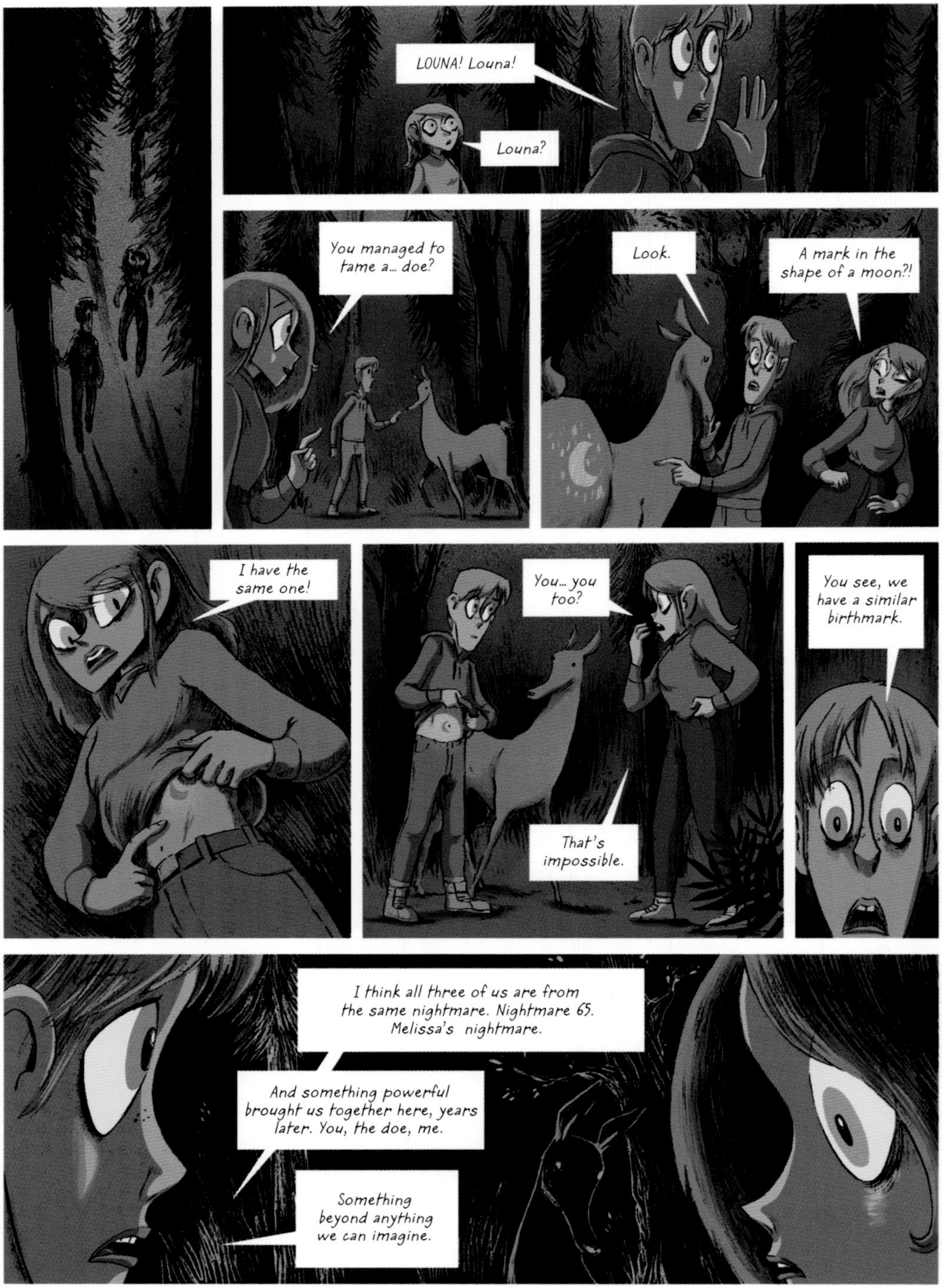

LOUNA! Louna!
Louna?
You managed to tame a... doe?
Look.
A mark in the shape of a moon?!
I have the same one!
You... you too?
That's impossible.
You see, we have a similar birthmark.
I think all three of us are from the same nightmare. Nightmare 65. Melissa's nightmare.
And something powerful brought us together here, years later. You, the doe, me.
Something beyond anything we can imagine.

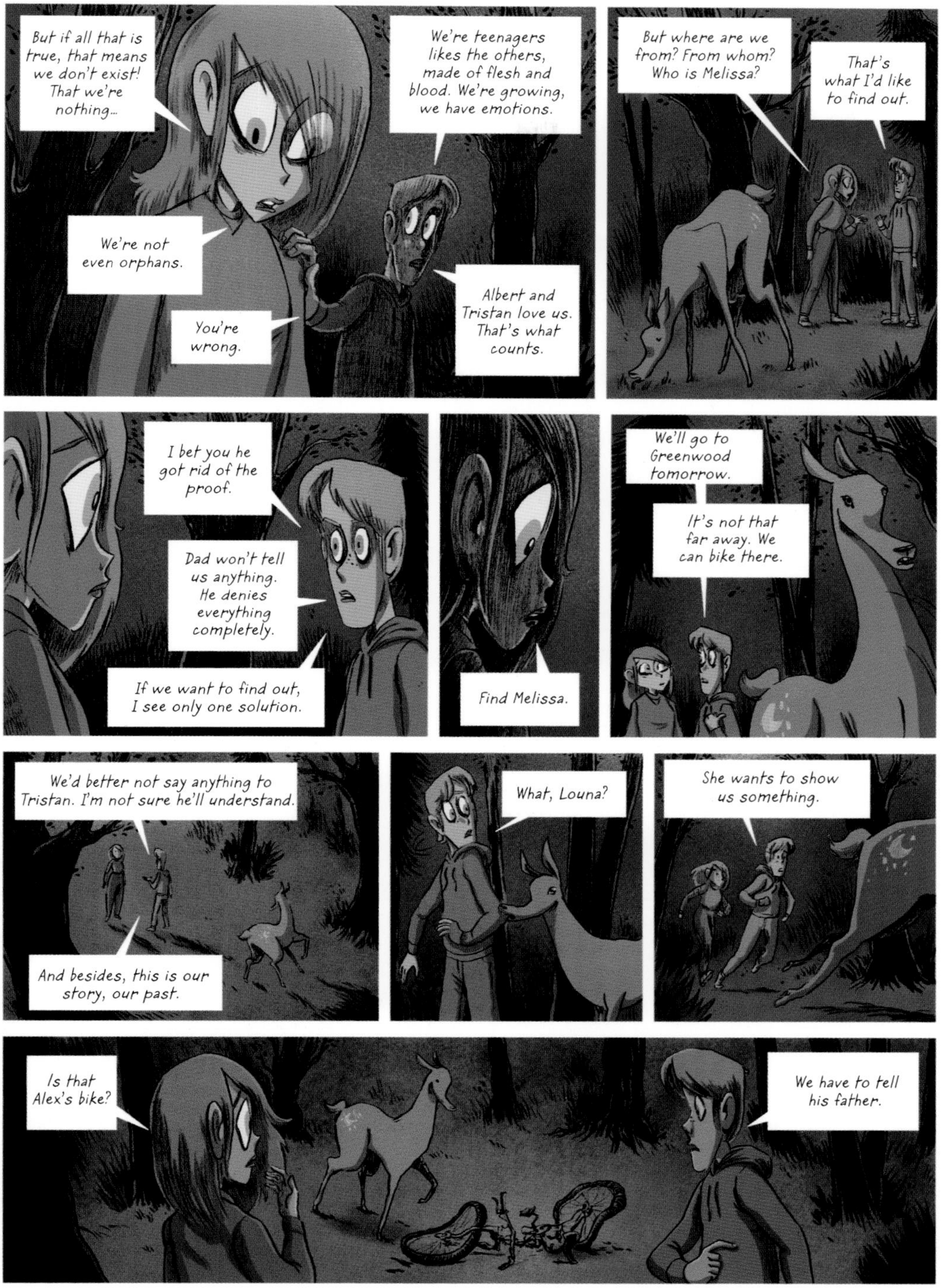
But if all that is true, that means we don't exist! That we're nothing...
We're teenagers likes the others, made of flesh and blood. We're growing, we have emotions.
We're not even orphans.
You're wrong.
Albert and Tristan love us. That's what counts.
But where are we from? From whom? Who is Melissa?
That's what I'd like to find out.
I bet you he got rid of the proof.
Dad won't tell us anything. He denies everything completely.
If we want to find out, I see only one solution.
Find Melissa.
We'll go to Greenwood tomorrow.
It's not that far away. We can bike there.
We'd better not say anything to Tristan. I'm not sure he'll understand.
And besides, this is our story, our past.
What, Louna?
She wants to show us something.
Is that Alex's bike?
We have to tell his father.

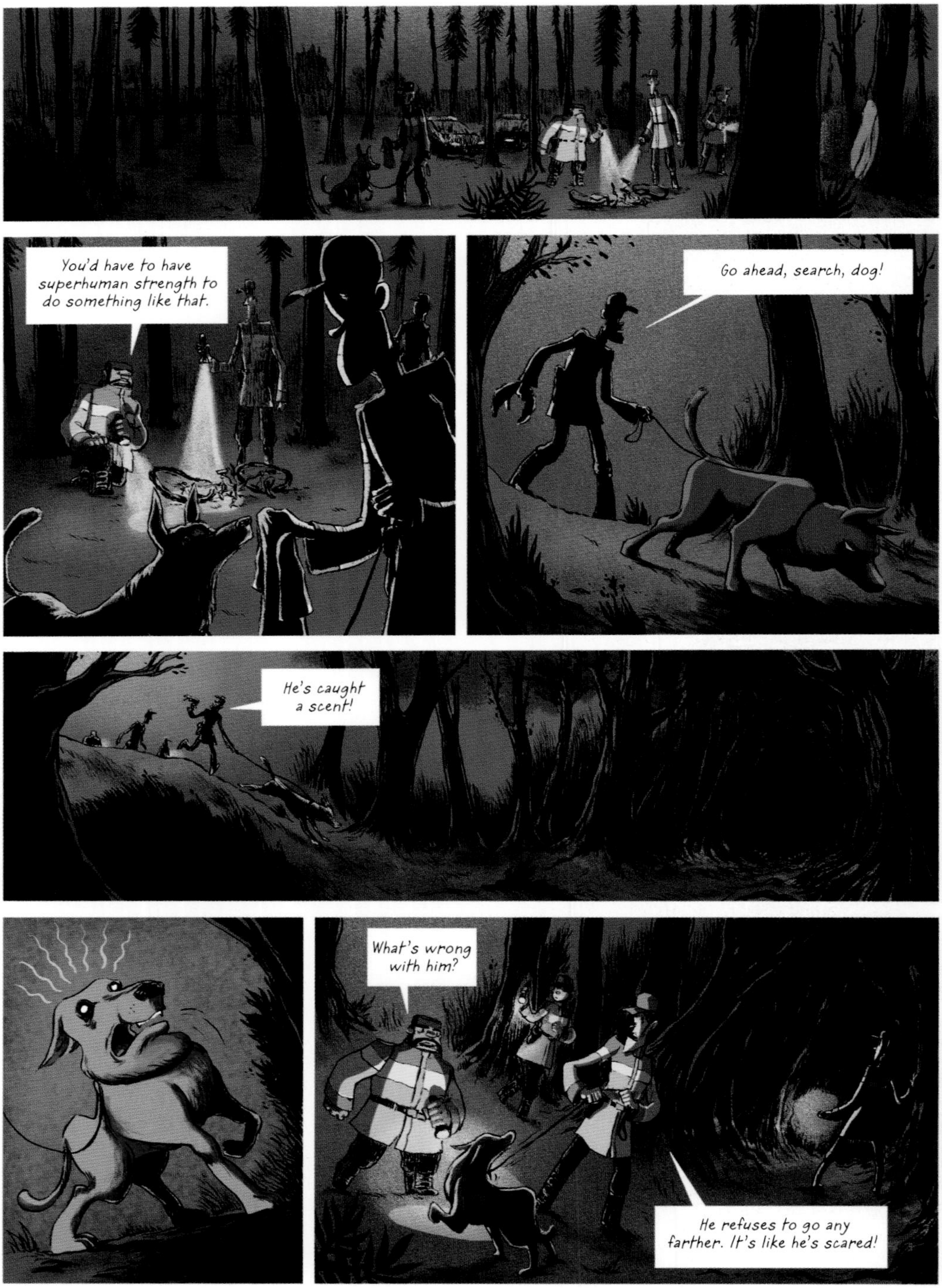
You'd have to have superhuman strength to do something like that.
Go ahead, search, dog!
He's caught a scent!
What's wrong with him?
He refuses to go any farther. It's like he's scared!

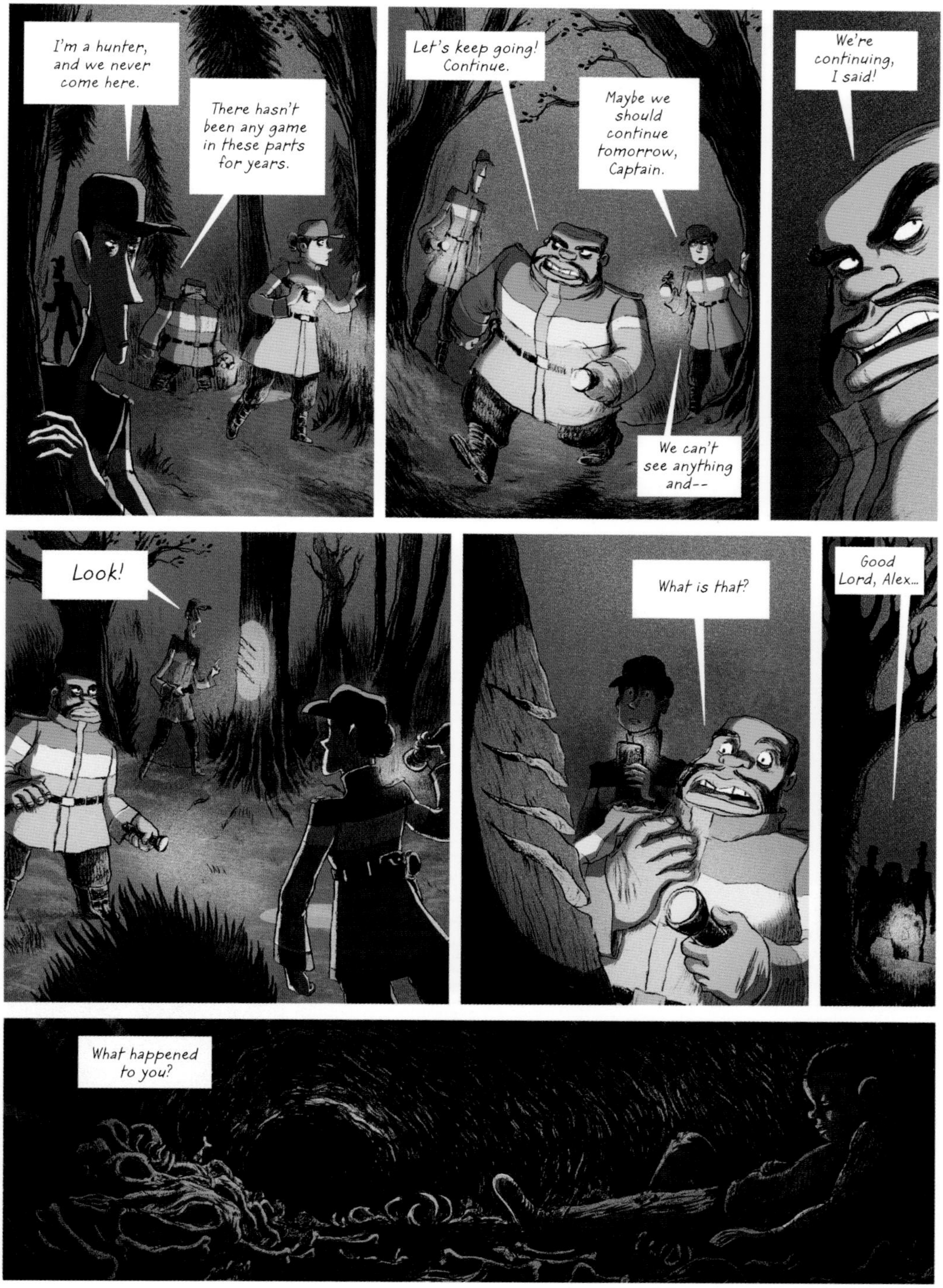
I'm a hunter, and we never come here.
There hasn't been any game in these parts for years.
Let's keep going! Continue.
Maybe we should continue tomorrow, Captain.
We can't see anything and--
We're continuing, I said!
Look!
What is that?
Good Lord, Alex...
What happened to you?

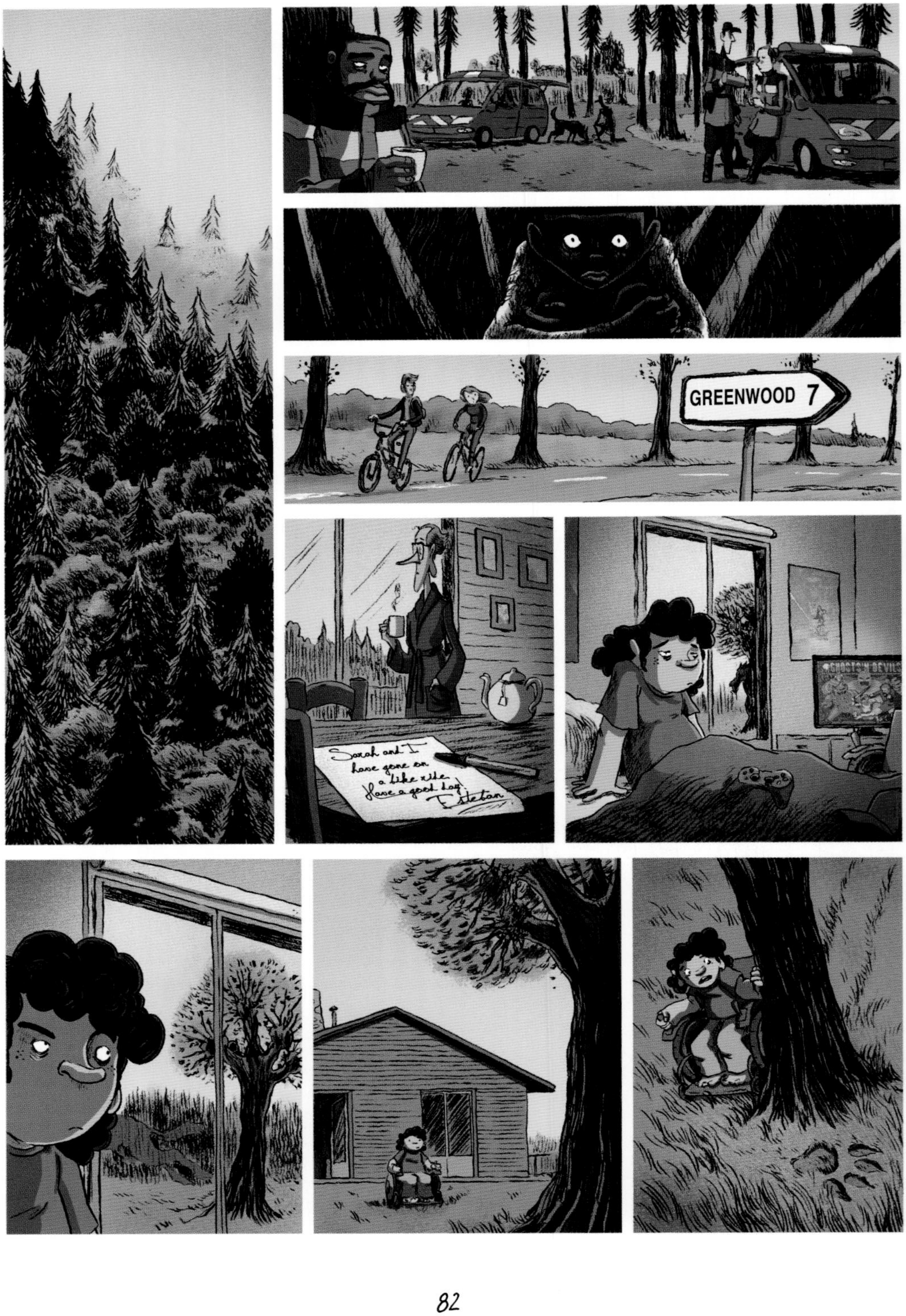
GREENWOOD 7
Sarah and I have gone on a bike ride. Have a good day! Stefan
GHOSTS'N DEVILS

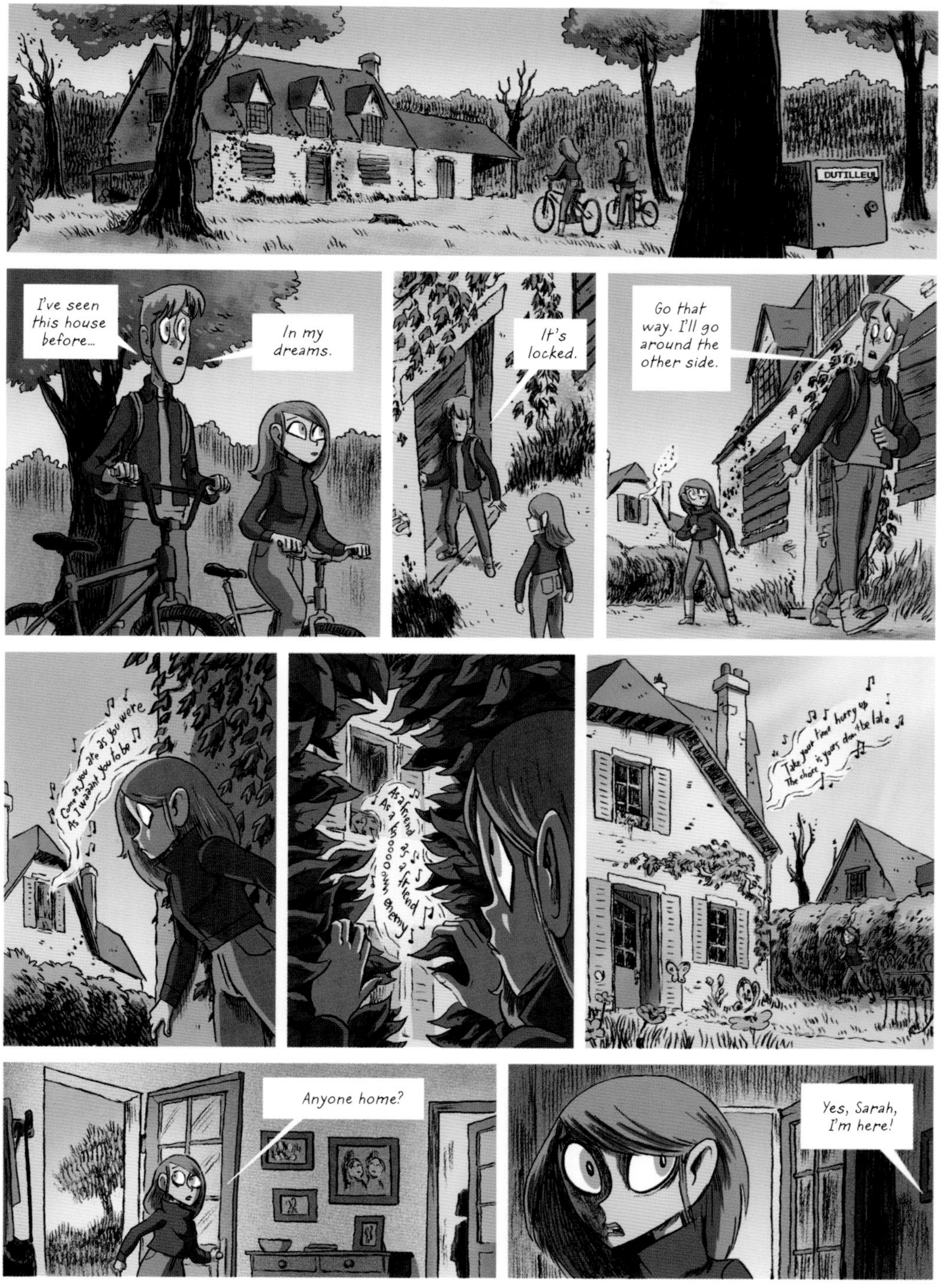
DUTILLEU
I've seen this house before...
In my dreams.
It's locked.
Go that way. I'll go around the other side.
Come as you are as you were
As I waaant you to be
As a friend as a friend
As a knoooown enemy
Take your time hurry up
The choice is yours don't be late
Anyone home?
Yes, Sarah, I'm here!

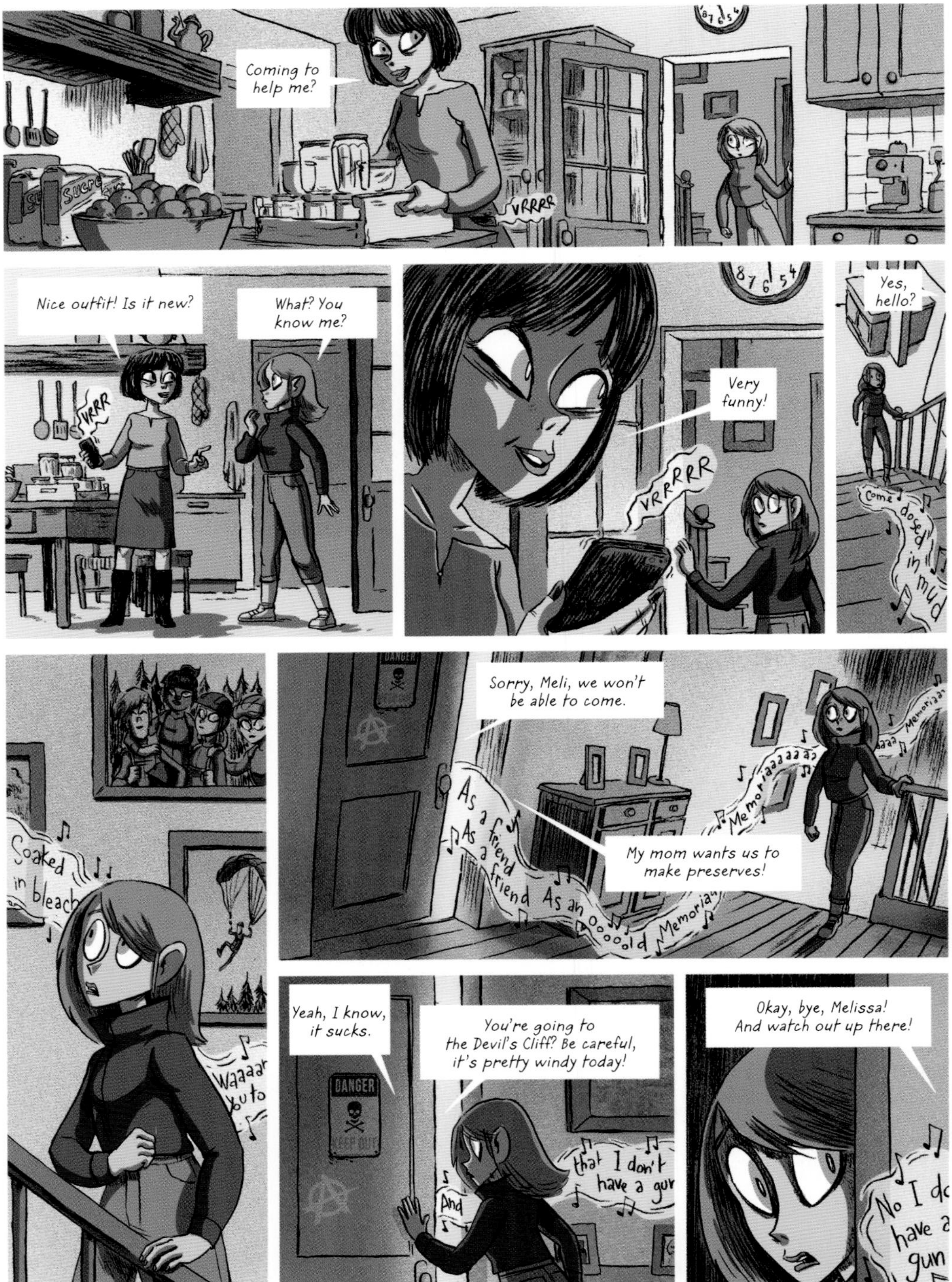
Coming to help me?
VRRRR
Nice outfit! Is it new?
VRRR
What? You know me?
Very funny!
VRRRRR
Yes, hello?
Come dosed in mud
Soaked in bleach
Waaaa you to
Sorry, Meli, we won't be able to come.
As a friend As a friend As a friend As an oooold Memoria
My mom wants us to make preserves!
Memoriaaaaaa
Memoriaa
DANGER
Yeah, I know, it sucks.
You're going to the Devil's Cliff? Be careful, it's pretty windy today!
DANGER
KEEP OUT
And
that I don't have a gun
Okay, bye, Melissa! And watch out up there!
No I do have a gun

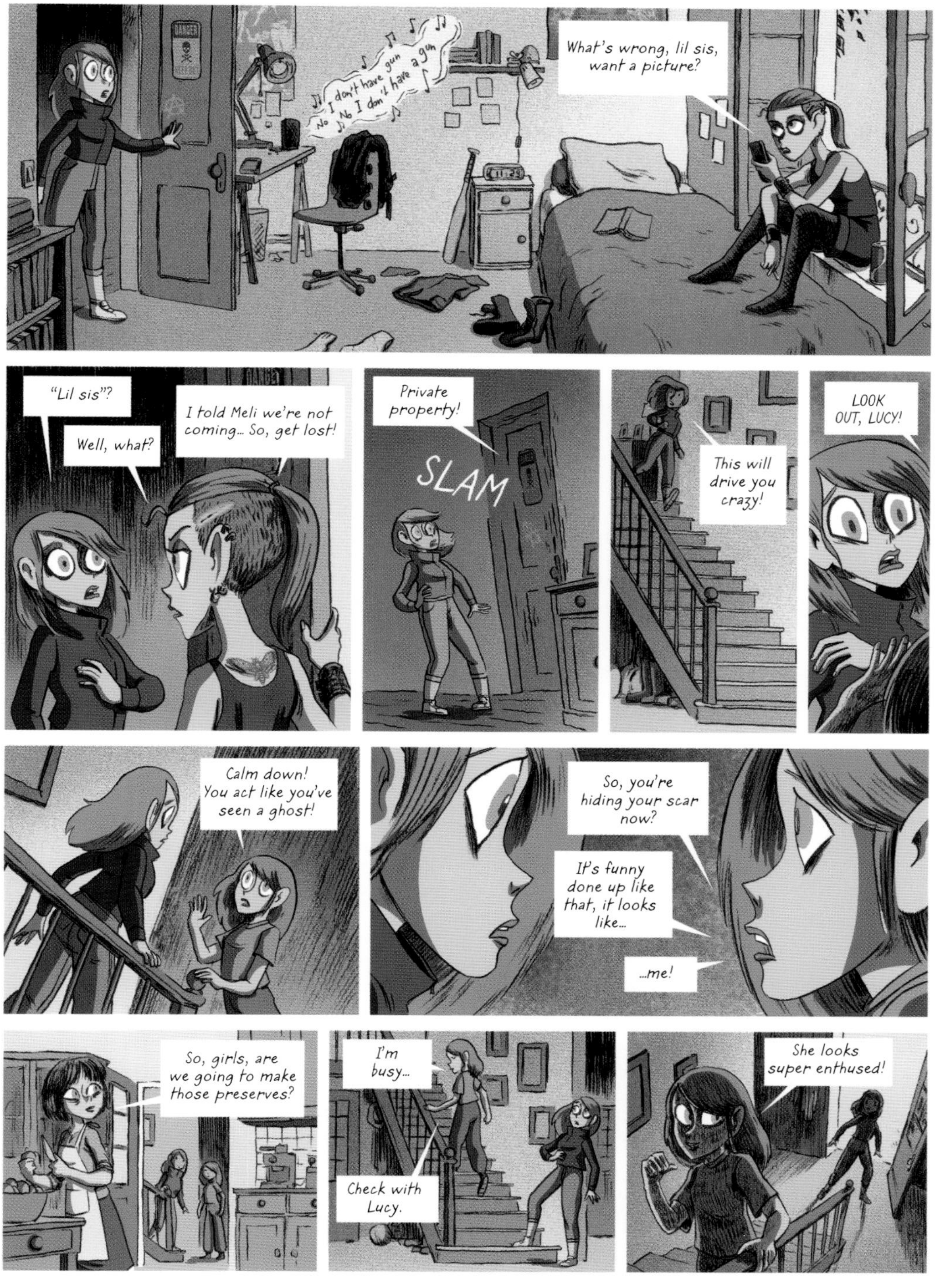
I don't have gun
No No I don't have a gun
What's wrong, lil sis, want a picture?
"Lil sis"?
Well, what?
I told Meli we're not coming... So, get lost!
Private property!
SLAM
This will drive you crazy!
LOOK OUT, LUCY!
Calm down! You act like you've seen a ghost!
So, you're hiding your scar now?
It's funny done up like that, it looks like...
...me!
So, girls, are we going to make those preserves?
I'm busy...
Check with Lucy.
She looks super enthused!

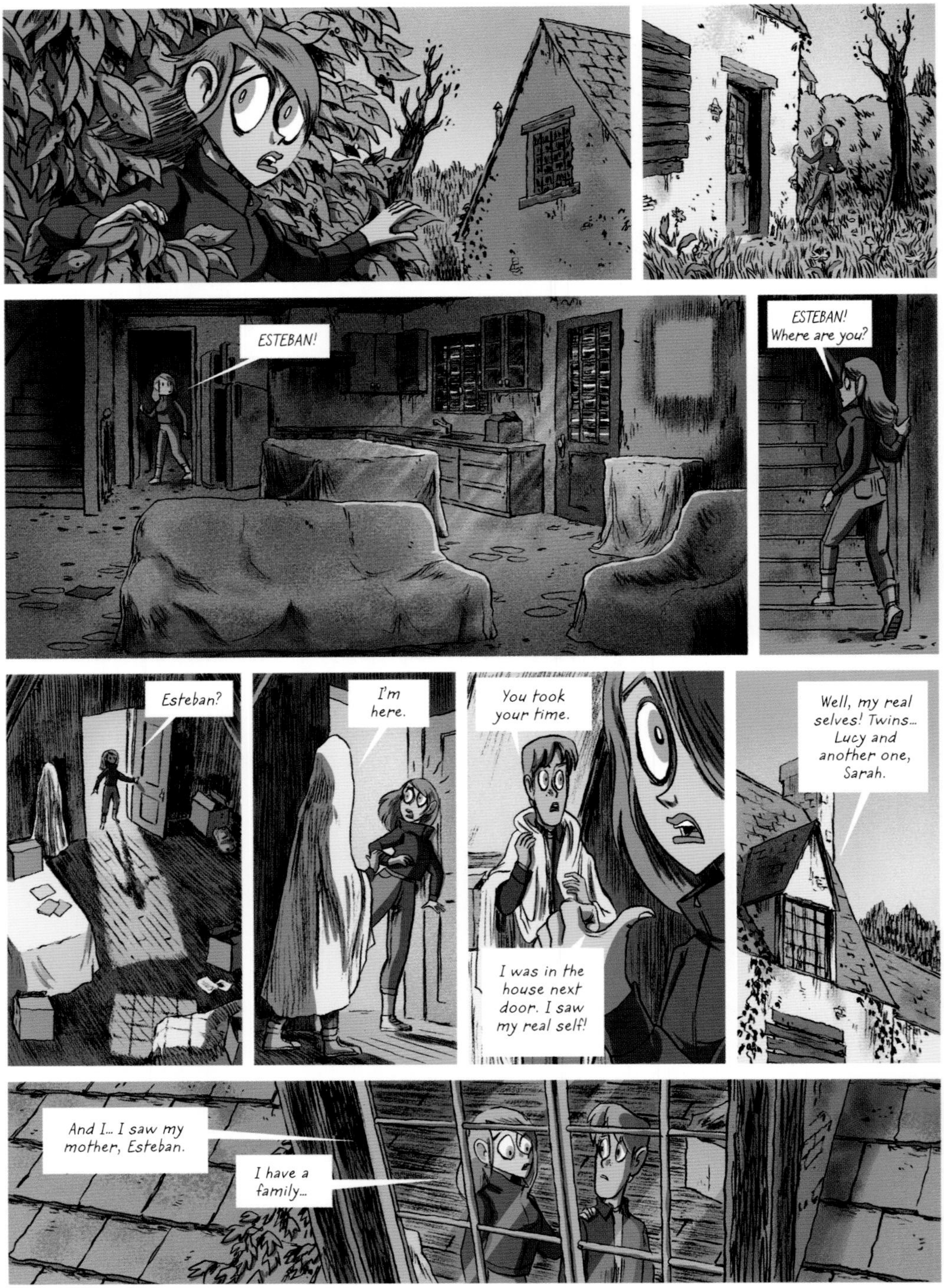
ESTEBAN!
ESTEBAN! Where are you?
Esteban?
I'm here.
You took your time.
I was in the house next door. I saw my real self!
Well, my real selves! Twins... Lucy and another one, Sarah.
And I... I saw my mother, Esteban.
I have a family...

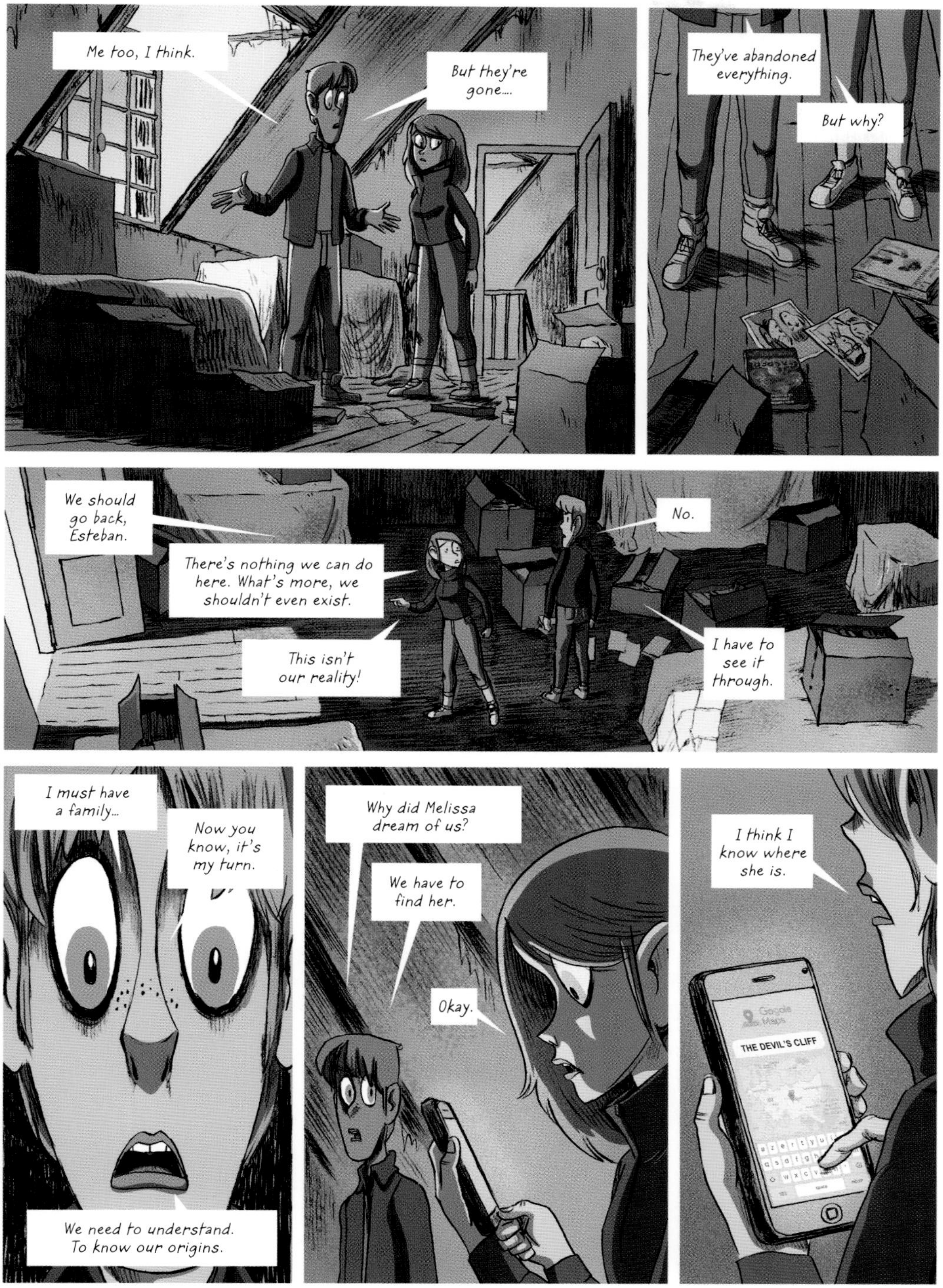
Me too, I think.
But they're gone....
They've abandoned everything.
But why?
CASPER
We should go back, Esteban.
There's nothing we can do here. What's more, we shouldn't even exist.
This isn't our reality!
No.
I have to see it through.
I must have a family...
Now you know, it's my turn.
We need to understand. To know our origins.
Why did Melissa dream of us?
We have to find her.
Okay.
I think I know where she is.
Google Maps
THE DEVIL'S CLIFF

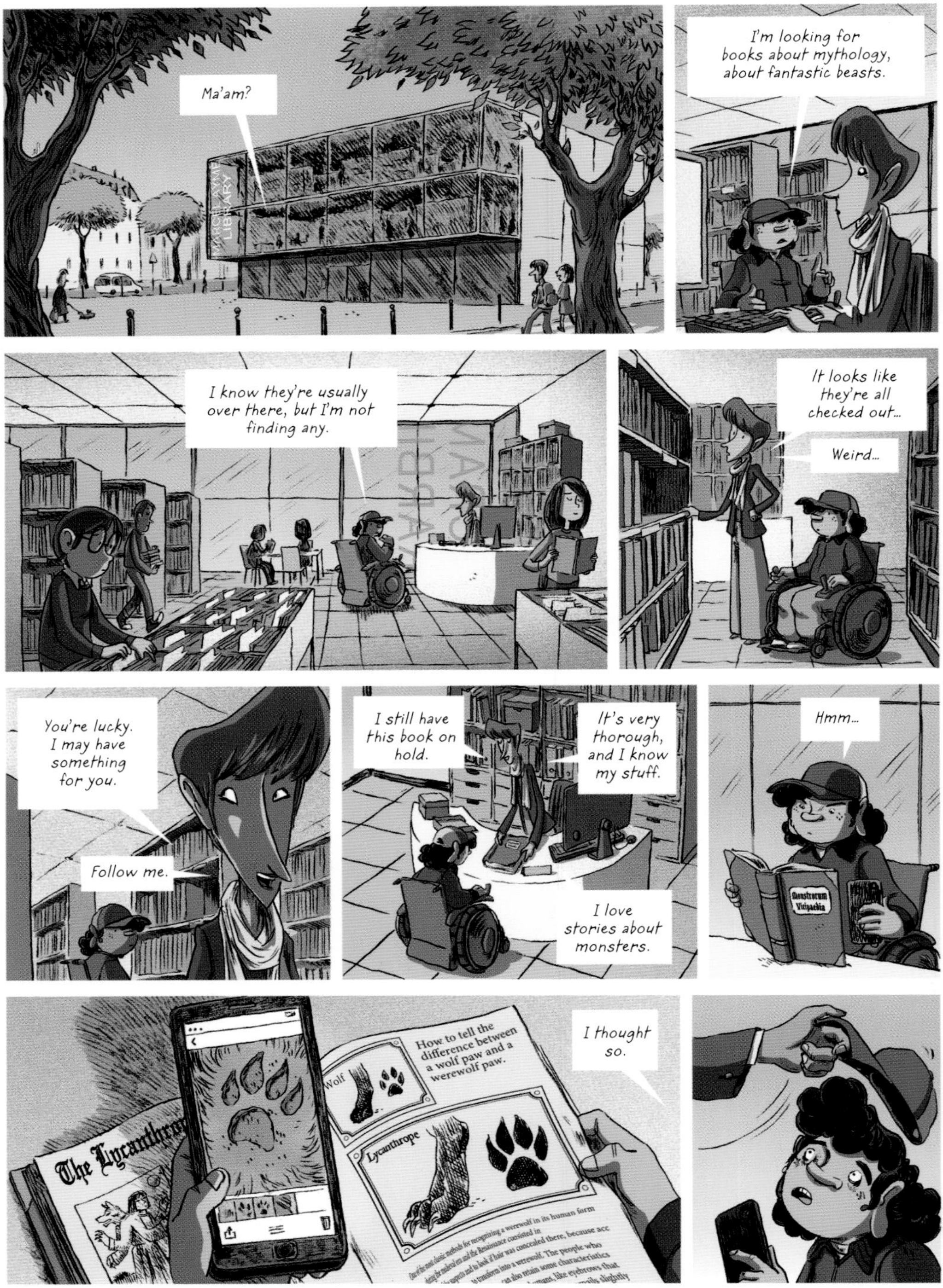
MARCEL AYMÉ LIBRARY
Ma'am?
I'm looking for books about mythology, about fantastic beasts.
I know they're usually over there, but I'm not finding any.
It looks like they're all checked out...
Weird...
You're lucky. I may have something for you.
Follow me.
I still have this book on hold.
It's very thorough, and I know my stuff.
I love stories about monsters.
Hmm...
Monstrorum Vicipaedia
The Lycanthrop
How to tell the difference between a wolf paw and a werewolf paw.
Wolf
Lycanthrope
I thought so.

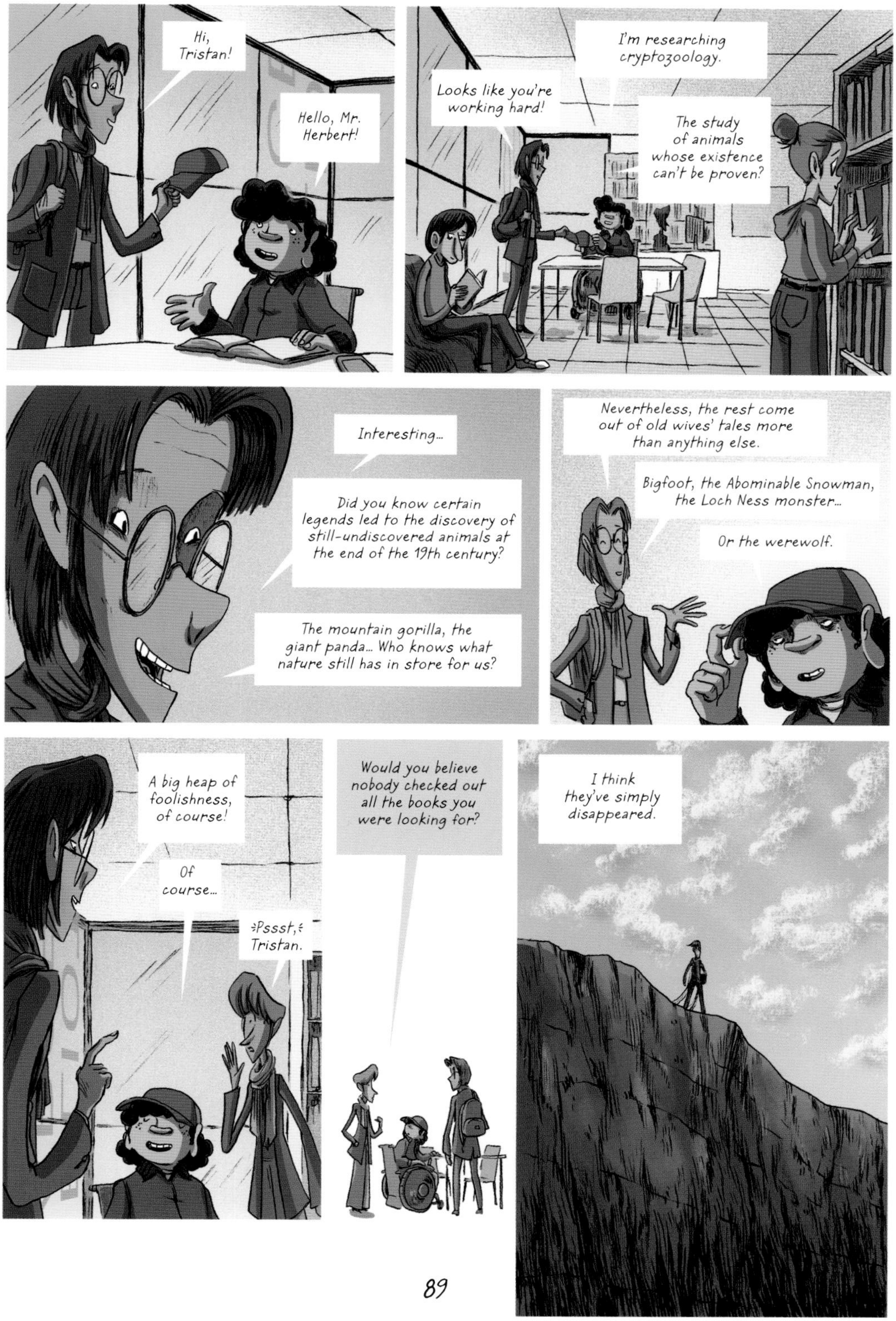

Hi, Tristan!
Hello, Mr. Herbert!
Looks like you're working hard!
I'm researching cryptozoology.
The study of animals whose existence can't be proven?
Interesting...
Did you know certain legends led to the discovery of still-undiscovered animals at the end of the 19th century?
The mountain gorilla, the giant panda... Who knows what nature still has in store for us?
Nevertheless, the rest come out of old wives' tales more than anything else.
Bigfoot, the Abominable Snowman, the Loch Ness monster...
Or the werewolf.
A big heap of foolishness, of course!
Of course...
Pssst, Tristan.
Would you believe nobody checked out all the books you were looking for?
I think they've simply disappeared.

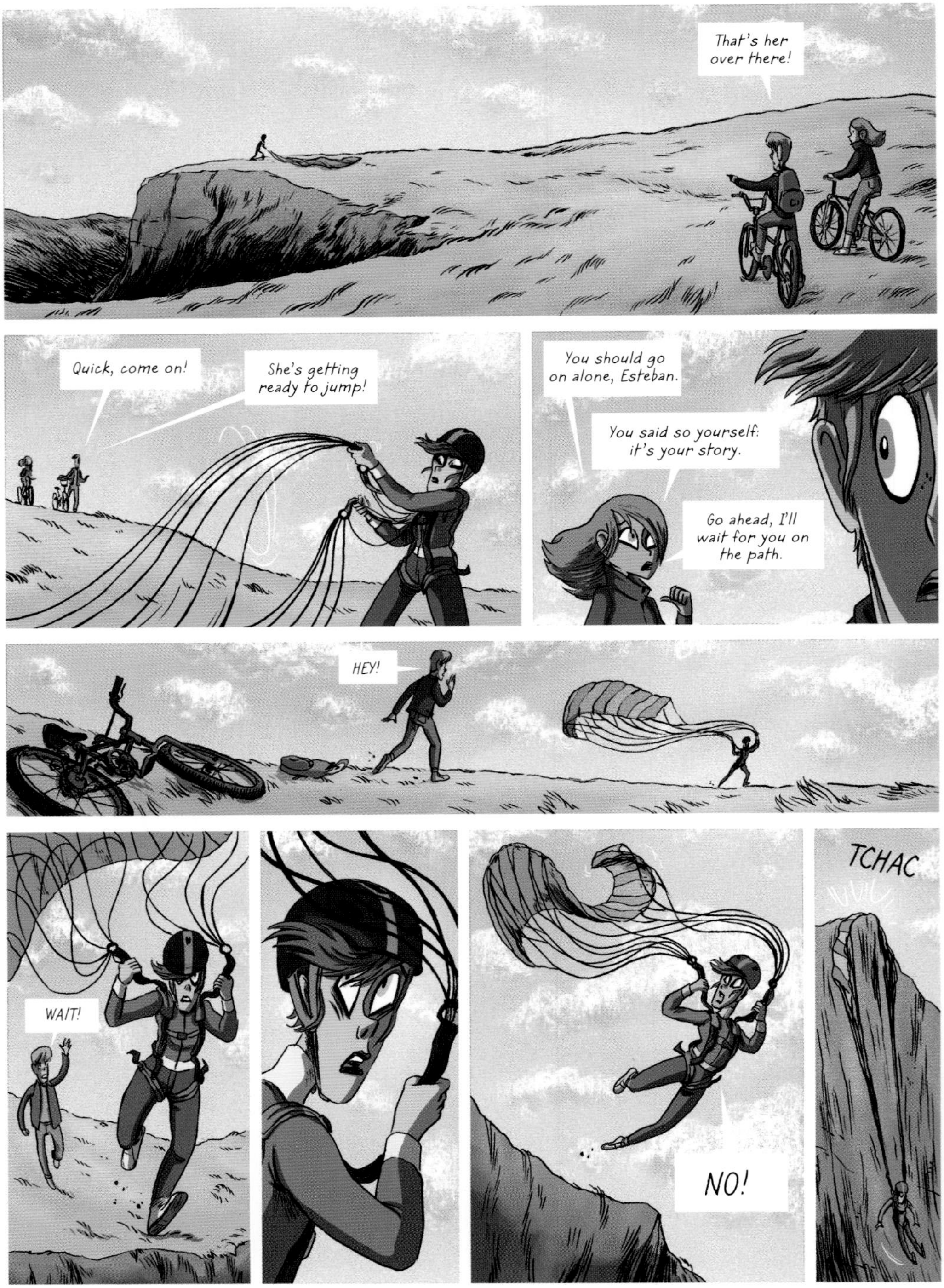
That's her over there!
Quick, come on!
She's getting ready to jump!
You should go on alone, Esteban.
You said so yourself: it's your story.
Go ahead, I'll wait for you on the path.
HEY!
WAIT!
NO!
TCHAC

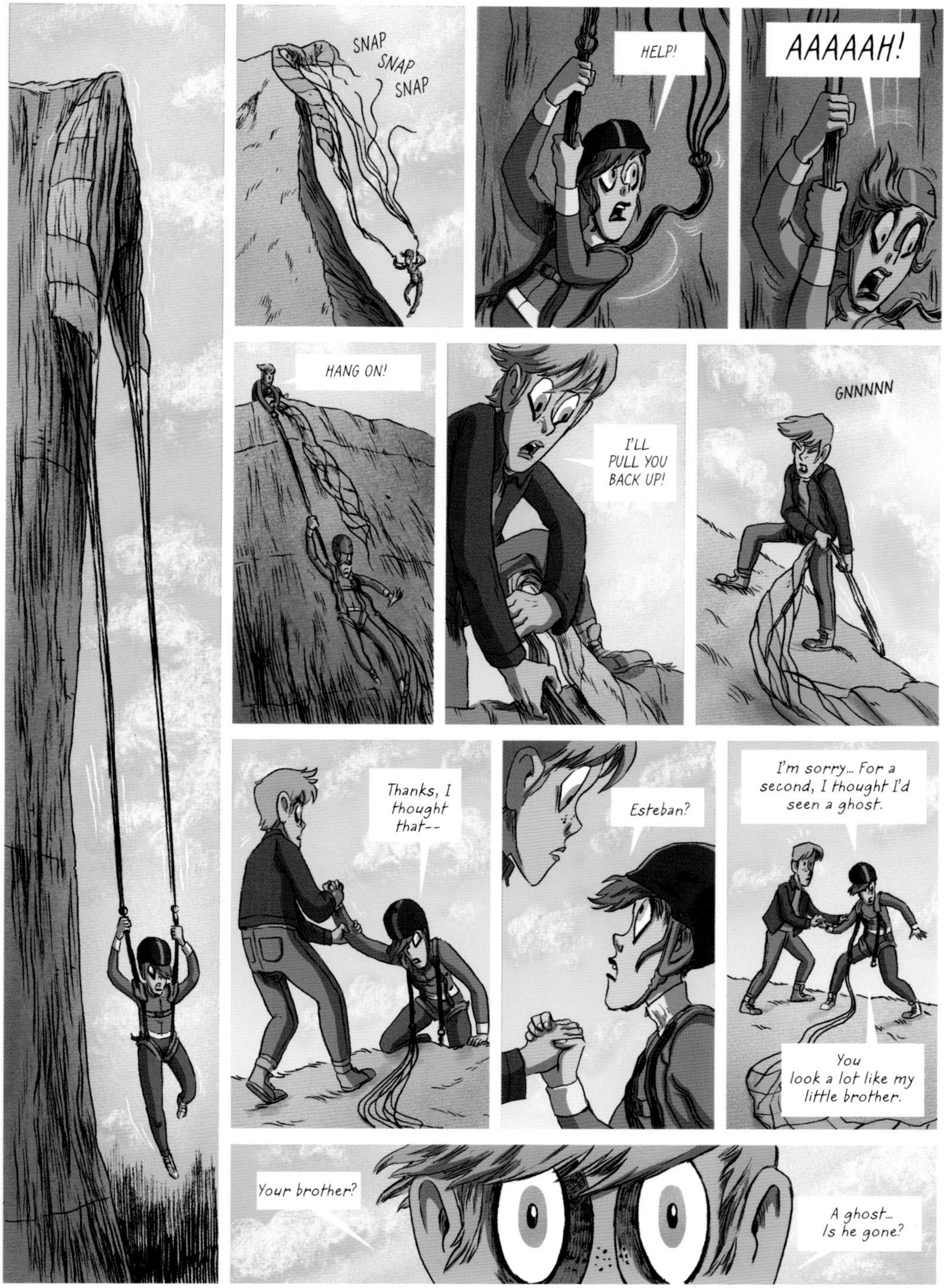
SNAP
SNAP
SNAP
HELP!
AAAAAH!
HANG ON!
I'LL PULL YOU BACK UP!
GNNNNN
Thanks, I thought that--
Esteban?
I'm sorry... For a second, I thought I'd seen a ghost.
You look a lot like my little brother.
Your brother?
A ghost... Is he gone?

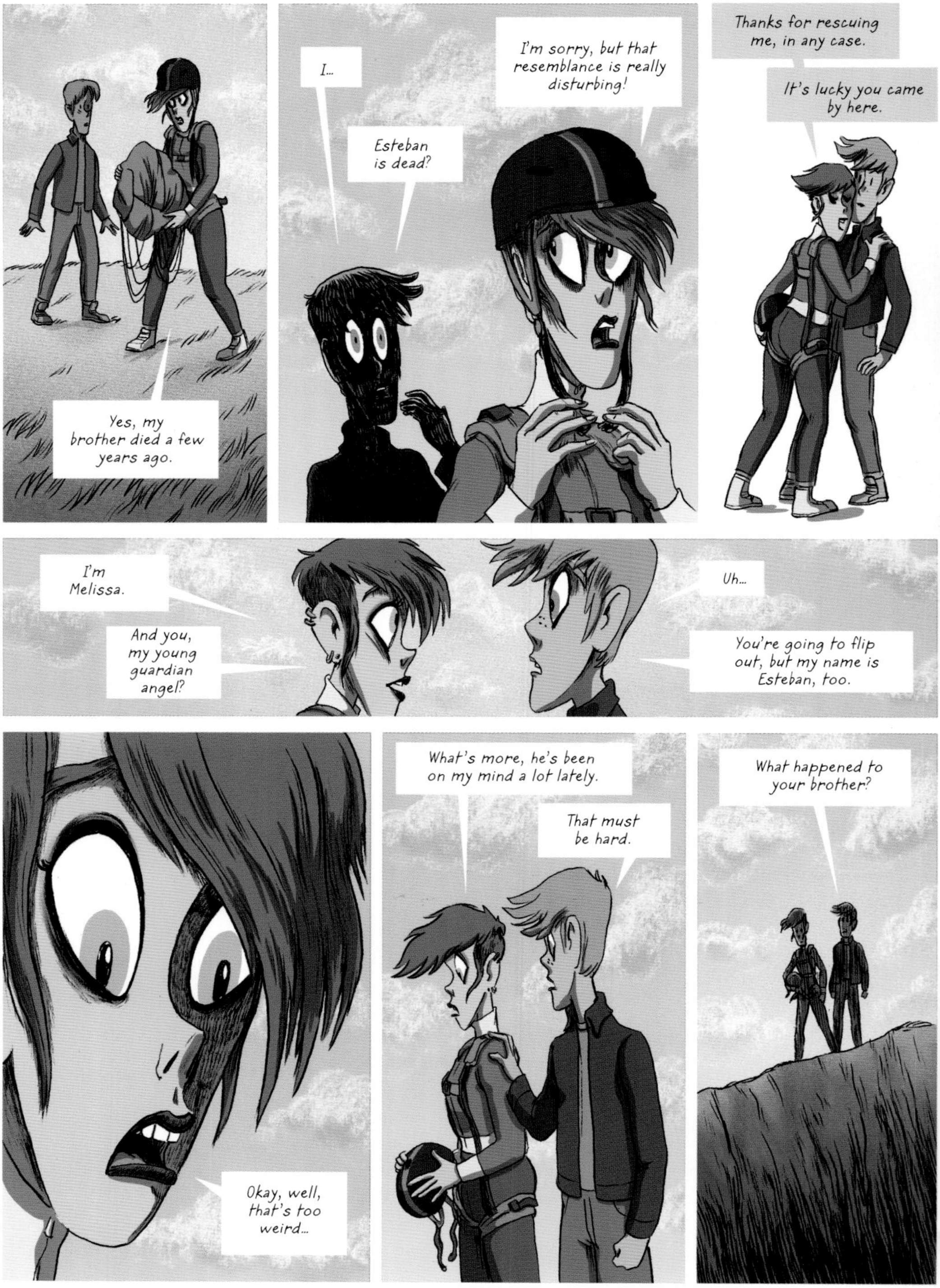
Yes, my brother died a few years ago.
I...
Esteban is dead?
I'm sorry, but that resemblance is really disturbing!
Thanks for rescuing me, in any case.
It's lucky you came by here.
I'm Melissa.
And you, my young guardian angel?
Uh...
You're going to flip out, but my name is Esteban, too.
Okay, well, that's too weird...
What's more, he's been on my mind a lot lately.
That must be hard.
What happened to your brother?

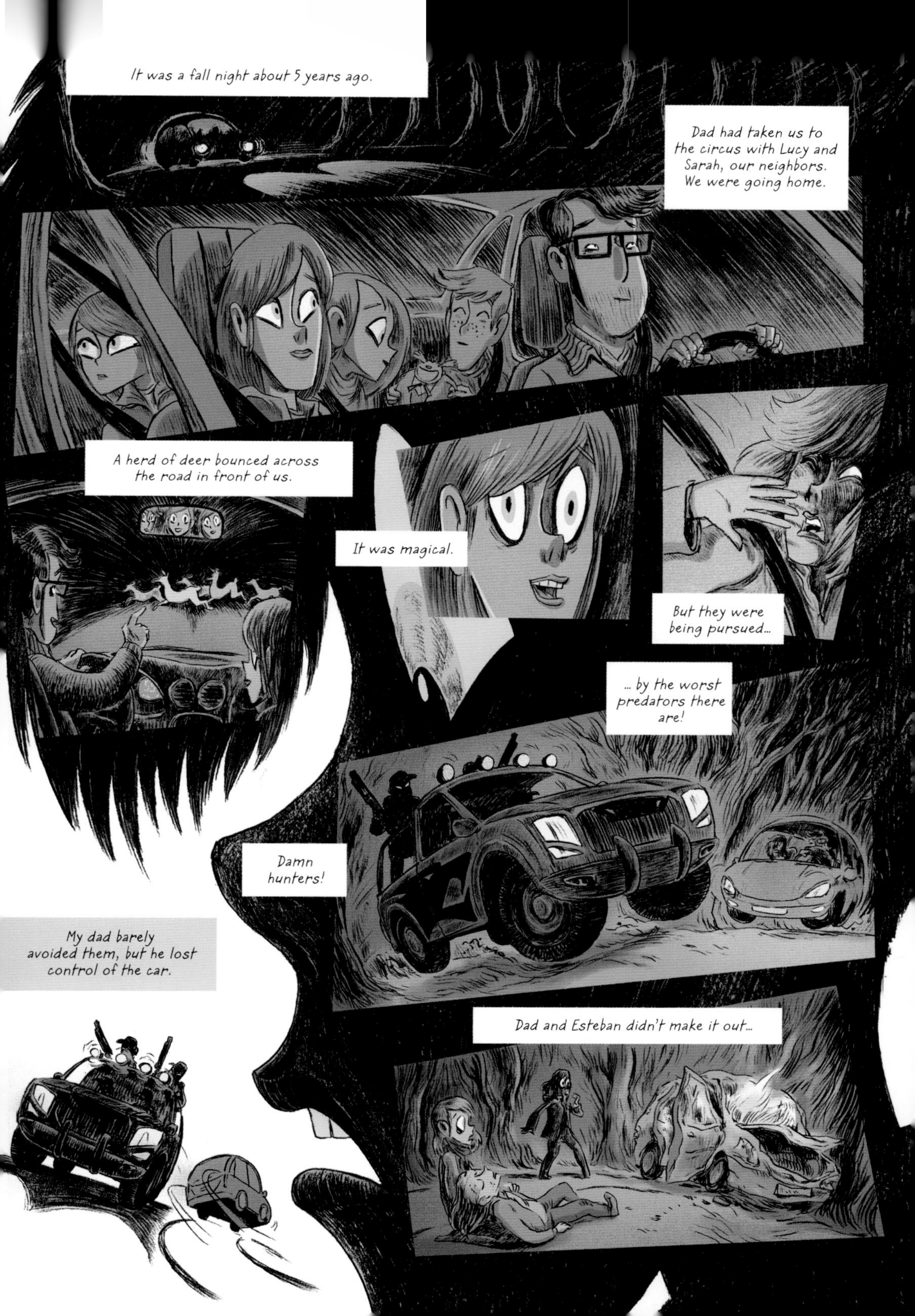

It was a fall night about 5 years ago.
Dad had taken us to the circus with Lucy and Sarah, our neighbors. We were going home.
A herd of deer bounced across the road in front of us.
It was magical.
But they were being pursued...
... by the worst predators there are!
Damn hunters!
My dad barely avoided them, but he lost control of the car.
Dad and Esteban didn't make it out...

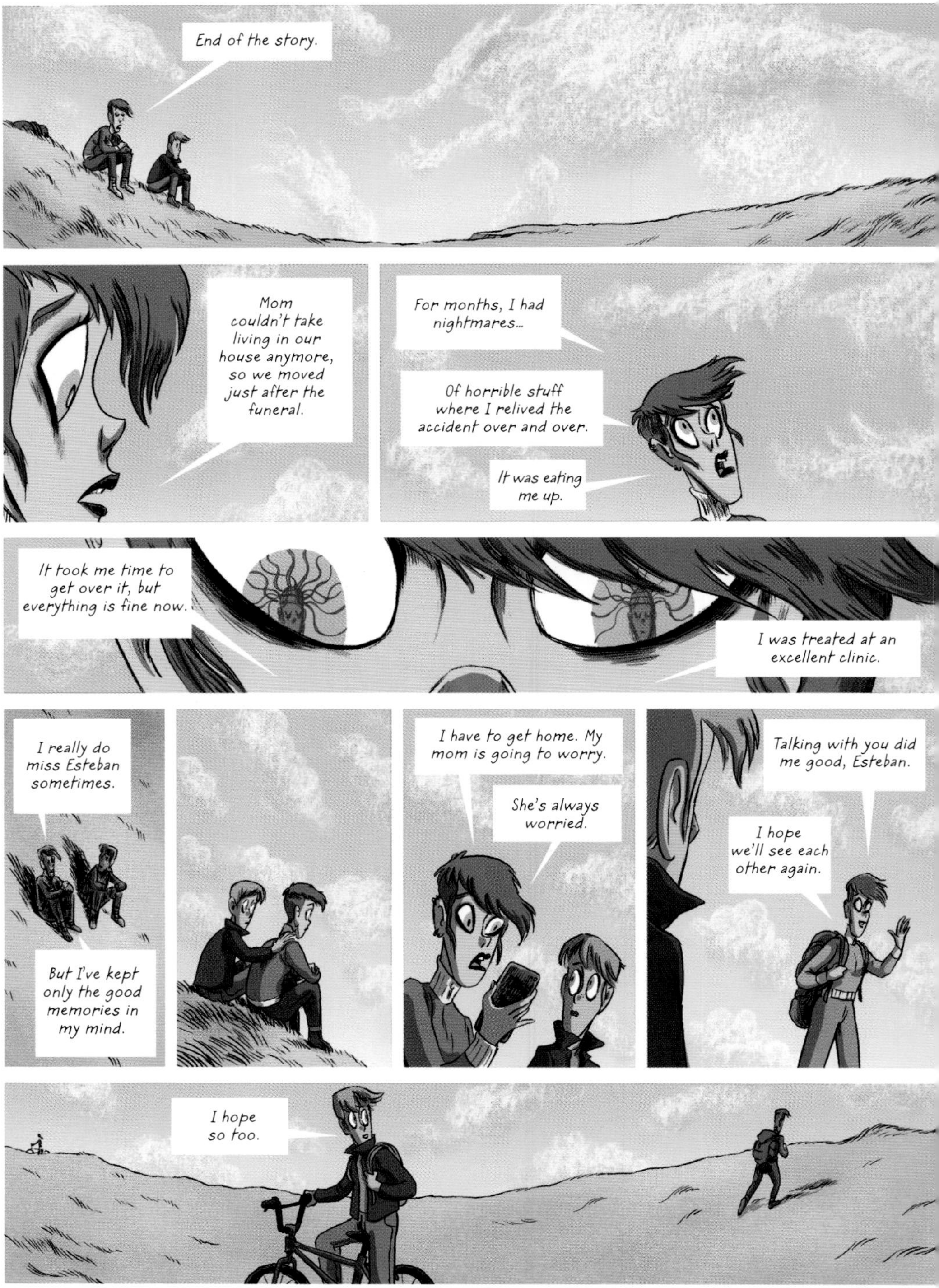
End of the story.
Mom couldn't take living in our house anymore, so we moved just after the funeral.
For months, I had nightmares...
Of horrible stuff where I relived the accident over and over.
It was eating me up.
It took me time to get over it, but everything is fine now.
I was treated at an excellent clinic.
I really do miss Esteban sometimes.
But I've kept only the good memories in my mind.
I have to get home. My mom is going to worry.
She's always worried.
Talking with you did me good, Esteban.
I hope we'll see each other again.
I hope so too.

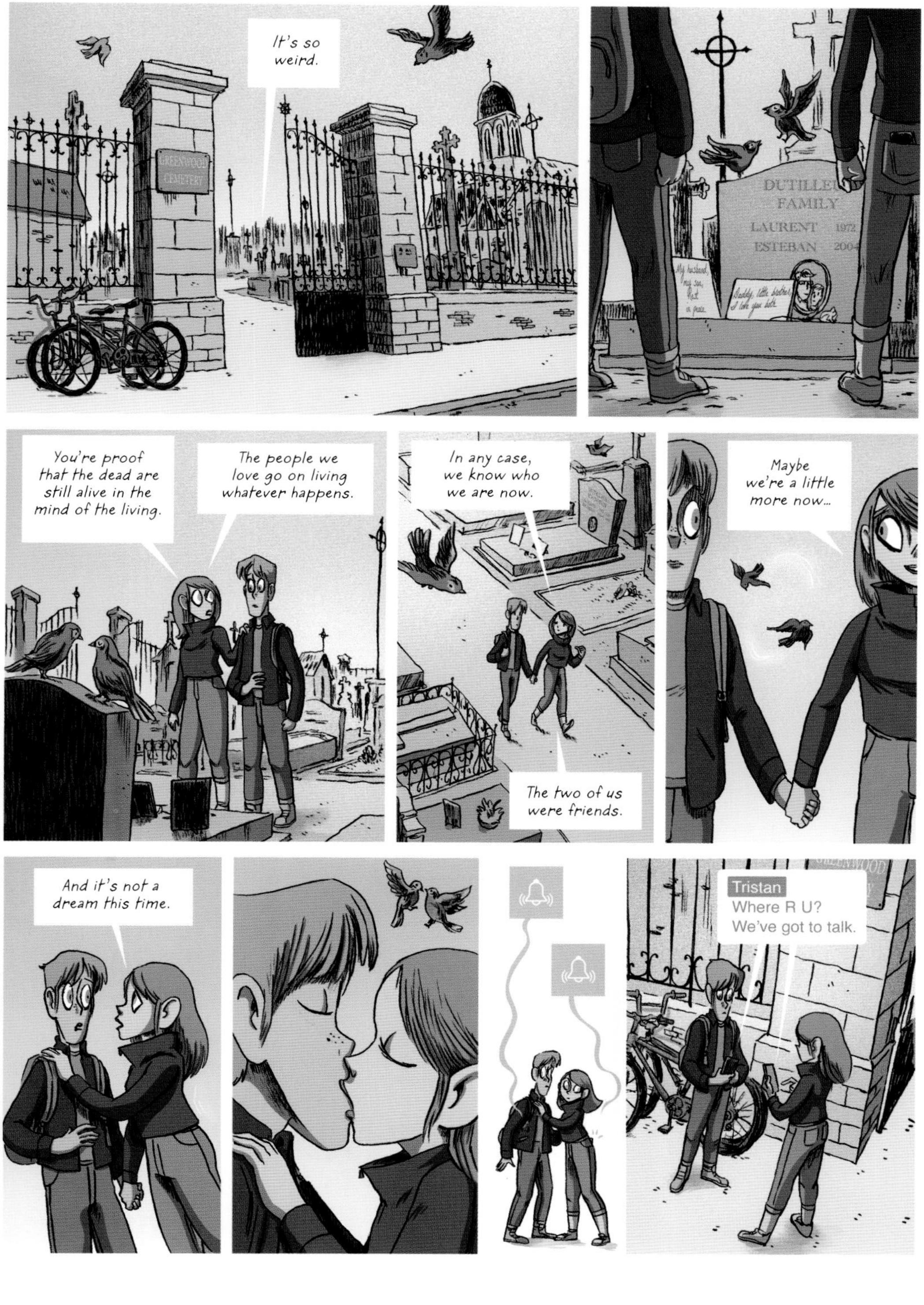
It's so weird.
GREENWOOD CEMETERY
DUTILLEUL FAMILY
LAURENT 1972
ESTEBAN 2004
My husband, my son, Rest in peace.
Daddy, little brother, I love you both.
You're proof that the dead are still alive in the mind of the living.
The people we love go on living whatever happens.
In any case, we know who we are now.
The two of us were friends.
Maybe we're a little more now...
And it's not a dream this time.
Tristan
Where R U?
We've got to talk.

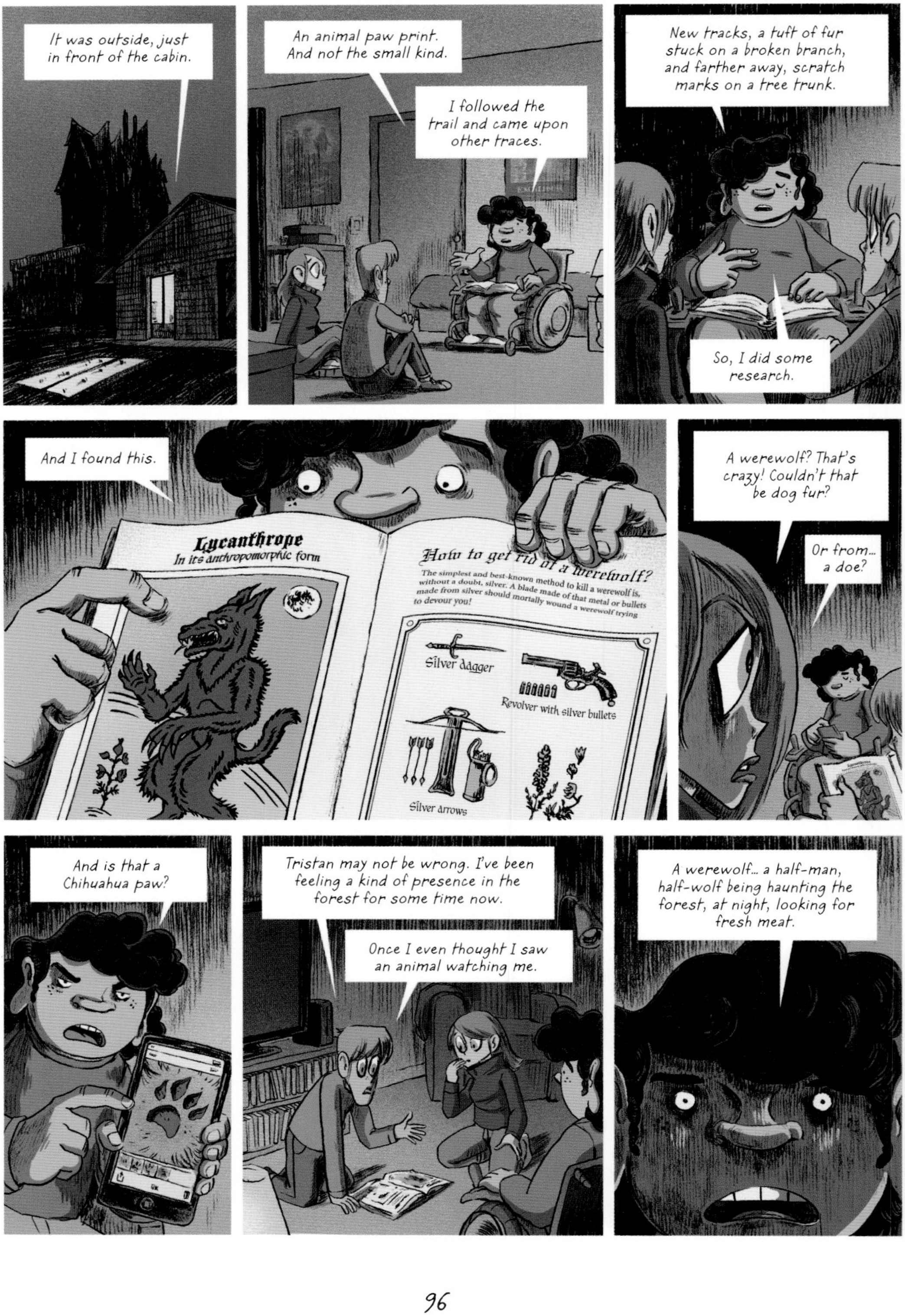
It was outside, just in front of the cabin.
An animal paw print. And not the small kind.
I followed the trail and came upon other traces.
New tracks, a tuft of fur stuck on a broken branch, and farther away, scratch marks on a tree trunk.
So, I did some research.
And I found this.
Lycanthrope
In its anthropomorphic form
How to get rid of a werewolf?
The simplest and best-known method to kill a werewolf is, without a doubt, silver. A blade made of that metal or bullets made from silver should mortally wound a werewolf trying to devour you!
Silver dagger
Revolver with silver bullets
Silver arrows
A werewolf? That's crazy! Couldn't that be dog fur?
Or from... a doe?
And is that a Chihuahua paw?
Tristan may not be wrong. I've been feeling a kind of presence in the forest for some time now.
Once I even thought I saw an animal watching me.
A werewolf... a half-man, half-wolf being haunting the forest, at night, looking for fresh meat.

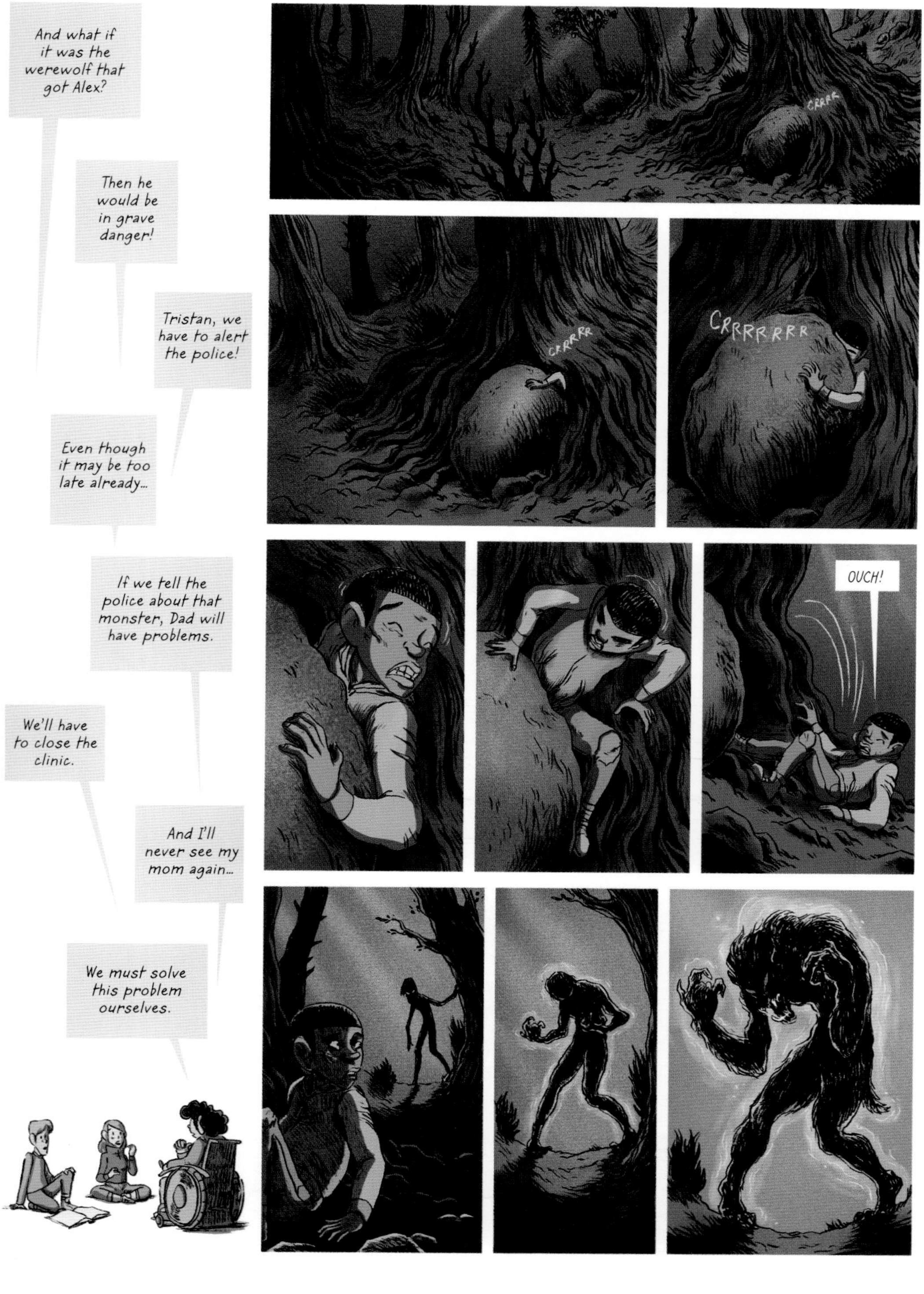
And what if it was the werewolf that got Alex?
Then he would be in grave danger!
Tristan, we have to alert the police!
Even though it may be too late already...
If we tell the police about that monster, Dad will have problems.
We'll have to close the clinic.
And I'll never see my mom again...
We must solve this problem ourselves.
CRRRR
CRRRRR
CRRRRRRRR
OUCH!

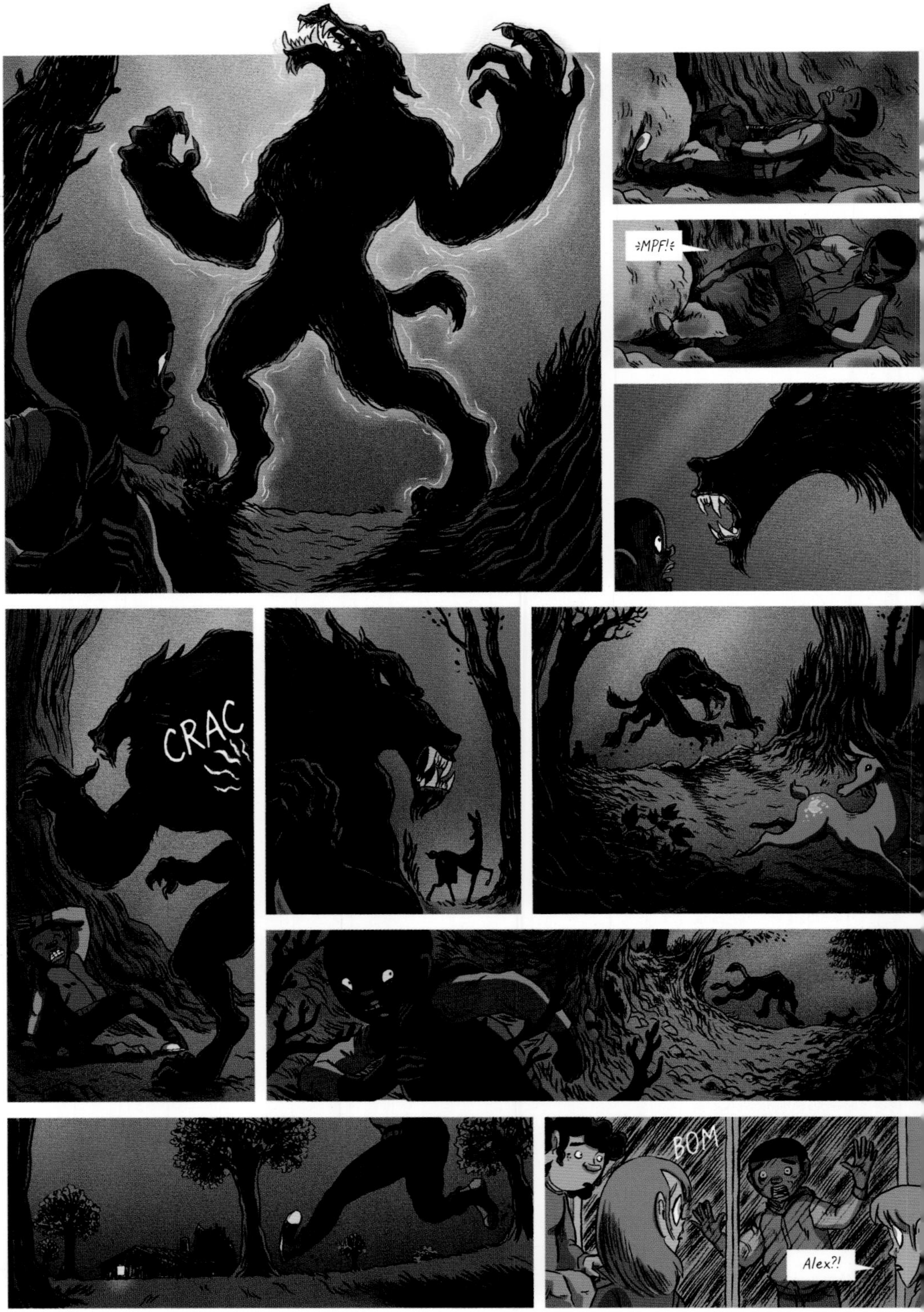
MPF!
CRAC
BOM
Alex?!

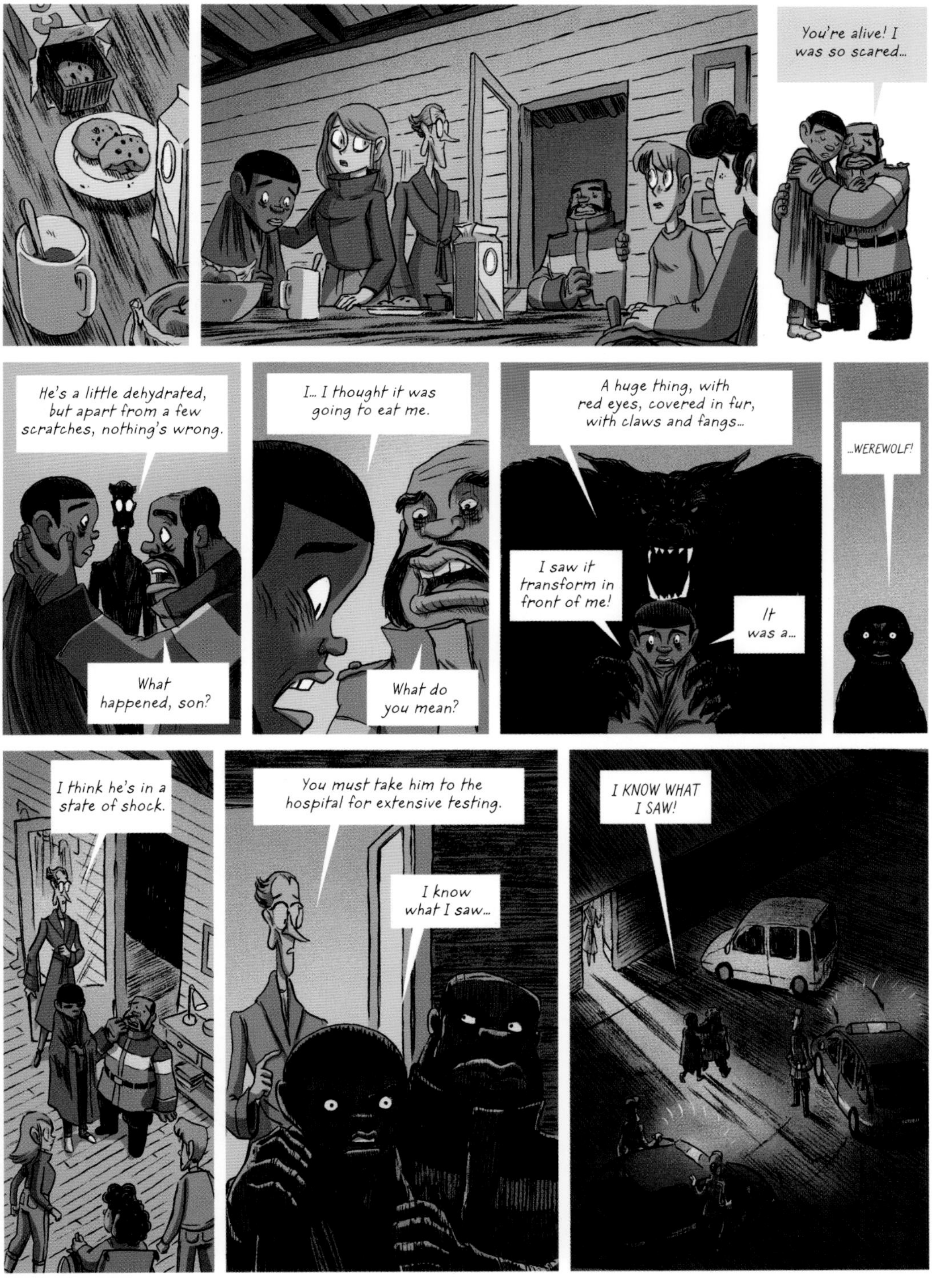
You're alive! I was so scared...
He's a little dehydrated, but apart from a few scratches, nothing's wrong.
What happened, son?
I... I thought it was going to eat me.
What do you mean?
A huge thing, with red eyes, covered in fur, with claws and fangs...
I saw it transform in front of me!
It was a...
...WEREWOLF!
I think he's in a state of shock.
You must take him to the hospital for extensive testing.
I know what I saw...
I KNOW WHAT I SAW!

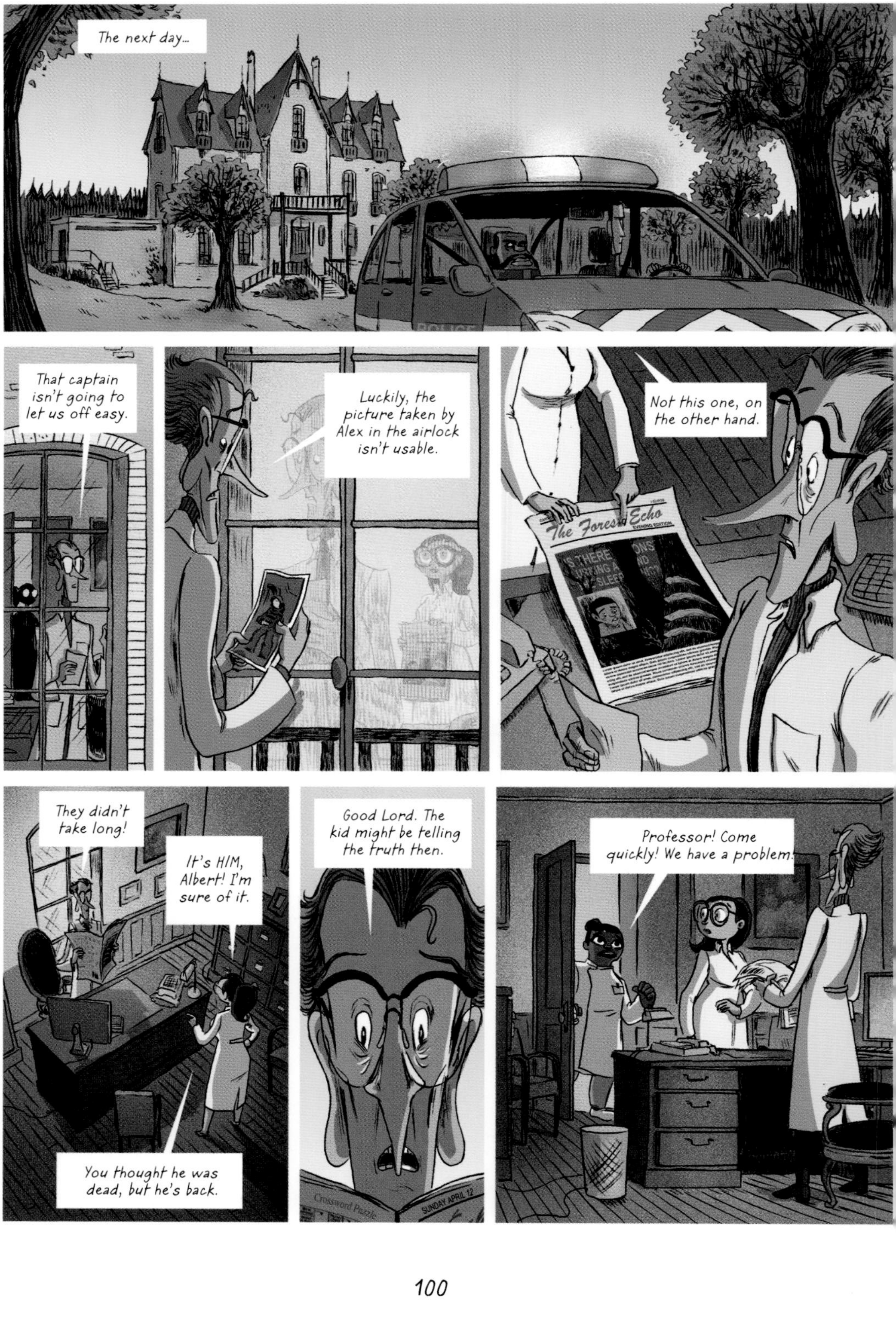
The next day...
That captain isn't going to let us off easy.
Luckily, the picture taken by Alex in the airlock isn't usable.
Not this one, on the other hand.
The Forest Echo
EVENING EDITION
They didn't take long!
It's HIM, Albert! I'm sure of it.
You thought he was dead, but he's back.
Good Lord. The kid might be telling the truth then.
Crossword Puzzle
SUNDAY APRIL 12
Professor! Come quickly! We have a problem!

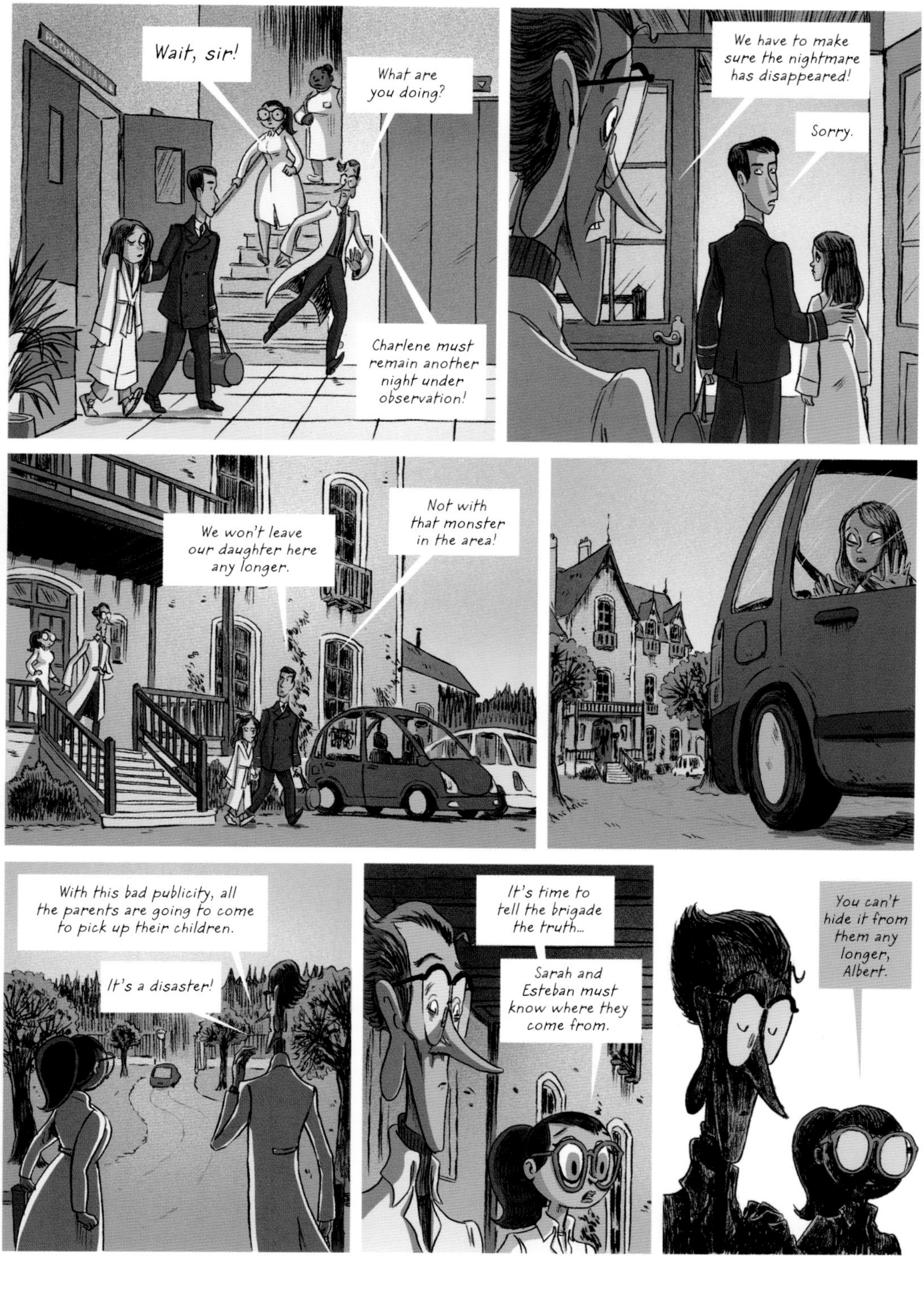
Wait, sir!
What are you doing?
Charlene must remain another night under observation!
We have to make sure the nightmare has disappeared!
Sorry.
We won't leave our daughter here any longer.
Not with that monster in the area!
With this bad publicity, all the parents are going to come to pick up their children.
It's a disaster!
It's time to tell the brigade the truth...
Sarah and Esteban must know where they come from.
You can't hide it from them any longer, Albert.

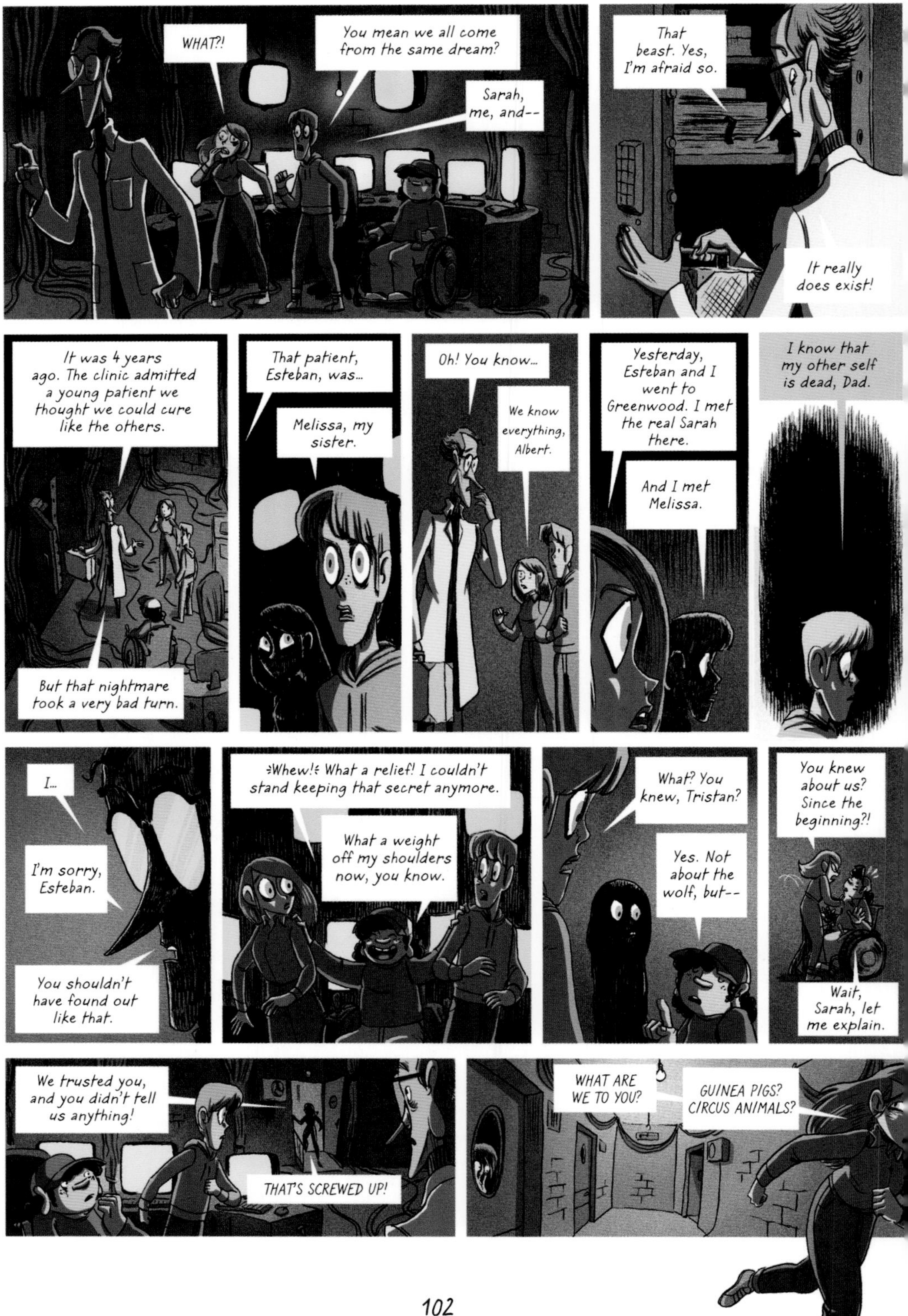
WHAT?!
You mean we all come from the same dream?
Sarah, me, and--
That beast. Yes, I'm afraid so.
It really does exist!
It was 4 years ago. The clinic admitted a young patient we thought we could cure like the others.
But that nightmare took a very bad turn.
That patient, Esteban, was...
Melissa, my sister.
Oh! You know...
We know everything, Albert.
Yesterday, Esteban and I went to Greenwood. I met the real Sarah there.
And I met Melissa.
I know that my other self is dead, Dad.
I...
I'm sorry, Esteban.
You shouldn't have found out like that.
Whew! What a relief! I couldn't stand keeping that secret anymore.
What a weight off my shoulders now, you know.
What? You knew, Tristan?
Yes. Not about the wolf, but--
You knew about us? Since the beginning?!
Wait, Sarah, let me explain.
We trusted you, and you didn't tell us anything!
THAT'S SCREWED UP!
WHAT ARE WE TO YOU?
GUINEA PIGS? CIRCUS ANIMALS?

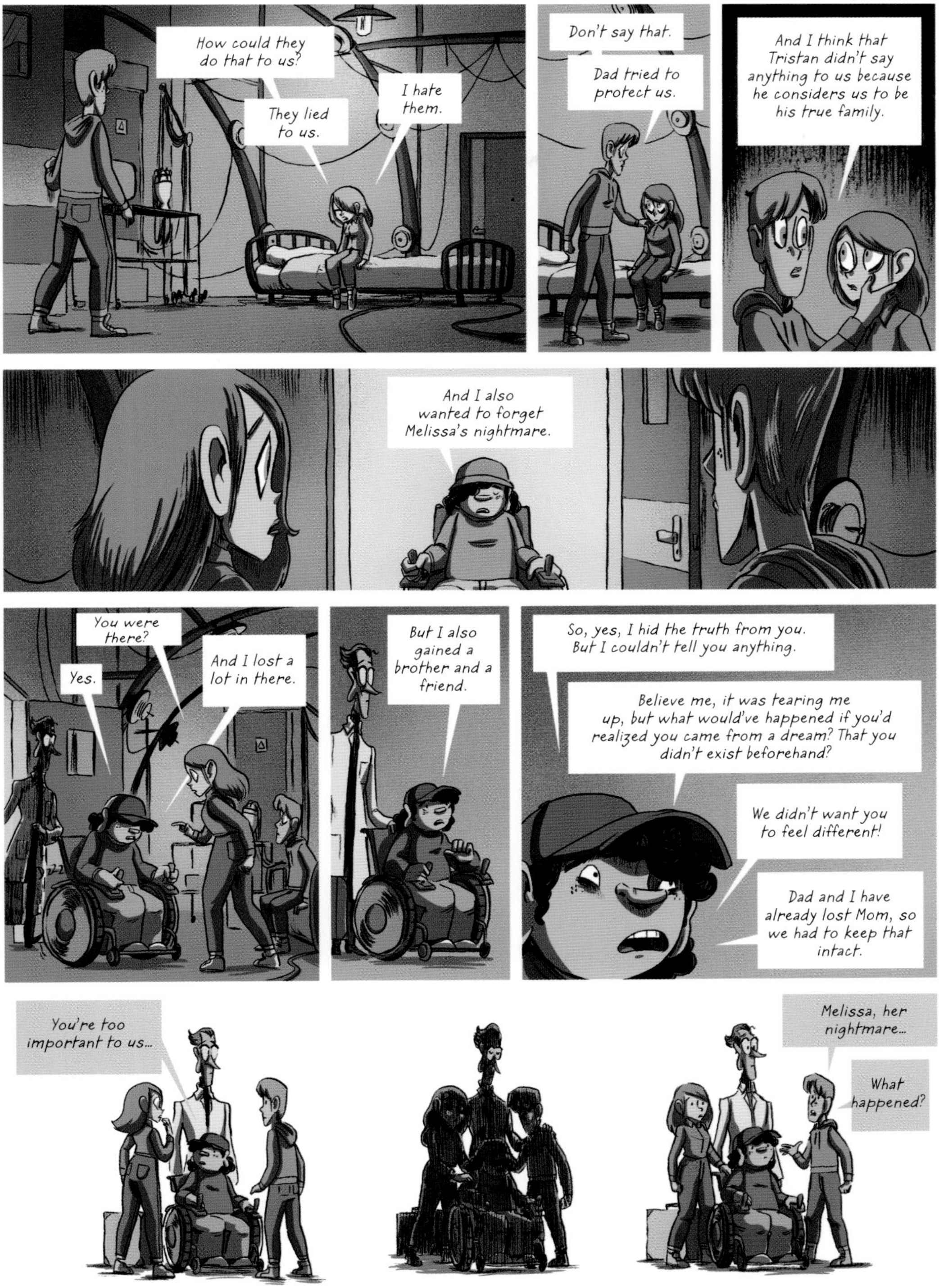
How could they do that to us?
They lied to us.
I hate them.
Don't say that.
Dad tried to protect us.
And I think that Tristan didn't say anything to us because he considers us to be his true family.
And I also wanted to forget Melissa's nightmare.
You were there?
Yes.
And I lost a lot in there.
But I also gained a brother and a friend.
So, yes, I hid the truth from you. But I couldn't tell you anything.
Believe me, it was tearing me up, but what would've happened if you'd realized you came from a dream? That you didn't exist beforehand?
We didn't want you to feel different!
Dad and I have already lost Mom, so we had to keep that intact.
You're too important to us...
Melissa, her nightmare...
What happened?

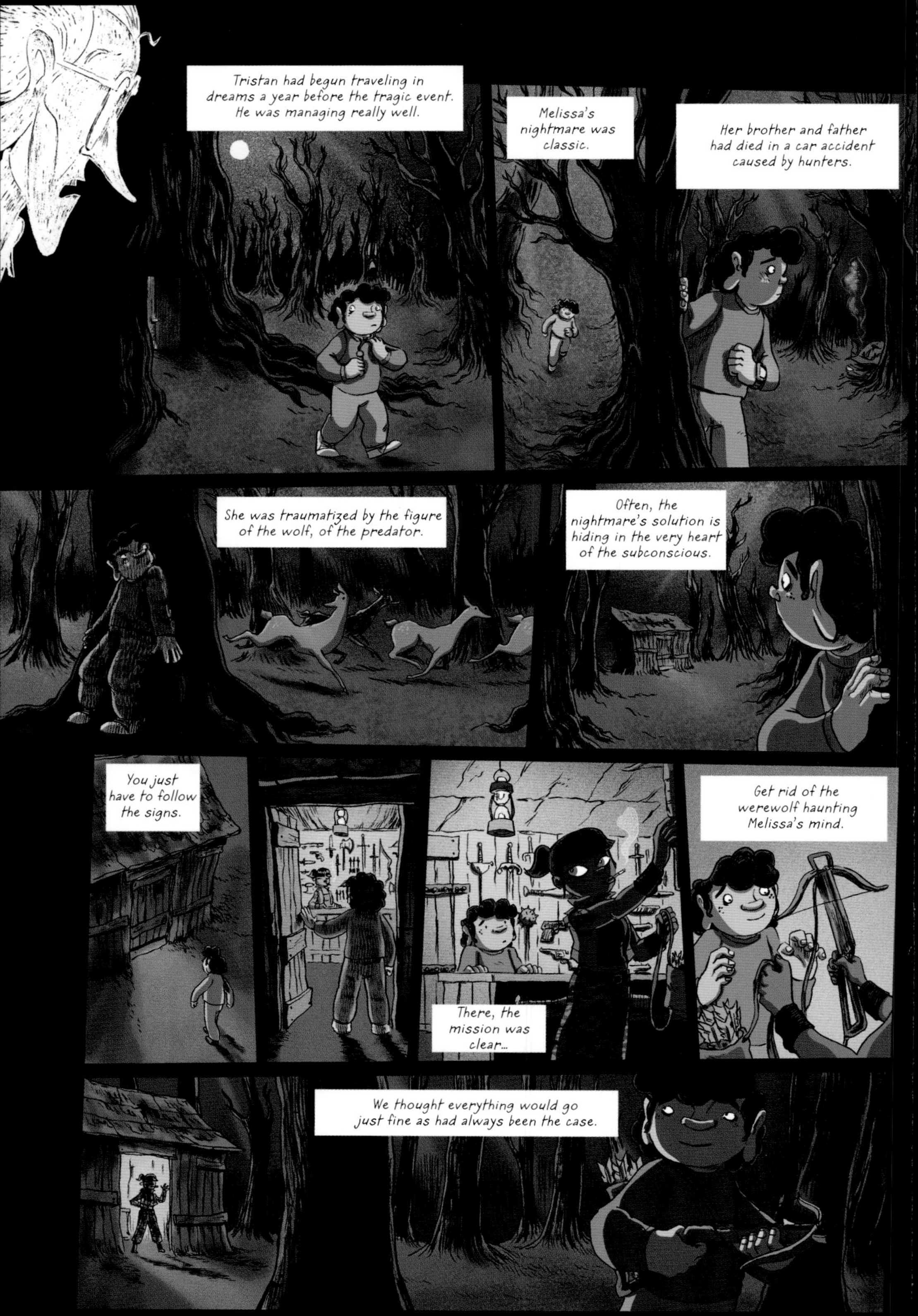
Tristan had begun traveling in dreams a year before the tragic event. He was managing really well.
Melissa's nightmare was classic.
Her brother and father had died in a car accident caused by hunters.
She was traumatized by the figure of the wolf, of the predator.
Often, the nightmare's solution is hiding in the very heart of the subconscious.
You just have to follow the signs.
There, the mission was clear...
Get rid of the werewolf haunting Melissa's mind.
We thought everything would go just fine as had always been the case.

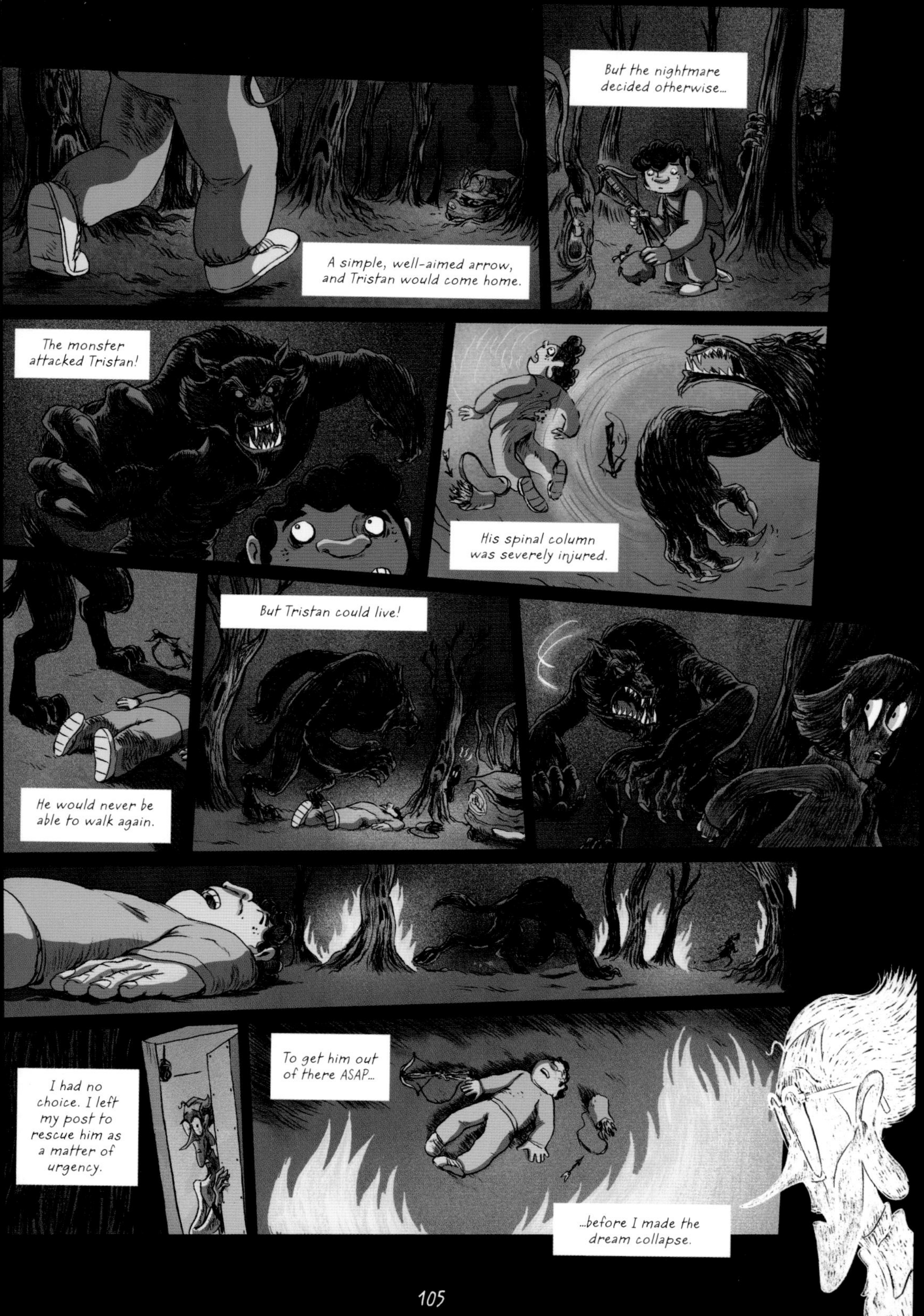
A simple, well-aimed arrow, and Tristan would come home.
But the nightmare decided otherwise...
The monster attacked Tristan!
His spinal column was severely injured.
He would never be able to walk again.
But Tristan could live!
I had no choice. I left my post to rescue him as a matter of urgency.
To get him out of there ASAP...
...before I made the dream collapse.

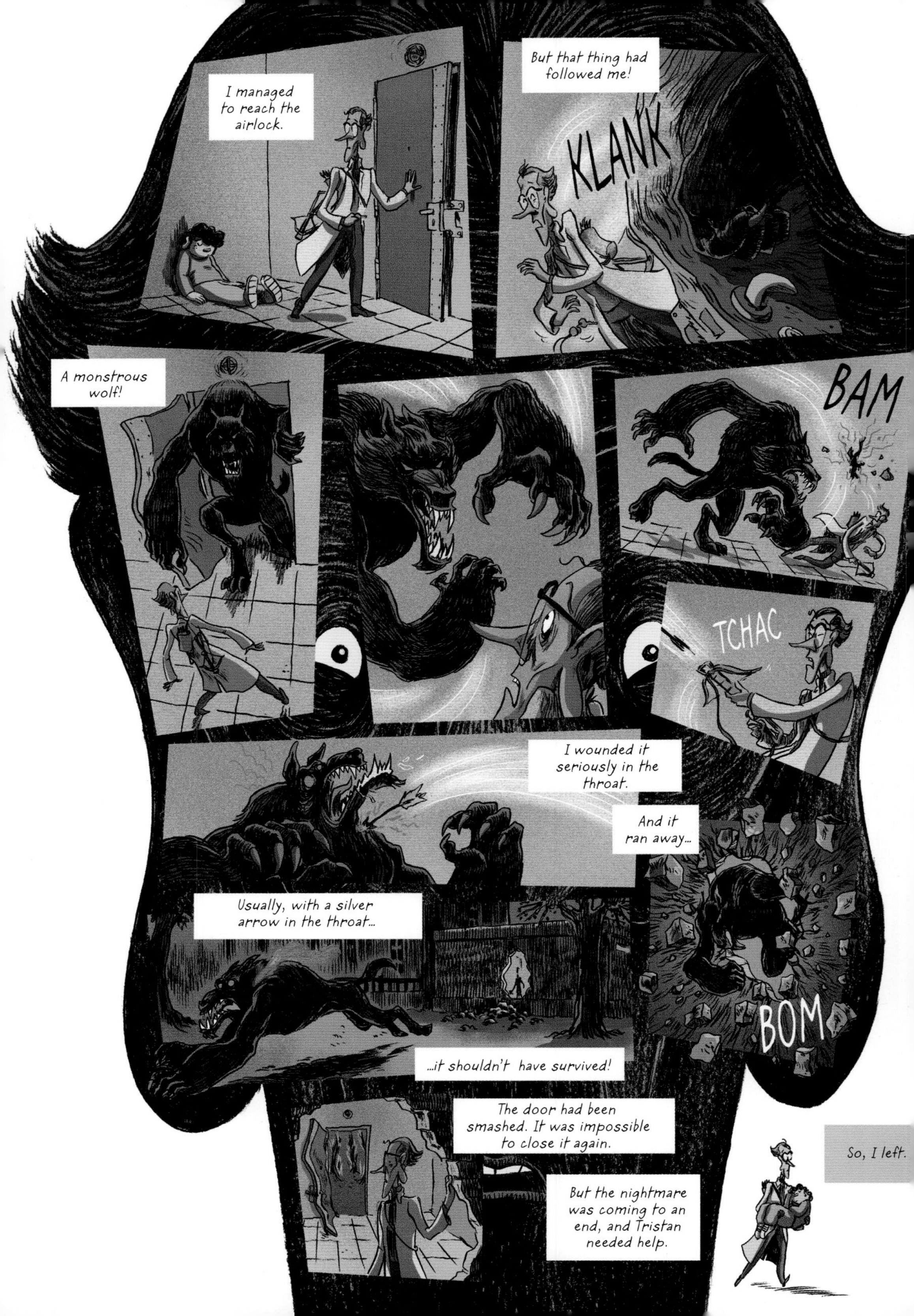
I managed to reach the airlock.
But that thing had followed me!
KLANK
A monstrous wolf!
BAM
TCHAC
I wounded it seriously in the throat.
And it ran away...
Usually, with a silver arrow in the throat...
BOM
...it shouldn't have survived!
The door had been smashed. It was impossible to close it again.
But the nightmare was coming to an end, and Tristan needed help.
So, I left.

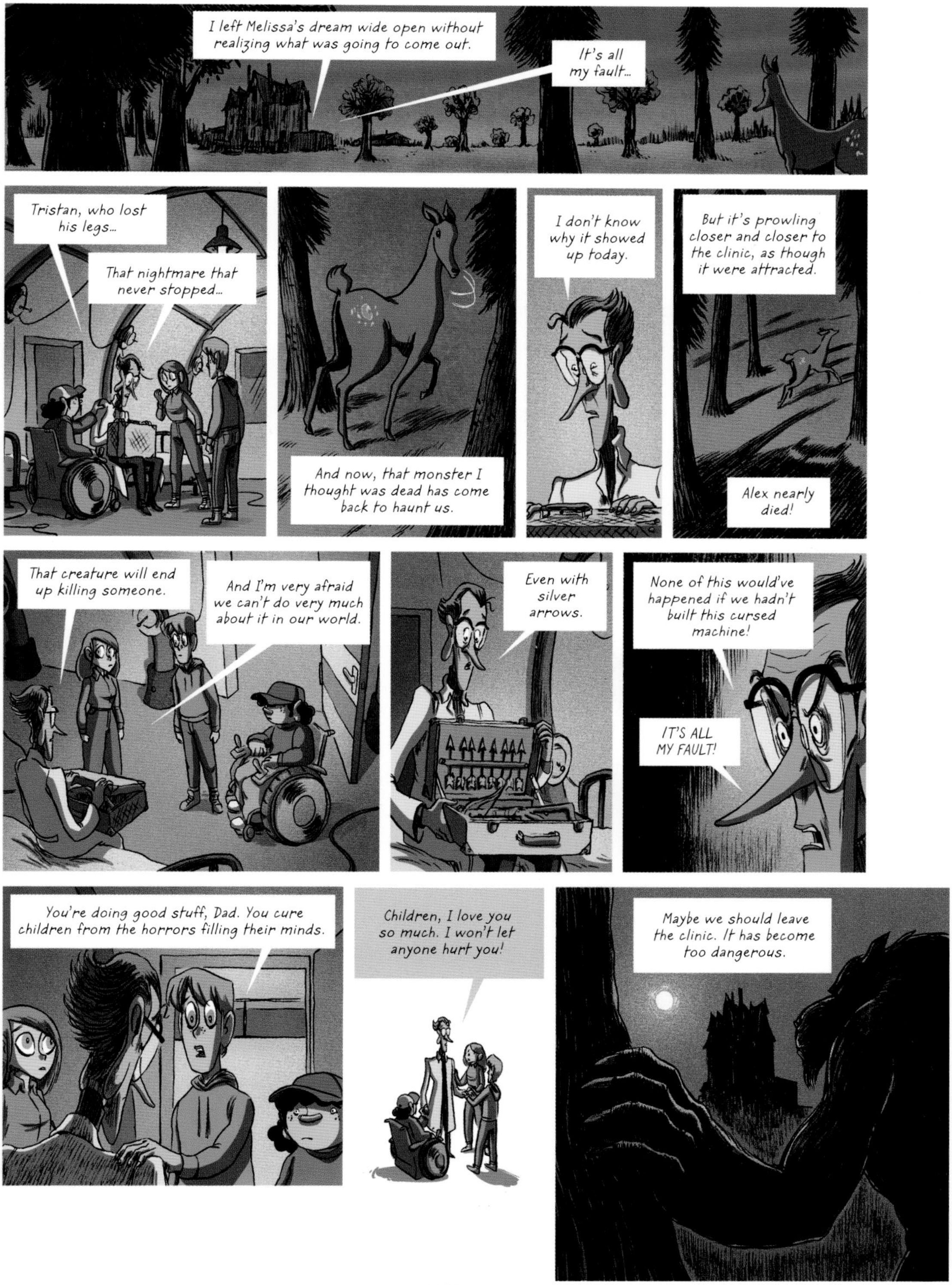
I left Melissa's dream wide open without realizing what was going to come out.
It's all my fault...
Tristan, who lost his legs...
That nightmare that never stopped...
And now, that monster I thought was dead has come back to haunt us.
I don't know why it showed up today.
But it's prowling closer and closer to the clinic, as though it were attracted.
Alex nearly died!
That creature will end up killing someone.
And I'm very afraid we can't do very much about it in our world.
Even with silver arrows.
None of this would've happened if we hadn't built this cursed machine!
IT'S ALL MY FAULT!
You're doing good stuff, Dad. You cure children from the horrors filling their minds.
Children, I love you so much. I won't let anyone hurt you!
Maybe we should leave the clinic. It has become too dangerous.

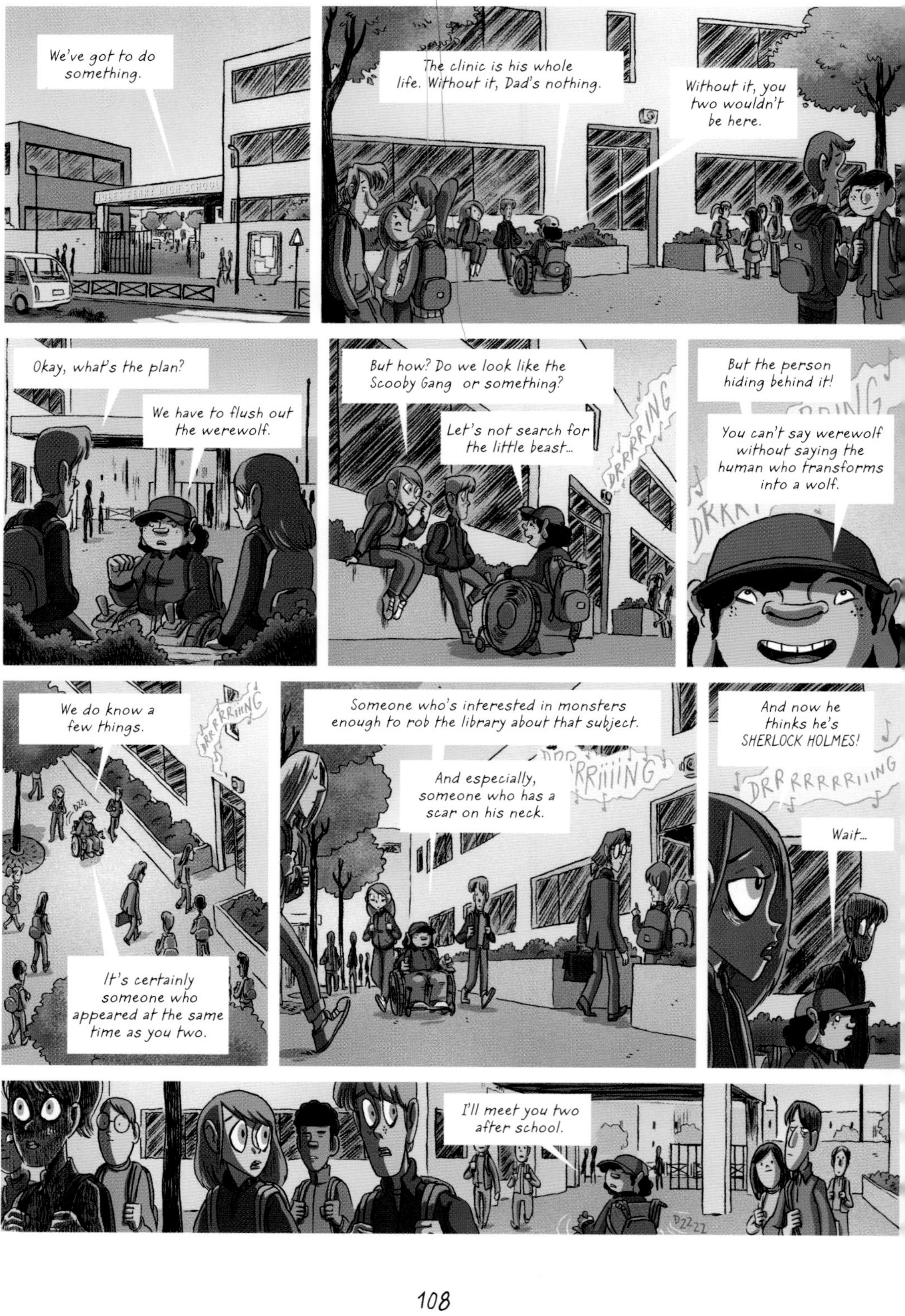
We've got to do something.
The clinic is his whole life. Without it, Dad's nothing.
Without it, you two wouldn't be here.
Okay, what's the plan?
We have to flush out the werewolf.
But how? Do we look like the Scooby Gang or something?
Let's not search for the little beast...
DRRRRING
But the person hiding behind it!
You can't say werewolf without saying the human who transforms into a wolf.
We do know a few things.
DRRRRRIIING
It's certainly someone who appeared at the same time as you two.
Someone who's interested in monsters enough to rob the library about that subject.
And especially, someone who has a scar on his neck.
DRRRRRIIING
And now he thinks he's SHERLOCK HOLMES!
DRRRRRRRRIIING
Wait...
I'll meet you two after school.
DZZZZ

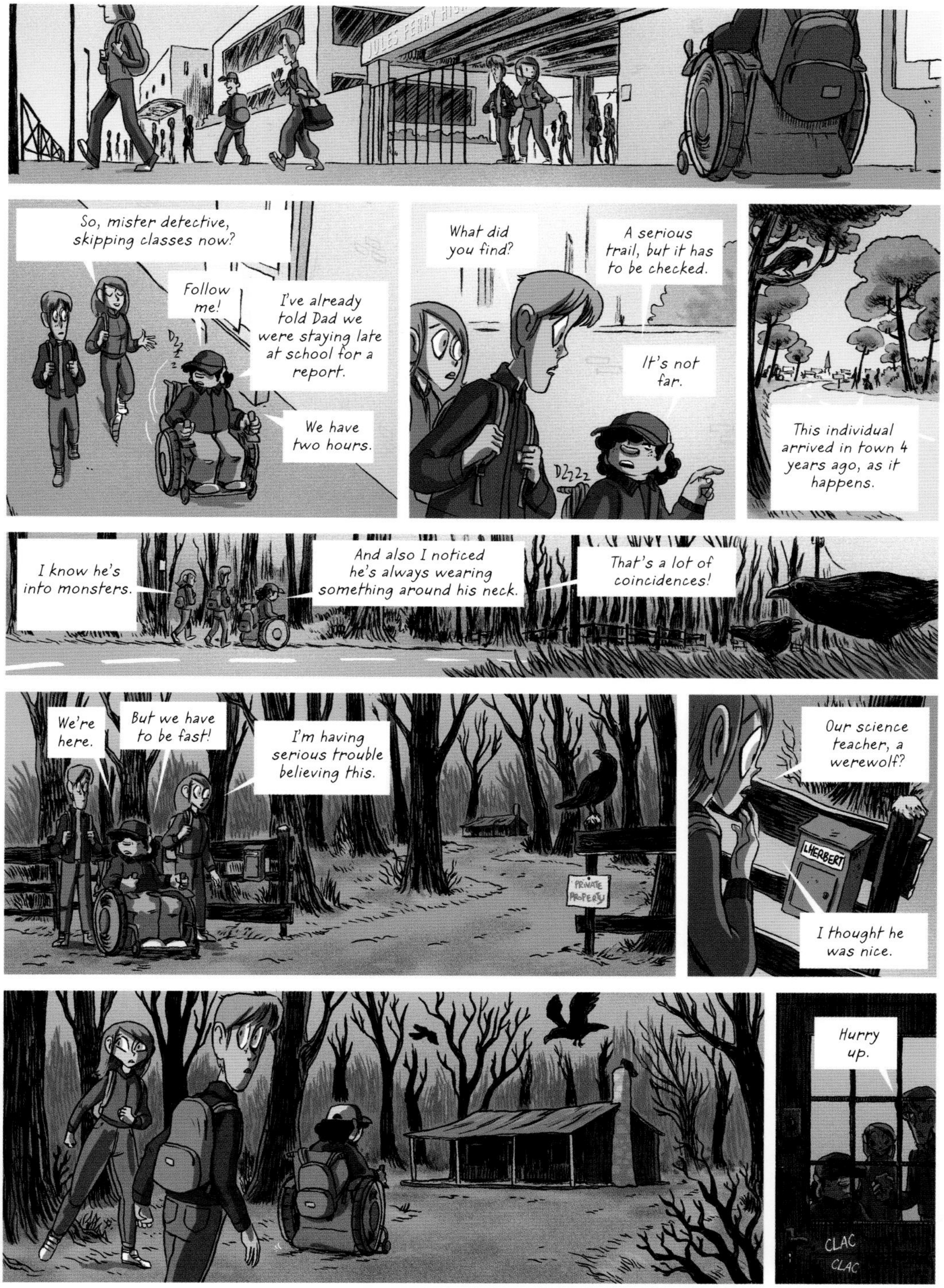
JULES FERRY HIGH
So, mister detective, skipping classes now?
Follow me!
I've already told Dad we were staying late at school for a report.
We have two hours.
What did you find?
A serious trail, but it has to be checked.
It's not far.
This individual arrived in town 4 years ago, as it happens.
I know he's into monsters.
And also I noticed he's always wearing something around his neck.
That's a lot of coincidences!
We're here.
But we have to be fast!
I'm having serious trouble believing this.
PRIVATE PROPERTY
Our science teacher, a werewolf?
L.HERBERT
I thought he was nice.
Hurry up.
CLAC
CLAC

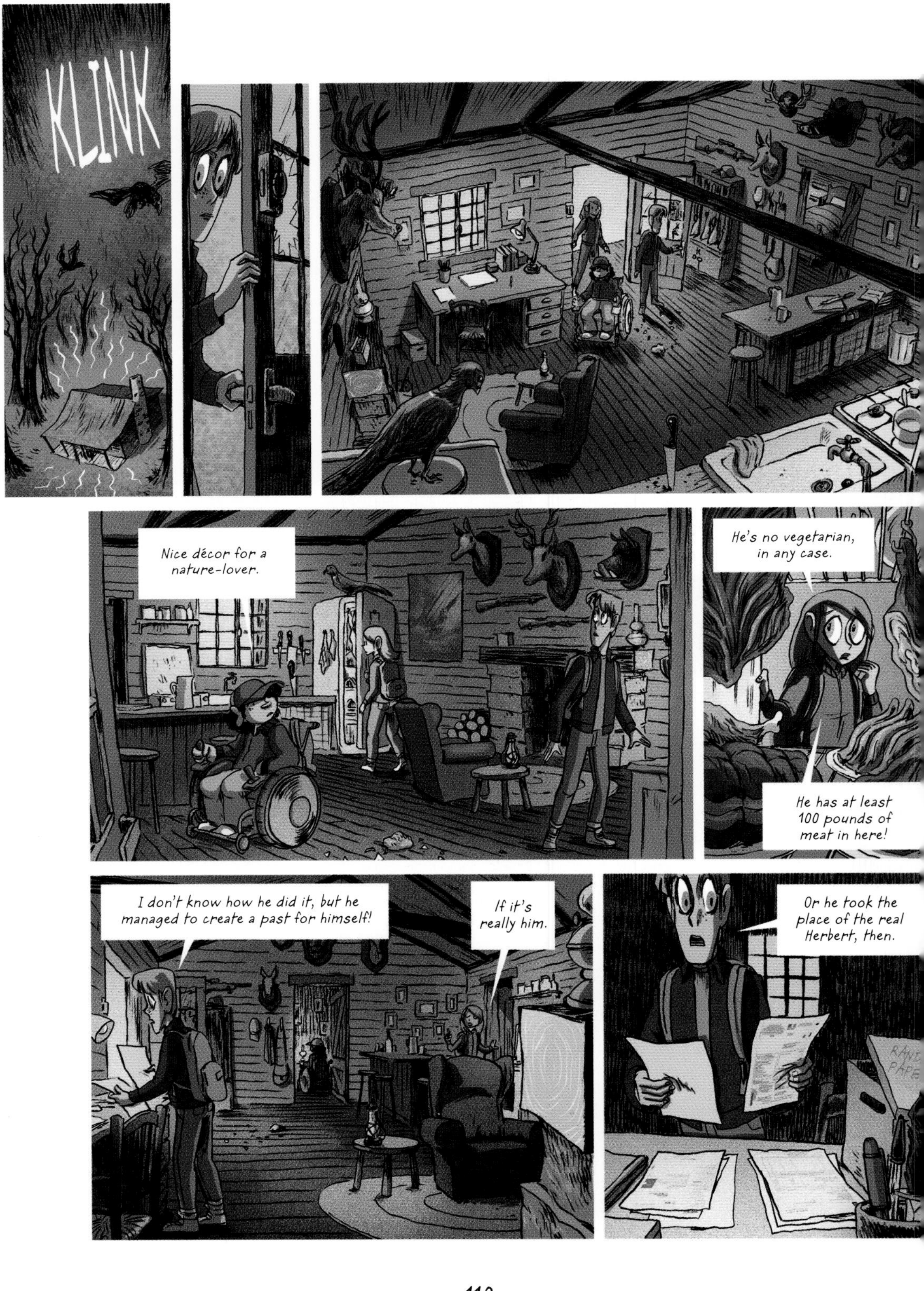
KLINK
Nice décor for a nature-lover.
He's no vegetarian, in any case.
He has at least 100 pounds of meat in here!
I don't know how he did it, but he managed to create a past for himself!
If it's really him.
Or he took the place of the real Herbert, then.

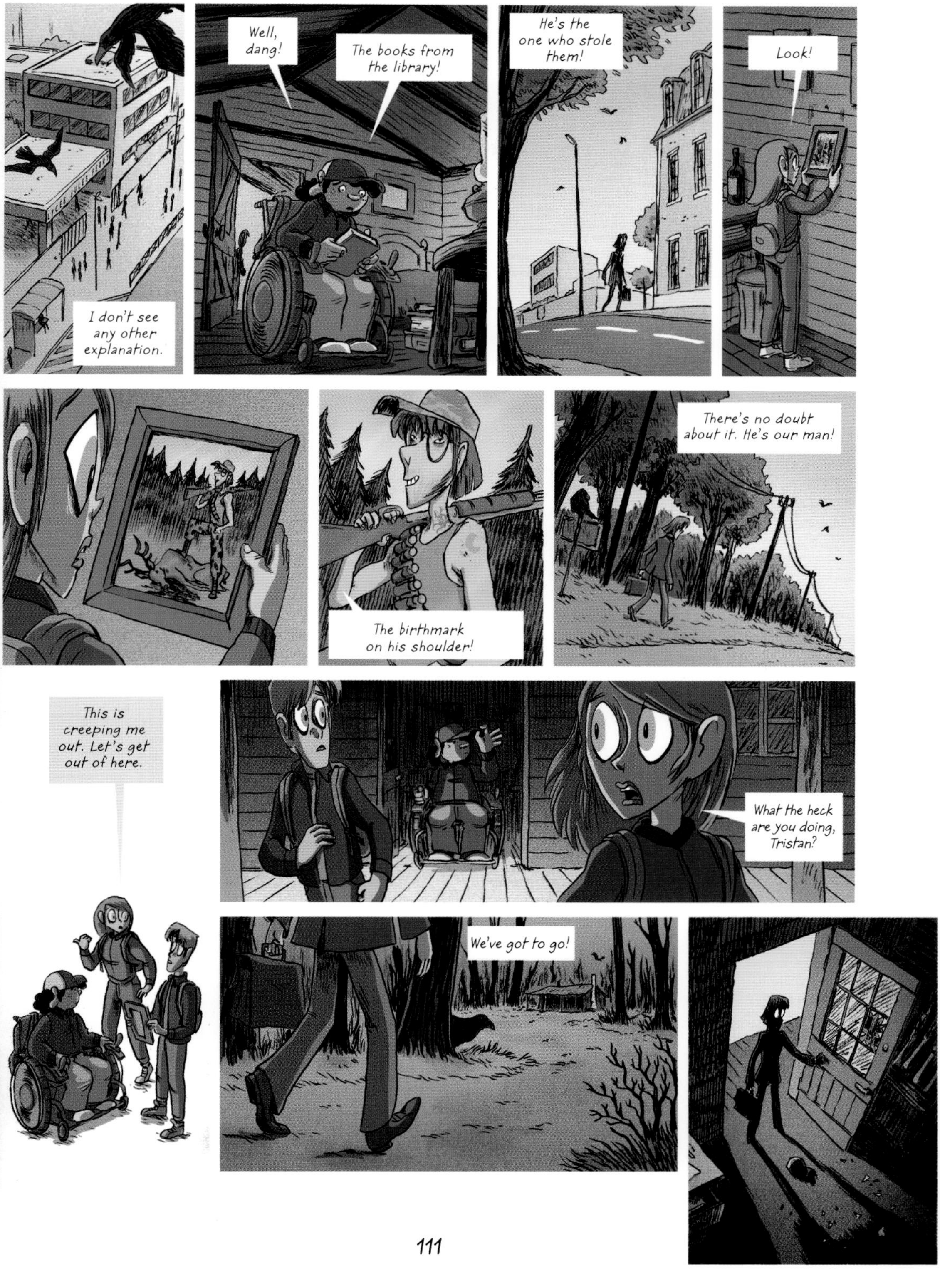
I don't see any other explanation.
Well, dang!
The books from the library!
He's the one who stole them!
Look!
The birthmark on his shoulder!
There's no doubt about it. He's our man!
This is creeping me out. Let's get out of here.
What the heck are you doing, Tristan?
We've got to go!

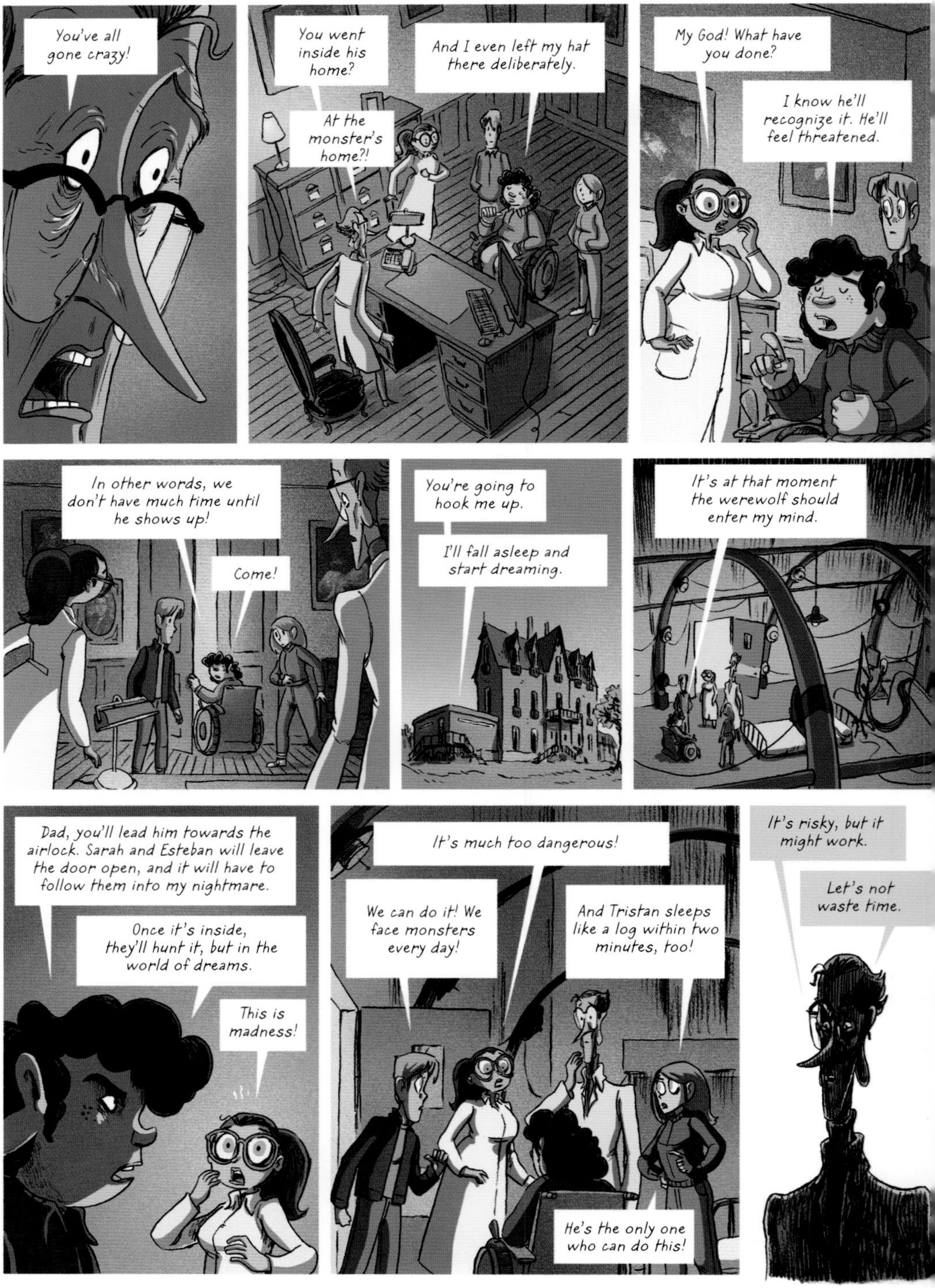
You've all gone crazy!
You went inside his home?
At the monster's home?!
And I even left my hat there deliberately.
My God! What have you done?
I know he'll recognize it. He'll feel threatened.
In other words, we don't have much time until he shows up!
Come!
You're going to hook me up.
I'll fall asleep and start dreaming.
It's at that moment the werewolf should enter my mind.
Dad, you'll lead him towards the airlock. Sarah and Esteban will leave the door open, and it will have to follow them into my nightmare.
Once it's inside, they'll hunt it, but in the world of dreams.
This is madness!
It's much too dangerous!
We can do it! We face monsters every day!
And Tristan sleeps like a log within two minutes, too!
He's the only one who can do this!
It's risky, but it might work.
Let's not waste time.

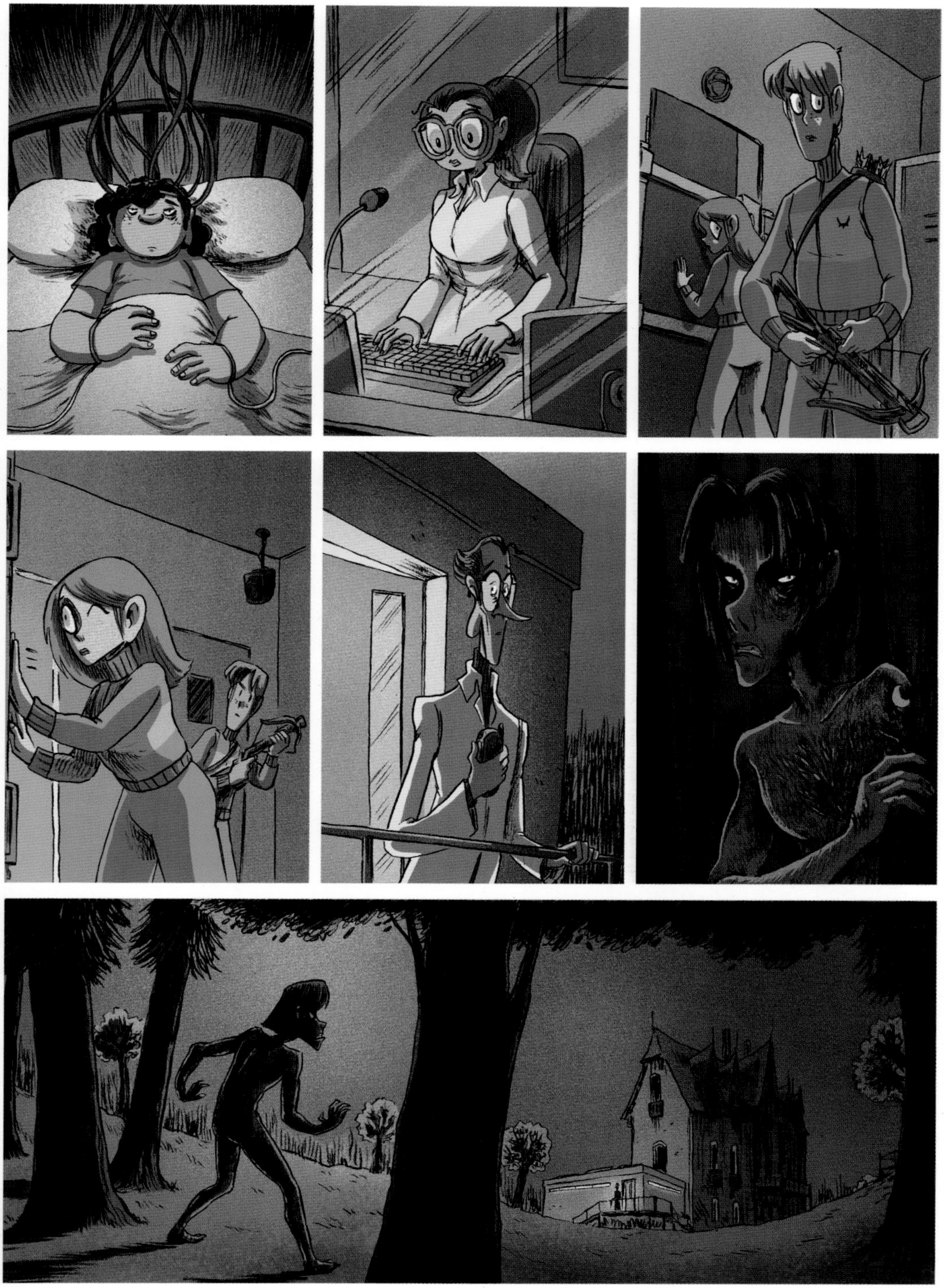

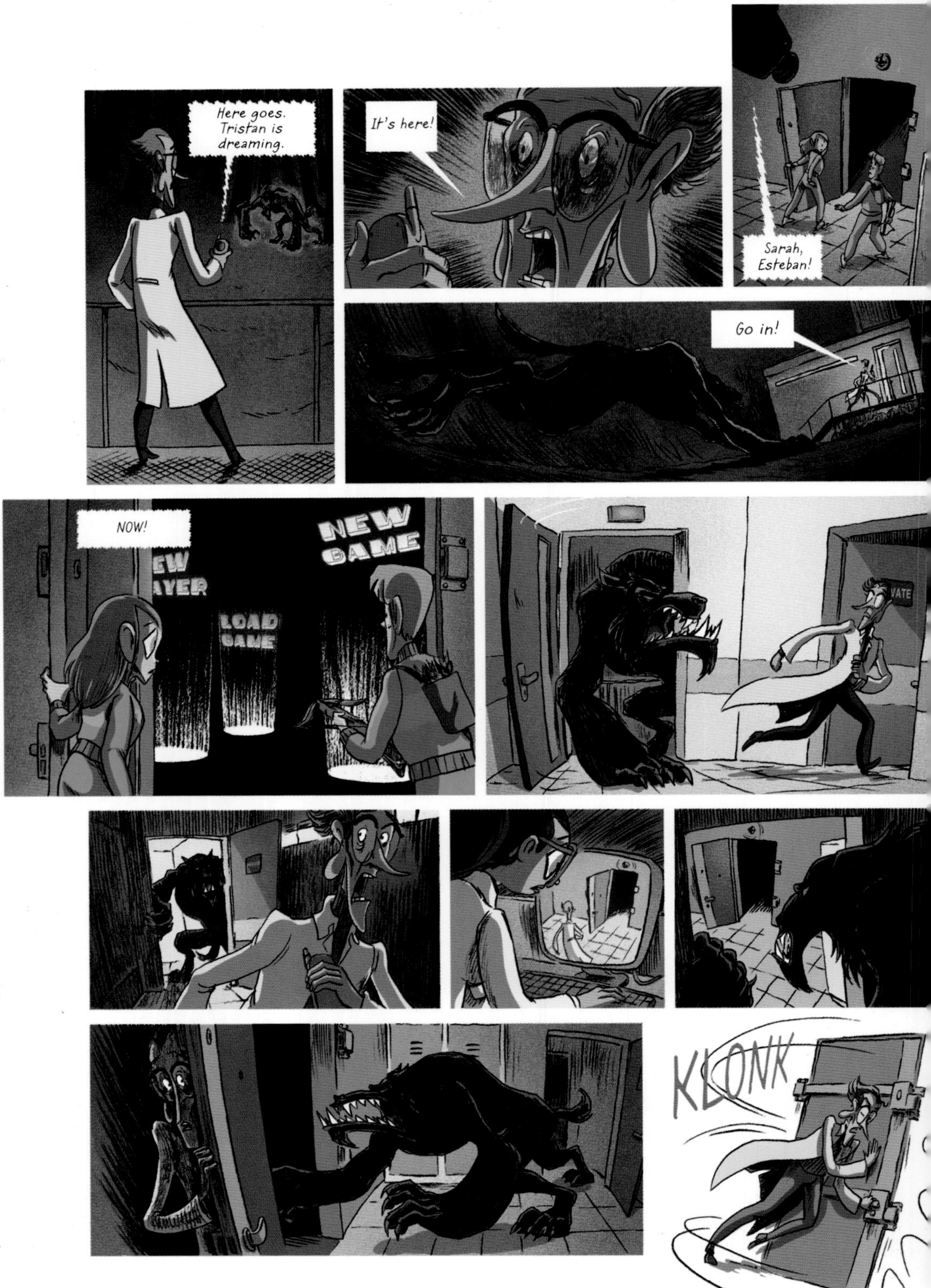
Here goes. Tristan is dreaming.
It's here!
Sarah, Esteban!
Go in!
NOW!
NEW GAME
LOAD GAME
KLONK

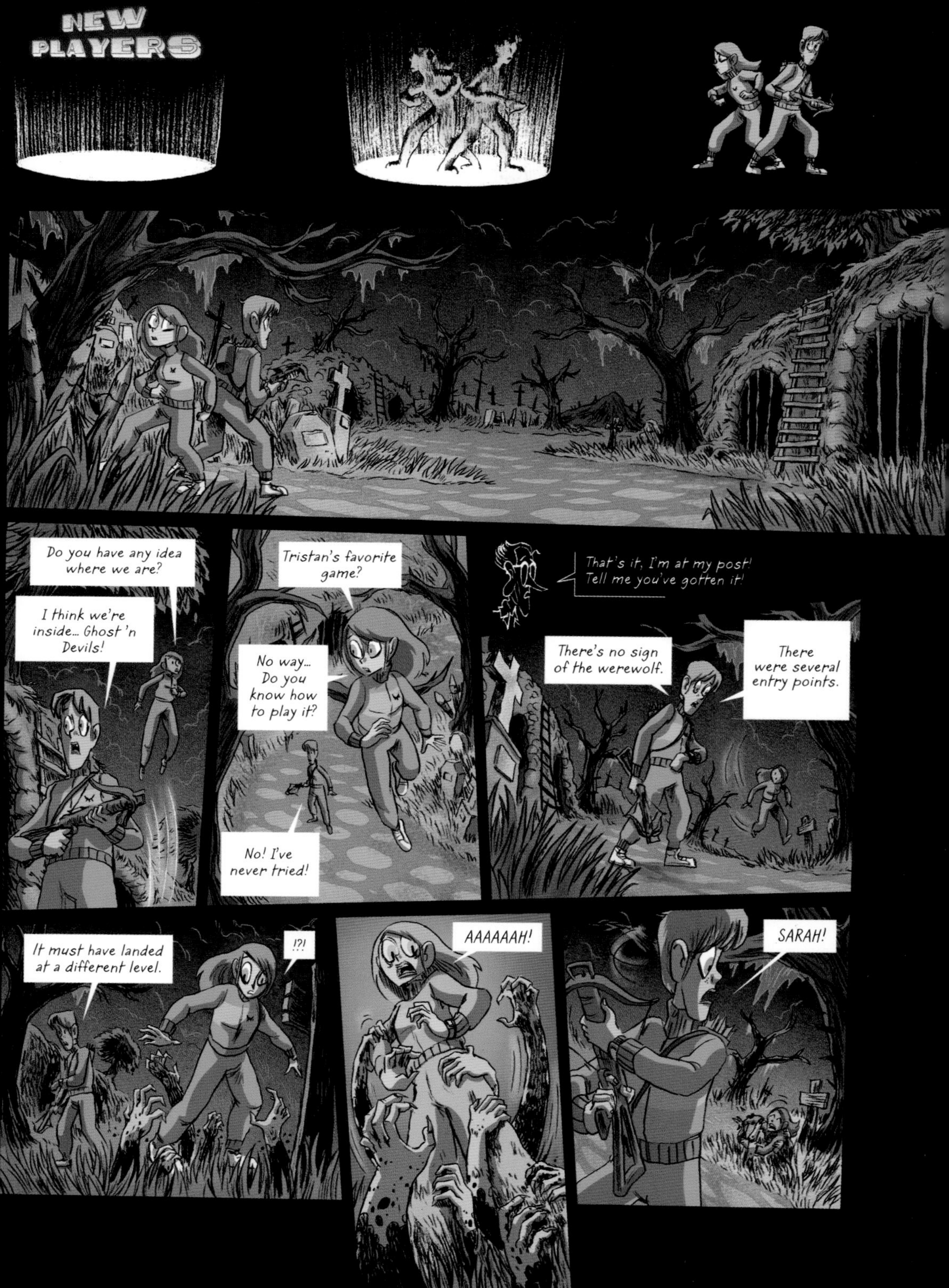
NEW PLAYERS
Do you have any idea where we are?
I think we're inside... Ghost 'n Devils!
Tristan's favorite game?
No way... Do you know how to play it?
No! I've never tried!
That's it, I'm at my post! Tell me you've gotten it!
There's no sign of the werewolf.
There were several entry points.
It must have landed at a different level.
!?!
AAAAAAH!
SARAH!

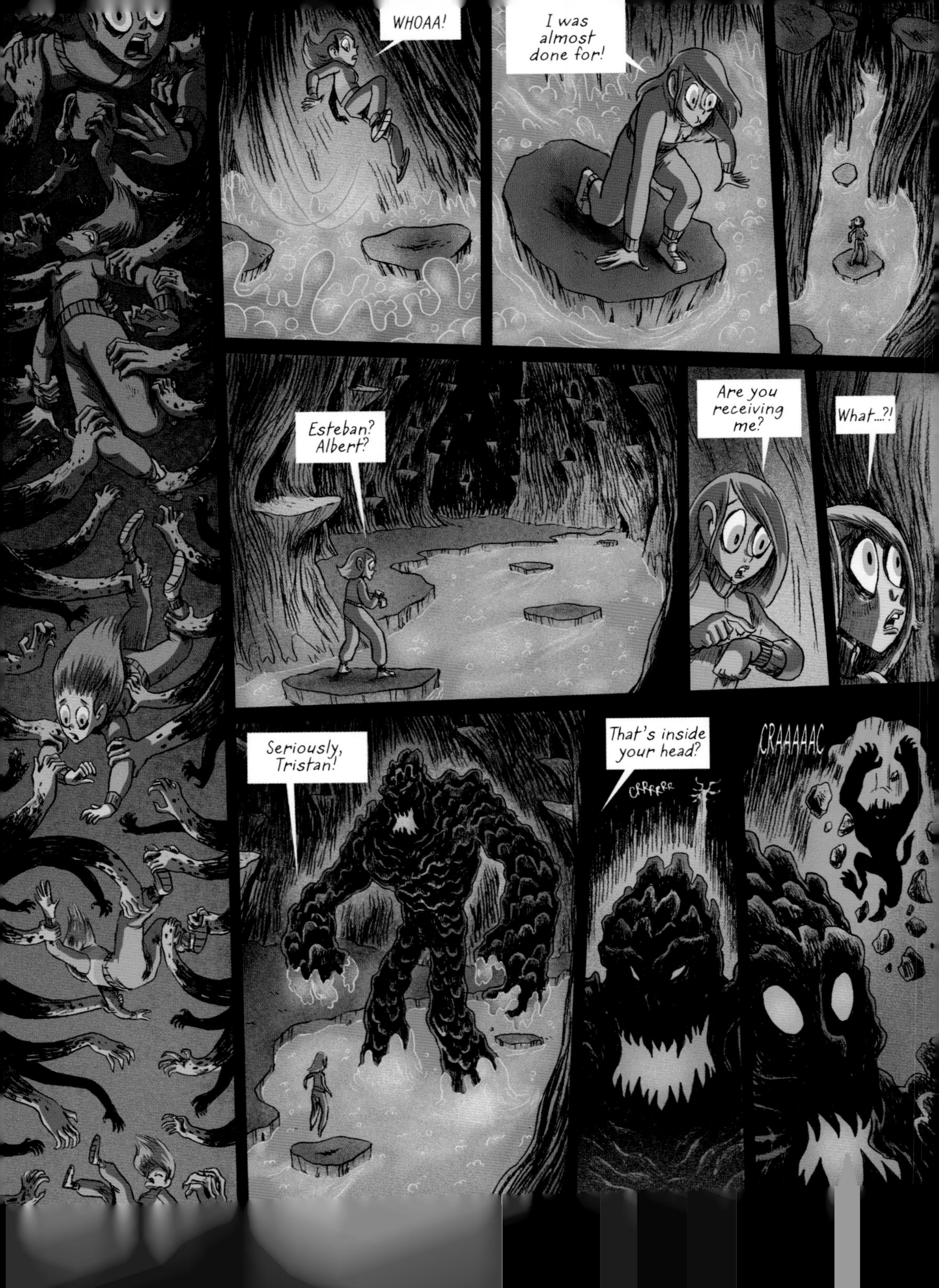
WHOAA!
I was almost done for!
Esteban? Albert?
Are you receiving me?
What...?!
Seriously, Tristan!
That's inside your head?
CRRRRR
CRAAAAAC

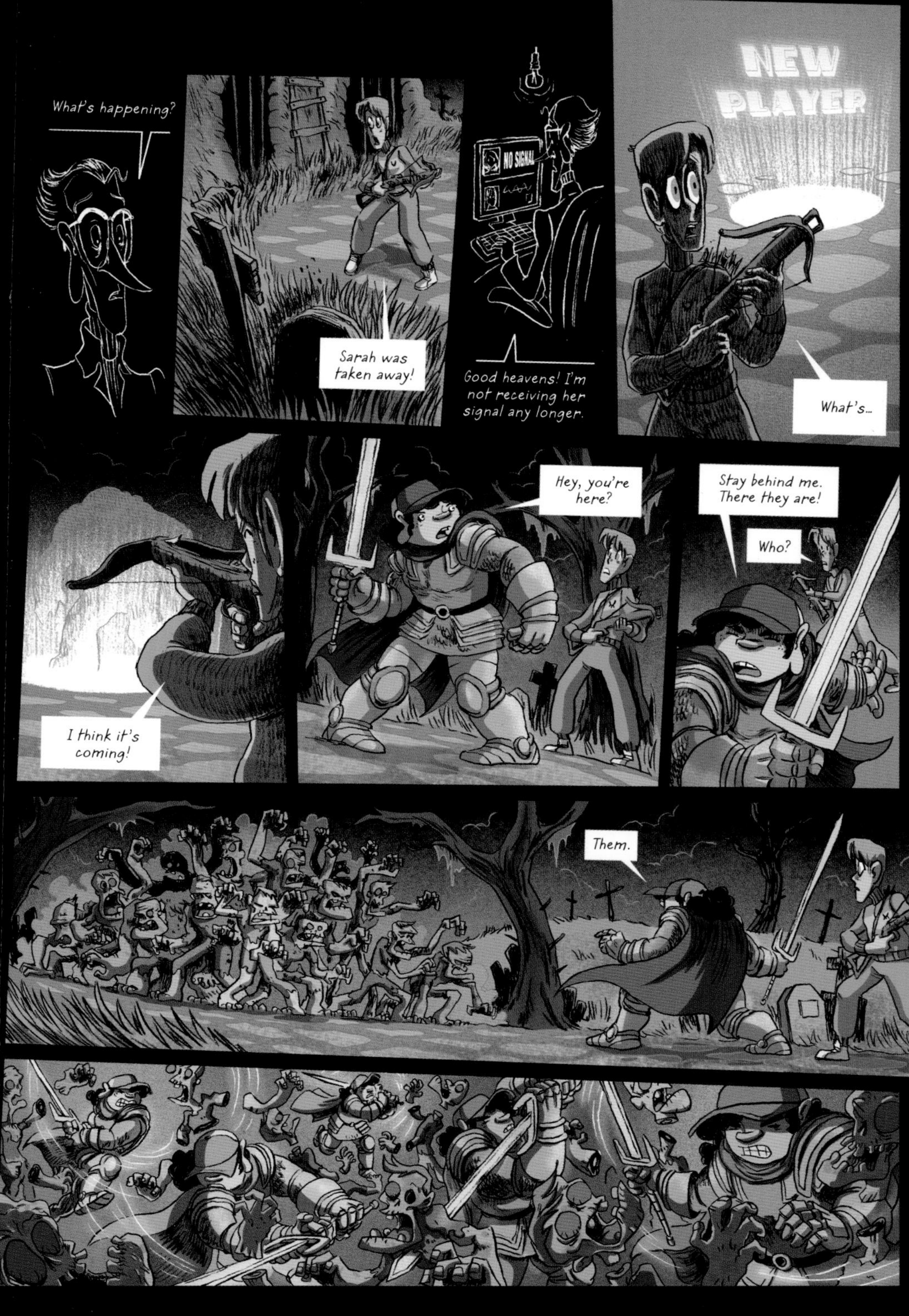
What's happening?
Sarah was taken away!
NO SIGNAL
Good heavens! I'm not receiving her signal any longer.
NEW PLAYER
What's...
I think it's coming!
Hey, you're here?
Stay behind me. There they are!
Who?
Them.

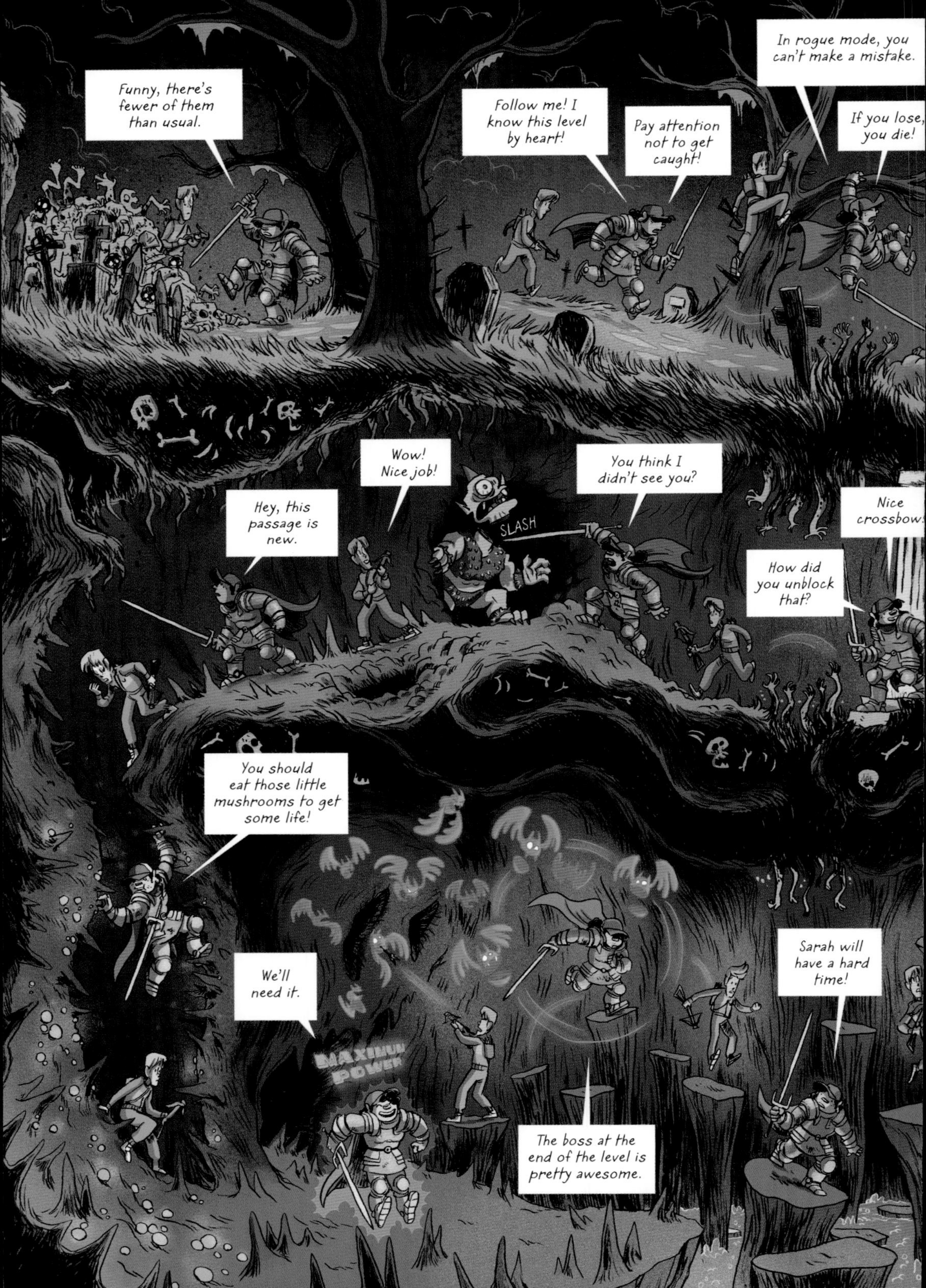

Funny, there's fewer of them than usual.
Follow me! I know this level by heart!
Pay attention not to get caught!
In rogue mode, you can't make a mistake.
If you lose, you die!
Hey, this passage is new.
Wow! Nice job!
SLASH
You think I didn't see you?
Nice crossbow
How did you unblock that?
You should eat those little mushrooms to get some life!
We'll need it.
MAXIMUM POWER
The boss at the end of the level is pretty awesome.
Sarah will have a hard time!

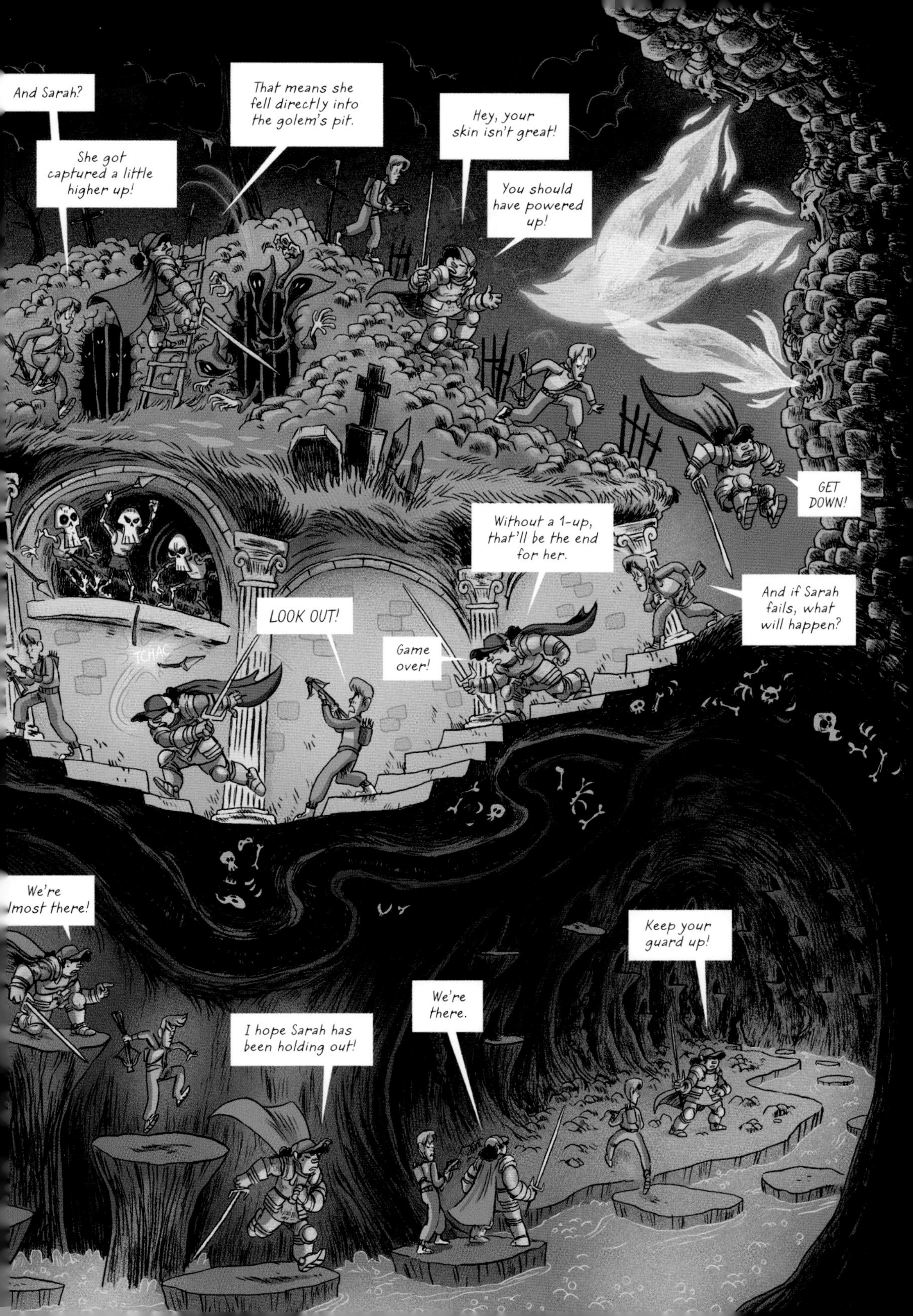
And Sarah?
She got captured a little higher up!
That means she fell directly into the golem's pit.
Hey, your skin isn't great!
You should have powered up!
GET DOWN!
TCHAC
LOOK OUT!
Game over!
Without a 1-up, that'll be the end for her.
And if Sarah fails, what will happen?
We're lmost there!
I hope Sarah has been holding out!
We're there.
Keep your guard up!

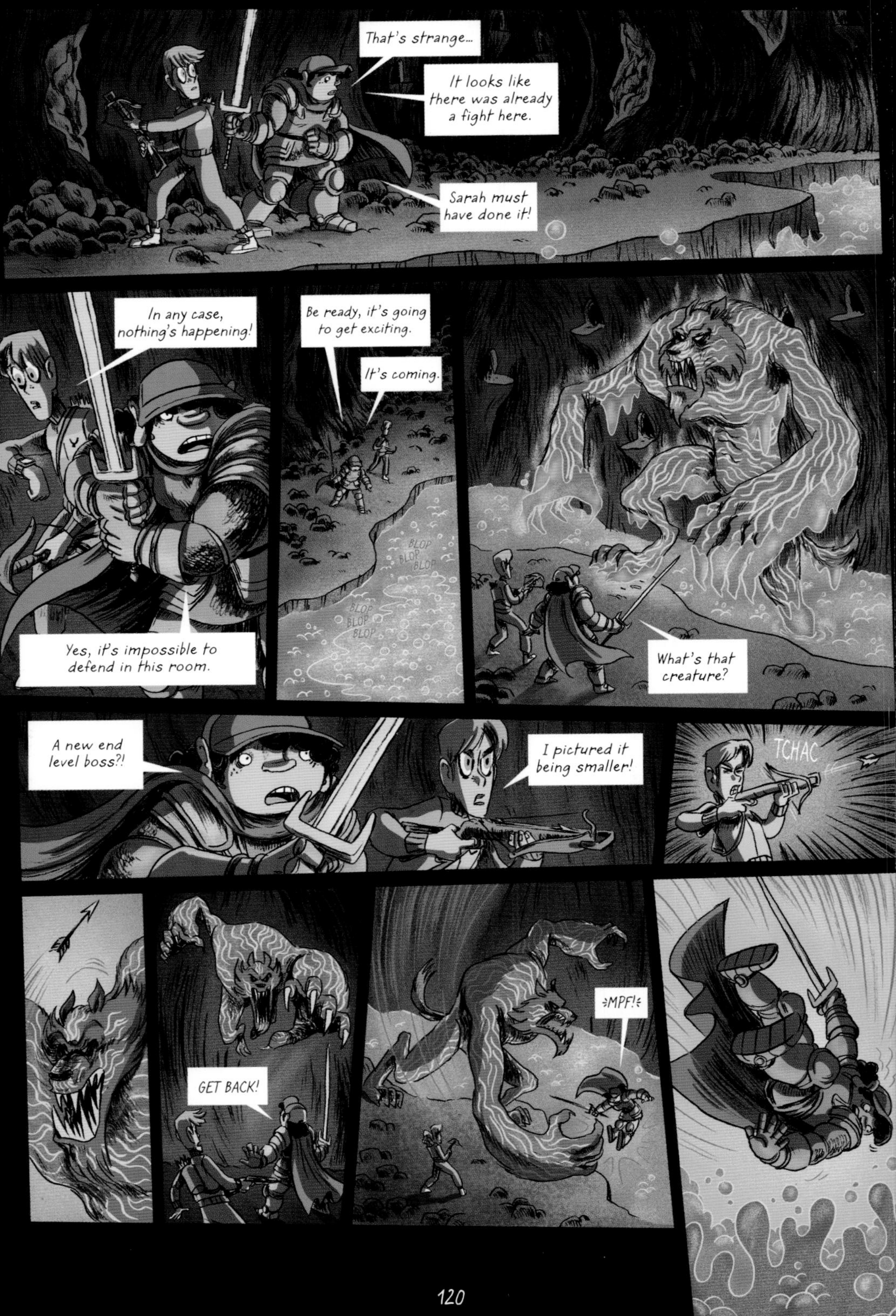
That's strange...
It looks like there was already a fight here.
Sarah must have done it!
In any case, nothing's happening!
Yes, it's impossible to defend in this room.
Be ready, it's going to get exciting.
It's coming.
BLOP BLOP BLOP
BLOP BLOP BLOP
What's that creature?
A new end level boss?!
I pictured it being smaller!
TCHAC
GET BACK!
MPF!

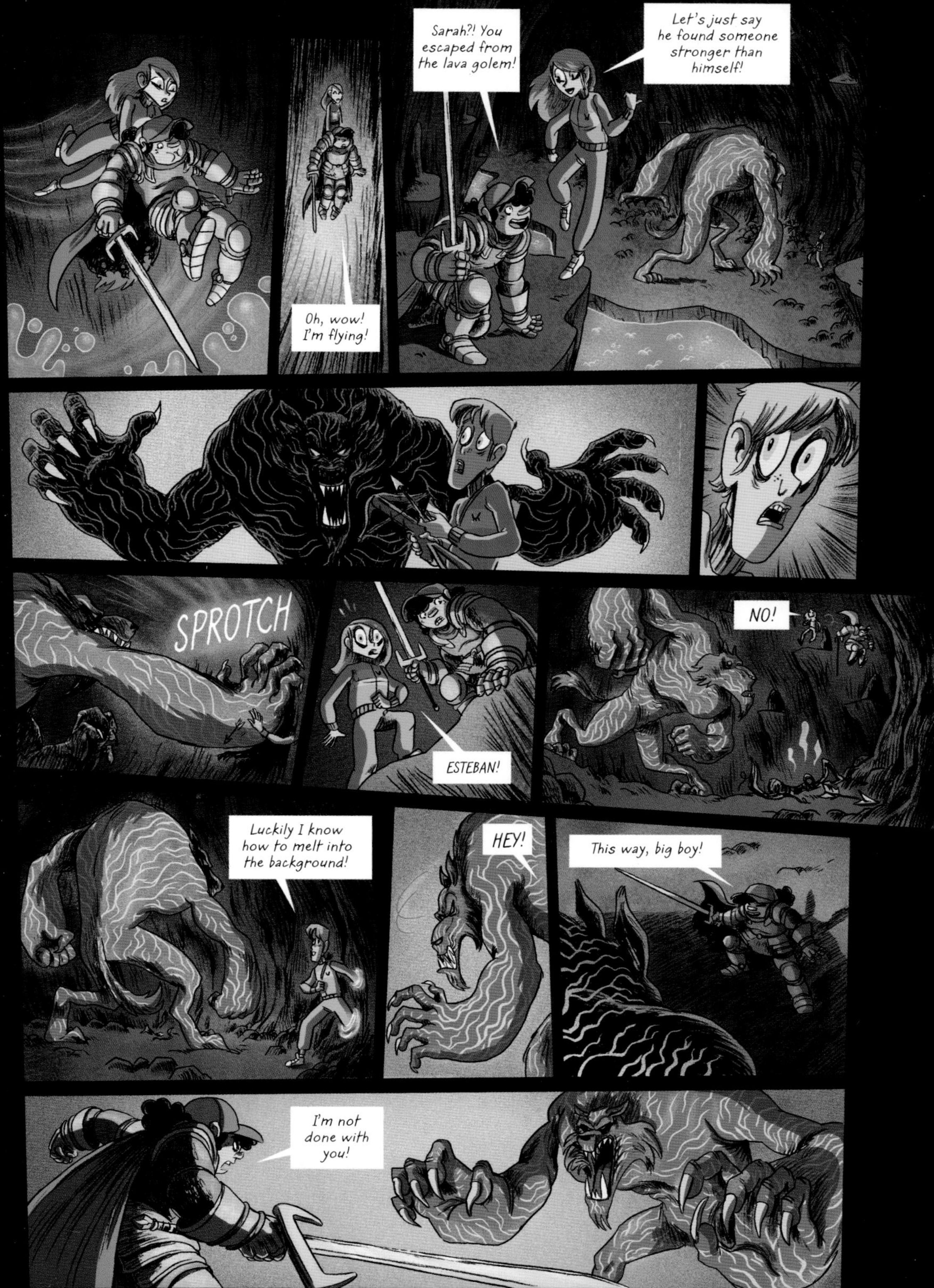
Oh, wow! I'm flying!
Sarah?! You escaped from the lava golem!
Let's just say he found someone stronger than himself!
SPROTCH
ESTEBAN!
NO!
Luckily I know how to melt into the background!
HEY!
This way, big boy!
I'm not done with you!

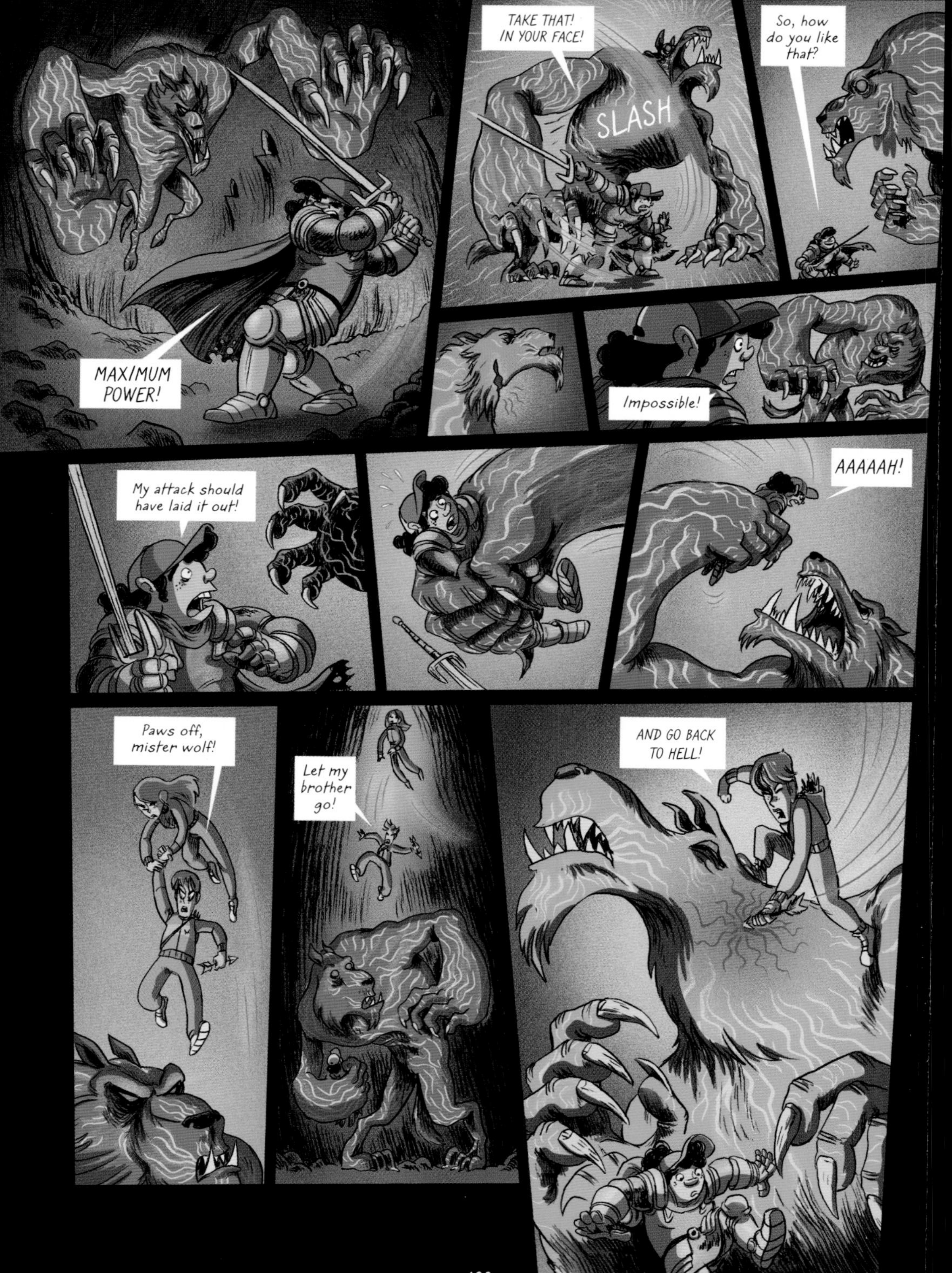
MAXIMUM POWER!
TAKE THAT! IN YOUR FACE!
SLASH
So, how do you like that?
Impossible!
My attack should have laid it out!
AAAAAH!
Paws off, mister wolf!
Let my brother go!
AND GO BACK TO HELL!

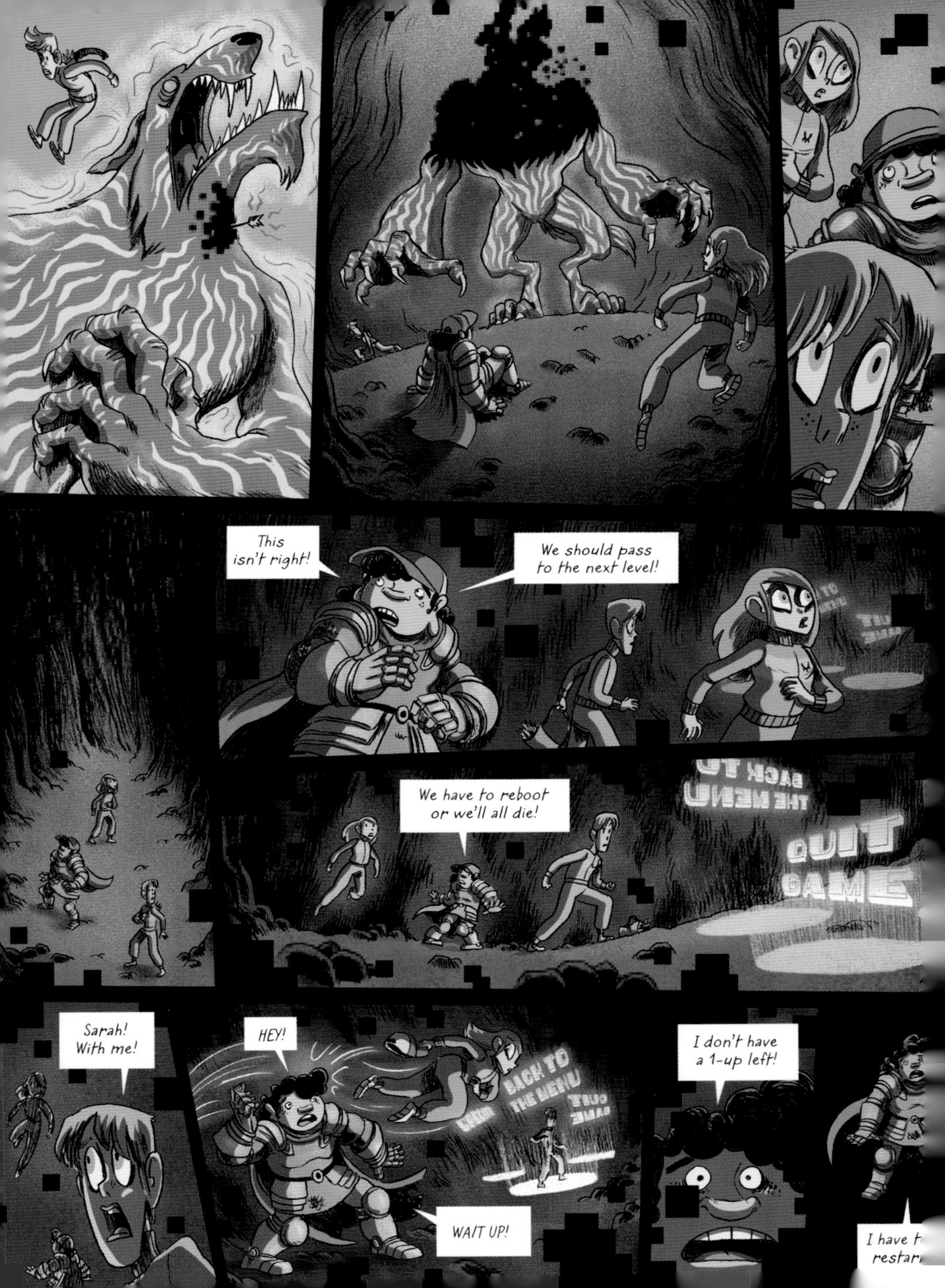
This isn't right!
We should pass to the next level!
We have to reboot or we'll all die!
Sarah! With me!
HEY!
BACK TO THE MENU
WAIT UP!
I don't have a 1-up left!
I have

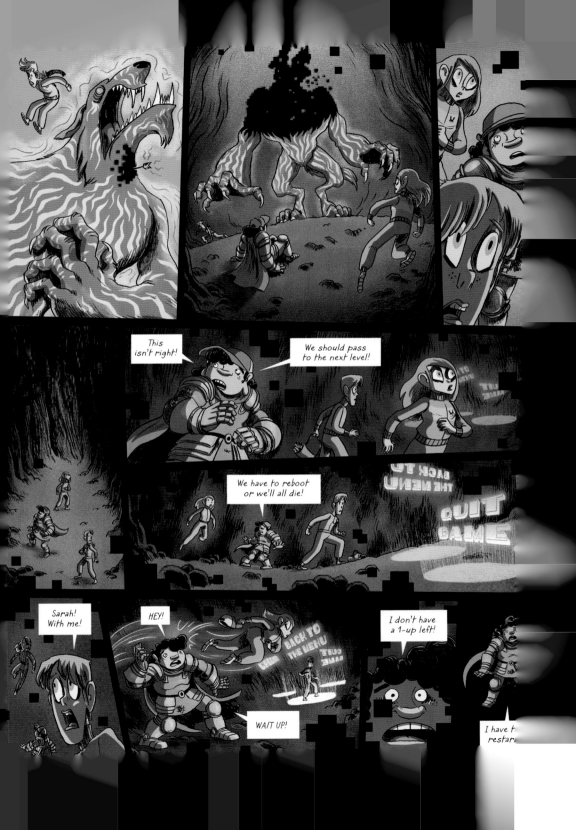

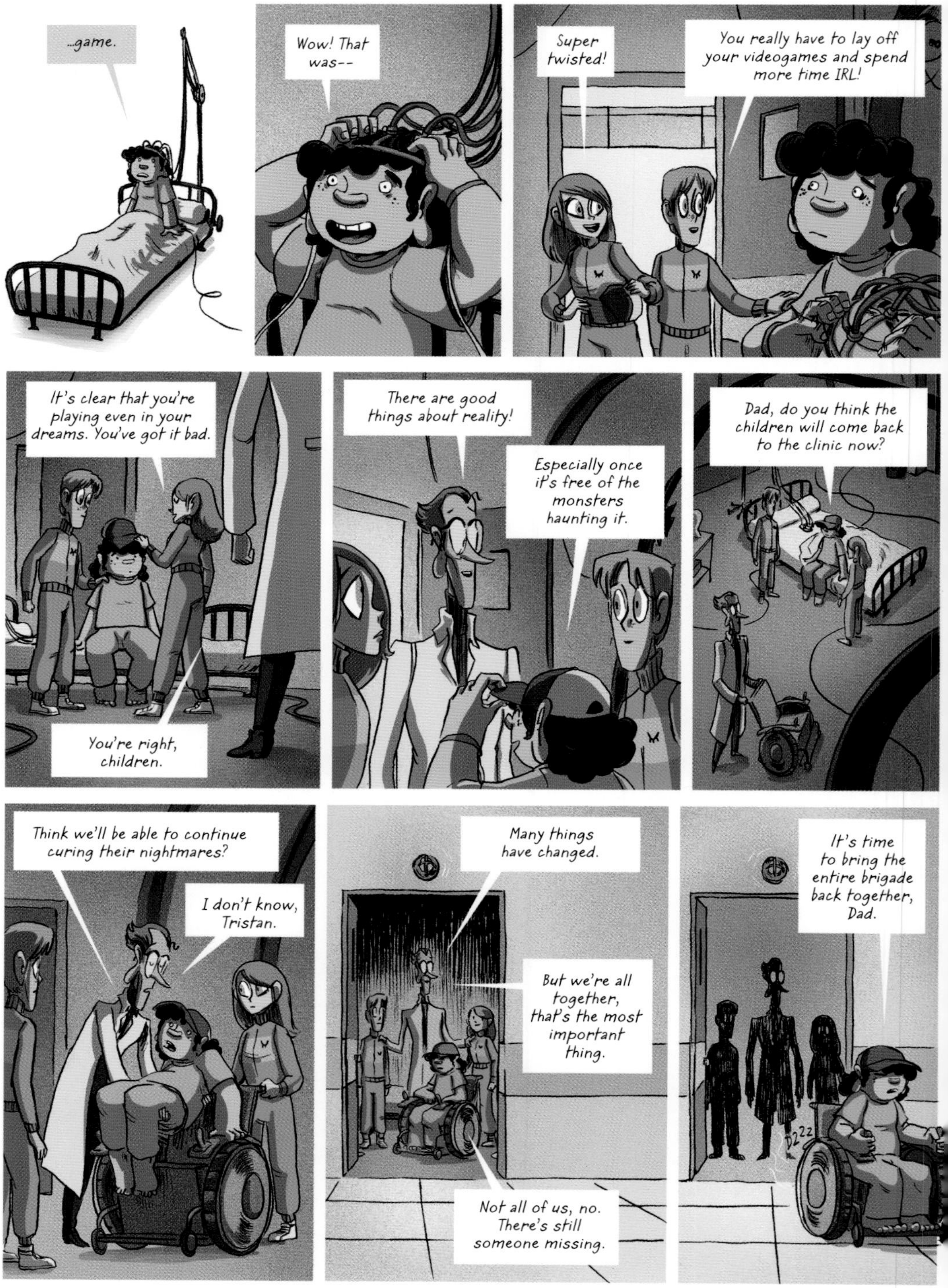
...game.
Wow! That was--
Super twisted!
You really have to lay off your videogames and spend more time IRL!
It's clear that you're playing even in your dreams. You've got it bad.
You're right, children.
There are good things about reality!
Especially once it's free of the monsters haunting it.
Dad, do you think the children will come back to the clinic now?
Think we'll be able to continue curing their nightmares?
I don't know, Tristan.
Many things have changed.
But we're all together, that's the most important thing.
Not all of us, no. There's still someone missing.
It's time to bring the entire brigade back together, Dad.
DZZZ

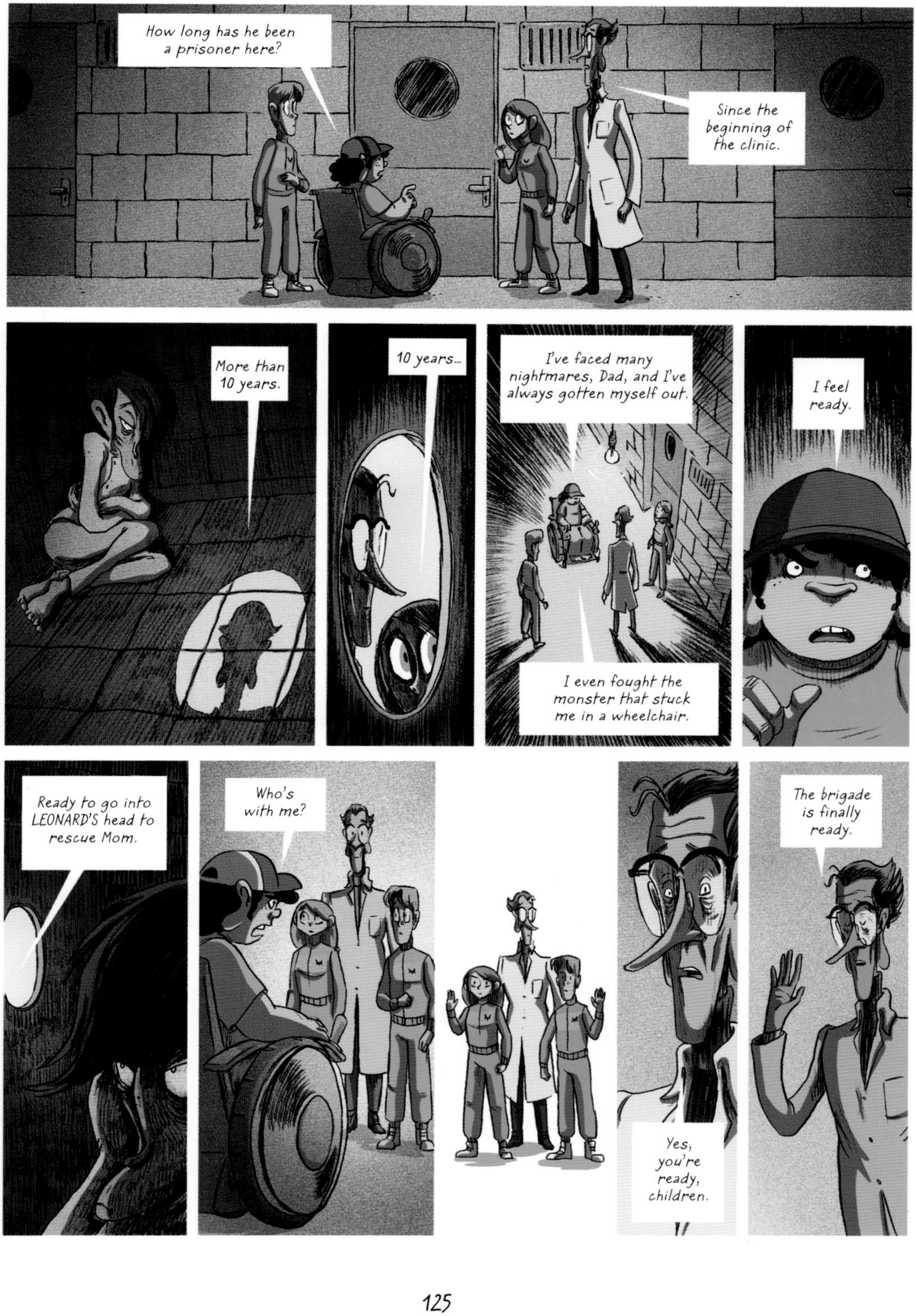
How long has he been a prisoner here?
Since the beginning of the clinic.
More than 10 years.
10 years...
I've faced many nightmares, Dad, and I've always gotten myself out.
I even fought the monster that stuck me in a wheelchair.
I feel ready.
Ready to go into LEONARD'S head to rescue Mom.
Who's with me?
Yes, you're ready, children.
The brigade is finally ready.

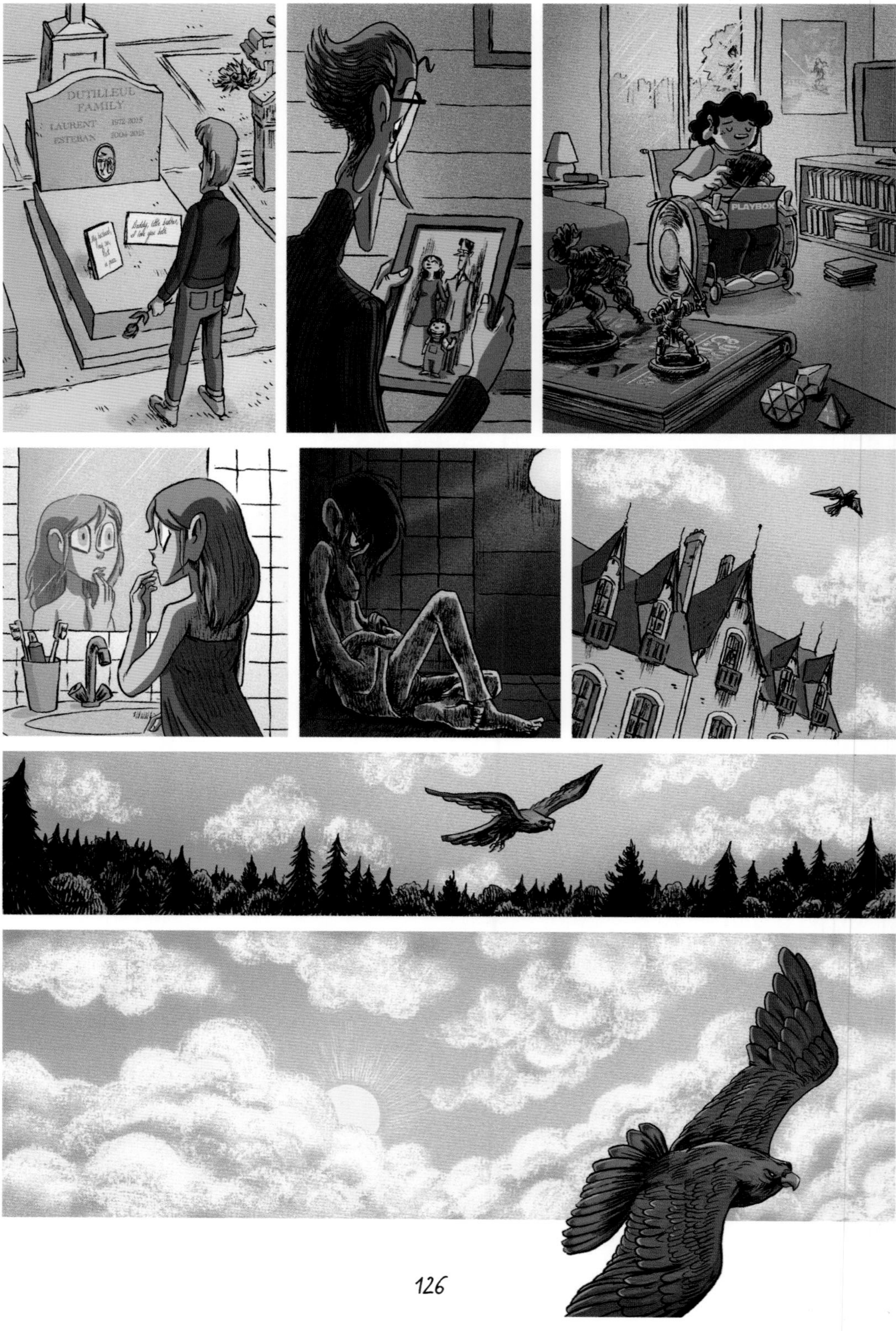
DUTILLEUL
FAMILY
LAURENT 1972-2015
ESTEBAN 2004-2015
Daddy, little brother, I love you both
PLAYBOX

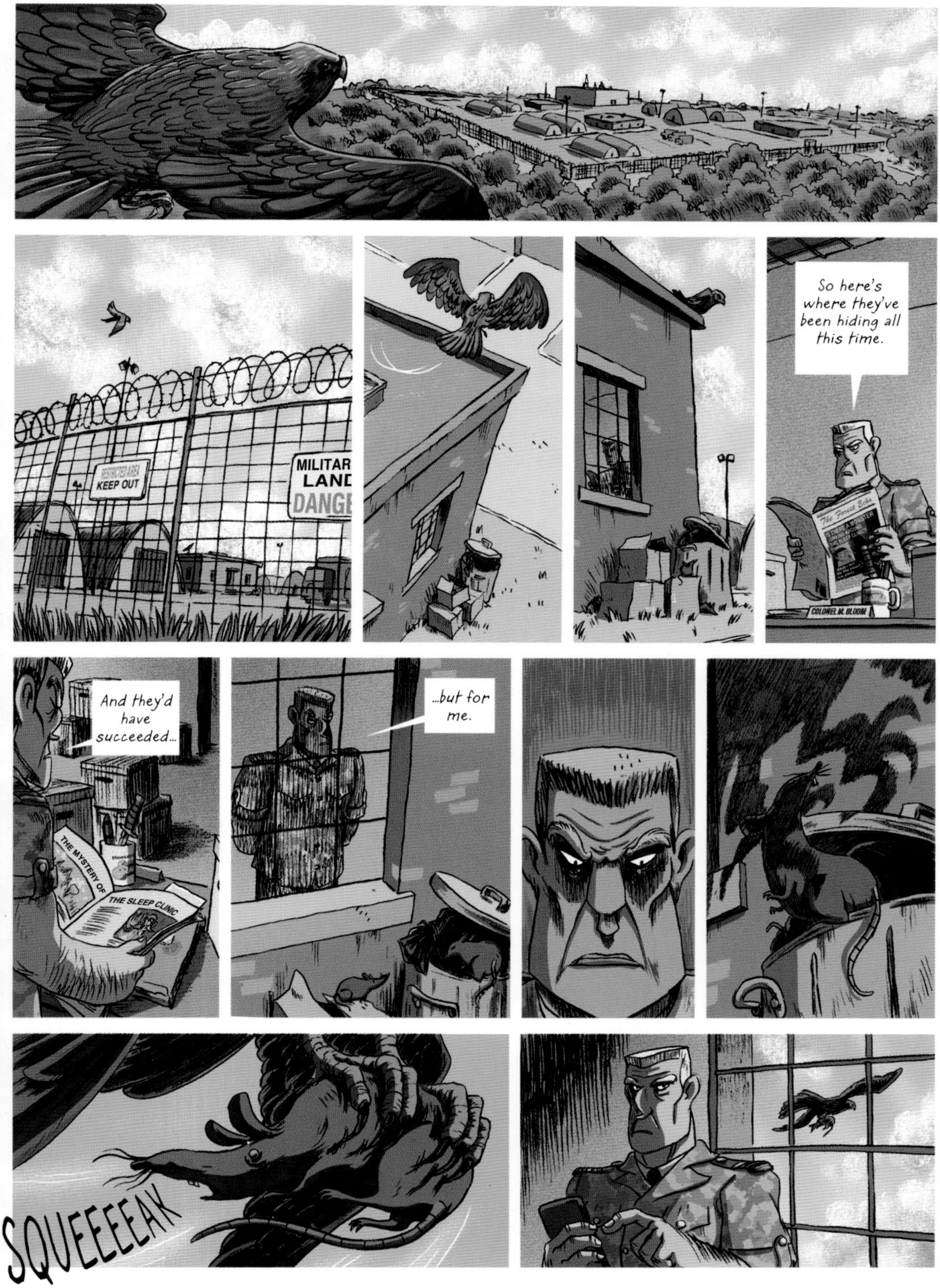
RESTRICTED AREA
KEEP OUT
MILITAR
LAND
DANGE
So here's where they've been hiding all this time.
The Forest Echo
COLONEL M. BLOOM
And they'd have succeeded...
THE MYSTERY OF
THE SLEEP CLINIC
...but for me.
SQUEEEEAK

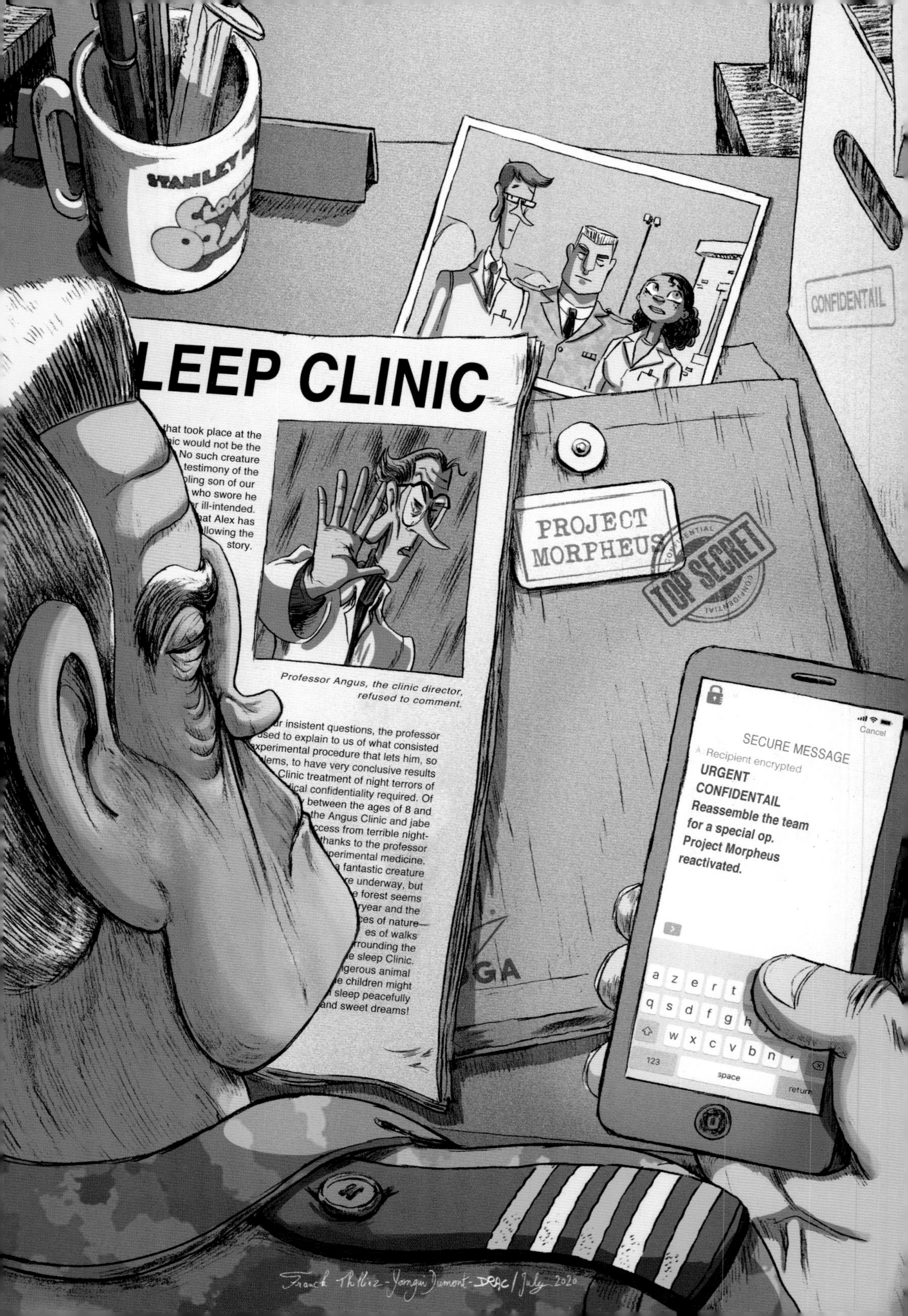

CONFIDENTAIL
LEEP CLINIC
that took place at the
ic would not be the
No such creature
testimony of the
pling son of our
who swore he
r ill-intended.
hat Alex has
llowing the
story.
Professor Angus, the clinic director, refused to comment.
r insistent questions, the professor
used to explain to us of what consisted
xperimental procedure that lets him, so
lems, to have very conclusive results
Clinic treatment of night terrors of
lical confidentiality required. Of
y between the ages of 8 and
the Angus Clinic and jabe
ccess from terrible night-
thanks to the professor
perimental medicine.
a fantastic creature
re underway, but
e forest seems
ryear and the
ces of nature
es of walks
rrounding the
e sleep Clinic.
gerous animal
e children might
n sleep peacefully
and sweet dreams!
PROJECT MORPHEUS
TOP SECRET
SECURE MESSAGE
Cancel
Recipient encrypted
URGENT
CONFIDENTAIL
Reassemble the team for a special op.
Project Morpheus reactivated.
space
return
123
Franck Thilliez - Yomgui Dumont - DRAC / July 2020